Clement Mansfield Ingleby

A Complete View Of The Shakespeare Controversy

Clement Mansfield Ingleby

A Complete View Of The Shakespeare Controversy

ISBN/EAN: 9783741186479

Manufactured in Europe, USA, Canada, Australia, Japa

Cover: Foto ©Andreas Hilbeck / pixelio.de

Manufactured and distributed by brebook publishing software
(www.brebook.com)

Clement Mansfield Ingleby

A Complete View Of The Shakespeare Controversy

A

COMPLETE VIEW

OF THE

SHAKSPERE CONTROVERSY,

CONCERNING

THE AUTHENTICITY AND GENUINENESS OF MANUSCRIPT MATTER
AFFECTING THE WORKS AND BIOGRAPHY OF SHAKSPERE,
PUBLISHED BY MR. J. PAYNE COLLIER
AS
THE FRUITS OF HIS RESEARCHES.

BY

C. M. INGLEBY, LL.D.

OF TRINITY COLLEGE, CAMBRIDGE.

LONDON:
NATTALI AND BOND, BEDFORD STREET,
COVENT GARDEN.
1861.
E.V.

G. NORMAN, PRINTER, MAIDEN LANE, COVENT GARDEN.

CONTENTS.

MANUSCRIPTS AND DOCUMENTS

TREATED OF IN THIS WORK.

Those to which an asterisk (*) is prefixed have been examined and adjudged spurious. Those to which a dagger (†) is prefixed are not to be ound, and are adjudged supposititious.

At Devonshire House.

*Manuscript alterations, corrections, additions, stage-directions, &c., in pencil and ink, contained in an edition of Shakspere, Folio, 1632, commonly called *The Perkins Folio*.

At Bridgewater House.

*Manuscript alterations and corrections in pencil and ink, contained in an edition of Shakspere, Folio, 1623, commonly called *The Bridgewater Folio*.

Six manuscript Documents in a folio volume, viz.:

*I. A statement of the value of the shares of Shakespeare and others in the Blackfriars property, upon avoiding the Playhouse. (n. d.)

*II. A letter addressed to Sir Thomas Egerton, signed "S. Danyell." (n. d.)

*III. A Memorial of the Blackfriars Players to the Privy Council. (Nov. 1589.)

*IV. A Report by two Chief Justices on the right of citizens within the precinct of the White and Black Friars to exemption from certain charges. (Jan. 27th, 1579.)

*V. A Warrant appointing Robert Daborne, William Shakespeare, and others, instructors of the Children of the Revels to Queen Elizabeth. (Jan. 4th, 1609.)

*VI. A letter to Sir Thomas Egerton, signed H. S. (n. d.) "*vera copia.*"

*A statement of account of rewards and payments for entertaining Queen Elizabeth at Harefield, signed Arth. Maynwaringe.

At Dulwich College.

*I. Verses on Edward Alleyn.

*II. A List of Players appended to a letter from the Council to the Lord Mayor.

*III. A letter addressed to Henslow, signed "John Marston."

*IV. A Complaint of certain inhabitants of the Liberty of Southwark.

*V. An Assessment for the poor of the Liberty of Southwark.

VI. A letter to Edward Alleyn from his wife.

---

†A Petition from the Owners and Players of the Blackfriars Theatre to the Privy Council, (assigned date 1596).

†A Certificate of the Justices of the Peace of the County of Middlesex about the Blackfriars, (assigned date Nov. 20, 1633).

†A letter from Samuel Daniel, the poet.

†A letter signed "W. Ralegh."

†A manuscript description of an impersonation in a masque.

†A Petition from the Inhabitants of the Liberty of the Blackfriars to the Privy Council, (assigned date 1576).

†A Petition from the Inhabitants of the Liberty of the Blackfriars to the Privy Council, (assigned date 1596).

†A letter from Lord Pembroke, (assigned date August 27th, 1624).

Manuscript notes concerning certain peculiarities of Marlow, supposed to be in the handwriting of Gabriel Harvey, in a copy of Marlow's *Hero and Leander*, 1629.

LIST OF FACSIMILES.

ADVERTISEMENT.

It has been from no desire unduly to extend this work that I have grafted upon it so many extracts from other books and articles on the same subject. In doing so my motive has been that in speaking of the writings of others I might ensure, if possible, a faultless accuracy, a point of great importance in a work which is at once critical and controversial. Nor have I rested satisfied with mere accuracy in quotation; but in all other respects I have sedulously endeavoured to give a complete view of the whole Shakspere Controversy, including, as far as my means of knowledge and my ability extend, (1) a narrative of the discovery of each volume or document in question, (2) a faithful description of its appearance and contents, and (3) an impartial discussion of each case in all its bearings, palæographic and critical. I have, accordingly, not scrupled to reprint such portions of my own previous publication, *The Shakspeare Fabrications*, as I found expedient for the completeness of the case against the authenticity and genuineness of the manuscript annotations of the Perkins Folio.

Readers or reviewers who may be disposed to impute it as a fault that I have to so great an extent traversed old ground, are reminded, that if it be a fault, it is a fault incident to the *design* of the work, and not to its execution. If, as my publishers believe, a succinct and exact account of the whole question is a *desideratum*, it can be no fault in such a work that it is thorough-going, leaving no period or feature of the Controversy unrepresented or unappreciated.

In the attempt to be *strictly* impartial, it is very likely that I have failed. It is true that I am personally a stranger to Mr. Collier, and I have no private interest in common with the staff of the Department of Manuscripts of the British Museum, nor have I any connexion with the officers of the Public Record Office: yet it may well be that my love for the works of Shakspere has warped my judgment. I have, however, endeavoured to follow the trail of evidence, and, as far as I know myself, I have not been induced to deviate from the course of impartiality which I have prescribed for myself, by the stimulus of personal motives of any kind.

That a case like the present, which rests entirely on circumstantial evidence, should affect all minds alike, is not to be expected. No evidence of a literary forgery has ever been found "as subtle as Arachne's woof." There has ever been some "orifex," through which a crotchetty, partial, or sceptical mind might escape the necessity of conviction. After the forgeries of Macpherson, Chatterton, and Ireland, there remained critics who having committed themselves to an opinion in favour of the authenticity or genuineness of the matter to which spuriousness was imputed, held with consistent tenacity to their original opinion, even after the spuriousness had been established beyond a rational doubt. In the late case of the forgeries of Constantine Simonides, Sir Thomas Phillips remained a convert to the genuineness of the two Greek manuscripts which he had purchased of Simonides (viz. one consisting of the poems of Hesiod, and another of portions of Homer), even after Sir F. Madden had pronounced against them, and Simonides had expiated one of his crimes in the dungeons of Berlin. And quite lately Mr. Mayer of Liverpool shewed his confidence in the integrity of the arch-forger by entrusting him with the unrolling of the papyri of a Greek manuscript which had been brought from Thebes. The result was as might have been anticipated. Simonides evolved from the folds of the papyri parts of three leaves of a papyrus scroll containing the 19th chapter of the Gospel of St. Matthew,—with new readings, of course! Simonides' skill in simulating a palimpsest is only too well known, as is also his craft in secreting what he intends to discover. Yet it would surprise no one who is acquainted with the history of literary frauds if Mr. Mayer should remain all his life a believer in the newly evolved papyrus and in the integrity of the famous Greek impostor.

The supreme importance of the questions arising out of the Perkins Folio, over all the other cases of forgery has obliged me to deal with that single case in a far more elaborate manner than with any of the others. It has been my aim to furnish a complete and nearly exhaustive analysis of the Perkins case, in all its aspects. The reader must not be offended with the apparent unimportance of some of the details. He must remember that the evidence is cumulative, and that in the chain with which I here present him the smallest link augments the weight of the integral mass that goes either to annihilate the authenticity and genuineness of the manuscript notes and emendations, or to identify their sponsor and their fabricator.

It would be disingenuous in me if I did not confess *in limine* my own hearty conviction of the spuriousness of all the annotations, and, with two exceptions, of all the documents which form the subject of the following examination; and further, my own opinion that at present Mr. Collier's character has not been vindicated from the presumption of complicity in so numerous and important a series of frauds. But in each case I have stated both sides of the question, and have not been slow to give full weight to such circumstances as have any tendency to relieve Mr. Collier from the suspicions which attach to his dealings with the matters in dispute. It is not, however, any part of my design to play the part of apologist or advocate for Mr. Collier, though, for matter of that, I have no doubt I could fill even that *rôle* with far more benefit to him than some of his blind adherents and partisans, who, to save him from the imputations of dishonesty, have not hesitated to do their best to blacken his reputation as an author, an editor, and a man of sense.[1] But while I repudiate the task of defending Mr. Collier, I must assure my readers that, out of the interests of truth, I have no inducement to impute discreditable conduct to one whose good faith I never doubted till the year before last, and whose services to literature, after deducting from his works those parts which relate to the alleged fabrications, I cannot but admit to be great and important.

With the exception of the facsimile from *Hamlet*, which faces the title-page, and is the work of Mr. Frederick G. Netherclift, the facsimiles from the Perkins Folio have been approved by a competent judge appointed for that purpose by the Duke of Devonshire, and are published with his Grace's express sanction.

My best thanks are hereby presented to the noble Duke for the permission to take and publish numerous and various facsimiles from the Perkins Folio, and for the means he has taken to ensure their fidelity—to the Earl of Ellesmere for unrestrained access to the manuscript treasures of the library at Bridgewater House, and for permission to take and publish numerous facsimiles therefrom—to the Governors of Dulwich College for a like permission in respect of

[1] I allude in particular to certain writers in "The Edinburgh Review" and "The Saturday Review."

the manuscripts in the library of that seminary—and in particular to the Master of the College for the trouble he has taken to afford my facsimilist access to the manuscripts—to Sir Francis Palgrave for a like permission in respect of the Petition of the Blackfriars Players to the Privy Council, which is in the State Paper Office—and to Mr. Francis Charles Parry for the use of his own memoranda of his interviews with Mr. Collier.

In order to enable my readers to see at a glance all the English literature relating to the Shakspere controversy, I have appended to this work a bibliographical list of separate publications, and of articles and reviews in periodicals, comprising nearly everything of interest (except mere letters and paragraphs), which has been published in this country on the subject of the alleged Shakspere forgeries. That list contains also some few American publications. I regret that I am not in possession of the means of making the list more complete in respect of works published out of England.

C. M. I.

Valentines, Ilford.
Oct. 10th, 1860.

INTRODUCTION.

Ever since July 2, 1859, on which day Mr. N. E. S. A. Hamilton's first letter appeared in "The Times," a literary controversy of more than usual importance has been maintained with an eagerness and a warmth which rarely extend beyond the sphere of private and personal disputes. While men of eminence in letters are found ranged on both sides of this controversy, it is note-worthy that the professional palæographists are not divided on the palæographic questions; but, on the contrary, that class of literary men, independently of any community of interest, are unanimous against the genuineness of the disputed documents.

Warmth of the Controversy.

Unanimity of the Palæographists.

Meanwhile the unskilled public look on in wonderment at the exhibition of so much animosity about a mere dry literary question. Some manuscript annotations are discovered in two printed books, and many manuscript documents are discovered bearing more or less on the contents of those books. The writing in the printed books and in the manuscripts is pronounced to be a modern fabrication, *i.e.* executed in modern times with a fraudulent purpose. It certainly seems at first sight that here there can be little or nothing to stir up personal strife: and I will take upon myself to affirm that if no reflections

Cause of the personal animus.

on moral character had been involved in the mere literary question, very few persons would have been found to defend the genuineness either of the annotations or of the documents; and that if controversy had been provoked, the discussion would have been conducted with the most respectable frigidity. The question of the genuineness of old-looking writing, or of the authenticity of the matter so written, could hardly have disturbed the moral equilibrium of palæographists, critics or reviewers. But simply because Mr. Collier was the discoverer of the annotations and of all the manuscripts whose genuineness is questioned, and because he has to a great extent identified his reputation with those alleged discoveries, it became difficult to prevent the intrusion of a personal animus into the literary question: and when Mr. Collier's connexion with these annotations and documents assumed a more serious complexion than that of their discoverer, or even their sponsor, the controversy on both sides became leavened with a bitterness which I do not believe to have had any other source than jealousy for the purity of our Elizabethan Literature on the one hand, and jealousy for the good name of Mr. Collier on the other.

Indifference of the periodical press to the purity of Shakspere's text.

From the first promulgation of the notes and emendations found on the margins of the Perkins Folio down to the present time nothing has moved me so much as the absolute indifference of nearly all the contributors to the periodical press of England to the purity of the text of England's greatest author. Judging from the indiscriminate praise which has been lavished on Mr. Collier's manuscript corrector, both while the question of the genuineness of the old writing had received no attempt at a solution, as well as since the publication of a mass of evidence against its genuineness comprised in the works of Mr. Hamilton and myself, it is difficult to believe that the majority of men of letters cared as much for having the text of Shakspere pure, as for having it intelligible. It is characteristic of the Englishman to be impatient alike of doubt, as of obscurity. He takes up his Shakspere, and reads some such sentence as the following:—

Cause of the indiscriminate praise which the public awarded to the "old corrector."

> And yet the spacious breadth of this division
> Admits no orifex for a point, as subtle
> As Ariachne's broken woof, to enter.[1]

If he thinks at all, he must certainly wonder how a point can be as subtle as a broken woof. How eagerly then does he accept any relief, that comes even in the shape of a conjecture, such as that of Mr. Keightley,[2] who would read,

> And yet the spacious breadth of this division,
> As subtle as Arachne's broken woof,
> Admits no orifex for a point to enter.

But what if the relief come in the shape of conjecture, confirmed by a manuscript emendation in a

[1] Troilus and Cressida. Act V. sc. 2.

[2] Notes and Queries, 2nd Series, vol. ix. p. 358.

handwriting of the middle of the 17th century? Common sense is satisfied, criticism is disarmed, doubt is removed, and grumbling is appeased. The Englishman can now read his Shakspere without a hitch or halt. That is too great a comfort for him to trouble himself about the purity of the text.

The necessity of a preliminary scrutiny of the MSS. overlooked by the public.

But plainly our Englishman is but gulled. How is it that he omitted the precaution of ascertaining, to the best of his skill, whether the writing was of that date to which its antique form appeared to belong. Specimens of the corrections in the Bridgewater Folio were made public in 1841, and a vast number of the notes and emendations of the Perkins Folio were, as I have said, promulgated in 1852; yet, notwithstanding the recommendation of Mr. Charles Knight[3] and that of Mr. Halliwell,[4] no palæographic examination of the Perkins Folio or of the Bridgewater Folio took place till the middle of 1859. Perhaps, on the whole, it has been favourable to our literature that the scrutiny was postponed; for in the meantime the notes and emendations, coming recommended by manuscript authority and, for the most part, endorsed by Mr. Collier, obtained a more favourable hearing than mere conjectures could have done; and the text of Shakspere received, in consequence, a thorough revision at the hands of verbal critics. But inasmuch as their judgment was, for the most part, adverse not only to the authority but also to the excellence

The interests of literature jeopardised but not compromised.

[3] Old Lamps or New, p. lix.

[4] Observations on the Shakspearian Forgeries, &c. p. 8.

of the emendations, even when so recommended and endorsed, it may be very satisfactorily concluded that few, if any, of these claimants on their favour and patronage would have enjoyed the most ephemeral reign in the text of the great Bard, had they, from the first, stood on their own intrinsic merits only.

Bridgewater House MSS.

The documents discovered by Mr. Collier in Bridgewater House, like the manuscript notes of the two folios, long escaped palæographic examination. They were made known to the public by him in 1835 and 1836; but it was not till 1853 that their genuineness was debated. The reason for the delay in this case was probably similar to that in the former case. Readers of the various biographies of Shakspere, knowing how scanty were the facts which formed the structure of those narratives, naturally devoured with eagerness any further materials, however meagre and unimportant, and, I may add, however wanting in authenticity. The *New Facts*, 1835, *New Particulars*, 1836, and *Further Particulars*, 1839, of Mr. Collier alike fed the popular craving, and the name of that editor was generally regarded as a guarantee of the genuineness of the materials communicated by him. Nor did Mr. Halliwell's two pamphlets[5] succeed in awakening the suspicions of the public. It was not, in fact, till evidence had been adduced against the genuineness of the manuscript notes of the Perkins

[5] Observations on the Shakspearian Forgeries, 1853, and Curiosities of Modern Shaksperian Criticism, 1853.

Folio that the public took any interest whatever in the other questions.

The Dulwich College MSS.

Most of the Dulwich documents which now lie under suspicion of forgery were published by Mr. Collier in his *Memoirs of Edward Alleyn*, 1841, and his *History of English Dramatic Poetry*, 1831. And these were not submitted to the scrutiny of palæographic experts till the autumn of 1859, and, as to some, not till the spring of the present year.

Petition of the Blackfriars Players to the Privy Council.

The Petition of the Blackfriars Players to the Privy Council, which is in the State Paper Office, was first published by Mr. Collier in his *History of English Dramatic Poetry*, vol. i. pp. 297-300. No palæographic examination of it took place till the spring of the present year.

The supposititious MSS.

The remaining documents of which I have given an account in the penultimate chapter, are not known to have had any existence, except from the statements of Mr. Collier: the fact being that they are not in the depositories where he professes to have found them.

COMPLETE VIEW

OF

THE SHAKSPERE CONTROVERSY.

CHAPTER I.

The Bridgewater Folio.

Authority of printed copies.

Till within the last score years, the only presumed authority to which editors of Shakspere's works had recourse, for the regulation or emendation of the text, was the printed text of the early quarto and folio editions of his plays, and the early impressions of his poems and sonnets. The text of a play founded on one of the folios, or on a quarto, was received as, in a certain sense, authoritative; and an eclectic text, formed on several early editions of the same play, though perhaps looked upon with some suspicion, was still regarded as having some claim to authority. Beyond such quasi-authoritative sources of the text, lay nothing but the region of conjecture. Conjecture, it is true, especially in the case of such a critic as Lewis Theobald, from the singular felicity and discretion with which it was employed, or from the perfect and absolute fitness of a proposed reading to the utmost exigence of the context, was a very frequent source of readings which maintained an unquestioned place in the text of Shakspere, and were regarded with as much admiration and respect as the most authoritative readings—in a word, they were received as *authentic*.

State of the text of the old copies.

To enable my readers to understand the condition in which an old editor found the text of Shakspere, it is necessary that I should call his attention to a few details of only technical interest. Shakspere wrote for the boards, and not for the table. The Globe Theatre was his book; and his admirers used their ears and eyes conjointly in the perusal of his immortal dramas. He died, and made no sign indicative of a care for the preservation of his works as classics for posterity. Up to and inclusive of the year 1622 *fourteen* of his plays had been published in *quarto* editions—viz.

Hamlet.	Much ado about nothing.
I. Hen. IV.	Richard II.
II. Hen. IV.	Richard III.
King Lear.	Romeo and Juliet.
Love's Labour's Lost.	Titus Andronicus.
Merchant of Venice.	Troilus and Cressida.
Midsummer-night's Dream.	Othello.[1]

[1] I ought to add that Mr. Collier mentions (Notes and Queries, 1st S. vol. viii. p. 74.) a unique 4to. of *The Taming of the Shrew*, "which came out some years before the folio 1623." He subsequently wrote, "Only three copies of this 4to. have yet come to light: one, (among Capell's books at Cambridge)

All these plays were published once or oftener in Shakspere's life-time, except Othello, which did not appear in print till 1622, *i. e.* six years after Shakspere's death.

There were also published in his lifetime *six* plays, bearing the names of *Hen. V.*, *King John* (in two parts), *The Merry Wives of Windsor*, *The Taming of a Shrew*, and *The Contention of the two Houses of York and Lancaster*, which last is in general equivalent to Parts II. and III. of Hen. VI. These *answer to* six of Shakspere's authentic plays; but in fact are *different*. The old plays of *Hen. V.* and *The Merry Wives of Windsor*, appear to be merely early sketches of the authentic

---

has the title page with the imprint of I. Smithwicke 1631: another (in the British Museum) has only a fragment of that title page, without the imprint; and the third (in the hands of the editor) has no title-page at all, but a memorandum in manuscript at the top of the first page (sign. A. 2), the upper half of which has been cropped away by a careless binder, so that only the lower half of the figures and letters remains; enough, however, to enable us to read, as well as the inscription can be made out, "1607 stayed by the author." The date may be 1609, but the top of the six, and of the seven or nine has fallen a sacrifice to the shears. What we are probably to understand is, that the publication of the comedy in 1607 or 1609 had been in some way stayed by the intervention of the author, on behalf of himself and the company to which he belonged; and that having in consequence been laid aside for a number of years, some copies of it, remaining in the hands of Smithwicke the Stationer, were issued in 1631, as if it had then been first published."—Collier's Ed. of Shakespeare, 1858, vol. ii. p. 437.

plays, like the *Hamlet* of 1603, and the *Romeo and Juliet* of 1597.

In the same year, his fellows Heminge and Condell issued the first folio edition of his plays complete, with the exception of *Pericles*, and *The Two Noble Kinsmen*, of considerable parts of which he was unquestionably the author. These plays could not have been excluded on the principle of including only those of his plays of which he was the undivided author; for the plays of II. Hen. VI. and III. Hen. VI. as well as Hen. VIII. appear in that collection, and in the first two it is certain that Shakspere worked up another man's labours,[2] while in the last it is highly probable that Fletcher worked upon an unfinished play of Shakspere's.[3]

Of this first folio edition of Shakspere, but one copy is known to be extant bearing the date 1622; all the other known copies bear the date 1623; and the edition is generally quoted as of the latter year. A second edition of Heminge and Condell's collection appeared in 1632; a third in 1663, and this third edition was re-issued, with the addition of seven spurious plays, in 1664. A fourth edition, comprizing these spurious plays, was published in 1685. These are the only early folio editions of Shakspere's plays.

The folio 1623 contained (a) the above mentioned

[2] See Boswell's Variorum Ed. 1821, vol. ii. p. 315. As to I. Hen. VI. and Titus Andronicus, the probability is that Shakspere had no hand in either of them.

[3] See Gentleman's Magazine, August, 1850.

fourteen authentic plays of Shakspere, (β) the *six* authentic plays corresponding with the *six* older plays, and (γ) *sixteen* plays which had not been previously published, in all thirty-six plays. The value of the first folio edition is, in fact, principally due to the circumstance of its being the earliest known edition of *sixteen* authentic plays of Shakspere.

Value of the folio 1623.

Of its value on any other ground, there is a remarkable difference of opinion. It is one of those questions on which critics must necessarily differ, pretty much in proportion to their knowledge of the facts of the case. By Mr. Knight, the folio of 1623 was originally regarded as an extremely well printed book for the time it was issued, and a text of unquestionable authenticity. But after the publication of his first Pictorial Edition, he saw how impossible it was to found a text upon the first folio edition only. Accordingly, in his National Edition, he was necessitated to deviate very considerably from the text of the folio; and I can only regret that in doing so he should have, not unfrequently, omitted to indicate by a foot-note his desertion of the folio reading and his adoption of that of the quarto.[4] Mr. Collier has pronounced it, with one exception, as well printed as any contemporary work of the kind.[5]

---

[4] Lest it should be thought that I overstate the case against Mr. Knight, I beg to refer the reader, for example, to the text of Hamlet, in the National Edition. In the first Act of that play he will find ten instances of silent deviation from the folios, and adoption of the quartos.

[5] Letter in The Athenæum, March 27th, 1852.

Professor Craik puts forward the most extravagant pretensions for this edition, and appears to regard it as one of the most accurately printed books of the period.[6] Mr. Bolton Corney, whose opinion is of more value than that of either of the last named gentlemen, has enacted[7] that "the text of the plays, *errors excepted* (!) shall," in all future editions, "be that of 1623, collated with that of such of the plays as had been published in a finished state." Now, without cavilling at the very wide signification of such a phrase as "errors excepted," I can by no means admit the canon in question: for this reason; that the execution of the edition of 1623 does not answer to the professions of Heminge and Condell. The entire text of the plays is certainly not derived, as, from their preface, they would lead their readers to believe, from any manuscripts of Shakspere's; nor indeed from any playhouse copies. The text of those plays which "had been published in a finished state," before 1623, *is, in the folio edition of that date, generally based upon the early quartos.* This is especially observable in the *First and Second Parts of Henry IV., Love's Labour's Lost, Merchant of Venice, Midsummer Night's Dream, Much ado about nothing, Richard II., Titus Andronicus,* and *Troilus and Cressida.* In each of these plays "there is," says the accurate, but clumsy Capell, "an almost strict conformity between the two im-

[6] The English of Shakspere.

[7] Notes and Queries, 1st S. vol. vi. p. 2.

pressions: some additions there are in the second, and some omissions; but *the faults and errors of the quartos are all preserved in the folio*; and others added to them."

This fact excludes the supposition that the editors of the folio had a manuscript authority for their text of these *nine* plays, or in fact any more trustworthy copies of them to print from, than the quartos which have come down to us. These remarks are true *in a less degree* of all the other *five* plays which we possess in early quarto editions. However, the facts, that the editors of 1623 printed additions to the quarto texts, and omitted passages from their folio which are contained in the quartos, are of great interest and importance for all future editors: but that no editor can be bound by the "text of the plays, errors excepted," as they are given in the folio of 1623, is a negative principle which does not admit of a rational doubt. As to the readings which are first found in the second, third, or fourth folio, it is self-evident that they can hardly carry more weight than the most recent conjectural emendations.[a]

Province of conjecture.

The conclusion from these premises is inevitably this, that we possess no authoritative text at all; and, of course, the door is open to legitimate conjecture as to the readings to be adopted, wherever the defective state of the text of the quartos or first folio renders emendation expedient. Let it be understood

---

[a] See Mr. Halliwell's tract on "Who smothers her with painting," 1852, pp. 6-8, where this point is ably discussed.

that a text shall be held to be defective, so long as the sense, if any, which it conveys is not such as it is probable a man like Shakspere would have put into the mouth of the speaker on the particular occasion in question. *Hic labor, hoc opus!* It will thus be evident to my readers that a very wide latitude is allowed to conjecture; in fact that nothing should be held to disqualify conjecture, but an ignorance in the conjecturer of the peculiar manners and customs, and the special idioms of the dramatic language of Shakspere's day.

However widely the opinions of competent and well-informed critics may differ as to what is to be taken as such a defective state of the text as to justify emendation, it is unfortunately true that in an enormous number of instances, the text of Shakspere, whether we find it in the quartos or the folio, is in such an abominably corrupt state, that emendation is a necessity, and must be acknowledged to be so even by those who regard it as an evil, and would never allow it where *any kind of sense* can be tortured out of the original words. Innumerable are the phrases out of which no possible sense can be tortured, by any kind of exegetical manœuvre. Every editor has his own favourite nostrums for many of these: but some cases are so hopeless, that it is an almost universal custom for editors to print the nonsense of the original text, in sheer despair of superseding it by any plausible emendations. Of these almost hopeless *cruces* the number does not exceed twenty-five. In some the difficulty lies in the construction of the sentence; in others, in the use of words which have not, and probably never had, any meaning. But these form but a drop in the "multitudinous seas" of misprints with which the text of quartos and folios are alike overwhelmed. In fact, it is not going too far to affirm the very reverse of Professor Craik's *dictum*, and aver that the first folio edition of Shakspere is the worse printed work, of any pretensions to permanent interest, dramatic or otherwise, that the first half of the seventeenth century produced.

Extremes of editorship.

Accordingly, the editors and conjectural critics of the two editions *cum notis variorum*, not unnaturally fell into the extreme of loose conjecture; they were more anxious to reform, than to understand: and the editions of our own day afford abundant evidence of a reaction upon that laxness of criticism, and almost universally err in the extreme of a too close adherence to the old copies. Against this blind deference to the printed authorities, the following protest of Mr. W. N. Lettsom cannot be too often repeated:—

"The earlier editors were no doubt far too ready to tamper with the original text; some of their successors have run into the other extreme; they perversely maintain the most ridiculous blunders of the old copies, and almost seem disposed to place conjectural criticism on a level with hap-hazard guess work. What is called conjecture, however, is neither more nor less than a particular application of circumstantial evidence, and if we receive such evidence when property or life is at stake, surely we should not reject it when we are sitting in judgment merely on words or syllables. At any rate, we should be sadly disappointed if we expected to escape the hazards of conjecture by a servile adherence to old copies. Scholars and critics are not the only persons who tamper with texts. Correctors, transcribers, and compositors have been much too ready to alter whatever they were unable to understand; their stupid sophistications have too often overlaid the genuine readings, and have been blindly received, as of paramount authority, by the unsuspecting simplicity of over-cautious commentators.

It would be well if the latter stopped here; unfortunately they are not satisfied with retaining corruptions; they must needs attempt to defend and explain them. In consequence they get into a bad habit of wresting and straining language, and finally become thorough proficients in the bewildering art of forcing any sense out of any words. In their desperate efforts to extract sense from nonsense, the poet himself has been too often sacrificed to the printer, and has thus gained a character for obscurity to a degree far beyond his deserts."[9]

Epoch of MS. authority.

In 1841 was published Mr. Collier's "Reasons for a New Edition of Shakespeare's Works, containing notices of the defects of former impressions and pointing out the lately acquired means of illustrating the plays, poems, and biography of the poet."

This tract forms an epoch in Shaksperian criticism. It was here that Mr. Collier first appealed to *manuscript authority* for the regulation and emendation of the text of Shakspere. We are here first introduced to a folio with manuscript corrections, viz. the first folio of the late Lord Ellesmere, (then Lord Francis Egerton.) This copy of the 1623 edition is perhaps

[9] Shakspeare's Versification, by W. Sidney Walker. Preface, p. xiv.

the finest extant. Its general condition is superior, and its margins larger than those of any other known copy; in fact it is in every respect in the same condition in which it was when it came from the printers in 1623 into the hands of Lord Chancellor Egerton, save only that a few deficient leaves have been supplied from an inferior copy,[10] and that its margins have some *manuscript notes*. The copy was known to bibliographers long before Mr. Collier had access to the Bridgewater Library. But no manuscript corrections had previously been seen upon its margins. Mr. Collier, to whom Lord F. Egerton had lent the volume, announces the discovery of these corrections in the following words:—

"certain corrections, in the margin of the printed portion of the folio, are probably as old as the reign of Charles I. Whether they were merely conjectural, or were made from original manuscripts of the plays, to which the individual might have had access, it is not perhaps possible to ascertain. * * * * these verbal, and sometimes literal, annotations are only found in a few of the plays in the commencement of the volume; and from what follows, it will be a matter of deep regret that the corrector of the text carried his labours no farther."[11]

Mr. Collier then proceeds to give *five* examples of these emendations. As the whole of the corrections in the volume number only *thirty-two*, with pencil suggestions for two others, I will give them all, premising that they will, most of them, be found in the notes to Mr. Collier's edition, 1841-1844.

[10] Mr. Collier says "supplied by manuscript." Where is this manuscript now?

[11] Reasons, 2nd edition, p. 14.

LIST OF MANUSCRIPT CORRECTIONS AND ERASURES IN THE BRIDGEWATER FOLIO.

Reference to Folio, 1623.	Reference to Play.	Text of Folio, 1623.	MS. correction or erasure in the Bridgewater Folio.	Substituted or amended word.
p. 63, c. 2.	Measure for M. Act i. sc. 4.	(The needfull bits and curbes to headstrong *weedes*,)	Steedes (erased)	steeds (*sic* Theobald and Perkins)
p. 69, c. 1.	„ Act ii. sc. 4.	Growne feard, and tedious:	(The cross of the "f" erased on the inside)	seard (*sic* Warburton; sear, Perkins)
p. 70, c. 1.	„ Act ii. sc. 4.	Owe, and succeed *thy* weaknesse.	this	this (*sic* Perkins)
p. 70, c. 2.	„ Act iii. sc. 1.	For thine owne bowels which do call thee, *fire*	s	sire (*sic* Rowe and Perkins)
p. 72, c. 1.	„ Act iii. sc. 1.	my minde promises with my habit,	(erased)	Liverie ?
p. 133, c. 1.	Love's L. L. Act iv. sc. 3.	Disfigure not his *Shop*.	shape	shape
p. 186, c. 2.	As you Like it, Act i. sc. 2.	who perceiueth our naturall wits	ing	perceiving (*sic* Fo. 1632)
p. 187, c. 2.	„ Act i. sc. 2.	I can tell you there is such oddes in the man:	e (erased)	men (*sic* Hanmer and Perkins)
(2nd) p. 187, c. 2.	„ Act i. sc. 3.	After my flight: now goe *in we* content	wo in	wo in (*sic* Fo. 1632)
p. 190, c. 2.	„ Act ii. sc. 3.	Why, what's the matter ?	Orl	Orl. (*sic* Fo. 1632)
p. 191, c. 2.	„ Act ii. sc. 4.	*Wearing* thy hearer in thy Mistris praise,	(erased)	Wearying ? (*sic* Fo. 1632)
p. 197, c. 2.	„ Act iii. sc. 2.	to a liuing humor of madnes,	o	loving (*sic* Johnson and Perkins)
p. 200, c. 2.	„ Act iv. sc. 1.	let me better acquainted with thee.	ance	acquaintance
p. 204, c. 1.	„ Act v. sc. 1.	I will ore-run thee with police:	y (erased)	policy (*sic* Fo. 1632)
p. 231, c. 1.	All's Well, &c. Act i. sc. 1.	within ten yeare it will make it selfe *two*,	10	ten (*sic* Hanmer)
p. 234, c. 1.	„ Act i. sc. 3.	The mistrie of your louelinesse,	n	loneliness (*sic* Theobald)
p. 236, c. 1.	„ Act ii. sc. 2.	Where hope is coldest, and despaire most *shifts*.	ffits	fits (*sic* Theobald and Perkins)
p. 237, c. 2.	„ Act ii. sc. 3.	I had rather be in this choise,	(erased)	chase ?
p. 240, c. 1.	„ Act ii. sc. 5.	*And* ere I doe begin.	E	End (*sic* Perkins)
p. 244, c. 2.	„ Act iii. sc. 7.	Resolue to carrie her:	ued	Resolved (*sic* Collier)
(2nd) p. 251, c. 1.	„ Act v. sc. 2.	You begge more then, word then.	a	a
(2nd) p. 252, c. 2.	„ Act v. sc. 3.	I wonder sir, *sir*, wiues are monsters	for	for
p. 278, c. 1.	Winter's Tale, Act i. sc. 2.	What Lady *she* her Lord.	shold	should (*sic* Perkins)
p. 279, c. 1.	„ Act i. sc. 2.	Of my Boyes face, me thoughts	y	my (*sic* Perkins)
p. 280, c. 1.	„ Act i. sc. 2.	My Wife's a Holy-Horse,	b	hoby-horse (*sic* Pope and Perkins)
p. 285, c. 2.	„ Act ii. sc. 3.	So sure as th*is* Beard's gray.	y	thy
p. 288, c. 2.	„ Act iii. sc. 3.	Hath made thy person for the Th,ower-out	r	thrower-out (*sic* Fo. 1632)
p. 289, c. 1.	„ Act iii. sc. 3.	You're a mad, olde man:	e	made (*sic* Theobald and Perkins)
p. 294, c. 1.	„ Act iv. sc. 3.	And hand,ed loue, as you do;	l	handled (*sic* Perkins)
p. 296, c. 2.	„ Act iv. sc. 3.	(For I doe feare eyes *over*)	e	ever (*sic* Perkins)
p. 299, c. 1.	„ Act v. sc. 1.	Aboue a better, gone; so must thy Graue	c	grace
p. 299, c. 2.	„ Act v. sc. 1.	Giue you all greetings, that a King (*at* friend)	s	as (*sic* Fo. 1632)

N.B. There are two pencil notes on the last board, as follows, "*His* for is, p. 349, col. 1; Heires for haires, 378, col. 1." These suggestions have not been acted upon in the emendations made with ink.

MS. Corrections in pencil & ink from the Bridgewater Folio.

l | And handed loue, as you do;
Winter's Tale. – page 294 col. 1.

| What Lady ſhe her Lord.
Winter's Tale. – page 278 col. 1.

| Disfigure not his Shop.
Love's Labour Lost. – page 133 col. 1.

fitts | Where hope is coldeſt, and deſpaire moſt ſhifts.
All's well that ends well. – page 236 col. 1.

now goe in we content | no in
As you like it. – page 187 col. 1

c | Aboue a better, gone; ſo muſt thy Graue
Winter's Tale. – page 299 col. 1.

that a King (at friend) | s
Winter's Tale. – page 299 col. 1.

a | *Laf.* You begge more then word then.
All's well that ends well. – page 251 col. 1

In the table given by Mr. Hamilton (*Inquiry*, 1850, pp. 74 and 75) entitled, " Manuscript Corrections in the Bridgewater Folio, 1623," there are only eighteen of those corrections, fourteen being omitted.[12]

In July, 1859, I called on Sir F. Madden, at the British Museum, for the express purpose of urging him to obtain the loan of the Bridgewater Folio, in order to submit it to a palæographic scrutiny. I need not detail the purport of our conversation: suffice it to say, that by one of those curious coincidences, which happen so often, and yet always strike one as so very unlikely, as I left the Museum Lord Ellesmere, accompanied by Dr. Kingsley, entered it, carrying with him the very folio in question,

Palæographic inquisition on the MS. notes.

[12] Mr. Collier has not been slow to avail himself of this circumstance, in his teply to Mr. Hamilton's charges against him of publishing scarcely half the emendations of the Perkins Folio, in his so-called " List of every Manuscript Note and Emendation in Mr. Collier's copy of Shakespeare's Works, folio. 1632." But Mr. Collier, in retaliating on his opponent, charitably reduces the number of Mr. Hamilton's omissions to *two*. (*Reply*, p. 23, note.) The fact is, as stated by Mr. Collier, that " few things are more difficult than to be utterly faultless in such extracts." But how that admission can help Mr. Collier's case, I do not perceive, since he tells us that he *never dreamed at any time of including many* of the corrections: yet he calls his List of 1856, " A List of every Manuscript Note and Emendation, &c." and challenges his readers to point out any sin of omission in his " Notes and Emendations," 1853, except two corrections which he specifies. (Preface to " Seven Lectures of Coleridge," &c. 1856, p. 79.)

which he had brought with the view of eliciting Sir F. Madden's opinion as to the genuineness of the writing in which the corrections are made. Accordingly the writing had the benefit of a palæographic scrutiny *sur le coup*, by Sir F. Madden and Mr. Hamilton, and that same morning it was discovered that in four cases of correction, viz. *this*, *a*, *handled*, and *as*, (*vide* foregoing table) pencil marks were more or less traceable,[13] to an extent which shewed that each of these emendations had been written in pencil, before they were inked in. Of course the inference is that others of the corrections had been inserted on a like principle. Furthermore, Sir F. Madden and Mr. Hamilton came to the conclusion that the ink-writing was not in a genuine, but a simulated character, and belonged, not to the time of the Commonwealth, but to the 19th century.

These circumstances will have greater significance as we advance in our examination of the general question. At present I simply call attention to them, in order to preserve the order of chronology in the history of each suspected document.

---

[13] Hamilton's Inquiry, pp. 72—75.

MS. Corrections in ink from the Bridgewater Folio.

perceiveth our naturall wits too dull | ing

As you like it. page 186. col. 2.

E | And ere I doe begin.

All's well that ends well. page 240 col. 2.

* thiz | Owe, and succeed thy weaknesse.

Measure for Measure. page 70. col. 2.

MS. Correction in ink from the Perkins Folio.

ing 3

All's well that ends well. page 242 col. 1.

From Collier's Catalogue of the Bridgewater Library.

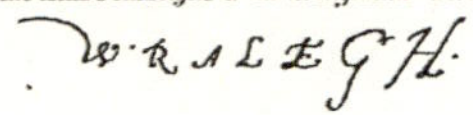

MS. Correction in ink from the Perkins Folio.

giz | And would ye not thinke |||

Henry VI part 2. page 124. col. 1.

* *Under this word there is a faint trace of the same word in pencil.*

CHAPTER II.

THE PERKINS FOLIO: ITS PURCHASE AND EXAMINATION BY MR. COLLIER.

Mr. Collier's Narratives.

BESIDES the manuscript corrections of the Bridgewater Folio, 1623, it was found that a copy of the folio, 1685, which had belonged to the poet Southerne, had a considerable number of manuscript notes. For a period of ten years from the publication of Mr. Collier's *New Facts*, these were the only manuscript sources from which any changes were publicly made in the text of Shakspere. Most of the corrections of the Bridgewater Folio and several of the annotations of Southerne's Folio were published by Mr. Collier in the text and notes of his edition of Shakspere, 1841-1844. Nothing more was heard of manuscript corrections till the year 1852. In "The Athenæum" for January 31, in that year, appeared a communication from Mr. Collier, dated "Maidenhead, Jan. 17," in which he gave the following account of a "find" which it had been his fortune to make:

"A short time before the death of the late Mr. Rodd, of Newport Street, I happened to be in his shop when a considerable parcel of books arrived from the country. He told me that they had been bought for him at an auction,—I think, in Bedfordshire; but I did not look on it as a matter of any importance to observe from whence they came. He unpacked them in my presence; and I cast my eyes on several that did not appear to me very inviting,—as they were entirely out of my line of reading. There were two, however, that attracted my attention:—one being a fine copy of Florio's Italian Dictionary, of the Edition of 1611,—and the other a much-thumbed, abused, and imperfect copy of the second Folio of Shakespeare in 1632. The first I did not possess,—and the last I was willing to buy, inasmuch as I apprehended it would add some missing leaves to a copy of the same impression which I had had for some time on my shelves. As was his usual course, Mr. Rodd required a very reasonable price for both:—for the first, I remember, I gave 12*s*.,—and for the last, only £1. 10*s*.

Your readers are no doubt aware that the second folio of Shakespeare, in 1632, is never, even when in good condition, a very dear book; but this copy was without the title-page (consequently without the portrait),—wanted several sheets at the end,—and was imperfect in the middle of the volume. With this last circumstance I was not acquainted at the time,—for I saw only the commencement and the conclusion; but I observed that some of the leaves were blotted and dirty,—and that although the rough calf binding was evidently the original, it was greasy and shabby. On the outside of one of the covers was inscribed,—"Tho. Perkins, his booke."

When the volume reached my house, I employed a person to ascertain whether any of the leaves in it would supply the deficiency in my other copy. Finding that I was disappointed in this respect (except as far as regarded two torn and stained pages), I put the book away in a closet,—somewhat vexed that I had mis-spent my money. I did not look at it again until shortly before I removed to this place; when I selected such books as I chose to take with me from those which I meant to leave behind in the Pantechnicon. Then it was that I for the first time remarked that the folio of 1632 which I had bought from Mr. Rodd contained manuscript alterations of the text as it stood printed in that early edition. These alterations were in an old handwriting—probably not of a later date than the Protectorate,—and applied (as I afterwards found, on going through the volume here) to every play. There was hardly a page without emendations of more or less importance and interest,—and some of them appeared to me highly valuable. The punctuation, on which of course so much of the author's meaning depends, was corrected in, I may say, thousands of places.

I did not come into possession of this volume—much less examine it minutely—until some years after I had completed the Shakespeare which I superintended through the press,—otherwise I should unquestionably have made great use of it in the notes;—and in particular instances the changes appear to me not merely so plausible, but so self-evident, that in spite of the principle I adopted of a close adherence to the old printed copies, I cannot help thinking that I should have availed myself of a few of these manuscript alterations in the text. Some of them may have been purely arbitrary or conjectural; but others seem to have been justified either by occasional resort to better manuscripts than those employed by the old player-editors, or as is not improbable, by the recital of the text at one of our old theatres when the corrector of my folio of 1632 was present, and of which recital he afterwards availed himself."

[Mr. Collier then gives a great number of examples of the old Corrector's "fancy," concluding his letter thus]:—

"It is my intention to place this relic before, and at the disposal of, the Council of the Shakespeare Society at its next meeting. The members will then be better able to judge of the date and of the peculiarity and importance of the alterations suggested on nearly every page; and if they agree with me, they will, in due time and as their funds allow, print such a selection of the manuscript notes as may best serve to explain, illustrate, or amend the acknowledged defects of the text of the plays of our greatest Dramatic Poet.

J. PAYNE COLLIER."

In "The Athenæum" for February 7, 1852, appeared a second communication from Mr. Collier on the subject of the manuscript corrections in his "folio of 1632;" he here remarks:—

"It is to me yet quite uncertain what character they [the corrections] really deserve,—that is to say, on what authority they were made:—whether they were adopted from purer manuscripts,—whether they were introduced by a person who had heard a better text recited on the stage than was given in the folios,—or whether they were merely conjectural. Perhaps all three methods were followed, as opportunity presented itself; and I cannot help thinking that the amendment in act i. sc. 1 of 'Othello,' which came last in my former letter, was an instance of speculative alteration, such as would occur to a person on reading the play. My chief reason is this:—that one of the words proposed, by the Manuscript Corrector of my folio of 1632, to be changed, seems to me on further reflexion clearly wrong. In the folios of 1623 and 1632, and in all the later editions that I have the means of consulting, the line stands thus:

'Who trimm'd in forms and visages of duty.'[1]

My folio of 1632 recommends the following change:—

'Who *learn'd* in forms and *usages* of duty.'

Now it strikes me forcibly, and it has struck friends of mine

---

[1] The context is this:

'Others there are,
Who trimm'd in forms and visages of duty,
Keep yet their hearts attending on themselves.'
Othello, act I., sc. 1.

whom I consulted, that "learn'd" is not the true word of the poet,—and that he must have written

'Who *train'd* in forms and usages of duty.'

The word "trimm'd" for *train'd* is not only an easier misprint, but *train'd* is the very word most fitted for the place, and which Shakespeare could hardly have avoided. If my corrector had employed a better manuscript than that used for the folios (the *second* being little more than a reprint of the *first*), he would, I think, have seen in it *train'd* for "trimm'd" as well as *usages* for "visages,"—but his sagacity does not appear to have suggested it to him. Still it is very possible that even a better manuscript contained this error of *learn'd* for *train'd*, while it showed, nevertheless, that *usages* ought to be substituted for visages." [2]

Mr. Collier then gives a further instalment of corrections from his "folio of 1632." In "The Athenæum," for March 27, 1852, is a third communication from Mr. Collier on the same subject. He writes:—

"Although I produced my copy of the folio of 1632 before a full assembly of the Council of the Shakespeare Society, and at a recent meeting of the Society of Antiquaries, I am informed—and can readily believe—that many members of the latter either had not an opportunity of examining it at all, or were able only to examine it so hastily that they wish to be

---

[2] A Correspondent of "The Athenæum," for March 6, 1852, affirms (but without any citation in support of his position) that in this place, *visages* means "*observances* or eye-service." "Their eye of observance," he writes, "is to their masters, but their hearts are kept waiting on themselves." Mr. Staunton more correctly explains the line to mean "Who *dress'd* in *shapes* and *masks* of duty."—Ed. vol. iii. p. 648.

allowed to inspect it again, under more favourable circumstances. I can have no hesitation in complying; because my desire is, that all who are interested should be gratified as far as possible, and enjoy the means of judging for themselves of the value and curiosity of the book. Therefore, if any of the Fellows of the Society of Antiquaries will do me the favour to meet me in the Library at Somerset House on Friday next, between the hours of 12 and 2, I shall have great pleasure in showing the volume to them. I need hardly add, that as the book is old and in a bad state of preservation, it will be necessary to be careful and cautious in handling it,—particularly as not a few of the emendations in the text are on the outer margins of the leaves. It must also be distinctly understood that no gentleman is at liberty to make memoranda, or in any way to give publicity to the notes or changes which he may inspect.

I have already mentioned, that this corrected copy of the folio 1632 unfortunately did not come into my hands until some years after I had completed and published my edition of the works of our great dramatist. In that edition I proceeded on the principle of adhering scrupulously to the text of the ancient printed Copies wherever it was possible to extract a meaning from it; and I ought perhaps to say here, that my corrected folio of 1632 does not remove by any means, all the difficulties of particular passages. Some it passes over, and others it erases,—although it alters and explains a great number of them. I have already given a variety of instances in former communications; but in consequence of a letter to which I have only replied this morning, I am tempted to add another,—and thus still farther to establish how incorrectly the first folio (followed by the second) of 1623 was printed, notwithstanding I am convinced that it was at least as well done as any book of the kind of that age, with one exception."

Mr. Collier then gives the now celebrated emendation *bisson multitude,* for "bosom multiplied," in *Coriolanus.*

The publication of these letters gave rise to a controversy on the value of these specimens of the old corrector's craft, both in "The Athenæum" and in "Notes and Queries."

Mr. Collier's *Notes and Emendations.*

In the summer of 1852 Mr. Collier superintended through the press a volume entitled "Notes and Emendations to the text of Shakespeare's Plays, from early manuscript corrections in a copy of the folio, 1632, in the possession of J. Payne Collier, Esq. F.S.A. forming a supplemental volume to the Works of Shakespeare by the same editor, in eight volumes, octavo. London: Printed for the Shakespeare Society. 1852."

A part of this impression was circulated among the members of the Shakespeare Society, but the work was not published till January, 1853,[1] when it was issued with a new title-page, and at the foot, "London, Whittaker & Co., Ave Maria Lane. 1853." These facts are inconsistent with the concluding statement in an article in "The Critic," of Aug. 27th, 1852, and which I have ascertained to have been written by Mr. F. Guest Tomlins, who was the Secretary and Treasurer of the Shakespeare Society. Mr. Tomlins writes:—

"In 1852 Mr. Collier, being director of the Shakespeare Society, produced the book to the council, and promised to let the society have the printing of a selection of the emendations, and his offer was cordially accepted. The emendations having

---

[1] I state this on the authority of Messrs. Whittaker & Co.

by this time excited much curiosity, the publishers of Mr. Collier's eight-volume Shakespeare were desirous to publish it as a supplemental volume, feeling that it was very likely to have a great effect on the sale of that edition. This was brought under Mr. Collier's notice, and mentioned by the secretary of the society to the council, who at once urged Mr. Collier to accept the publisher's offer, as it would put a hundred and twenty pounds in his pocket; whereas if the society published it, he would only get his trouble of editing for his pains, all the works of the society being edited gratuitously. Mr. Collier for a long time resisted any such arrangement; but the society insisting upon it, it was agreed, very handsomely on the part of the publishers, that they would let the society have the requisite number of copies for their subscribers at bare cost price, and thus in 1852 the society issued it with their title-page simultaneously with the public edition."

It is in reference to this explanation of Mr. Tomlins that Mr. Collier thus speaks in his Reply (p. 37):—

"It ["The Critic"] has only done me justice in the matter; and I thank it, in perfect ignorance, as far as my own knowledge is concerned, of what it may have said about me at other times and on other subjects."

What kind of ignorance a person may have, which is not a want of knowledge in him, Mr. Collier does not explain: nor does he tell his readers that a personal ally is couched under the *nom de guerre* of his deadly opponent, "The Critic."

The Introduction to the first edition of Mr. Collier's *Notes and Emendations* contains a narrative of the purchase of the Perkins Folio and discovery of the manuscript notes in it, which differs from the foregoing but very slightly in one or two particulars, omitting the allusion to the amanuensis, and adding to the facts narrated in "The Athenæum" the circumstances of the volume being taken home by Mr. Collier, and his parting with the copy of the second folio, on the chance of completing which he had purchased the Perkins Folio. There is, however, in this Introduction a candid retractation of his first judgment as to the date of the binding. These few remarks being premised, Mr. Collier shall speak for himself:—

"In the history of the volume to which I have been thus indebted, I can offer little that may serve to give it authenticity. It is very certain that the manuscript notes in its margins were made before it was subjected to all the ill-usage it has experienced. When it first came into my hands, and indeed for some time afterwards, I imagined that the binding was the original rough calf in which many books of about the same date were clothed; but more recent examination has convinced me, that this was at least the second coat it had worn. It is, nevertheless, in a very shabby condition, quite inconsistent with the state of the interior, where, besides the loss of some leaves, as already mentioned, and the loosening of others, many stains of wine, beer, and other liquids are observable: here and there, holes have been burned in the paper, either by the falling of the lighted snuff of a candle, or by the ashes of tobacco. In several places it is torn and disfigured by blots and dirt, and every margin bears evidence to frequent and careless perusal. In short, to a choice collector, no book could well present a more forbidding appearance.

I was tempted only by its cheapness to buy it, under the following circumstances:—In the spring of 1849 I happened to be in the shop of the late Mr. Rodd of Great Newport-street, at the time when a package of books arrived from the country: my impression is that it came from Bedfordshire, but I am not at all certain upon a point which I looked upon as a matter of no importance. He opened the parcel in my presence, as he had often done before in the course of my thirty or forty years' acquaintance with him, and looking at the backs and title-pages of several volumes, I saw that they were chiefly works of little interest to me. Two folios, however, attracted my attention, one of them gilt on the sides, and the other in rough calf: the first was an excellent copy of Florio's "New World of Words," 1611, with the name of Henry Osborn (whom I mistook at the moment for his celebrated namesake, Francis) upon the first leaf; and the other a copy of the second folio of Shakespeare's Plays, much cropped, the covers old and greasy, and, as I saw at a glance on opening them, imperfect at the beginning and end. Concluding hastily that the latter would complete another poor copy of the second folio, which I had bought of the same bookseller, and which I had had for some years in my possession, and wanting the former for my use, I bought them both, the Florio for twelve, and the Shakespeare for thirty shillings.

As it turned out, I at first repented my bargain as regarded the Shakespeare, because when I took it home, it appeared that two leaves which I wanted were unfit for my purpose, not merely by being too short, but damaged and defaced: thus disappointed, I threw it by, and did not see it again, until I made a selection of books I would take with me on quitting London. In the mean time, finding that I could not readily remedy the deficiencies in my other copy of the folio, 1632, I had parted with it; and when I removed into the country, with my family, in the spring of 1850, in order that I might not be without some copy of the second folio for the purpose of reference, I took with me that which is the foundation of the present work.

It was while putting my books together for removal, that I

first observed some marks in the margin of this folio; but it was subsequently placed upon an upper shelf, and I did not take it down until I had occasion to consult it. It then struck me that Thomas Perkins, whose name, with the addition of "his Booke," was upon the cover, might be the old actor who had performed in Marlowe's "Jew of Malta," on its revival shortly before 1633. At this time I fancied that the binding was of about that date, and that the volume might have been his; but in the first place, I found that his name was Richard Perkins, and in the next I became satisfied that the rough calf was not the original binding. Still, Thomas Perkins might have been a descendant of Richard; and this circumstance and others induced me to examine the volume more particularly: I then discovered, to my surprise, that there was hardly a page which did not present, in a handwriting of the time, some emendations in the pointing or in the text, while on most of them they were frequent, and on many numerous."[4]

This account was reprinted in the second edition of *Notes and Emendations,* which also bears the date 1853. For this edition, which, up to p. 200,[5] is little more than a reprint of the first, Mr. Collier received £100.[6] Of the Preface to this Edition I shall have to speak hereafter. Hitherto, as we have seen, Mr. Collier's narratives of the purchase of the Perkins Folio, and of the discovery of the manuscript corrections on its margins, are uniform and con-

---

[4] Notes and Emendations: Introduction, 2nd Ed., pp. xiii—xvi. 1st Ed., pp. v—viii.

[5] In my little work on "The Shakspeare Fabrications," Preface, p. xiii., I stated that the two Editions are identical up to p. 200. This is not correct.

[6] The Critic. Aug. 27th, 1859.

sistent, containing only such discrepancies as are sure to arise when an intelligent and veracious witness is giving two *independent* accounts of the same transactions.

Mr. Collier's affidavit in the matter of *Literary Cookery.*

In 1856 Mr. Collier prosecuted Mr. John Russell Smith for the publication of a pseudonymous pamphlet, entitled "Literary Cookery, with reference to matter attributed to Coleridge and Shakespeare. 1855."[7] The prosecution was founded on an affidavit by Mr. Collier, dated Jan. 8th, 1856, from which I will make an extract of such parts as refer to the Perkins Folio:—

"I, John Payne Collier, of Maidenhead, in the County of Berks, Esquire, Barrister-at-law, and one of the Vice-Presidents of the Society of Antiquaries of London, make oath and say:—

1. That in the years 1841, 1842, 1843, and 1844, I prepared for the press and published an edition of the Works of Shakespeare:—that in the spring of the year 1849 I purchased of the late Mr. Rodd, of Great Newport Street, bookseller, a copy of the second folio of Shakespeare's Plays, bearing the date of, and which I believe was published in the year 1632; and which copy contained, when I so purchased it, a great number of manuscript notes, purporting to be corrections, alterations, and emendations of the original text, made, as I believe, by the

---

[7] *Literary Cookery*, I learn, has been attributed to me by a writer in "The Critic" for July 21st, 1860. Mr. H. Merivale, in the "Edinburgh Review" for April, 1860, seems to have fallen into the same mistake. The fact is that I did not know who the author of that pamphlet was till long after the publication of my "Shakspeare Fabrications."

same person, and at a period nearly contemporaneous with the publication of the said folio itself.

2. In order that any person interested in the subject might have an opportunity of inspecting the said book, and examining the said manuscript notes, I exhibited the said book to and before the Shakespeare Society, and three times before the Society of Antiquaries, and it was inspected and examined by a great number of persons. The said folio has, since the publication of the volume next hereinafter mentioned, become, and is now, the property of his Grace the Duke of Devonshire.

3. In the year 1852 I published a volume containing some, but not all, of the said manuscript corrections, alterations, and emendations, and a facsimile of a part of one page of the said folio, with the manuscript emendations thereon; and an "Introduction," setting forth the circumstances under which I became possessed of the said folio edition, and which induced me to publish the said volume.

4. In the year 1853 I published a second edition of the said notes and emendations, containing, besides the said "Introduction," a statement, in the form of a Preface to the last-mentioned edition, of facts and circumstances which occurred subsequently to the publication of my first edition of the said "Notes and Emendations,"—a copy of which second edition is now shewn me and marked with the letter A. And I say, that all the statements in the said Preface and Introduction, relative to the discovery, contents, and authenticity of the said folio copy, and the manuscript notes, corrections, alterations, and emendations thereof are true; and that every note, correction, alteration, and emendation in each of the said two editions, and every word, figure, and sign therein, purporting or professing to be a note, correction, alteration, or emendation of the text, is, to the best of my knowledge and belief, a true and accurate copy of the original manuscript in the said folio copy of 1632; and that I have not, in either of the said editions, to the best of my knowledge and belief, inserted a single word, stop, sign, note, correction, alteration, or emendation of

the said original text of Shakespeare, which is not a faithful copy of the said original manuscript, and which I do not believe to have been written, as aforesaid, not long after the publication of the said folio copy of the year 1632."

Literary Cookery was an able attempt to impugn the genuineness of the Lectures published by Mr. Collier in *Notes and Queries*, in 1855, and in an octavo volume in 1856, purporting to be printed from Mr. Collier's short-hand notes of those delivered by Coleridge, in Scots' Corporation Hall, Crane Court, Fleet Street. But that tract, by a side-wind, threw imputations on the genuineness of the manuscript notes of the Perkins Folio. These imputations Mr. Collier, in the 9th clause of his affidavit, affirms to be "wholly, and I believe maliciously false."

Having presented my readers with Mr. Collier's several accounts of his acquisition of the Perkins Folio and of his discovery of the manuscript notes therein, (to the truth of one of which he has deposed upon oath), I now proceed to state the exceptions which have been taken to this narrative, and to examine their validity.

Weight of Mr. Collier's character.

To have doubted the truth of Mr. Collier's narrative prior to his affidavit of its truth, was simply to charge him with gross inaccuracy, or to impute to him the offence of fabricating an account of his connexion with the Perkins Folio for a dishonest purpose. But to doubt the truth of that narrative after Mr. Collier has deliberately sworn to it, under circumstances which must have called his attention to the minutest point connected with it, is to charge him with perjury. No man of honourable feeling, or indeed of common humanity, could lightly bring such a charge against a personal enemy, much less against a time-honoured man of letters, to whose learning and patient research, through half a century, the world of letters is indebted for a great number of publications, illustrating the Life, Times, and Works of Shakspere.

The first question one meets with, then, in harbouring a doubt of the truth of Mr. Collier's narrative (allowing for mere inaccuracies of description, or lapses of memory, from which no man is wholly exempt), is this:—Is not Mr. Collier's good name a sufficient guarantee of the truth of his narrative? It is the duty of one who assumes the office of arbitrator on the questions between Mr. Collier and his opponents, to acquire such information as will enable him to allow the affirmative of that interrogatory, or to meet it conclusively with a negative. The arbitrator is thus involved in a most invidious inquisition on Mr. Collier's literary career, if not on his private character. While Mr. Collier's partizans obstruct inquiry, it is not reasonable in Mr. Collier to complain that his opponents "have hunted in every dirty hole and obscure corner for information" (Reply, p. 5). However, to set the question at rest, it is not necessary to go back more than twenty years. Far be it from me to play the part of detective or censor of Mr. Collier's moral lapses. But it is necessary that I should point out that he has, in a manner, pleaded guilty to one act of fraud, of the heinousness of which I will leave the reader to judge. Be it a serious or a light offence, it clearly establishes this, that Mr. Collier's good name is not a sufficient guarantee of the truth of any statement of his,—*i. e.* cannot be held to preclude suspicion and inquiry into the veracity of the statement. The facts of the case to which I allude will be fully investigated in a future chapter: let it here suffice to say that Mr. Collier tampered with a letter addressed to Edward Alleyn, the actor, by his wife, to the extent of interpolating a long passage about Shakspere which not only is not in the letter (which may now be seen by any one in the library of Dulwich College), but, as no entire line of it is lost, we are able to affirm never formed any part of the letter. The motive which induced Mr. Collier to commit this petty fraud could have been nothing else than the *pruritus* of turning to the account of Shakspere's life an exceedingly interesting document which contained nothing about him. Let the offence be called venial, if my reader please. But whatever he may call it, he will not go so far as to say that Mr. Collier's honour is of that scrupulous character which can be held to constitute a valid plea in bar of challenging the veracity of that narrative, to which he has deposed on oath: and I say this with a full recognition of the fact that perjury is a greater crime than such a fraud as I have mentioned can possibly be esteemed.

Examination of alleged improbabilities in Mr. Collier's narrative.

Mr. Collier's narrative involves several suppositions which, by some of his opponents, have been pronounced incredible, by all highly improbable :—

1st. That Mr. Rodd should have sold a folio Shakspere in such haste that he did not examine it to see what it contained, but contented himself with observing that it was defective at the beginning and end, and that it was ill-conditioned.

It may be assumed that Mr. Rodd did not discover the missing leaves in the middle; for to have found out that deficiency he must have *carefully* examined the book : and that he did not so examine it is inferable from the circumstance, that he was not staggered by the quantity of the manuscript notes.

All who knew Mr. Rodd knew that he was a quick seller : that whereas some dealers in old books treasure up a curiosity, or a fancied curiosity, for leisurely examination, on the chance of making a usurious per-centage out of it, Thomas Rodd did nothing of the kind. He bought and sold, and was content with his ordinary profit: so that I now attach no weight to this objection. That he did not examine the volume more than cursorily is not in evidence; and it is hardly a just inference from the fact that he ignored the notes,—at least, did not mention them to his purchaser, nor raise his price on their account. The notes, indeed, are so thick on almost every page of the book, that, supposing those notes have not been added to, since Mr. Rodd possessed the book, I do not believe he could have turned it over in the most cursory manner without observing them. But what if he did observe them? How do we know that the old bibliopole did not regard them as a blemish? A bookseller of my acquaintance once had a Plato, with venerable Greek annotations; but, instead of taking the opinion of Dr. Donaldson or Prof. Thompson upon their value, he had them washed out before binding! My readers must remember that in 1849, the alleged year of the purchase, manuscript notes on folio Shakesperes had not acquired any *prestige*, as witness Mr. Parry's lost first folio, Mr. Singer's annotated second folio, and several others, which one never heard of till the Perkins Folio had become famous.[a] I accordingly disallow this first alleged improbability.

2. That Mr. Rodd should have sold the Perkins

[a] Nothing can be more unhappy than Mr. Collier's replies, when hard pressed by his opponents. To meet the objection in question, he now affirms that "neither Rodd nor [himself were] aware of the existence of any manuscript notes in it" [the folio]. (Reply, p. 8.) That Mr. Collier, looking only at the beginning and end of the folio, should have failed to see the corrections (if they were there) is credible. That Rodd so far examined the book as to discover the deficiency in the middle, and yet failed to see some sign of upwards of 20,000 manuscript corrections, is past belief.

Folio (even allowing that it contained no manuscript notes) for so low a price as 30*s*.

I urged this as an improbability in my *opusculum* on "The Shakspeare Fabrications."[9] But I have changed my opinion on further knowledge, and now regret my hasty expressions on that and some other points, which it is happily not too late to recall. The Perkins Folio in 1849, if free from notes, would, in its present condition, be worth but little more than 30*s*;[10] that Mr. Rodd would have valued the book more on account of the few manuscript notes which he might have observed, I can hardly believe: and why he should not have sold a book cheap to an old and valued customer and friend, I cannot see.

3. That Mr. Collier should have examined the Perkins Folio in Rodd's shop sufficiently closely to discover that it was a copy of the *second* impression, and yet should have failed to see the manuscript notes.

This is a point which strikes me as very improbable. Unless Mr. Collier judged hastily, from the size of a leaf, that this could not be a copy of the first folio, he must have subjected the volume to a tolerably close scrutiny, before he could have concluded positively that it was a copy of the second folio; and in that case he *must* have seen the manuscript notes.

[9] Preface, p. viii.

[10] The Perkins Folio has no title, has lost four leaves at the end, and in the middle wants pp. 87-88, and 89-90 (II. Hen. IV.), pp. 101-102 (I. Hen. VI.), pp. 111-112 (Ibid.), and pp. 223-224 (Hen. VIII.): *i.e.* two leaves in one place, and one leaf in three places.

But, on the other hand, he may have taken Mr. Rodd's word for its being a copy of the edition of 1632; or he may have inferred that from the low price.

4. That Mr. Collier having become the possessor of the book, and found that it would not serve to supply the deficiency in his other copy of the second folio, should have put it by in a closet without examination: that when he did at last, after the lapse of a year (or a little more), observe "marks in the margin," his curiosity should have been so little excited, that he placed the book upon an upper shelf, and did not take it down till he had occasion to consult it: that even then he was not struck with the abundance of corrections, but with the name of "Tho. Perkins:" and that he was only induced to examine the corrections by a fancy that "Tho. Perkins" might be a descendant of Richard Perkins the actor of the reign of Charles I.

Here, at last, is a case of apparent improbability. I cannot do otherwise than allow it to have weight.

5. That within two years Mr. Rodd should have had two second folios of Shakspere, both wanting the title and *four* leaves at the end, and both priced 30*s*.[11]

I am disposed to think that this improbability has been over-rated. Second folios of Shakspere

[11] In a catalogue of Rodd's, dated January 1st, 1847, appears the following entry:

"Shakespeare (W.) Comedies, Histories and Tragedies, *wanting the title and four leaves at the end, cut and in soiled condition*, £1. 10*s* . . . . fol. 1632."

are *very* common, and the beginning and end are just those places in which they are mostly deficient. If 30*s* were about the price of such a second folio as the Perkins Folio (without the notes), it would be also about the price of the one specified in Rodd's catalogue. The only improbability, as it appears to me, is in the fact of the leaves wanting at the end of both volumes being the same. Of course the object, with which this case of improbability has been set up, is to lead to the conclusion that it is the Perkins Folio which is specified in Rodd's catalogue of Jan. 1st, 1847; and that since no manuscript notes are mentioned, none (of any consequence) existed in it then; and that, therefore, the manuscript notes have been added to it since; and further to suggest the inference that Mr. Collier fixed upon a false year of purchase, in order to assure himself of the impossibility of producing *positive* evidence from Rodd's sale-books. We shall see that there is, in point of fact, no foundation to support such serious conclusions. For all we know to the contrary the copy specified in Rodd's catalogue may have been the one which was sold by auction by Messrs. Sotheby and Wilkinson, after Mr. Rodd's death. It is a fact that the auctioneer's books shew that a copy of the *second*[12] folio of Shakspere, "wanting the

[12] It was originally entered in the sale catalogue of Rodd's stock as the *first* edition, but Mr. Wilkinson (Mr. Rodd's executor) altered it at the sale to "second."

title and four leaves at the end, soiled," was sold on that occasion to the late Mr. Pickering for 10*s*. If we suppose this not to be the copy specified in Rodd's catalogue, we are then reduced to the necessity of accepting a still more improbable position, viz.: that Mr. Rodd had on sale, during a period of about eighteen months, *three* copies of the second folio edition of Shakspere, each wanting title and four leaves at the end. So that here we have simply a choice of improbabilities.[13]

6. That those very sale-books of Mr. Rodd, which contained the entry of the sale of the Perkins Folio, whether purchased in 1847 or 1849, and those only, should be irrecoverably lost.

The series of sale-books in the hands of Mr. Wilkinson, Mr. Rodd's executor, are complete to the end of the year 1840. Mr. Collier, it seems, had access to the books some years ago, and searched them for a trace of the sale of the Perkins Folio to himself in 1849. Finding no trace of the transaction, he searched the earlier books, but, he says,[14] without success. Subsequently a gentleman of the bar in Lincoln's Inn, who was engaged in searching for a

---

[13] While I write Messrs. Willis and Sotheran have on sale an annotated copy of the second folio of Shakspere, originally wanting the title, and *four* leaves at the end, all of which have been supplied from other copies. This copy, however, never belonged to Mr. Rodd.

[14] Notes and Emendations, Introd. p. 7, note.

missing pedigree, and who thought that some traces of it might be found among Rodd's books, borrowed his sale-books from 1847 to 1849, inclusive; one Roberts, formerly a clerk of Mr. Rodd's, was the agent for procuring the books for, and the bearer of them to, the barrister in question, who says that Roberts subsequently took them away, professedly to return them to Mr. Wilkinson; Roberts himself cannot be found, nor the books.

To say the least, it is a remarkable coincidence that the only sale books we want to inspect, are the only sale books lost."[11]

My conclusion is that positions 4 and 6 are admissible as probabilities against the truth of Mr. Collier's narrative.

Mr. Collier's attempt to corroborate his narrative.

In corroboration of that narrative, Mr. Collier contents himself with calling a witness, who gives his evidence in the most slipshod manner, finally refuses to be cross-examined, and thus seriously damages his correspondent's case. It seems that Mr. Collier, in consequence of a rumour that had reached him, wrote to ask Dr. Wellesley, the amiable and learned Principal of New Inn Hall, Oxford, what he could say to confirm his (Mr. Collier's) account of the purchase of the Perkins Folio of Rodd in 1849; and thereupon, the Principal wrote Mr. Collier the following letter, which is thought, by Mr. Collier and his partizans, to be as conclusive,

[11] See The Critic, Ap. 21, May 5th and 26th, 1860.

as a revelation written on the broad back of Fo-Hi's sea-horse.

"Woodmancote Rectory, Hurstpierpoint,
August 13th, 1859.

"Sir,

Dr. Wellesley's letter to Mr. Collier.

"Although I do not recollect the precise date, I remember some years ago being in the shop of Thomas Rodd on one occasion when a case of books from the country had just been opened. One of those books was an imperfect folio Shakspeare, with an abundance of manuscript notes in the margins. He observed to me that it was of little value to collectors as a copy, and that the price was thirty shillings. I should have taken it myself; but, as he stated that he had put it by for another customer, I did not continue to examine it; nor did I think any more about it, until I heard afterwards that *it had been found to possess great literary curiosity and value.* In all probability, Mr. Rodd named you to me; but whether he or others did so, *the affair was generally spoken of at the time,* and I never heard it doubted that *you had become the possessor of the book.*

I am, Sir,
Your faithful and obedient servant,
H. Wellesley.

"To J. P. Collier, Esq."

Mr. Collier's conclusion from this is:—

"Dr. Wellesley, *therefore,* saw the Perkins folio, with "an abundance of manuscript notes in the margins," in 1849, *for* Rodd died in that year;" * * *.

In other words, begging two of the points to be established,—that the Perkins Folio was purchased of Mr. Rodd in 1849, and that it was the Perkins Folio that Mr. Rodd shewed Dr. Wellesley,—it evidently follows that, as Rodd died in 1849, Dr. Wellesley must have seen the book in that year.

Ambiguous points in Dr. Wellesley's letter.

Now I must ask the reader to reperuse the parts of Dr. Wellesley's letter which I have printed in italics, and to resolve the following questions for his own satisfaction,—

1st. What does Dr. Wellesley mean by the phrase, "put it by for another customer?" Are we to understand by this that it was "put by" for another customer to *look at*, or that it was "put by" for another customer to *purchase (i.e.* that it was bespoke), or that it was actually sold?

2nd. Which book was it, the one he saw, or some other, which had been found to possess great literary curiosity and value? ("IT" is an ambiguous middle).

3rd. What affair was generally spoken of at the time?

4th. At what time? At the time Dr. Wellesley saw that folio Shakspere which Mr. Rodd shewed him, or at the time the ambiguous "IT" had been found to possess great literary curiosity and value?

5th. Of which book had Dr. Wellesley never heard it doubted that Mr. Collier had become the possessor?

I say, my readers must determine these points as best they may: for Dr. Wellesley has unequivocally refused to submit to cross-examination, in a very polite letter which he has addressed to me. This is to play the partisan of Mr. Collier with an amiable candour. But, in the meantime, what is his evidence worth? Not a rush. It is worthless from ambiguity and partisanship. In saying this I do not intend to insinuate the faintest doubt of Dr.

Wellesley's veracity: I accept his statement, that he saw at Rodd's some years ago an imperfect folio Shakspere, with an abundance of manuscript notes in the margins; that he wished to purchase it, but that it had been already "put by." But as to whether it was in, before, or after the year 1849, that he paid this visit to Rodd's shop,[16] and as to whether it was a first, second, third or fourth folio Shakspere that he saw there, we are quite in the dark. The rest of the letter is ample evidence to prove that he had mixed up in his memory the book he had seen there with the book about which he had heard and read so much. "Nor did I," he writes, "think any more about "IT," until I afterwards found that "IT" had been found to possess great literary curiosity and value." This is the equivocation that slurs over the fact of the non-identification of the two books.

[16] Dr. Wellesley, I understand, has since told Mr. Foss that he should think the circumstances which he relates must have taken place before 1849.

CHAPTER III.

THE PERKINS FOLIO.—ITS SUPPOSITITIOUS PEDIGREE.

Mr. J. Carrick Moore's letter to Mr. Collier.

SOON after the publication of the first edition of his *Notes and Emendations*, Mr. Collier, who seems at the first to have been more struck by the superscription, "Tho. Perkins his Booke," than by the abundance of the manuscript corrections, was gratified by the receipt of the following letter.[1]

"Hyde Park Gate, Kensington,
25th April, 1853.

"SIR,

You will, I trust, forgive one who has not the honour of knowing you, for intruding on your leisure, when I state that the subject on which I am about to trouble you is the copy of the folio 1632 of *Shakespeare*, with the MS. emendations, which you have lately given to the world, and for which every lover of Shakspeare is so deeply indebted to you.

The information which I wish to give you may, if followed up, enable you to trace the ownership of that copy for at least a century back.

A friend of mine, Mr. Parry, with whom I was lately conversing on your extraordinary and interesting discovery, told me he many years ago possessed a copy of the folio 1632[2] which had marginal notes in manuscript, and which, being in bad order, he never consulted. This copy he lost, he did not know how, and gave himself no concern about it.

When I showed him the fac-simile of the page out of *Henry*

[1] Mr. Collier's "Reply," p. 12.

[2] Mr. Parry denies ever having mentioned this, either to Mr. Moore or Mr. Collier, as the date of his folio; and argues that he could not have done so, as he had the strongest impression that it was lettered outside 1623.

VI., which forms the frontispiece to your work, Mr. Parry told me he had no doubt that the copy was the same as that which he lost, as he remembered very well the hand-writing, and the state of preservation. I pressed him to give me all particulars about the work, and how it came into his possession. He told me that it was given him, with many old books,[3] by an uncle of the name of Grey [*sic*], who was a literary man, and fond of curious works.[4] Mr. Parry believes that Mr. Grey got the copy at the sale of the Perkins library;[5] and all I could learn of these Perkins's is, that they were related to Pope's Arabella Fermor, and that all the family were dead when the sale of their library took place. I urged Mr. Parry to inform you of these circumstances, thinking that they might interest you greatly, and hoping that if you could once trace the copy into the hands of one of the name of Perkins upwards, it might be a clue to further discovery. Whether from indolence or from modesty, Mr. Parry, I find, has not communicated with you; and I therefore told him that I assuredly would, as every fragment of information on such a subject has its value.

Trusting to your indulgence, and your zeal for our great poet, to excuse the liberty I have taken, believe me to be, sir,

Your faithful and obedient Servant,

JOHN CARRICK MOORE.

"J. Payne Collier, Esq."

---

[3] Mr. Parry says that Mr. Gray never gave him any book besides the folio Shakspere, and that he never misled Mr. Moore on this point.

[4] Mr. Parry denies having told Mr. Moore that Mr. Gray was his uncle, or that he was "fond of curious works." On the contrary, Mr. Parry says that Mr. Gray was only a distant relation of his mother's: that he was not a book-collector, and Mr. Parry believes that he parted with the folio Shakspere and the other books, simply because he had no interest in them.

[5] Mr. Parry says that he never *believed* this; but merely threw out an antiquarian suggestion that the folio might have been obtained from Ufton Court.

In a letter dated the 4th May, 1853, (*i. e.* 19 days after the date of Mr. Moore's letter) which Mr. Collier addressed to me, he says,

Mr. Collier's letter to Dr. Ingleby.

"Having been called to London in some haste, I did not return hither until last evening, and find your note of the 9th Inst. awaiting me. * * * * *

My chief reason for visiting London was to follow up an inquiry respecting my folio 1632, which has ended more satisfactorily than I could well have anticipated: I have seen a gentleman to whom the book belonged thirty years ago, if not more, and who, through a connexion obtained it he believes from the library of a family of the name of Perkins formerly residing at Ufton Court, in this county. Whether that family was in any way connected with Richard Perkins, the actor of the reign of Charles I. I have yet to ascertain—if I can.

If the possessor of the volume 30 years ago be not mistaken in his memory, that a distant member of his family procured the book from Ufton Court library, it will carry back its history for 120 or 130 years.

I may hereafter be able to carry the question even farther, but there I am, at present, obliged to stop."

I quote from this private letter, not to tax Mr. Collier with inconsistency in his statements, (for the letter would not serve this purpose, and if it would have done so, I should not have made any use of it,) but to shew how early Mr. Collier had fixed in his mind that Mr. Parry *believed* that Mr. Gray obtained his folio from Ufton Court, which Mr. Parry emphatically denies he ever did, as he does that he knowingly led Mr. Collier or Mr. Moore to believe that such was his impression.

In "The Athenæum" for June 4th, 1853, Mr. Col-

Mr. Collier's antiquarian

speculation in The Athenæum.

lier publishes the following narrative of the supposed pedigree of his corrected folio. It is an antiquarian curiosity, in its way.

"Your readers who have taken so lively an interest in the emendations and alterations of the text of Shakespeare contained in my copy of the folio, 1632, will be glad to hear that I have just advanced an important step towards tracing the ownership and history of that remarkable book. The proof that it was in existence, in its annotated state, fifty years ago is clear and positive; and upon the foundation of strong probability I am able to carry it back almost to the period when the volume was published. The facts are these.—John Carrick Moore, Esq., of Hyde Park Gate, (nephew to Sir John Moore, who fell at Corunna, in Jan: 1809), being in possession of a copy of the 'Notes and Emendations' founded upon my folio, 1632, happened to show it to a friend of the name of Parry, residing at St. John's Wood. Mr. Parry remarked, that he had once been the owner of a folio, 1632, [see note [3] p. 53], the margins of which were much occupied by manuscript notes in an old handwriting; and having read my description of the book, both externally[6] and internally, and having looked at the facsimile which accompanied that description, he declared, without a moment's hesitation, that this very copy of the folio, 1632,[7] had been given to him, about fifty years since, by Mr. George Gray, a connexion of his family,—who, he believed, had procured it, some years before, from the library of a Roman Catholic family of the name of Perkins, of Ufton Court, Berkshire, one member of which had married Arabella Fermor, the heroine of 'The Rape of the Lock.'

---

[6] Mr. Parry denies having then spoken of the external part of the book.

[7] Mr. Parry denies having used such words as "this very copy," &c.

Those particulars were, as kindly as promptly, communicated to me by Mr. Moore, with whom I was not personally acquainted,—and he urged Mr. Parry also to write to me on the subject; but that gentleman was prevented from doing so by a serious fall, which confined him to his bed. Being, of course, much interested in the question, I soon afterwards took an opportunity of introducing myself to Mr. Moore; who, satisfied that Mr. Parry had formerly been the proprietor of my copy of the folio, 1632, advised me to call upon that gentleman at his house, Hill Road, St. John's Wood,—assuring me that he would be glad to give me all the information in his power.

I was, I think, the first person whom Mr. Parry saw after his accident,—and in a long interview he repeated to me the statements he had previously made to Mr. Moore, respecting the gift of Mr. Gray, half a century ago, and his conviction of the identity of the volume.[8] He could not prove the fact, but he had always understood and believed [see note [5] p. 54], that Mr. Gray had become possessed of it on the dispersion of the library of the Perkins's family at Ufton Court,[9] and that it had been in his hands some years[10] before the conclusion of the last century. Mr. Parry had himself had the curiosity to visit Ufton Court about 1803 or 1804; when a Roman Catholic Priest, not less than eighty years old, shewed him the library, and the then empty shelves, from which the books had been removed.

On referring subsequently to the 'Magna Britannia' of Lysons, under the head of "Berkshire," I found various particulars regarding the Perkins family at Ufton Court, between

---

[8] This is certainly correct. Mr. Parry did believe in the identity of the volume, judging solely from the facsimile which Mr. Moore had shewn him!

[9] Mr. Parry now believes that this library had been dispersed before Mr. Gray was born.

[10] Mr. Parry denies having used the expression "some years."

1635 and 1738; but I did not meet with any mention of Thomas Perkins, whose name, it will be remembered, is on the cover of the folio, 1632, in question. The name of the distinguished actor of the reigns of James the First and Charles the First, was Richard Perkins; and Ashmole's Collections, according to Lysons, speak of a Richard Perkins as the husband of Lady Mervin, of Ufton Court. It is just possible that this Richard Perkins was the actor; for although the 'Historia Histrionica' tells us that he was buried at Clerkenwell, that authority is by no means final: just before it notices the death of Perkins, it speaks of Lowin as having expired in great poverty at Brentford, when we know that this "player" (so designated in the register) was buried at St. Clement Danes, Strand, on the 24th of August 1653. However, it is a mere speculation that the Richard Perkins who married Lady Mervin may have been the actor,—and I am not yet in possession of any dates or other circumstances to guide me.

Having put in writing the particulars with which Mr. Parry had so unreservedly favoured me, I took the liberty of forwarding them to Mr. Moore,—and he returned the manuscript with his full approbation as regarded what had originally passed between himself and Mr. Parry. After it was in type, I again waited upon Mr. Parry, only three days ago, in order that I might read the proof to him and introduce such additions and corrections as he wished to be made. They were few, but not unimportant; and among them was the fact (confirming the probability that Mr. Gray had obtained this copy of the folio, 1632, from the Perkins library) that Mr. Gray resided at Newbury, not far from Ufton Court,—a circumstance which Mr. Parry had previously omitted. The connecting link between the book and this library is, therefore not complete—and we have still to ascertain, if we can, who was Thomas Perkins, aud by whom the notes and emendations were introduced into the folio 1632. A Mr. Francis Perkins died at Ufton Court in 1635,—and he may have been the first purchaser, and owner, of this second folio of the works of

Shakespeare. At all events, however, it is certain that this very volume was for many years in the possession of Mr. Parry (how he lost it he knows not),—who obtained it from his connexion, Mr. George Gray, of Newbury. Mr. Parry was well acquainted with the fact that various leaves were wanting; and he so perfectly recollects its state and condition, the frequent erasures of passages, as well as the handwriting of the numerous marginal and other corrections, that when I asked him, just before I wished him good morning, whether he had any doubt on the point of his previous ownership, he answered me most emphatically in these words—" I have no more doubt about it, than that you are sitting there."

J. Payne Collier.

Maidenhead, May 28.

P.S. I ought not to omit the expression of my warmest acknowledgments to both Mr. Moore and Mr. Parry, for the zealous and ready assistance which they have afforded me. I hope that if any of the readers of the *Athenæum* are in possession of information that may tend to the further elucidation of the subject, they will communicate it with equal alacrity.

Since writing what precedes, I am informed by a letter from a friend, who has just made a search at the Heralds' College, that in the pedigree of the family of Perkins of Ufton Court several members are named Thomas, especially in the earlier dates,—but that latterly Francis was the prevailing name. Richard Perkins, who married Lady Mervin, as a younger son, is not mentioned."

This communication, it will be observed, records only two visits to Mr. Parry, one of which occurred immediately after his accident; and the other subsequently, when Mr. Collier read to him the proof of the Preface to the second edition of *Notes and Emendations*. It has excited universal admiration, as well it might, that on neither occasion did Mr. Mr. Collier's strange omission.

Collier take with him the corrected folio, 1632. If Mr. Collier's *bona fides* is to be defended, we must presume that the identification of the volume by Mr. Parry was the very thing Mr. Collier wanted to establish. On that identification depended the whole antiquarian fabric that he had been raising; if the Perkins Folio, and Mr. Parry's folio were two distinct books, neither Mr. Parry, nor Mr. Gray, nor Ufton Court library, nor the Perkins's of Ufton Court, had anything to do with Mr. Collier's book. Now the identification could only be established by one means—viz., the production of the book to Mr. Parry. Yet, knowing all this, Mr. Collier twice leaves his house, where the Perkins Folio is lying on its shelf, and pays two visits to Mr. Parry, for no other conceivable purpose than to identify the volume, yet omits to take it with him. At Maidenhead is the folio; at St. John's Wood are Mr. Collier and Mr. Parry face to face; and Mr. Parry who has never seen the book says, "I have no more doubt [that your corrected folio was once mine] than that you are sitting there;" and Mr. Collier says "Good morning," and returns to Maidenhead under the strange delusion that Mr. Parry has identified the volume, and forthwith proceeds to publish the second edition of his *Notes and Emendations*, with a Preface, from which the following is an extract:—

Preface to Notes and Emendations.

"John Carrick Moore, Esq., of Hyde Park Gate, Kensington * *, was kind enough to address a note to me, in which he stated that a friend of his, a gentleman of the name

Fac simile of M^r. Collier's Letter to M^r. Parry. Sheet Nº III.

Gays House
Maidenhead
26 April 1853

Sir

M^r. J. Carrick Moore has done me the favour of communicating to me that you can give me some clue to the history of my copy of the folio 1632. If I can recover the first link in the chain of evidence, I may be able to make out others.

M^r. Moore says that the book was once in your possession — or at all events that you had a copy of the

To face p. 60

Ashbee & Dangerfield, Lith.
[illegible]

folio, 1632, with manuscript annotations, which you more than suspect to be the identical book now in my hands.

Can you at all describe the book to me? How was it bound, and was it shabby and defective? Had it title-page or conclusion?

Had it the name of Tho. Perkins on the cover?

If so, can you be good enough to inform me who were the Perkins family mentioned by Mr Moore, & when & where were their books sold?

Can you at all bear in mind the character & nature of the M.S. notes & were they almost entirely written in the cropped margins of the book?

These questions will, I fear occasion you trouble, but Mr Moore encourages me to hope that you will excuse it.

I am very near the conclusion of a new edition of my vol. of "Notes and Emendations", so that the sooner I receive any information on the subject, the greater will be my obligation.

Trusting that you will pardon my importunity upon this subject, I am

Sir,

Your most obedient
& faithful Svt.
J. Payne Collier

— Parry Esq.

of Parry, had been at one time in possession of the very folio upon which I founded my recent volume of "Notes and Emendations"—that Mr. Parry had been well acquainted with the fact that its margins were filled throughout by manuscript notes, and that he accurately remembered the hand-writing in which they were made. On being shown the fac-simile, which accompanied my first edition, and which is repeated in the present, he declared his instant conviction that it had been copied from what had once been his folio, 1632. How or precisely when it escaped from his custody he knew not, but the description of it in my "Introduction" exactly corresponded with his recollection.[11]

I lost no time in thanking Mr. Moore for these tidings, and in writing to Mr. Parry for all the particulars within his knowledge.[12] Unfortunately the latter gentleman, just before he received my note, had met with a serious injury,[13] which confined him to his bed, so that he was unable to send me any reply.

For about ten days I remained in suspense, but at last I determined to wait upon Mr. Moore to inquire whether he was aware of any reason why I had not received an answer from Mr. Parry. He accounted for the silence of that gentleman on the ground of his recent accident; and as Mr. Moore was confident that Mr. Parry was correct in the conclusion that my folio 1632, had formerly belonged to him, he advised me to call upon him, being sure that he would be glad to satisfy me upon every point. I accordingly hastened to St John's Wood, and had the pleasure of an interview with Mr. Parry, who, without the slightest reserve, gave me such an account of the book as made it certain that it was the same which, some fifty years ago, had been presented to him by a connexion of his family,

[11] This is denied by Mr. Parry.

[12] A facsimile of this letter is given on sheet III.

[13] This was an injury to the knee by a fall which most ominously took place on the 23rd April, (1853). Mr. Collier afterwards (Reply, p. 16) calls this "serious" accident, a "slight" one.

Mr. George Gray. Mr. Parry described both the exterior [see note [5], p. 56] and interior of the volume, with its innumerable corrections and its missing leaves, with so much minuteness that no room was left for doubt.

On the question from whence Mr. Gray, who resided at Newbury, had procured the book, Mr. Parry was not so clear and positive: he was not in a condition to state any distinct evidence to show out of what library it had come; but he had always understood and believed that it had been obtained, with some other old works (to the collection of which Mr. Gray was partial), [see note [4], p. 54] from Ufton Court, Berkshire; [see note [5], p. 54] formerly, and for many years before the dispersion of the library, the residence of a Roman Catholic family of the name of Perkins, one member of which, Francis Perkins, who died in 1736, was the husband of Arabella Fermor, the heroine of "The Rape of the Lock."

This information has been communicated to me so recently, that I have not yet been able to ascertain at what date, and in what way the books at Ufton Court were disposed of. Mr. Parry is strongly of opinion that Mr. Gray became the owner of this copy of the folio, 1632, considerably[14] before the end of the last century; and Mr. Parry was himself at Ufton Court about fifty years since, when a Roman Catholic clergyman, eighty years of age, who had remembered the books there all his life,[14] shewed him the then empty shelves upon which they had been placed in the library.

A Mr. Francis Perkins died at Ufton Court three years after the publication of the folio, 1632; and if Mr. Parry's belief be correct, that the copy which Mr. Gray gave to him had once been deposited there, it is not impossible that Francis Perkins was the first purchaser of it. If so, we might be led to the inference, that either he, or one of his immediate descendants was the writer of the emendations; but, as has been men-

[14] Mr. Parry repudiates both the "considerably," and the "all his life."

tioned elsewhere, the present rough calf binding was not the original coat of the volume; and, as far as my imperfect researches have yet gone, I do not find any Thomas Perkins recorded as of Ufton Court.

The Christian name of the great actor of the reign of Charles I. was Richard; and a Richard Perkins, called Esquire in Ashmole's Collections, at a date not stated, married Lady Mervin, a benefactress of that parish. Why should we deem it impossible that Richard Perkins, having attained eminence on the stage, subsequently married a lady of title and property? However, this and other points, dependent chiefly upon dates, remain to be investigated, and upon any of them I shall be most thankful for information.

The only facts that I am yet able to establish are, that my folio, 1632, with its elaborate corrections, about half a century since came into the possession of Mr. Parry from Mr. George Gray, who, it is possible, obtained it from Ufton Court (about eight miles from his residence), where it is unquestionable that at an early date there was a library, likely to have contained such a book, which library was afterwards dispersed. The name of "Tho. Perkins" on the cover is a strong confirmation of the opinion, that it once formed part of that library;[15] and as to the identity of the volume, and hand-writing of the notes, Mr. Parry feels absolutely certain."

General remarks on Mr. Collier's narratives.

I have now given at length Mr. Collier's two published narratives of his excursion in search of a pedigree for his folio. I say of these, as I said of his two published narratives of the purchase of the folio,

[15] This is an amusing example of a vicious circle. Mr. Parry assuming his folio to be that at Maidenhead, learns that the latter has the name of "Perkins" on it, and thence suggests that his folio may have come from Ufton Court the seat of the Perkins; and the fact that the one at Maidenhead has that name, is, says Mr. Collier, a strong confirmation of Mr. Parry's suggestion.

and discovery of the manuscript corrections, that they are uniform and consistent, and contain only such discrepancies as are incident to erring human nature when telling the same story twice. Looking at these narratives out of connexion with subsequent events, I see nothing in them to excite suspicion of the truthfulness of their author; but I see much to excite the gravest doubt as to the accuracy of the statements, and abundant evidence to shew that the historical explorer has lost himself in the antiquarian dreamer. When I know that a man of short sight has ascended a mountain in order to sketch the surrounding scenery, and yet has not taken his spectacles with him, I should be astonished if I found that he had actually made the sketch with as much minuteness as if he had taken his glasses with him: but I should be ten-fold more astonished if he treated his sketch as authentic; and however great might be my respect for his virtues, I am sure I should not receive his sketch as authentic, though he made an affidavit of its truth. Similarly, I must refuse to accept Mr. Collier's conclusions regarding the pedigree of his folio, when I find that those conclusions are dependent on an identification which Mr. Collier had the means of substantiating or of disproving, and which yet he did not take the trouble to employ.[16]

[16] The only explanations vouchsafed by Mr. Collier of this strange omission, are that he "was in haste to get [his] Preface to the printer," (Reply, p. 16) and that "owing to the late

Having weighed dispassionately Mr. Collier's several narratives, and also Mr. Parry's most valuable evidence on the questions involved, I can only come to the conclusion that Mr. Collier's wish had been all along the father of his facts, and that on Mr. Parry's shoulders must rest a share of the blame, for having, through carelessness, incautiousness, and want of precision, done his best to put an F.S.A. on the scent of a mare's-nest. Most providential is it that "Mr. Parry has not gone the way of the old bibliopole,"[17] Mr. Rodd; and much to Mr. Parry's credit is it that, unlike Dr. Wellesley, he does not refuse to be cross-examined.

Having thus given Mr. Collier's version of his two visits to Mr. Parry, I will now give Mr. Parry's version of those events. I am far from wishing to assume that Mr. Collier's memory is weak and un- *Relative values of Mr. Collier's and Mr. Parry's testimony.*

---

date at which I had heard of his [Mr. Parry's] recognition of the volume by its notes, and to a slight (!) accident which had befallen him, I was not able to exhibit to him the folio itself, &c." (The Athenæum, Feb. 18, 1860.) One does not very clearly see how Mr. Collier would have been delayed by bringing the folio with him from Maidenhead in the first instance; nor how Mr. Parry's accident, which did not prevent Mr. Collier visiting him, and discussing the folios with him, would have prevented him looking at the folio itself. To say the least, Mr. Collier's conduct was not that of a man desirous of ascertaining whether his folio had ever belonged to Mr. Parry, but rather that of a man anxious to give his folio a pedigree which, he knew, was not likely to stand the simple test of identification.

17 The Saturday Review for July 23rd, 1859.

trustworthy, and that Mr. Parry's is retentive and faithful. But I cannot but think it probable, that Mr. Collier's judgment as to what passed at those interviews was more likely to be warped by his interest in the circumstances surrounding his corrected folio, than that of Mr. Parry was by any of the incidents connected with his lost book. Mr. Collier was confessedly anxious to find a pedigree for his folio, if for no other reason, to obviate the risk of incurring the suspicion of having fabricated the manuscript notes himself. He would thus naturally catch at any hint, however vague or indefinite, that could be turned to the account of his folio. Mr. Parry, on the other hand, could have had no conceivable inducement for heightening the colour of his story, or for drawing on his imagination to supply the defects of his memory. At the same time I can readily believe that to save trouble he may have allowed Mr. Collier to draw inferences from what was actually communicated to him, which may have put Mr. Collier on a false scent, and that thus Mr. Parry's silence may have operated as a confirmation of Mr. Collier's prepossessions.

Mr. Parry's narrative.

Mr. Parry's version, which I take from his own manuscript, is to the following effect.

Some years before Mr. Parry first saw Mr. Collier, in the course of pruning some trees in his garden, he cut a branch of holly, and a shoot of barberry. Thinking they would make good walking sticks, he put them aside to dry.

In the month of April, 1853, being at the house of the father of Mr. John Carrick Moore, (No. 9, Clarges Street,) Miss Moore shewed him the first edition of Mr. Collier's *Notes and Emendations*, with the facsimile of part of a page of Hen. VI. Mr. Parry immediately remarked that the facsimile in question was taken from a folio edition of Shakspere that was once his. The Moores wished him to write to Mr. Collier about it; but he declined doing so to avoid trouble, but said he had no objection for Mr. John Carrick Moore to write to Mr. Collier on the subject, which he understands he did on the 25th of that month. Some time before, happening to see the sticks to which allusion has been made, it occurred to him to trim and varnish them. He completed this labour on the 22nd April; and on the following day he fell and severely hurt his knee.

At the beginning of the month of May, he received a visit from Mr. Collier in his bed-room. Mr. Collier had no book with him. In reply to Mr. Collier's questions, Mr. Parry gave him, to the best of his memory, an account of the *interior* of his lost folio. He did not speak of this folio as of any particular date. Mr. Collier did not ask him any question as to the exterior of the book, nor did Mr. Parry volunteer any statement about it; but, had allusion been made to it, his memory would have served him to tell Mr. Collier that the binding of his lost folio was *dark, clean, and shiny.* Of the inside he could not have spoken with as much precision as of the outside, as he does not recollect ever having read a page of it. He told Mr. Collier, that he believed the facsimile which Miss Moore had shewn him,[18] was from his lost folio; and that the folio in Mr. Collier's possession must be that he had lost. He inferred this from the facsimile only; and not dreaming that there was more than one annotated folio Shakspere in the world, he jumped to the conclusion that his folio and Mr. Collier's were identical.

He further told Mr. Collier that his lost folio had been given him by a relative named George Gray; that he did not positively know where Mr. Gray had obtained it; but, as Mr. Collier had informed him that the folio at Maidenhead had on it the name of Thomas Perkins, he thought it not unlikely that his relative might have got his folio from the library at Ufton Court, the seat of the Perkins's; he added that Mr. Gray must have become the owner of the folio before the end of the last century; and that it was thirty or forty years since it had been in his (Mr. Parry's) possession.

On the 25th May, Mr. Collier paid him a second visit, on this occasion bringing with him the proof of the Preface to the second edition of *Notes and Emendations*. Mr. Parry did not except, as he

[18] Mr. Parry and Mr. Collier are at issue too, on the question, whether *Mr. Collier* ever shewed Mr. Parry a facsimile. I believe Mr. Parry's memory is, as Mr. Collier says, at fault here. (Reply, p. 17.)

might have done, to some of the statements in it: for being still under the impression that Mr. Collier had the folio which he (Mr. Parry) had lost, he did not think it material to be precise in the details of his conversation with Mr. Collier on his first visit.

Mr. Collier's narratives of his street interview with Mr. Parry.

Mr. Collier's first narrative of his third interview with Mr. Parry is given in his letter to "The Times," of July 20th, 1859. After cutting down his two visits to Mr. Parry, at the house of the latter gentleman, to *one*, Mr. Collier continues thus:—

"Very soon afterwards [i.e. after the first visit to Mr. Parry at his house], for greater satisfaction, I brought the corrected folio of 1632 from Maidenhead to London, and took it to St. John's-wood, but I failed to meet with Mr. Parry at home. I therefore paid a third visit to that gentleman, again carrying the book with me. I met him coming from his house, and I informed him that I had the corrected folio of 1632 under my arm, and that I was sorry he could not then examine it, as I wished. He replied—"If you will let me see it now, I shall be able to state at once whether it was ever my book." I therefore shewed it to him on the spot, and, after looking at it in several places, he gave it back to me with these words:—"That was my book, it is the same, but it has been much ill-used since it was in my possession."

Mr. Collier's second narrative of this third interview is given with still greater detail in his *Reply*, p. 16-17. It is necessary to premise that Mr. Hamilton, in his *Inquiry*, p. 63, states that

"on the occasion alluded to he [Mr. Parry] was, in consequence of an accident, halting along the road on two crutches, the management of which occupied both his hands, and must certainly have totally prevented his handling a folio volume."

Mr. Collier replies thus:—

"I was in haste to get my Preface to the printer, and I did not, on that occasion, carry the volume itself to St. John's Wood with me; but I afterwards did so, and met Mr. Parry a short distance from his house, walking lame, and aided by a stick. Mr. Parry has since said he was "using *sticks*;" but this is a slight mistake, which Mr. Hamilton has, possibly only by error, exaggerated into *crutches*,—a word employed by nobody. Mr. Parry was walking with *a* stick; and after expressing my regret at his recent accident,[19] and stating that I had the Perkins folio under my arm, I said that, under the circumstances, I could not think of asking him to return home in order to examine it: he replied, "If you will let me see it now, I shall be able to state at once, whether it was ever my book." I therefore produced it to him on the spot, and held his stick while he looked at the book in several places, including the cover: he then returned it to me with these words, "That was my book; it is the same, but it has been much ill-used since it was in my possession." I then gave him back his stick, and thanking him for his most satisfactory assurance, I wished him good morning.

Very soon after reaching home, that is to say, within a day or two, it occurred to me that I ought to record Mr. Parry's expressions, and I did so with a pencil at the foot of page iv. of my Preface to the second edition of *Notes and Emendations*, in these words, which, it will be observed, differ from those above used, by having "This" for *That*, and "mis-used" for *ill-used*, but the meaning is of course exactly the same.[20]

"'I afterwards shewed him [i.e. Mr. Parry,] the book itself,

---

[19] Mr. Collier having already called on him twice since his accident!

[20] These synonymous emendations have a strong family likeness to the proposed correction of *contiguity* for "continuity," in the *Seven Lectures*, 1856, p. 83.

and having looked at it in several places, he said "This was my book: it is the same; but has been much misused since it was in my possession.'' "

This is in nearly the same words as Mr. Collier's prior account of the same interview in "The Athenæum" of February 18, 1860, with some amplifications. Thus, instead of "including the cover," Mr. Collier in "The Athenæum" wrote, "and I am very sure looked also at the cover." This, however, is a detail not borne out by Mr. Collier's manuscript note, which records Mr. Parry's remark with the simple introduction, "and having looked at it *in several places.*" This addition I can only look upon as an evidence of that eagerness in Mr. Collier to press all possible contingencies into the service of his folio. If such a variation were all the discrepancy between Mr. Collier's narratives and Mr. Parry's version of the third interview, that not over-scrupulous eagerness, which is natural to a man of antiquarian tendencies, would serve to explain it away. But unfortunately the difference between Mr. Collier's and Mr. Parry's versions is one of *diametrical opposition;* and if both accounts had been deposed to on oath, the inevitable inference would have been *that one of them had perjured himself.*

Mr. Parry's narrative of that interview.

From Mr. Parry's manuscript I take the following narrative of that interview:—

One day in the month of June (1853), Mr. Parry, wishing to have a little fresh air, (and perhaps without the doctor's leave,) got up, and took the *two sticks*, of which mention has been made, and remarking that he had prophetically prepared them against his accident, sallied forth from his house. Before he had gone far he met Mr. Collier in the street, and they walked a short distance together, and entered into conversation. He well remembers that with one of his sticks he shoved a stone out of the path, when Mr. Collier told him an anecdote of a friend of his who had been thrown down by a stone in the path; and this was more the subject of their conversation than anything else during that short walk. Mr. Parry says that, to the best of his recollection, Mr. Collier had no book with him, and that he (Mr. Parry) certainly should not have forgotten the incident had he been shewn the corrected folio in the street. He does not remember any other than these three interviews with Mr. Collier.

What conclusion are we to draw from this most extraordinary oppugnancy of testimony? It is, indeed, a most painful task that devolves on one who has undertaken to decide upon the merits of this portion of the controversy. I cannot see how it is possible to reject Mr. Parry's evidence, since he is not an interested witness. Whatever motive Mr. Collier may have had in making a false or incorrect statement as to what passed at this third interview, it is plain that Mr. Parry had none. If his version be incorrect, it is so by a lapse of memory. But such a monstrous lapse of memory is quite inconceivable in a man of Mr. Parry's clear faculties. In his letter to Mr. Hamilton, which appeared in "The Times" of August 1, 1859, Mr. Parry modestly says, "I may be wrong and Mr. Collier may be right;" but that is the qualification of a man who is as far removed from dogmatism as the poles are asunder. At the same time, Mr. Parry has the best possible corroboration of his recollection of what passed at this interview, for, as we shall see, when he did see the Perkins Folio at the British Museum, he saw a book which he was certain he had never seen before.

Evidence of Mr. Collier's want of veracity.

If, then, we accept the other alternative, and say that Mr. Collier's account is false or inaccurate, we are bound to inquire whether the facts of the case countenance the supposition of a mere freak of memory, or of a positive falsification of facts. I am sorry to have to say that I find in the correspondence in "The Times" the clearest indication of moral delinquency on Mr. Collier's part. It is this: In his letter to "The Times" of July 7th, 1859, Mr. Collier writes :—

"I have shown and sworn that this very book was in the possession of a gentleman named Parry about half a century ago, given to him by a relation named George Gray. *Mr. Parry recognized it instantly, annotated as it is now;*"

Mr. Collier may congratulate himself that the first of these two statements is not correct. If he had sworn to *that*, he would have committed perjury. But the fact is that he simply deposed to *this*—viz.

"that all the statements in the said Preface and Introduction, relative to the discovery, contents, and authenticity of the said folio copy, and the manuscript notes, corrections, alterations, and emendations thereof are true;"

and that Preface did not contain any dogmatic statement "that this very book was in the possession of a gentleman named Parry," &c.

But let me call my reader's attention to the sentence which I have printed in italic type. Let him remember that this is an allusion to facts *already made public.* Mr. Collier is not vouchsafing new facts; but reverting to old. Now it is not the fact that any of Mr. Collier's published narratives contained any account of Mr. Parry recognizing the volume, or of even seeing it. This is, I conceive, the introduction of the narrow end of the wedge. Mr. Collier well knew that, whatever opportunities Mr. Parry had enjoyed of seeing the Perkins Folio, the public had not been made aware of any identification of the volume itself, *but of a facsimile of part of a page of it* only. Knowing this, he seems to me to be saying to the public in this letter, "You all know that Mr. Parry saw this volume, and recognized it; at any rate you may read all about it in my preface; and I have sworn to the truth of that." The rejoinder which the well-informed public would naturally make, and which Mr. Hamilton[21] and others did make, is to this effect: "We know all about your preface and affidavit; but you do not tell us

[21] Letter to The Times, July 16th, 1860.

there that Mr. Parry ever saw the folio at all." This opens the way for Mr. Collier's second letter to "The Times" (July 20, 1859), wherein he favours the public with a circumstantial narrative of the production of the folio to Mr. Parry in the street, of which production Mr. Parry has not the most distant recollection. Mr. Hamilton having unfortunately hampered Mr. Parry with *crutches*, so as to prevent the possibility of his having handled a huge folio, and "looked at it in several places," Mr. Collier, by the law of "action and reaction," flies to the other extreme, and reduces Mr. Parry's holly and barberry sticks to *one* stick, which he held while Mr. Parry examined the folio: and then, in order that Mr. Parry's exact words may not depend on Mr. Collier's recollection, we have an *inaccurate* (it appears to me a *purposely* inaccurate) version of them from Mr. Collier's memory, and a *verbatim* report of them from Mr. Collier's notes made immediately after the interview.

All this hangs together in a perfectly consistent tale of circumstances. No other hypothesis that I have tried will stand the slightest crucial test. Unfortunately, but none the less indisputably, the most probable explanation is one that is incompatible with Mr. Collier's truthfulness.

Mr. Parry's inspection of the Perkins Folio.

I have now only to record the visit of Mr. Parry to the British Museum, on July 13th, 1859. On this occasion Sir Frederic Madden shewed Mr. Parry *one* book—viz. the Perkins Folio, expecting that he would immediately recognize it. But Mr. Parry, instead of seeing a book that had once been his own, or one that had been shewn to him by Mr. Collier, saw one that was a perfect stranger to him in every way. Thereupon, he wrote down, at Sir Frederic Madden's request, the following statement:—

"British Museum, July 13th, 1859.

and his evidence thereupon.

"On being shewn an old edition of Shakespeare's plays, I think I can positively say that it is not the book which Mr. Gray gave me in or about 1806. Sir Frederick Madden stated to me that this copy of Shakespeare, which he now produces to me, was once in Mr. Collier's possession.

(Signed) FRA.^s CHAS. PARRY."

Mr. Parry further stated to Sir Frederic Madden, in the hearing of Mr. Hamilton (as he has subsequently done to me and others) that he believed that his "volume was of the edition 1623; that it was in smooth dark binding, with a new back lettered with that date; that it had no writing on the upper cover, was not so thick, and had a broader margin."

Mr. Collier's attempt to undermine this evidence.

Mr. Collier's mode of meeting this conclusive evidence that Mr. Parry had never seen the Perkins Folio till the 13th July, 1859, is utterly inconsistent with the supposition of his own ingenuousness. These are Mr. Collier's words:—

"He [Mr. Parry] is, like myself, advanced in years, and certainly little able to compete with the imposing authorities at the British Museum. When he went there on the 14th (*sic*) July last, for the purpose of inspecting the Perkins folio, in the presence of Sir F. Madden, Mr. Hamilton, Mr. Maskelyne, and others, he may easily have been confused by the rapid passing and repassing of the folios of 1623 and 1632 before his eyes; and at last he may not have been able to remember which edition had really been his own book," * * * and, he may have been, as it were, cajoled out of his own conviction."[81]

To this most discreditable charge of playing off on the infirmity of an old man, a juggling trick with two folios, a sort of game of book-rig, I shall simply give Mr. Parry's own reply addressed to Sir F. Madden.

"March 12, 1860.

"I have this instant received your note requesting me to say whether the statement made by Mr. Collier in the *Athenæum* of Feb. 18 last, namely, that you had confused me by passing and repassing folio Shakespeares before me, was true. I have no hesitation whatever in flatly contradicting that assertion. While I was conversing with you on the subject, you brought a large old book and placed it on the table. I looked at it several times whilst we were speaking together, and was greatly surprised when at length you took it up and said that was the book in question. I felt perfectly assured that I had never seen that book before. I also now must add that you did not show me any other book whatever, or speak of any other book on that occasion.

I am, &c.

(Signed) F. C. Parry."

Recovery of fly-leaf of Mr. Parry's Folio.

Since writing this Mr. Parry found among his papers the loose fly-leaf of his lost folio, and he kindly forwarded it to me for examination. It is a quarter of an inch shorter, and about as much

---

[80] Reply, p. 18, and The Athenæum, Feb. 18, 1860.

[81] Reply, p. 19.

broader, than the leaves of the Perkins Folio. It is covered with writing in a hand of the last century, and among other notes is an extract from Pope's preface to his edition of Shakspere.[24]

---

[24] The proof sheets containing Mr. Parry's evidence were revised by him before being sent to press. He is answerable for every statement I have made about him.

CHAPTER IV.

THE PERKINS FOLIO.—MR. COLLIER'S ACCOUNT OF ITS MANUSCRIPT NOTES.

MR. COLLIER'S *Notes and Emendations* was not intended to contain all the manuscript notes of the Perkins Folio. The second edition of that work, after page 200, contains considerable additions to the corrections published in the first edition. But still it was not put forward as anything else than what Mr. Tomlins calls "a selection of the emendations."[1] For my part, I do not see what could have been gained by publishing all the corrections of the Perkins Folio. Certainly for the reading public a judicious selection was all that could be desired. I cannot say I think Mr. Collier's selection by any means judicious. On the contrary, a tenth part of that selection would have been sufficient for all conceivable purposes. But when Mr. Collier, in 1856, undertook the publication of a complete list of the manuscript corrections, he was certainly bound to publish a list which should be as nearly exhaustive

Mr. Collier's Notes and Emendations.

Mr. Collier's "List of every manuscript Note and Emendation," &c.

[1] The Critic, Aug. 27, 1859.

as practicable. To Mr. Hamilton is due the merit[2] of pointing out and establishing one of the most curious facts in the history of book-making, viz. that Mr. Collier's complete list *does not contain half* the manuscript corrections in the Perkins Folio. Of course this would not be remarkable, if Mr. Collier's advertisement of his list had fairly stated that he had restricted himself to *certain classes* of corrections, or that he purposed to omit from his list *a certain class* of corrections. But this was not the case. Mr. Collier presents his list of 1856 to his readers with this notice :—

Mr. Collier's pretension for the completeness of his List.

"These 'Notes and Emendations' are before the world in two separate editions; but as the whole of the alterations and corrections were not included, and as those interested in such matters are anxious to see *the entire body* in the shortest form, I have appended them to the present volume in one column, while in the opposite column I have placed the old, or the received text."[3]

Again :—[4]

"I have gone over *every* emendation in the folio 1632 recently, for the purpose of the last portion of my present volume;" . . .

and again[5] he writes,

"I have often gone over the *thousands of marks of all kinds* in its margins; but I will take this opportunity of pointing out two emendations of considerable importance, which happening not to

[2] Inquiry, p. 30.
[3] Preface to "Seven Lectures," p. lx.
[4] At p. lxxiii. [5] At p. lxxix.

be in the margins, and being written with very pale ink, escaped my eye until some time after the appearance of my second edition, as well as of the one-volume Shakspeare. For the purpose of the later portion of my present work, I have recently re-examined *every line and letter* of the folio 1632, and I can safely assert that no other sin of omission on my part can be discovered."

Inasmuch as the Complete List contains a great many corrections which are not in either edition of the *Notes and Emendations*, we might infer from the last extract that the two corrections which he proceeds to specify are not in that list. But such an inference would be wrong, as both are there. So we must needs conclude that Mr. Collier puts forth his list as absolutely exhaustive of the stores of his "old corrector." The list itself is entitled, "A list of *every* manuscript note and emendation in Mr. Collier's copy of Shakespeare's Works, Folio. 1632."

"Yet," says Mr. Hamilton,[6]

"in spite of these reiterated assertions, the *literal* fact is, that the Complete List does not contain one *half* of the corrections, many of the most significant being among those omitted."

Mr. Hamilton's List of every note and emendation in Hamlet.

Mr. Hamilton then gives a list of every manuscript correction in the play of *Hamlet*. In this list, omitting cancels of passages for the purpose of shortening the piece, there are, (if I have counted accurately, which it is not easy to do) 426 corrections. Of these only 125 are said to be in Mr. Collier's complete list. But of these 426, not a few are

[6] Inquiry, p. 31.

cases of corrections obliterated, but still legible,[7] and one is a pencil correction.

But, though I have no doubt Mr. Hamilton's table (for the collations of which he is indebted to the more practised eye of Mr. Staunton) is a very close approximation to accuracy, I do not think it fairly states the case against Mr. Collier. I find that some corrections, not contained in Mr. Collier's Complete List, are yet in the *Notes and Emendations*, and those are not marked with a "C" in Mr. Hamilton's table. But after making this addition to the catalogue of Mr. Collier's acknowledgments, I still find that, taking into consideration all his works on these corrections, he has actually ignored altogether considerably more than *two thirds* of the manuscript corrections in *Hamlet*. It would be very strange indeed if, taking all the plays in the Perkins Folio, it should be found that Mr. Collier had acknowledged anything like half of the alterations and additions of his old corrector.

The charge of misrepresentation against Mr. Collier stated.

Now this does appear to me to be a most extraordinary fact. An editor of high character and position in literature announces that *he has recently gone over every emendation in his corrected second folio*, expressly for his list,—*and* (for that and other publications) *has often gone over the thousands of marks of all kinds in its margins; and has recently reëxamined every line and letter of his folio, and*

[7] I have not counted two cases of obliteration, where the corrections cannot be wholly deciphered.

challenges his readers to bring against him a single sin of omission. He then professes to publish a list of every manuscript note and emendation in his folio. Such is the flourish of trumpets and prologue. Then the theme comes on; and we find in the list less than half the notes and emendations which actually exist in ink, and in a legible state on the margins and between the lines of his corrected folio!

Mr. Collier's dilemma.

If this omission were *intentional* on Mr. Collier's part, all I can say is, that society has a very expressive word to designate such conduct. Among the Houyhnhnms, it would be called "saying the thing which is not," without any imputation of wilful misrepresentation. If the omission were accidental,—a mere oversight—what an editor have we here! Such is the dilemma, the horns of which are presented to Mr. Collier; and apparently thinking lightly of the moral delinquency, he accepts the first. He coolly tells us,[8] that "many of ["the real or supposed omissions in Hamlet,"] I never dreamed at any time of including." It should be noted here that there are no "supposed omissions" in Mr. Hamilton's table which are not "real." So Mr. Collier obliges his readers to conclude that he has made a special point of introducing his "List" as a complete and exhaustive one, when he had intentionally omitted a majority of the notes and emendations.

That Mr. Collier should have done this is, indeed,

[8] Reply, p. 23, note.

passing strange. But it is far more extraordinary to find him bringing forward the fact of *intentional omission* on his part as his *exculpation* for the unexampled shortcomings of his Complete List!

No principle seems to have guided Mr. Collier in his rejections.

What class of corrections can that be which Mr. Collier "never dreamed at any time of including?" Was it "literal corrections"—*i.e.* where there is only a change of the letter, without change of the sense? Certainly not; for the Complete List teems with such corrections: as *usuries* for "usances" in *Measure for Measure*, and *grisled* for "grisly" in *Hamlet*. Why then did he omit *honoured* for "honourable" in the latter play? Was it "changes of punctuation or spelling?" No; for Mr. Collier makes a point of such changes in his *Notes and Emendations*; and besides, they form but a small proportion of the "old corrector's" alterations. Nor could it have been Mr. Collier's intention to omit only such "corrections" as were not new: for in that case he would have omitted more than half those in his Complete List: and then how are we to account for the omission of such emendations as the insertion of the word "but," in the line "The suppliance of a minute; ^ No more." In one page of the corrected folio (*Hamlet*), Mr. Arnold has mentioned[9]

---

[9] See Fraser's Magazine, Feb. 1860, p. 181, where this point is very well enforced. See also Mr. Halliwell's observations on some of the Manuscript Emendations, &c. p. 11, where the reader will find a very remarkable instance of Mr. Collier's default.

that there are fourteen alterations, of which only five are given by Mr. Collier; of the nine ignored by him, the one quoted above is a novelty; another was given by Hanmer; another was proposed by Johnson; and six had been adopted by Mr. Collier in his edition, 1841-1844, without any note.

In short no guiding principle of exclusion is discoverable.

Another omission pointed out by Mr. Arnold is still more remarkable. I give that writer's own words:—[10]

Examples of discrepancies between the Perkins Folio and Mr. Collier's account of it.

I. Michael Hopkins *v.* Nicholas Henton.

"In *Hen. VIII.*, act i. sc. I, where Brandon is enumerating to the Duke of Buckingham 'the limbs o' the plot' against him, this line occurs, as printed in the folio:—

BRAN. A monk of the Chartreux.
BUCK. Oh! *Michael Hopkins?*
BRAN. He.

In sc. 2 this same person is, by the Duke's surveyor, called *Nicholas Henton.* Theobald was the first to point out, from Holingshed's *Chronicle*, that this person's real name was *Nicholas Hopkins*, and that he was a monk of a house 'beside Bristow, called Henton.' He altered the name, however, in both places, 'for perspicuity's sake,' to *Nicholas Hopkins*, though he admitted he might sometimes have been named Henton from the place. Theobald's alteration has been adopted by modern editors. Mr. Knight, indeed, retains the reading of the folio, ingeniously attributing the mistake made by the Duke in the Christian name to his precipitation; Mr. Collier himself, in his eight-volume edition, although he professes to adhere so closely to the old copies, retains Theobald's emendation, and explains

[10] Fraser's Magazine, Feb. 1860, p. 182.

the mistake in a note, though he seems to take the credit of the discovery to himself. In the corrected folio, 1632, in the first cited passage, the name *Michael Hopkins* is erased and *Nicholas Henton* is written by the side, so as to make the name correspond with that given in sc. 2, as to which no alteration was made. Mr. Collier does not notice this emendation. Why not? It was important, as shewing that, according to the lights vouchsafed to the 'Old Corrector,' *Nicholas Henton* was the proper appellation in both places. The alteration could not have been overlooked. It happens, indeed, 'not to be in the margin;' it is in the body of the book, in a blank space, but written with anything but 'very pale ink;' and being the only alteration on a remarkably clean page it could not 'escape the eye' of any one who merely opened the page, much less of a person who examined and 're-examined every line and letter of the folio.'"

II. Fire v. sire.

In "Notes and Queries,"[11] Mr. Collier calls the attention of the readers of that periodical to a passage in *Measure for Measure*, act iii. sc. 1:—

"For thine own bowels, which do call thee, fire
The mere effusion of thy proper loins,
Do curse the gout, &c."

"The above," he writes, "is as the passage is given in every other copy of the folio 1632 I have inspected, but that in my hands with early manuscript corrections; there the second of the above lines stands as follows:

"For thine own bowels, which do call thee sire,"

most clearly and unmistakably printed. Is any other copy known with the same peculiarity?"

This is entirely incorrect. The comma after "thee," is cancelled in ink, and the cross of the f is, on the

[11] First Series, vol. vi. p. 141.

inside, erased with a knife, and the erasure is as plain as an erasure can be.

In the same communication Mr. Collier also calls attention to a passage in *Richard II.* act i. sc. 3:— III. Sly *v.* fly.

> "The sly slow hours shall not determinate
> The dateless limit of thy dear exile."

which he believes to be the reading of "all copies of the folio 1632, excepting [his]." He continues:

"It has been customary, I believe, to print "sly slow," *fly-slow*, on the example and recommendation of Pope; but Steevens questions the propriety of doing so, and I, hastily perhaps, adopted his opinion, from an anxiety to adhere to the old impressions in all cases where it was possible to make sense out of the original reading. My folio 1632 did not come into my possession until long afterwards, and there to my surprise I found "sly slow" printed *fly slow*, the old manuscript-corrector having, moreover, placed a hyphen between the two words, so as to make the line read—

> "The fly-slow hours shall not determinate."

The statement that "fly slow" is so *printed* is incorrect. Mr. Collier himself confesses that "the cross-stroke from the f to the l in "fly-slow" is rather faint:" I may add that it is unmistakably written with a pen.

Mr. Hamilton,[12] calls attention to another singular discrepancy. In the line, "Keepes on his wonder, keepes himself in cloudes,"[13] the "old corrector" has cancelled the letters *keep*; "but," says Mr. Hamilton, "the margin on which the correction is made has IV. Keeps *v* feeds.

---

[12] Inquiry, p. 48. [13] Hamlet, act v. sc. 3.

been carefully torn away." Then follows a note in these words:—

"In the *Complete List* we are told by Mr. Collier that the 'corrected' Folio has '*Feeds* for *keepes*;" *Feeds* being the reading of the 4tos. Consequently the margin must have been intentionally mutilated *since* 1856, when the *List* was published, in order to get rid of the reading of the 4tos! Similar instances of recent mutilation occur throughout the 'Folio.'"

I must confess my utter inability to understand what a mutilator could propose to himself in tearing away this emendation. Any one who suspects Mr. Collier of doing this, must have a very low estimate of that gentleman's wit. How he was to get rid of the reading of the quartos, after he had himself made it public in his Complete List, surpasses my comprehension. Still, the mutilation, which no doubt exists, is a singular fact, and creates a discrepancy between the book itself and Mr. Collier's account of it. If the mutilation have been perpetrated since Mr. Collier reëxamined the page, who, in the household of Mr. Collier, or in that of the Duke of Devonshire did it, and why? If it were done before, whence did Mr. Collier obtain the emendation?

V. The statue scene in Winter's Tale.

In the sixth chapter of my *opusculum* on *The Shakspeare Fabrications*, I have given the following five cases of "remarkable discrepancies," between the Perkins Folio and Mr. Collier's account of it. In *Winter's Tale*, act v. sc. 3, occurs this passage,

"Let be, let be!
Would I were dead, but that methinks already——
What was he that did make it?"

Mr. Collier comments thus upon it:—

"'Let, let be!' is addressed to Paulina, who *offers to draw the curtain* before the statue of Hermione, as we find from a manuscript stage direction, and the writer of it, in a vacant space adjoining, thus supplies a missing line, which we have printed in *italic* type:—

Let be, let be!
Would I were dead, but that, methinks, already
I am but dead, stone looking upon stone.
What was he that did make it?"

It should be remarked that there is no comma after the word "dead," in the manuscript. The introduction of that comma is an emendation of Mr. Collier's on the manuscript line. Besides, the mention of a "vacant place" is disingenuous, for the space on which the line is written was not altogether vacant, and had once been occupied by a previous attempt of the "old corrector," of which the words "looking upon deade stone" are still legible,[11] though they have been erased with a penknife. There can be little doubt that the line which formerly occupied this space was,

"I am but dead looking upon deade stone:"

upon the erasure of this line, but not coincident with it, has been written this line:

"I am but dead stone looking upon stone."

The merits of this manufacture I shall have to discuss in another place.

[11] To Sir F. Madden and Mr. Hamilton I am indebted for deciphering these words.

VI. Controul v. reproof.

In *Coriolanus*, act iii. sc. 2, occurs this passage :—

"VOLUMNIA. . . . Pray be counsell'd ;
I have a heart as little apt as yours,
But yet a brain, that leads my use of anger
To better vantage."

The "old corrector" interpolates a line after "yours,"

"To brook controul without the use of anger."

So, in fact, the line stands in the Perkins Folio; and so Mr. Collier gave it in *Notes and Emendations*,[15] in the facsimile which was subsequently made for private distribution, in his one-volume edition of Shakespeare, and in his Appendix to the *Seven Lectures*. And yet with a strange obliviousness, he thus gives the line in his edition of 1858,[16]

"To brook *reproof* without the use of anger ;"

and tells us in a note,

"This line is from the corrected folio 1632, and is clearly wanted, since the sense is incomplete without it."

VII. Reserves v. reserve *vice* resumes.

In *Timon of Athens*, act ii. sc. 2, Flavius laments that Timon

". . . . . takes no account
How things go from him, nor resumes no care
Of what is to continue. Never mind
Was to be so unwise, to be so kind."

Mr. Collier tells us in his *Notes and Emendations*,[17] that the "old corrector" reads the passage thus :—

[15] 1st Ed. pp. xxiv. and 357; 2nd Ed. pp. xxxi. and 361.
[16] Vol. iv. p. 686 (!)
[17] 1st Ed. p. 389; 2nd Ed. p. 300.

" . . . Takes no account
How things go from him; *no reserve;* no care
Of what is to continue. Never mind
Was *surely* so unwise, to be so kind."

And so, indeed, it stands in the Perkins Folio; but I must add, that "so" has once been struck through, and *too* has been put in the margin, and been partially erased. Mr. Collier gives the same version of these two emendations in his one-volume edition of Shakespeare, and in the Appendix to the *Seven Lectures.* And yet in his edition of 1858,[18] he gives the passage thus:—

" . . . takes no account
How things go from him; *no reserves,* no care
Of what is to continue;"[19]

In *Much ado about Nothing,* act ii. sc. 1, Benedict speaks of Beatrice "huddling jest upon jest with such impossible conveyance." The "old corrector" appears to have first drawn his pen through "possible," and in the margin written *portable,* thus making the word *importable;* which is a word in use in Shakspere's day. But not satisfied with this, he scratched out the dot of the "i," and turned the "im" into *un,* thus making the word *unportable.* And in remarkable harmony with this work of the "old corrector," we find that in *Notes and Emendations,*[20] Mr. Collier tells us that the "old cor- VIII. Importable v. unportable vice impossible.

[18] Vol. v. p. 231.
[19] This discrepancy, and the last, were first mentioned to me by Mr. Staunton.
[20] 1st and 2nd Ed. p. 68.

rector's" word was *importable;* but in the *Seven Lectures,*[21] he tells us that the "old corrector's" word is *unportable;* while in his edition of 1858,[22] he installs *importable* in the text, and tells us, in a note, that such is the word of the corrected folio 1632. I must say this has the very ugly appearance of Mr. Collier having forgotten that the "old corrector" had altered his word, between 1853 and 1856.

IX. The skull scene in 2 Hen. VI.

I will give one more instance of discrepancy. In 2 *Hen. VI.* act iv. sc. 7, after the stage direction, "*Re-enter* Rebels, *with the heads of* Lord Say *and his Son-in-law,*" Jack Cade says, "But is not this braver?—Let them kiss one another, for they loved well, when they were alive." On this Mr. Collier has this note:—[23]

> "Here the corrected folio 1632, adds as a stage direction, 'Jowl them together,' and no doubt the rebels suited the action to the word. The fact is related by Holinshed."

Now, where did Mr. Collier get the word "together"? The "corrected folio 1632," has simply *Jowle them.*

If we are to regard these cases of discrepancy as mere errors of deciphering (!) or of citation, I must regard it as unfortunate that we cannot conjure up Congreve's ghost, and move him to write a second treatise, to be entitled "Amendments of Mr. Collier's False and Imperfect Citations, &c. 8vo. 1860," instead of 1698, which is the date of Congreve's retaliation, *so entitled.*

[21] p. 168. [22] Vol. ii. p. 27. [23] Ed. 1858.

CHAPTER V.

The Perkins Folio.—The Museum Inquisition on its Manuscript Notes.

The preceding three chapters relate merely to the discovery of the folio, its supposititious pedigree, and its contents. The question as to whether the manuscript corrections are, what from their character they pretend to be, in a handwriting of the 17th century, or whether they are in a handwriting of the 19th century, intended to simulate one or more handwritings of the 17th century, remains to be examined.

Is the ink-writing in a genuine hand of the 17th century?

It is obvious that there are three kinds of evidence which may be brought to bear on the manuscript corrections, with a view to the settlement of that question: 1st, That which is called *external* evidence—viz. the peculiarities of the forms of the letters and signs employed, and of the ink or colouring matter in which they are written; 2ndly, That which is called *internal* evidence—viz. the peculiarities of the corrections themselves, irrespective of the writing; and 3rdly, That which I may call the *collateral* evidence—viz. the peculiarities of the conduct of some person or persons in respect of the folio, and its

The three kinds of evidence available.

manuscript corrections. It is obvious that if the manuscript notes can be proved to be of the 19th century by the sagacity of palæographists and record-readers, (though "the general," who know nothing of the art of palæography, may possibly not be convinced by their testimony,) the notes are at once condemned forgeries, however free from anachronism the corrections themselves may be, and however free from the taint of modern dealing by this or that person. Accordingly, it was felt by all persons interested in the question of the genuineness of the manuscript notes, that the first thing to be done with them was to submit them to a palæographic scrutiny. While the volume was in Mr. Collier's possession, there were insuperable difficulties in doing this: for that gentleman having shewn his folio, under restrictions, on two occasions to the members of the Shakspere Society, and at two evening meetings of the Society of Antiquaries, and further having invited the Fellows of that Society to inspect it by daylight, under restrictions,[1] considered that he had done all that could be desired to court and facilitate examination.

Presentation of the Perkins Folio to the late Duke of Devonshire.

When the volume had passed into the possession of the late, and afterwards had become the property of the present Duke of Devonshire, there were still

[1] See page 32. "It must also be distinctly understood that no gentleman is at liberty to make memoranda," &c. Now it is only by copious and laborious "memoranda" that a palæographic scrutiny of the Perkins Folio can be performed.

great obstacles in the way of a palæographic scrutiny. Mr. Herman Merivale, indeed, says,[1]

"It lay in his Grace's library for two or three years, open to inspection by respectable persons with very little difficulty."

Difficulty of access to it.

But this is simply untrue. I myself was more than a year, using every means of seeing the book; but the Duke's librarian refused to exhibit it, and the Duke himself did not know where it was; and I never could get a sight of it until it had been deposited in the Department of Manuscripts of the British Museum.

The occasion of its being sent to the British Museum.

The circumstances which ultimately led to the Perkins Folio being submitted to a palæographic scrutiny were these: Among other means of getting a sight of the once mysterious volume was the one of calling upon Sir F. Madden, the Keeper of the Manuscripts of the British Museum, to use his influence in getting the folio deposited there. This course was suggested to me by the following incident. In the year 1856 I accidentally met Mr. W. J. Thoms (the editor of "Notes and Queries") in a bookseller's shop in the Strand or Fleet-street, and in the course of half an hour's pleasant conversation with him, I stated my conviction that the Perkins notes were not genuine. He replied that he believed them to be so, and fortified his own opinion by citing those of other men of letters. In particular he assured me that Sir F. Madden believed the notes to be genuine. Having

[1] Edinburgh Review, April, 1860, vol. CLI. p. 478.

great doubts about the correctness of Mr. Thoms' statement, I went, accompanied by Mr. A. F. Mayo (the son of Dr. Thomas Mayo), to call on Sir F. Madden, in order to learn his opinion of the notes from his own mouth. He told me that he had never expressed any opinion whatever about the notes, and had never so much as seen the folio. I did not mention Mr. Thoms' name in connexion with the subject. This visit put it into my head to apply to Sir F. Madden for the use of his influence in procuring the deposit of the Perkins Folio at the British Museum. Accordingly, in the autumn of 1858, I again called on Sir F. Madden. I told him that I had been unsuccessful in seeing the Perkins Folio at Devonshire House. I said that judging from the use of certain words, and from Mr. Collier's conduct in respect of a stage direction in one play (*Hamlet*), and an emendation in another (*All's well that ends well*), I was convinced that the manuscript notes were spurious. Sir F. Madden's reply was, that he could not believe that so large a number of corrections could have been fabricated in modern times; and added, with some warmth, that he was a friend of Mr. Collier's, and was satisfied that Mr. Collier's faith was above suspicion. I then inquired whether he (Sir Frederic) would have any objection to write to the Duke of Devonshire, and ask his Grace for the loan of the folio, in order to submit it to a palæographic examination. He said that he had no objection to do so, but that he was then so fully occupied that he must postpone for the present making the application. I understand that Mr. Staunton also called on Sir Frederic Madden with the same object, and received substantially the same reply. In consequence of these two applications, Sir Frederic Madden, with true courtesy, on Sept. 6, 1858, addressed a request to Mr. Collier, (rather than apply immediately to the Duke), that he would procure him (Sir Frederic) a sight of the folio. To this request—in fact to the letter in which it was contained, and which related to other subjects—Sir Frederic Madden received no answer. Official and other business intervening, he did not act on his resolution of writing to the Duke till May 1859, when Professor Bodenstedt was introduced to him by Mr. Watts of the British Museum, and the learned Bavarian having expressed a great desire to see the folio, Sir Frederic promised to meet his wishes, and at the same time to give several of his Shaksperian friends an opportunity of examining the volume. Accordingly on May 13th, he wrote to the Duke requesting the loan of the volume for a short time, and by his Grace's liberality it was sent to him on the 26th of the same month, late in the day. In the evening of the same day Sir Frederic wrote letters to Professor Bodenstedt, the Rev. A. Dyce, Mr. W. J. Thoms (a friend of Mr. Collier's), and Mr. Staunton, inviting them to see the volume.

On the following morning Sir Frederic Madden and Mr. Bond proceeded to examine the manuscript Sir F. Madden and Mr. Bond examine the MS. notes. notes on palæographic grounds, and they were both struck with the very suspicious character of the writing—certainly the work of one hand, but presenting varieties of forms assignable to different periods—the evident *painting* over of many of the letters, and the artificial look of the ink. The day had not passed before Sir Frederic had quite made up his mind that the "old corrector" had never lived in the 17th century, but that the notes were fabricated at a recent period. On the 28th May, Mr. Dyce came to see the volume in Sir Frederic's study; on the 30th, Mr. Forster; on the 31st, Professor Bodenstedt; and on the 1st and 2nd of June, Mr. Bruce, a friend of Mr. Collier's. On the latter day Mr. Hamilton called his chief's attention to the numerous words deleted in the margin, either with an acid or rubbed out, apparently with the finger, and many more half effaced. From the commencement of June not a day passed without the volume being inspected constantly in Sir F. Madden's study by literary and other persons, and almost always in his presence.

Sir F. Madden's opinion.

The volume in frequent request.

On the 4th June I went to the Department of Manuscripts with Mr. Staunton, and examined a great number of previously selected passages in Mr. Hamilton's presence; but as the time for closing the Museum had passed, and Sir F. Madden was not there, I postponed all further examination of the book till the Monday following, viz. the 6th June.

On the morning of that day I again visited the

Department of Manuscripts, and saw the book in Sir Frederic Madden's presence. Sir Frederic now told me that, after a brief examination, he had come to the conclusion that the manuscript notes were not in the handwriting of any known period, but were exceedingly clumsy imitations of some handwritings prevalent in the 17th century. Sir Frederic, however, still very earnestly expressed his belief in Mr. Collier's *bona fides*, and refused to allow his opinion to be publicly expressed, lest such an expression might be used by Mr. Collier's opponents to prejudice that gentleman's character.

Discovery of pencilling by Dr. Ingleby.

During this visit, while I was very closely examining certain passages in the folio, I was surprised by the appearance of a pencil mark or line; and on tracing it by the eye I concluded, perhaps hastily, that it passed under the ink word. I accordingly directed Sir Frederic Madden's attention to it. But Sir Frederic Madden did not appear to attach any importance to the remark, and did not pursue the inquiry I had suggested.

Discovery of the correspondence between words in ink and words in pencil by Mr. Hamilton.

Within a week after this occurred Mr. Hamilton, while poring over the volume, discovered that its margins were covered with minute and half obliterated pencil marks, some of which appeared to underlie the ink, and, what was a new feature, that all of them appeared to correspond with the ink writing. He at once called Sir Frederic Madden's attention to these circumstances. Sir Frederic accordingly again looked through the volume page by page, and was inexpressibly astonished to discover hundreds of marks of punctuation and corrigenda in pencil, more or less distinct, in an apparently modern hand, which were evidently intended as a guide to the "old corrector," *in nearly all cases* followed by a corresponding alteration of the text in ink. Entire words were also found written in pencil, and to the eyes of Sir F. Madden, Mr. Bond, and Mr. Hamilton, it seemed clear that some of these pencillings did *underlie the ink*.[3] Mr. Hamilton writes:—[4]

Mr. Hamilton's account of his first examination of the MS. notes.

"In the first place, they have none of the feigned antiquity about them of the ink corrections, either in form or spelling. They are in a bold, clear handwriting of the present day, are evidently executed by one hand throughout, and have been placed on the margins to direct the alterations afterwards made in ink, and with which they invariably correspond. They are of various kinds. Amongst the most common are crosses and ticks, apparently used to call attention to words or letters requiring correction. Some of them may, of course, be the "crosses, ticks, or lines" which Mr. Collier acknowledges he introduced himself; but as cases occur where such pencil-ticks actually *underlie* corrections in ink, some of them at least must have been placed on the margins before the "Old Corrector" commenced his labours. The ordinary signs in use to indicate *corrigenda* for the press are of common occurrence in the margins, while the corrections indicated thereby are made in the text in the *quasi-*

[3] To save "Indagators" of the Periodical Press the trouble of finding a mare's-nest, I beg to call attention to the circumstance that I have derived most of the particulars of this narrative from Sir Frederic Madden's letter to "The Critic" of the 24th March, 1860, which is reprinted in the appendix to this book.

[4] Inquiry, p. 24.

antique ink.[5] Again, whole syllables or words occur in pencil, partially rubbed out, but still legible, and in which the character of the modern handwriting is plainly visible; while in near neighbourhood to them, the same syllable or word is repeated in ink in the antique hand. In some cases the ink word and the pencil word occupy the same space in the margin, and are written one upon the other; and in these instances the naked eye readily detects the fact that the pencil has been written prior to the ink. As, however, the most positive evidence on this head was desirable, its decision forming one of the turning-points of the inquiry; Mr. Maskelyne, by permission of the Duke of Devonshire, undertook to institute a series of microscopic and chemical experiments on the subject. The importance of the point lay in this: that since the pencil alterations were undeniably recent * * *, it followed that the ink corrections, if written subsequently to these, must be modern likewise, however carefully an antique appearance might have been simulated for them."

Professor Maskelyne's experiments were of three descriptions—*optical*, *chemical*, and *mechanical*. To determine whether a given pencil line is above or beneath an ink line, it is necessary to observe whether the former is traceable through the latter where they cross, which can only be satisfactorily done by the aid of the microscope; or it is still better to remove the ink, mechanically or chemically (according to its nature), and then to observe whether the continuity of the pencil line is restored: if so, the pencil was under the ink; if not, the ink was under the pencil.

Prof. Maskelyne's three classes of experiments.

[5] See sheet no. IV., where I have presented the reader with examples of the old corrector's mode of altering the punctuation of the Perkins Folio.

Prof. Maskelyne suggests the use of the microscope.

This chemist, in calling public attention to his mode of manipulation, and its results, in "The Times" of July 16th, 1859, says:—

"I suggested the use of an instrument which has already done good service in an analogous case (that of the Simonides' Uranius)—the microscope."

Mr. Collier, in his Letter to "The Athenæum" of Feb. 18th, 1860, writes thus:—

Mr. Collier mistakes the Simonides' Uranius for a microscope.

"In this undertaking he [Mr. Hamilton] was avowedly aided by Sir F. Madden and by Mr. Maskelyne, of the Mineral Department, who brought for their use a microscope bearing the imposing and scientific name of the Simonides Uranius."

That the public should have mistaken the meaning of "the Simonides' Uranius," was perhaps not improbable; but it certainly provoked no little ridicule to find Mr. Collier ignorant of one of the most notorious literary forgeries that the world has ever known, and perpetrating a blunder from which, in the absence of a knowledge of letters, his knowledge of English grammar ought to have saved him. On the mistake being brought to his notice, he excused himself by confessing,[6] "I have no pretensions to *science* of any kind, and I mistook Mr. Maskelyne's parenthesis." "Why this is a more excellent *fault* than the other." It was not Mr. Collier's ignorance of science that provoked the smile, but his ignorance of an incident in letters which is as widely known as his Perkins Folio. As Mr. Maskelyne says, it is "an analogous case." Constantine Simonides, a Greek by birth, and at present resident in Liverpool, after per-

[6] Reply, p. 23.

petrating a long series of forgeries of Greek manuscripts, professed to have discovered a palimpsest[1] of a history of Egypt by Uranius. It consisted of 71 leaves, and each page comprised two columns. In all there were 284 columns. That it was a palimpsest was evident from the fact that four other manuscripts had originally been written, apparently over the obliterated, or partially obliterated, work of Uranius:—viz. 1. A work of Flavius Josephus; 2. A history of the Virgin Mary; 3. A work of the Emperor Constantine; and 4. A history of St. John the Baptist. All these were written in a 12th century hand; and through them Simonides pretended to have discovered an underlying manuscript work of Uranius. The palimpsest was submitted to the ablest scholars of Germany; and with the single and most honourable exception of Alexander von Humboldt, all of them, including the erudite Dr. Dindorf, were completely convinced of the genuineness of the Uranius manuscript. A large sum of money was given to Simonides as the price of the palimpsest. At last, the suspicions of Professor Lepsius having been aroused by the extraordinary confirmation which Uranius gave throughout to his own system of Egyptian chronology, he called in the aid of Professor Ehrenberg, who applied to the manuscript his powerful microscope, and at once discovered the fact

The Uranius forgery of Simonides.

The forgery discovered by the use of the microscope.

[1] That manuscript is called a palimpsest which has been written on the papyrus or parchment from which a previously written manuscript has been expunged.

that wherever the writing of the so-called palimpsest was crossed by the 12th century writing, the ink of the apparently old uncial letters in reality overlay the writing of the other works.[8] The result of this discovery to Simonides, was his residence for a length of time in the dungeons of Berlin. The result of Professor Maskelyne's scrutiny of the manuscript in the Perkins Folio affords, as yet, no parallel to the dungeon catastrophe.

Optically; Professor Maskelyne reports thus:—

The result of the application of the microscope to the Perkins notes.

"The microscope reveals the particles of plumbago in the hollows of the paper, and in no case that I have yet examined does it fail to bring this fact forward into incontrovertible reality. Secondly the ink presents a rather singular aspect under the microscope. Its appearance in many cases on, rather than in the paper, suggested the idea of its being a water-colour paint rather than an ink; it has a remarkable lustre, and the distribution of particles of colouring matter in it seems unlike that in inks, ancient or modern, that I have yet examined."[9]

The chemical test.

Chemically; Professor Maskelyne informs us that the ink has a taste—

"unlike the styptic taste of ordinary inks, which it imparts to the tongue, and by its substance evidently yielding to the action of damp." But that "its colouring matter resists the action of chemical agents which rapidly change inks, ancient or modern, whose colour is due to iron."

The mechanical test.

Mechanically; Professor Maskelyne informs us that the seeming ink—

"proves to be a paint removable, with the exception of a slight

[8] I take this account from "The Athenæum," Feb. 16, 1856.
[9] Letter in The Times of July 16, 1859.

stain, by mere water," and that "its prevailing character is that of a paint formed perhaps of sepia, or of sepia mixed with a little Indian ink." "I have nowhere been able to detect the pencil-mark clearly overlying the ink, though in several places the pencil stops abruptly at the ink, and some seems to be just traceable through its translucent substance, while lacking there the generally metallic lustre of the plumbago. But the question is set at rest by the removal by water of the ink in instances where the ink and the pencil intersected each other. The first case I chose for this purpose was a *u* in *Richard II.*, p. 36. A pencil tick crossed the *u*, intersecting each limb of that letter. The pencil was barely visible through the first stroke, and not at all visible under the second stroke of the *u*. On damping off the ink in the first stroke, however, the pencil-mark became much plainer than before, and even when as much of the ink-stain as possible was removed the pencil still runs through the ink line in unbroken even continuity. Had the pencil been superposed on the ink, it must have lain superficially upon its lustrous surface and have been removed in the washing. We must, I think, be led by this to the inference that the pencil underlies the ink—that is to say, was antecedent to it in its date; while, also, it is evident that the "old commentator" had done his best to rub out the pencil writing before he introduced its ink substitute.

General results of Prof. Maskelyne's examination.

Now it is clear that evidence of this kind cannot by itself establish a forgery. It is on palæographical grounds alone that the modern character of the pencillings can be established; but this point once determined in the affirmative, the result of the physical inquiry certainly will be to make the "old commentator" far less venerable."

There are thus two questions, quite independent of each other, for the solution of palæographists:—

The two questions for the solution of palæographists.

1st. Are the ink-notes in a genuine 17th century hand?

2nd. Are the pencillings in a modern cursive?

Before entering on the consideration of the importance of keeping these questions distinct, a point which has been fully recognized by the palæographists, but strangely lost sight of by the critics, I will proceed to consider the features of the Perkins Folio, of which Sir F. Madden and Mr. Hamilton took especial cognizance, and which are clearly detailed by the latter gentleman in his letter, published in "The Times" of July 2nd, 1859. He writes:—

Mr. Hamilton's account of the Perkins Folio, and its MS. notes.

"The volume is bound in rough calf (probably about the middle of George II.'s reign), the water-mark of the leaves pasted inside the cover being a crown surmounting the letters "G. R." (*Georgius Rex*), and the Dutch lion within a paling, with the legend *pro patriâ*; and there is evidence to shew that the corrections, though intended to resemble a hand of the middle of the 17th century, could not have been written on the margins of the volume until after it was bound, and consequently not, at the earliest, until towards the middle of the 18th.

I should enter more minutely into this feature of the case, did not the corrections themselves, when closely examined, furnish facts so precise and so startling in their character that all collateral and constructive evidence seems unnecessary and insignificant.

They at first sight seem to be of two kinds,—those, namely, which have been allowed to remain, and those which have been obliterated with more or less success, sometimes by erasure with a penknife or the employment of chymical agency, and sometimes by tearing and cutting away parts of the margin. The corrections thus variously obliterated are probably almost as numerous as those suffered to remain, and in importance equal to them. Whole lines, entire words, and stage directions, have been attempted to be got rid of, though in many instances without success, as a glance at the various readings of a first portion of *Hamlet*, which I subjoin, will shew.

Of the corrections allowed to stand, some, on a hasty glance, might, so far as the handwriting is concerned, pass as genuine, while others have been strangely tampered with, touched up, or painted over, a modern character being dexterously altered by touches of the pen into a more antique form.[10] There is, moreover, a kind of exaggeration in the shape of the letters throughout, difficult, if not impossible, to reconcile with a belief in the genuineness of the hand; not to mention the frequent and strange juxta-position of stiff Chancery capital letters of the form in use two centuries ago with others of quite a modern appearance, and it is well here to state that all the corrections are evidently by one hand; and that, consequently, whatever invalidates or destroys the credit of a part must be considered equally damaging and fatal to the whole.

At times the correction first put in the margin has been obliterated, and a second emendation substituted in its stead, of which I will mention two examples which occur in *Cymbeline* (fol. 1632, p. 400, col. 1):—

"With Oakes unshakeable and roaring Waters,"

where *Oakes* has first been made into *Cliffes*, and subsequently into *Rockes*.[11] Again (p. 401, col. 2),

"Whose Roof's as low as ours: Sleepe Boyes, this gate,"

---

[10] As an instance, I may refer to the play of *The Tempest*, where the "old corrector," has first written some *ks* in modern character, and then, in a different coat of paint, prolonged the downward strokes, so as to give the letters a more ancient form. See also *Othello*, p. 357—where the *g* of the stage direction *on the ground*, has two tails intersecting one another.

[11] The writer of the article in Notes and Queries, (second Series, vol. ix. p. 210), asserts that "Cliffes" is written in pencil, in an antique character, and founds on that fact a charge of disingenuousness against Mr. Hamilton. The assertion only demonstrates the utter incapacity of the writer to tell one kind of writing from another. A few months apprenticeship to

on the margin (a pencil cross having been made in the first instance) *Sleepe* is corrected into *Sweete*, afterwards *Sweete* has been crossed out, and *Stoope* written above.

There is scarcely a single page throughout the volume in which these obliterations do not occur. At the time they were effected it is possible the obliteration may have appeared complete; but the action of the atmosphere in the course of some years seems in the majority of instances to have so far negatived the chymical agency as to enable the corrections to be readily deciphered. Examples of these accompany this letter, and I shall be surprised if in the hands of Shakspearian critics they do not furnish a clue to the real history of the corrector and his corrections.

I now come to the most astounding result of these investigations, in comparison with which all other facts concerning the corrected folio become insignificant. On a close examination of the margins they are found to be covered with an infinite number of faint pencil marks and corrections, in obedience to which the supposed old corrector has made his emendations. These pencil corrections have not even the pretence of antiquity in character or spelling, but are written in a bold hand of the present century. A remarkable instance occurs in Richard III. (fol. 1632, p. 181, col. 2), where the stage direction, "with the body", is written in pencil in a clear modern hand, while over* this the ink corrector writes in the antique and smaller character, "with the dead bodie," the word "dead" being seemingly inserted to cover over the entire space occupied by the larger pencil writing, and "bodie" instead of "body" to give the requisite appearance of antiquity." Further on, in the tragedy of *Hamlet* (fol. 1632, p. 187, col. 1),

* i.e. on the top of.

---

record-reading might possibly dispel a few of his illusions, which so happily blind him to every fact which prejudices his friend Mr. Collier. Truth often suffers from the indulgence of an "amiable weakness."

" "The Athenæum" of Feb. 18th, 1860, devotes a column and

"And crooke the pregnant Hindges of the knee,"

"begging," occurs in pencil in the opposite margin in the same modern hand, evidently with the intention of superseding "preg-

---

a half of the Review of Mr. Hamilton's *Inquiry*, to the proof of the positions that *body* is an older orthography than *bodie* and that the latter mode of spelling did not come into fashion till the reign of Charles II.

The establishment of these points is intended as an answer to the following argument. "Bodie," says our Manuscript Department, "is an old form, Body a new form of the word. *Ergo*, the rascal who wrote "bodie" in ink upon "body" in pencil must have been a very recent rascal—"still alive" is the charitable supposition,—and his adoption of the ancient spelling in his ink is neither more nor less than a fraudulent mystification." Having first stated this gloss on Mr. Hamilton's position, (to prepare the reader's mind!) the reviewer proceeds to quote Mr. Hamilton's own words. "On a close examination," &c. &c. The reviewer makes it appear that Mr. Hamilton's inference that the pencil writing is recent, is derived from the modern character of the spelling. But this is not the case. That inference is *solely* derived from the fact that the pencil writing is "in a bold hand of the present century." Now Mr. Maskelyne has established that the ink writing is over the pencil writing. Therefore the ink writing is *of the present century*. But it is in a 17th century hand, (or rather it is a mixture of several distinct styles of that century.) Therefore the antique character of the ink writing is not genuine. Now is the spelling consistent with the supposition that the writer assumed the 17th century hand *fraudulently?* Yes. For while the pencil words are always spelled as they are in the present day, the spelling of the ink words corresponding to such pencil words is sometimes obsolete. Thus where the pencil word is *body*, the corresponding ink word is *bodie*. Such a fabricator would in all probability have preferred the spelling *bodie* to nant" in the text. The entire passage from, "Why should the poore be flatter'd?" to "As I doe thee. Something too much of this" was afterwards struck out. The ink corrector, probably thrown off his guard by this, neglected to copy over and afterwards rub out the pencil alteration, according to his usual plan, and by this oversight we seem to obtain as clear a view of the *modus operandi* as if we had looked over the corrector's shoulder and seen the entire work in process of fabrication. I give several further instances where the modern pencil writing can be distinctly seen underneath the old ink correction, and I should add that in parts of the volume page after page occurs, in which commas, notes of admiration and interrogation, &c., are deleted, or inserted in obedience to pencil indications of precisely the same modern character and appearance as those employed in correcting the press at the present day. *Twelfth Night* (fol. 1632, p. 258, col. 1):—"I take these Wisemen, that crow so at these set kind of fooles,

---

body (in the ink word). 1st, Because the former was the spelling of the period succeeding the date of the 2nd folio—to which period the "old corrector" professed to belong. 2nd, Because by choosing *bodie*, rather than *body*, he would obviate an objection which might (however untenable) be derived from *body*; for though *body* is an archaic form, it is also the most modern: whereas *bodie* is an archaism, and is not modern.

This reply is *sufficient* to rebut the argument of "The Athenæum." But I might go still farther: I might, consistently with facts, deny the writer's statement, that the spelling *body* is older than *bodie*. I believe *bodie* to be the older form. Certainly both were used indifferently in Shakspere's day. Thus in "Dialogical Discourses of Spirits and Divels," 1601, in the third dialogue (pp. 64—98, inclusive), *bodie* occurs *one hundred and twenty three* times, and *body* only *five* times: while in "A Treatise of Specters," &c. 1605, in chapter 5 (pp. 43—49), *bodie* occurs *twenty five* times, and *body sixty times.*

no better than the fooles Zanies." The corrector makes it "*to be* no better than," &c. Here the antique "to be" is written over a modern pencil "to be" still clearly legible. A few lines further down the letter *l* is added in the margin over a pencil *l*.

In *Hamlet* (fol. 1632, p. 278, col. 1):—

"Oh, most pernicious woman!"

is made into—

"Oh, most pernicious and perfidious woman!"

but here, again, the "perfidious" of the corrector can be seen to be above a pencil "perfidious" written in a perfectly modern hand.[13]

In *Hamlet* (fol. 1632, p. 276, col. 2), the line

"Looke too't, I charge you; come your way,"

has been altered by the corrector into

"Looke too't, I charge you; *so now* come your way,"

in the inner margin. The words "so now," in faint pencil and in a modern hand, on the outer margin, are distinctly visible. Immediately below this, and before

"Enter Hamlet, Horatio, Marcellus,"

the corrector has inserted "Sc. 4." This would seem to have been done in obedience to a pencil "IV." in the margin.

In *King John* (fol. 1632, p. 6, col. 2),

"Austria and France shoot in each other's mouth."

The corrector adds, as a direction, at this line "aside;" the same word "aside" occurs likewise in pencil in a modern hand on the outer margin."

This most excellent description of the actual state of the Perkins Folio cannot be too often repeated.

---

[13] *See* facsimile facing title-page.

It is a picture of the actual fact; and not a statement in it has ever been, or to the best of my judgment can be, impugned. I have devoted much time to the examination of the once mysterious volume: and though I could from my own original resources give an exact and faithful description of its contents, I am satisfied I could not improve on Mr. Hamilton's portraiture, and therefore avail myself of his language and examples; and his inferences, drawn with professional skill, and brought forward with as much modesty as is consistent with confidence in his own judgment, I most conscientiously endorse.[14]

I will simply call attention to the selection of words and phrases which I have made from the manuscript annotations of the Perkins Folio, for the sheet of facsimiles, no. IV. Here the reader will observe several examples of the pencil-writing underlying the ink; and many more would have been added but for the over-scrupulousness ("hyper-

---

[14] It is noteworthy that in one place, viz. *Comedies*, p. 278, the bottom of the page, comprizing nearly the whole margin, has been cut away with a knife, probably to get rid of some lengthy addition of which the old corrector had repented. Mr. Collier speaks of the book as having suffered from "the falling of the lighted snuff of a candle, or the ashes of tobacco."—(*Notes and Emendations*, 1st ed. Introduction, p. vi.) Now at pp. 325-8, in *King Lear*, it seems to me that the paper has been wilfully burnt in order to get rid of some corrections, or still more probably of a suspicious erasure.

M.S. Corrections in pencil & ink from the Perkins Folio

Sheet No. IV.

A G written by Mr. Collier in pencil for the direction of his facsimilist

An.
Seb.
bled
I could

Twelfth Night _ page 260 col. 1.

(1)
Go Go
Go Go
Iobbt,

Merchant of Venice _ page 167 col. 2

(2)
Gra.

Merchant of Venice
page 175 col. 2

(3)
Alls well that ends well.
page 247 col. 1

(4) Both
King Henry VI. part 2.
page 129 col. 2

(5) Enter Duke angerly
Two Gentlemen of Verona
page 36 col. 2

(6)
ing | Kin. The extreme parts of
Love's Labour lost _ page 143 col. 1

Twelfth Night _ page 275 col. 2

(7) South
King John page 6 col. 2

(8) Surgeon! send one pre-

(9) is! You broke my head

Merchant of Venice _ page 169 col. 1

(10) Venice still

(11) Bohemia

Merchant of Venice.

(12) offer.
Twelfth Night.
page 274. col. 2

(13) Yonder she comes.
Midsummer Night's Dream... page 160 col. 2

(18) ing | Shew duty, as mistaken all this while,
Coriolanus _ page 56 col. 1.

* This very modern mode of indicating the insertion of a 'full-stop' occurs on almost every page of the Perkins Folio

(14) And pitch our evils there? oh fie, fie, fie :

offall?

Measure for Measure _ page 68 col. 2

(15) of
Comedy of Errors.
page 92. col. 2.

(16) of | to
Mt. of Venice.
page 165 col. 1.

Short-hand in pencil, according to Palmers system, 1774

(19) Fluellen | Thif.
M. Night's Dream.
page 159 col. 1.

(Struggles or instead noise.)
Coriolanus _ page 55 col. 2.

(17)
Twelfth Night.
page 274 col. 2.

1, 2 & 3 Examples of a G occasionally employed by the "Old Corrector."
4, 5, 6, 18 & 19 Examples of pencil written under the ink.
7, 8, 9 & 12 Examples of the "Old Corrector's" mode of correcting punctuation, in pencil & ink.
13, 14, 15, 16 & 17 Examples of the "Old Corrector's" corrections in pencil & ink.
10 & 11 Specimens of the "Old Corrector's" slanting handwriting

Ashbee & Dangerfield Lith.

Before p. 147

squeamishness," Mr. Collier would call it) of Mr. Ashbee, who positively refused to attempt the fac-simile of any pencil-writing, *however legible,* that was not *distinct,* and as the reader already knows, the great mass of the pencil instructions of the folio are "half obliterated." Mr. Collier complains[18] of Mr. Hamilton for having given only *fifteen* of the "infinite number" of pencil words and marks. Instead of that he should have given Mr. Hamilton and Mr. Frederick G. Netherclift credit for not attempting the representation of pencil-writing which in thousands of places is very indistinct, even where it is perfectly legible. The question was not "what pencil words can be read?" but, "what pencil words can be represented by lithography?" In the sheet referred to the reader will observe traces of *th* in pencil under the *th* of the word *both;* portions of *Enter Duke* in pencil under the stage-direction, *Enter Duke Angerly,* and under the correction *ing,* for *s* in the word "parts," are traces of the same correction in pencil, while the *pa* which protrudes from the left of the ink correction shews that the whole word *parting* was first written in pencil.

In the stage-direction *Venice still,* the reader will observe that the "old corrector" has yielded to his *habitual* inclination to the right, and has thus fallen into the pseudo-antique cursive of the letter signed "S. Danyell," which is given in facsimile in sheet no. IX.

[18] Reply, p. 21.

The fundamental mistake of Mr. R. Grant White and "Scrutator."

Reviewers of Mr. Hamilton's letters and book, have fallen into a strange mistake, which was first committed by Mr. R. Grant White in "The Atlantic Monthly Advertiser" for October 1859, and has since been repeated, and still more strenuously urged by a writer who calls himself "Scrutator," in a pamphlet which is characterized only by disingenuousness, feebleness, and inconsequence. The mistake is this. These writers assume that the primal evidence of forgery, in the case of the ink corrections, is the fact that they correspond with pencil-writing. of a more or less modern character, some of which respectively underlie the ink corrections with which they correspond. It is then attempted to be shewn either that the pencil-writing may be a cursive of the 17th century, or that there are two pencil hands, of which the older only is ever found to underlie the ink. It is therefore inferred that, since that pencil-writing, which must have been written before the ink-writing, may be of the 17th century, the ink-writing itself may be as old as its character would lead one to believe.

The primal evidence of forgery.

This is all wrong. *The primal evidence of forgery lies in the ink-writing,* AND IN THAT ALONE. All evidence that rests on the judgment of palæographists is necessarily of a kind which is not susceptible of verification by any but palæographic experts. If Mr. Hamilton presents his readers with a facsimile by Mr. Frederick G. Netherclift, any one who has an eye and a pair of compasses may, by comparing the facsimile with the original, arrive at an independent judgment on the fidelity of the representation. But if Sir Frederic Madden pronounces an opinion that a particular piece of antique-looking writing is not a genuine antique, but a modern simulation, the public have but the alternative of accepting Sir Frederic's *ipse dixit*, or rejecting his skill as a palæographist. In the case in question, *all* the palæographists who have examined the manuscript are of one opinion. Sir Frederic Madden, Mr. Bond, and Mr. Hamilton of the British Museum; Sir Francis Palgrave, Deputy Keeper of Her Majesty's Public Records; Mr. W. H. Black, formerly Assistant Keeper of ditto, and Mr. T. Duffus Hardy, Assistant Keeper of ditto; Professor Brewer, Reader at the Rolls, and several others of less note, have unhesitatingly pronounced the ink-writing spurious, on palæographic grounds, not a single palæographist having yet ventured to dissent from that decision. This conclusion having been arrived at, the discovery of the pencil-writing, which indeed throws every other feature of this case into the shade, becomes significant. With the knowledge *already* acquired that the ink-writing is a modern simulation, it becomes obvious that the pencil marks and notes are the suggestions for corrections which in the vast majority of cases have been followed. The only motive which could induce a critic to charitably suppose, on the one hand, that the pencil-writing—especially where it underlies the ink (!)—is a cursive

The secondary evidence of forgery.

of the 17th century, or, on the other, that one hand wrote the corresponding pencil-writing (long after the ink-writing had been executed) for purposes of interpretation, and that another and an older hand wrote those pencil corrections, which underlie the ink, for the direction of the scribe,—the only conceivable motive for such kindly, but far-strained suppositions vanishes, when we know (as palæographists do), or believe (as the public must do, if they have any faith in palæography), that, by the ink corrections alone, the fabrication is proved. We are then at liberty to dismiss from our minds the question—how can we reconcile these pencil marks with a belief in the genuineness of the ink corrections?.and instead, we have to consider how to explain the pencil marks and corrections, on the assumption that the ink corrections are in a simulated hand. We are thus left to the conclusions of our senses, which are these :—

Conclusions on the palæographic questions.

1st, That all the pencil marks and corrections are in one handwriting.

2nd, That that handwriting is one of our own day.

There is as much intrinsic reason for doubting these conclusions, as for doubting whether a letter which has been addressed to me by a stranger, is all in one handwriting, and in a handwriting of my own day.

CHAPTER VI.

THE PERKINS FOLIO.—THE WEAK POINTS IN MR. COLLIER'S REPLIES RESPECTING IT.

As was expected, Mr. Hamilton's assaults on the genuineness of the "old corrector" called Mr. Collier himself into the field. In reply to the former gentleman's letters, and that of Professor Maskelyne, Mr. Collier wrote two letters to the editor of "The Times," which were published in the impressions of that Journal of July 7th and 20th, 1859. In the first of these letters he plaintively says,

Mr. Collier's four replies.

"I am determined not to make the poor remainder of my life miserable by further irritating contests; this is the last word I shall ever submit to say upon the subject in print; but if the matter be brought before a proper legal tribunal I shall be prepared in every way to vindicate my integrity."

In despite of this somewhat petulant vow, he writes a second letter to "The Times" eight days later; and after the publication of the *Inquiry* of Mr. Hamilton, he publishes two replies, one in "The Athenæum" of Feb. 18th, 1860, and the other in the form of a pamphlet, in order, to use his own words, "that the bane and the antidote may be taken together."[1]

As I cannot reprint these replies at length, I

[1] Reply, p. 1.

shall adopt the plan of extracting from them such remarks as bear upon the various questions involved in the discussion of the Perkins Folio, allowing all Mr. Collier's observations on other disputed manuscripts to stand over for separate examination.

In the course of a careful consideration of Mr. Collier's replies, I have found many points on which his rejoinders are most unsatisfactory, and some on which they are certainly entitled to weight. I purpose to deal with the former class only. With these deductions, the readers of Mr. Collier's replies, so far as they concern the Perkins Folio, may take them for what they profess to be. The points to which I am bound to except are the following:—

I. The manuscript corrected folio seen by Dr. Wellesley in Rodd's shop.

II. The pencil-writing in the Perkins Folio.

III. Mr. Maskelyne's examination of the manuscript notes and emendations of the Perkins Folio.

IV. The alleged similarity between the handwritings in the Bridgewater Folio and the Perkins Folio.

V. The "G. R. and Dutch Lion."

VI. Mr. Hamilton's "Hamlet" collations.

VII. Mr. Collier's capacity for fabrication.

VIII. The testimony of Mr. Dyce to the excellence of the emendations, and Mr. Collier's option of appropriating them.

What Folio Shakspere did Dr. Wellesley see in Rodd's shop?

I. What folio it was that Dr. Wellesley saw at Rodd's shop it is impossible to say with certainty.

Dr. Wellesley has informed me that he has inspected the Perkins Folio, and is of opinion, that it is the identical book: but he is not certain; nor does he speak of any special mark by which he is enabled to establish the identity. But whether there be any such mark or not, we cannot tell, owing to Dr. Wellesley's refusal to be cross-examined.

One reason there is which would lead to the belief that the Perkins Folio is not the book he saw at Rodd's shop. If, as we learn from the *Notes and Emendations*,[2] Mr. Collier *took* the folio home, it would seem that Dr. Wellesley could not have seen it in Rodd's shop, unless he and Mr. Collier were there together. Mr. Collier did not deviate from this statement till after he had received Dr. Wellesley's letter. Then he writes,[3]

"It so happened, that just after I had left Rodd's, and had secured my purchase by paying for it, *leaving the volume to be sent home*, the Rev. Dr. H. Wellesley entered the shop, looked at the book, and seeing the MS. notes, which I had not seen, wished to become the possessor. Rodd informed Dr. Wellesley that the old folio had been already sold[4] for the very price I had given for it."

In his *Reply*[5] Mr. Collier gives us this version of the incident:—

"My frequent course was to call at Rodd's on my way from Kensington, to see what he might have that was new and inte-

---

[2] 1st Edition, Introduction, p. vii.

[3] The Athenæum, Feb. 18, 1860.

[4] This is Mr. Collier's *construction* of an ambiguous phrase in Dr. Wellesley's letter.

[5] Page 8.

resting to me, and if the book or books I had bought were of any size, to go on towards the City, and on my return to carry away my purchase by an omnibus. I did not ordinarily give Rodd the trouble of sending all the way to my house. Such I feel pretty sure was the case with the Perkins folio: I left it in the shop until my return, and then "took it home" with another folio."

Without wishing to be hypercritical, I must say, this looks something like *cooking evidence*. The expression, "It so happened, that *just after*—" does not rest on Mr. Collier's memory (for, by his own account he "had left Rodd's"), nor on the testimony of any one else. Dr. Wellesley is unable to say when it was that he paid Mr. Rodd this visit, on the date of which so much depends. But, says Mr. Collier, it was just after he had left the volume *to be sent home*. This is testimony *pro re natâ* with a vengeance. In *Notes and Emendations*, Mr. Collier *takes* the folio home. But when Dr. Wellesley's evidence turns up, and it becomes possible to make that gentleman's visit synchronize with Mr. Collier's departure from Rodd's shop, then the testimony undergoes a *rifacimento*; and it then turns out, that Mr. Collier *left* the folio behind him: else how could Dr. Wellesley have seen it then and there?

When Mr. Collier wrote his letter to "The Athenæum," he forgot having said in his *Notes and Emendations* that he *took* the book home. His attention having been called to the discrepancy, he finds that he left the book in Rodd's shop until his return from the city, and then took it home! What is this but an *ex post facto* history? In theology it is called a *harmony*. But Mr. Collier's hypothesis fails to harmonize one discrepancy. If the book were left to be called for, it was not left to be sent home.

The fact and origin of the pencil-writing.

II. Mr. Collier nearly goes the length of denying the very existence of pencil-writing in the Perkins Folio:—

"What I mean to say is, that if such specks and spots of plumbago be made, there is no word in our language to which, with the smallest ingenuity, they may not be adapted."[6]

He says "made," because he will hardly admit that they have been *found*. Again:—[7]

"All I maintain is that the pencil-marks are so few, so small, and so indistinct, that it is only by the exercise of the most tortuous ingenuity that they can be transformed into words and letters;"

It is useless and childish to contend with facts. In reply to these denials of Mr. Collier's, I need only cite three writers on his own side.—Mr. H. Merivale[8] writes thus:—

"But then the mysterious pencil marks! There they are, most undoubtedly, and in very great numbers too."

The "Saturday" reviewer[9] assumes their existence, though he very grossly errs in saying that they are not legible to the naked eye. "Scrutator" says,

"The presence of the pencil no one who has examined the book lately, at least with the aid of a glass, has denied."[10]

[6] Reply, p. 21.
[7] Reply, p. 26.
[8] The Edinburgh Review, Ap. 1860.
[9] April 21, 1860.
[10] Strictures, p. 7.

It is impossible to doubt that Mr. Collier really believes in the existence of the pencillings; else why should he nearly go the length of charging the officers of the Museum with having first inserted them, and then seduced Mr. Frederick G. Netherclift to torture them into words in imitation of Mr. Collier's handwriting?[11]

At any rate he is sure he never wrote in pencil in the folio. He writes:—[12]

"I never made a single pencil mark on the pages of the book, excepting crosses, ticks, or lines, to direct my attention to particular emendations."

And he further says,[13]

"If there be upon the volume any pencillings by me, beyond crosses, ticks, and lines, they will speak for themselves; they have escaped my recollection."

This is certainly a very curious instance of defect of memory. The simple fact is that, irrespective of pencil emendations, notes, and suggestions, of which I shall speak hereafter, Mr. Collier has made very free with the margins of the book, in writing upon them in pencil such remarks as most editors, and all methodical ones confine to their common-place books. I have never kept any strict account of these remarks; but, to substantiate my assertion, I have jotted down a few of them, which will serve as a sample of the mass, whose name is "legion."

---

[11] Reply, p. 23. [12] The Times, July 7th, 1860.
[13] The Times, July 20th, 1859.

Measure for Measure p. 70. c. 2 fire note this.
Love's Labour's Lost. p. 133. c. 2 *fasting* | *l* See Hamlet. 277.
" p. 139. c. 1 *kill'd by* | *kingly* See above "pure scoffe".
All's well that ends well. p. 234. c. 2. to‸success | *try* So 1623
" p. 256. c. 2. and beare bating | yet see 273
Hamlet. p. 277. c. 2. fast in | lasting See LLL 133. This is in Smith's—1765.

That all these pencil observations and scores of others are in Mr. Collier's handwriting I cannot for an instant doubt, as they are obviously in the same hand in which the notes on the last board are written, and these Mr. Collier acknowledges to have been written by himself.[14]

It must be borne in mind that all such pencil observations are of a distinct class from those which are connected with the ink notes and emendations, or those which appear to be suggestions for emendations not actually adopted. All I wish to say of these in this place is that inasmuch as Mr. Collier's memory has been shewn to be fallacious in respect of the one class, surely it may be so in respect of the other.

It is of the latter class that Mr. Collier endeavours to discredit the existence at the time the book was in his possession. He writes:—[15]

"I exhibited the Perkins folio by candle light and by daylight,[16] and it was turned about in every possible direction by

[14] Letter to The Times of July 7th, 1860.

[15] Reply, p, 25.

[16] "It was not perhaps convenient," writes Mr. Collier, (Reply, p. 10) to Mr. Hamilton, "to notice this *daylight* exhi-

those who inspected it, and I never heard of an individual who saw pencil-marks, until after the volume had been deposited in the Manuscript Department of the British Museum."

We are further told that Mr. Collier never saw any pencil marks while the Perkins Folio was in his hands;[17] that the late Duke of Devonshire never saw any, nor a certain "intelligent Shakespearian friend" of Mr. Collier's, nor Mr. Netherclift, senior; nor yet were they observed at the meetings of the Shakspeare Society or the Society of Antiquaries in 1852-3.[18] But surely all these statements are consistent with Mr. Hamilton's theory. Do they not actually form a part of it? Of course, if Mr. Collier, as has been insinuated, did fabricate the notes, having previously written in the pencil directions, he would surely have rubbed out the latter (*i. e.* for a time have rendered them invisible), before exhibiting the folio for any one's inspection, or inviting scrutiny to the manuscript notes. The fact that the pencillings were invisible in 1852-3, is quite consistent with the fact that they became visible again after the lapse of five or six years: for what is called rubbing out, is merely removing some portions of the plumbago, and rubbing up the fibre of the paper over the other portions of the plumbago. The atmosphere which affects the fibre

bition at all." The fact is, that no report of such an exhibition has been found. All we have is Mr. Collier's invitation in "The Athenæum," March 27, 1852, and his mention of *three* exhibitions, before the Society of Antiquaries, in his affidavit.

[17] Reply, p. 24.

[18] Reply, pp. 25 and 26.

of the paper, will, it is well known, disclose some of the plumbago so covered over: and thus

"Time will unfold what plighted cunning hides;"

and pencil writing which has been rubbed out may after a few years become legible again.

Mr. Collier has another method of discrediting the pencillings:—

"Is it not strange," he asks, "if pencil-marks can be pointed out, as supposed instructions for such words, and fragments of words, as Mr. Hamilton has given us, that not the smallest trace of pencil is to be found in connexion with the entire lines, sentences, and parts of sentences, which abound in the Perkins folio?"[90]

He then goes on to shew that this circumstance favours the supposition of the officers of the British Museum having fraudulently inserted, in pencil, "specks and spots for the purpose of discrediting the ink emendations," inasmuch as it would have been easy to have applied them as hints for a lithographer in forming short words, but impossible to have done so by whole lines and sentences.[91] Mr.

[90] Reply, p. 28.

[91] Mr. Collier's insinuations and charges of fraud against his opponents are none the less discreditable to himself because, "*more suo*," he qualifies them by such phrases as "I only suppose it," or "I cannot for a moment suppose," &c., or "I do not at all mean purposely," or "I do not impute it," or "I am bound here to acquit," &c., or "unknowingly I believe," and various other "shows" of the like flimsy texture. They do not serve to dissemble the malice of his charges; but they amply protect the writer against actions at law, which, I conceive, was one reason why they were displayed.

Collier must have taken leave of his senses if he supposed that by retorting the charge of fraud, merely by way of speculation and without adducing any evidence, he could divert the public eye from the facts of this case, and their bearing on his own character. The public, as I have found from experience, are slow to believe anything that discredits the good name of a public man: but when once their suspicions are aroused, no legerdemain can distract their attention: they are then exacting judges of evidence, and unrelenting censors of him whom that evidence condemns. Nor will public connexions or private friendships avail him long:—

> "When Fortunes in her shift and change of mood,
> Spurns down her late belov'd, all his dependents
> Which labour'd after him to the mountain's top,
> Even on their knees and hands, let him slip down,
> Not one accompanying his declining foot."

Putting aside Mr. Collier's irrelevant retort, it is easy to answer his objection. It is not the length but the *fewness* of the "whole lines and sentences," that, in all probability, occasions the absence of the pencillings. A corrector using his pencil, as Mr. Collier and many others have done before, and will do again, would find it necessary to pencil in the short corrections as a guide to the ink scribe (himself or another) because they are so exceedingly numerous (from twenty to thirty thousand), while the "whole lines and sentences," amounting only to *eleven* in all, would be more conveniently inserted from pencil riders. This would be far preferable to writing so much in pencil on a single margin, the obliteration of which might be difficult or even impossible, and the detection of which would be the ruin of the speculation. Surely this is the true, as it is the obvious, explanation.

Inferences from Prof. Maskelyne's examination of the MS. notes.

III. But Mr. Collier would have us believe that, even admitting that the pencillings are *bonâ fide*, and of a modern character, it has never been satisfactorily shewn that they underlie the ink. Mr. Collier writes:—[22]

"He [Prof. Maskelyne] is mysteriously great upon the question, whether in some places the pencil overlies the ink, or the ink the pencil, apparently forgetting that if the pencil mark overlies the ink, the pencil mark must have been made last:[!] he admits, however, without reserve, that '*in several places the pencil stops abruptly at the ink.*' Is not this decisive? Why does it "stop abruptly at the ink," but because the ink had been previously written, and the person who made the pencil-mark went no further than the ink would allow him? Truly, all this discussion about "the lustre of the plumbago," and about the plumbago "just traceable under the ink," is too paltry and puerile for a man of Mr. Maskelyne's scientific attainments; and it almost makes one smile to read his grave and authoritative denunciation of the *u* in *Richard II.*, and of the "tick" which "intersects each limb of that letter." If as, he tells us, the pencil sometimes *stops at the ink*, there is an end of the question, as far as every word so circumstanced is concerned."

Not at all. Mr. Maskelyne instances the case of "a *u* in Richard II."

"A pencil tick," he says, "crossed the *u*, intersecting each limb of that letter. The pencil was barely visible through the

[22] Reply, p. 27.

first stroke, *and not at all visible under the second stroke of the u.* On damping off the ink in the first stroke, however, the pencil mark became much plainer than before, and even when as much of the ink-stain as possible was removed the pencil still runs through the ink line in unbroken even continuity. Had the pencil been superposed on the ink, it must have lain superficially upon its lustrous surface and have been removed in the washing."[53]

Here then is a case in which the pencil line *stopped abruptly at the ink,* as to one limb of the *u,* and yet must have been written before that limb was written, because that pencil line was found to underlie the other limb of the *u.*

The question of identity of the writer of the ink-notes in the Perkins Folio and the writer of the ink-notes in the Bridgewater Folio.

IV. Mr. Hamilton states that the manuscript corrections in the Bridgewater Folio,

"are not only modern, but, decidedly, *by the same hand* as those in his [Mr. Collier's] more famous copy of the second edition."[54]

To use "Scrutator's" elegant phrase, Lord Ellesmere "has knocked over one of the nine-pins," in the following words, for permission to make use of which Mr. Collier thanks his Lordship:—

"There is *no pretence, whatever,* for saying that the emendations in the Perkins Shakespeare are in the same handwriting as those in my first folio: on the contrary, except as they are (or profess to be) of the same period, *they are quite different.*"[55]

But I have authority for stating that this is a garbled extract from the opinion which Lord Ellesmere wrote for Mr. Collier, and which (in its perfect state) he permitted Mr. Collier to make public.

---

[53] Letter in The Times of July 16, 1859.

[54] Inquiry, p. 72.

[55] Reply, p. 45.

But even if it were Lord Ellesmere's ungarbled opinion of the writing, what is it worth? Lord Ellesmere is entitled to his own opinion on the subject, and with that I have no wish, as I have no right, to interfere. The question, however, for the public to consider is this—Is Lord Ellesmere a better judge of handwriting than the skilled palæographists of the British Museum? Is it likely he can be? But to settle once for all the point of likeness or unlikeness between the manuscript of the Perkins Folio and that of the Bridgewater Folio, I have given facsimiles of both in illustration of what appear to me some striking features of resemblance.[36]

The date of the watermark in the paper of the binding.

V. We have seen that Mr. Hamilton found on the paper pasted within the cover of the Perkins Folio the watermark of "a crown surmounting the letters "G. R." and the Dutch lion within a paling, with the legend *pro patriâ*." In addition to what he says of this device in his first letter in "The Times," he writes, in his *Inquiry*:—[37]

"I have recently investigated this point minutely, and am of opinion that the binding is even later than I had at first imagined. Paper of the same texture, and with the same watermark, was in common use from 1760 to 1780. See Haldimand Correspondence, in the British Museum. I have seen a watermark almost identical in Dutch foolscap of the present day."

The point is not of much importance. But Mr. Col-

[36] See sheet of facsimiles, no. II.

[37] Page 133.

lier has hung upon it a charge of dishonesty against the officers of the Manuscript Department. He says,—[28]

"The fly-leaf, with its "G. R. and Dutch Lion," so exultingly dwelt upon by Mr. Hamilton, may easily have been inserted even later; but later or earlier, *it has been abstracted from the book;* and when it came from the Manuscript Department, no fly-leaf was found in it. I do not deny the "G. R." nor the "Dutch Lion;" but, for aught that appears, all this was a pure invention by Mr. Hamilton. He, or somebody else, has deprived us of the means of testing his assertion: as his "calf" has been metamorphosed into a "sheep,"[29] so his "G. R." may by this time have been turned into C. R., and his "Dutch Lion" into an English one. Hence possibly, the present absence of the fly-leaf."

Here is a charge of theft,—theft of the most odious kind; purloining a fly-leaf, because it bore evidence against an opinion to which the purloiner had committed himself. With such apparent recklessness does Mr. Collier prefer the most serious charges against the character of a rising writer, whose only offence is that he has been inconveniently zealous in investigating the origin of various manuscripts which, according to his opinion, have for years vitiated the biography and corrupted the language of Shakspere. Now on what do Mr. Collier's charges rest? On the absence from the

[28] Reply, p. 28.

[29] This remark is in allusion to Mr. Hamilton's second letter, where he gives it as his revised opinion that the binding was not in calf but sheep.

Perkins Folio of a fly-leaf to which Mr. Hamilton expressly referred in his first letter in "The Times." What are the facts? In that letter Mr. Hamilton did *not* refer to any fly-leaf. His words are:—

"The volume is bound in rough calf (probably about the middle of George II.'s reign), the water-mark of the *leaves pasted inside the cover* being a crown" &c.

In his second letter he corrects the expression "rough calf," and describes the binding as in "rough sheep." "The fly-leaf with its 'G. R. and Dutch lion,'" is an *ex post facto* invention of Mr. Collier's. It is ingenious, as it enables him to retort a charge of purloining and dishonesty against Mr. Hamilton, and no doubt has had its effect with general readers, for whom it was expressly intended. It is sufficient to say that Mr. Hamilton never mentioned a fly-leaf at all: that the Perkins Folio had no fly-leaf when it left the library at Devonshire House: but that "the leaves pasted inside the cover," are still there to witness to the "G. R. and the Dutch lion."

The bearing of the Hamlet collation in Mr. Hamilton's *Inquiry* on the question of forgery.

VI. No reader of Mr. Hamilton's book, who has the slightest interest in the Perkins Folio, can feel otherwise than grateful to him and Mr. Staunton for the table of the "Hamlet" collations. We have divers versions of the contents of the Perkins Folio from the pen of Mr. Collier, from not one of which is it possible to gather a correct notion of the book. The collations of that single play are a perfect picture of the contents of the original, and a just sample of the other plays in that volume. Read that table through, and you will have a thoroughly correct notion of the whole book. Irrespective of the question of genuineness of the manuscript notes, the table is of the greatest value. But it has a bearing on that question also, which Mr. Collier fails to perceive. On the "twenty-two pages with the Old Corrrector's emendations of 'Hamlet,'" [and he should have added *King Henry VI.* Part II.] he remarks,[30]

"all that were really important [have] been pointed out eight years ago. What bearing this useless repetition can have upon the question of authenticity, it would puzzle abler men than Mr. Hamilton to explain. His real object was only to prove my omissions;"

It is, indeed, true that these collations have not, nor were they intended to have, any *direct* bearing on the authenticity or genuineness of the Perkins manuscript notes. Their indirect bearing is soon shewn. Mr. Collier, as we have seen, calls the List of Emendations appended to the *Seven Lectures*, 1856, "A list of *every manuscript note and emendation*," &c.; and in the Preface to the same work, he speaks of this list as complete, and challenges his readers to find so much as a single omission. The fact is, as I have already shewn, that his Complete List does not contain half the notes and emendations which are legible in the Perkins Folio. Mr. Hamilton's object, clearly, was not merely to prove Mr. Collier's omissions, but to substantiate one of two things: either that the Perkins Folio had received

[30] The Athenæum, Feb. 18, 1860. See also Reply, p. 23.

large additions since 1856, or that Mr. Collier had deliberately and systematically stated what he must have known to be untrue; and I can only assume that Mr. Collier would accept the latter alternative; for he assures us that the omissions were *intentional:* and from this it would appear that he does not regard the want of veracity as a very serious defect.[31]

The indirect bearing of this alternative on the questions of authenticity and genuineness is this: If the first alternative be true, more than half the emendations are not older than 1856; and the rest, being in the same hand, are thus proved to be modern fabrications: If the second alternative be true, no statement of Mr. Collier's can be believed.

---

[31] Mr. Collier's notions of right and wrong seem very different from those of other honest men. Thus, at p. 58 of his *Reply*, he says, "Whatever I may be, in the opinion of my adversaries, I feel sure that he [Malone] was a man of honour and principle;" having first told us (p. 47), that his (Malone's) books, "the title pages of which he decorated with the old autographs [which he had cut from the Dulwich manuscripts], had belonged to Dulwich College; for he contrived to persuade the Master, Warden and Fellows, of that day, that Old Plays and Old Poetry did not half so well become their shelves, as the musty divinity, dull chronicles, and other volumes of the same sort which he substituted. Hence the bulk of his collection; and he must have chuckled amazingly at his success in persuading unsuspecting people to make an exchange of works, which would sell for hundreds of pounds, for others not worth so many shillings." That is, according to Mr. Collier, a man may be a swindler, and at the same time be "a man of honour and principle"!

One of the two must be true. Either is fatal to Mr. Collier's pretensions for his folio.

Apart from the moral question, could Mr. Collier have written the MS. notes?

VII. Mr. Collier, of course, repudiates the charge of fabricating the manuscript notes, &c. He says,[32]

"I have had too much to do with my own plain round English hand (from which I never, even for a playful purpose, attempted to vary) to be able to devote my time to the manufacture of public or private documents, and, as in the case of the Perkins Folio, to fill a volume of about a thousand pages with innumerable notes, to say nothing of changes of punctuation in tens of thousands of places."

The statement in the parenthesis is untrue, if we may believe what Mr. Collier himself tells us in the Preface to the *Seven Lectures*, 1856.[33] He there says,

"My father taught me at an early age the use of abbreviated characters, and I hardly know any species of instruction that in after-life has stood me in greater stead."

To write short-hand is surely to vary from his "own plain round English hand."

"Neither," he writes,[34] "have I ever enjoyed facilities absolutely necessary to such elaborate trickery. In five out of the eight houses I have occupied, since I married forty-five years ago, I never had a study to myself: * * and when I have had a study, I defy the world to show an instance in which I ever turned the key of the door to prevent intrusion:"

Where was the occasion? For he says in the same letter:—

"For many years I seldom went to bed until other people were rising."

[32] The Athenæum, Feb. 18, 1860. [33] p. v.
[34] The Athenæum, Feb. 18, 1860.

And for other facilities, he informs us that he was an adept in removing ink-stains, an art so profusely displayed by the "old corrector," though time has often undone him in that respect. He says,

"I myself have taken envelopes sent from different hemispheres east and west, and have obliterated the addresses by the simplest application."[35]

However innocent Mr. Collier may be of the charge of fabrication, surely these replies cannot be said to give his case a better complexion.

What is the value of Mr. Dyce's testimony, and that of other critics, to the excellence of the MS. emendations?

VIII. In his letter published in "The Times" of July 7, 1859, Mr. Collier writes:—

"I shall say nothing of the indisputable character of many of the emendations. The Rev. Mr. Dyce has declared, in his own handwriting, that "some of them are so admirable that they can hardly be conjectural," and, in the course of his recent impression of the works of Shakespeare, he has pronounced such as he unavoidably adopted, irresistible, indubitable, infallible, &c."

Now, to this I must say that whatever weight may be accorded to the opinion of so ripe a scholar as Mr. Dyce, I do not see how it becomes overwhelming, or irrevocable, because he has written it down! Mr. Dyce's opinion, however, on more than one of the Perkins emendations, has been revoked.[36] Surely a critic may change his opinion, despite the *litera scripta*. Special and plausible emendations generally provoke love at first sight, and ensure a favourable reception, too often a hasty adoption. But these are just the very emendations

[35] Reply, p. 55.
[36] Dyce's Few Notes, p. 81.

which are generally treated as paramours—embraced as sources of gratification, and cast off as sources of corruption. Mr. Halliwell and the late Mr. Singer have been as susceptible to the charms of the Lights of the Perkins Harêm as Mr. Dyce himself, and with a like speedy repentance.[37] But Mr. Dyce has in his edition of Shakspere, finally adopted several of the Perkins novelties. No doubt of it. But he has adopted, besides some novelties which *are* indisputable and undisputed,[38] others which many critics believe to be utterly wrong; and some which are the cast-offs of Messrs. Halliwell and Singer. So that Mr. Dyce's judgment, even as to the few which he has finally adopted, is far from conclusive evidence that those few are worthy to remain in the text.

Could Mr. Collier have appropriated them by burning the folio in the first instance?

But Mr. Collier continues:—

"All this I might have appropriated to myself; and having burnt the corrected folio, 1632, I might have established for myself a brighter Shakespearian reputation than all the commentators put together."

The answer to this is obvious. Mr. Collier could not, by having in the first instance destroyed the Perkins Folio, have appropriated to himself the vast bulk of the manuscript emendations therein, simply *because the vast bulk of them are not new.* As to

[37] Notes and Queries, 1st Series, vol. v. pp. 436, 485, 556, and the Editions of Halliwell and Singer.

[38] Such as "continue *them*," *vice* "continue *then*," in *Love's Labour's Lost*, act v. sc. 2.

those which are new, how many of them does Mr. Collier believe that, *in that case,* the editors would have adopted *of absolute necessity* into the text? I say 'of absolute necessity,' "because"—I quote from Mr. Arnold's first article in "Fraser's Magazine"—[39]

"corrupt as the text of Shakespeare is acknowledged to be in many places, few editors would venture to incorporate conjectural emendations, except in passages where no sense could be made of the original; or where the alteration manifestly recommends itself by its harmony with the context, and the small amount of violence done by it to the printed text. Very few of Mr. Collier's emendations are of this character; but even as to those of less value, when they are brought forward with the stamp of authority, we accept them, perhaps too blindly, though often with reluctance, because we feel the authority is too strong to contend against."

But destroy the source of the presumed authority, *i. e.* annihilate the authority, and all these emendations "of less value," are at once rejected: and with the few stragglers that would then remain, no editor or critic, not even one of Mr. Collier's "stuffed sufficiency," could create the reputation of a Jackson or a Beckett.

Mr. Collier puts the case somewhat differently in his Reply:—[40]

"To have suggested them would have made the fortune of any man; and, if I were the real author of them, what could have induced me *to foist them into an old folio and to give anybody else the credit of them?*"

The answer is simply this; that of the emendations that are new, *very few indeed* are of the indis-

[39] January, 1860. [40] Page 63.

putable character. For the mass of those that were new, Mr. Collier, if he had invented them, could not have obtained any consideration, unless he had invested them with the prestige of authority. *By foisting them into an old folio* he might, certainly, have given to emendations which, regarded as conjectures, are bad enough, sufficient weight *with those who accepted the authority*, to supplant really sound conjectural emendations, and, in most cases, to supersede a better reading which was already in possession of the old printed text. And besides this, he might, by a like insertion, have *traded on the gross capital of all the commentators that ever lived*, by putting a prodigious number of their emendations on the margin of his folio (as the "old corrector" has done); while the new emendations would scarcely have afforded him a basis for a reputation that could vie with even the third-rate editors, such as Hanmer, or the third-rate commentators, such as Grey. This is capable of direct proof.

Mr. Collier is not just or accurate in speaking of his rival editors. He says,—[41]

"Mr. Singer inserted many with very grudging acknowledgment, and adopted others, as if they were his own improvements: Mr. Knight behaved in a more straightforward way, but availed himself of them. The Rev. Mr. Dyce has been driven to the hard necessity of doing nearly the same, with this salvo, that in order to discredit the Perkins folio, he has asserted, unknowingly I believe, [!] that some of the best changes of the text were contained in Mr. Singer's corrected

[41] Reply, p. 63.

folio, when Mr. Singer never had a corrected folio that presented them, or anything like them." * * * [speaking of "diseases" for *degrees*, "mirror'd" for *married*, and two other emendations][42] "The two first of these changes of text the Rev. A. Dyce vindicates on the ground that *they are supported by corrections in Mr. Singer's folio*, as well as in the Perkins folio, when the fact is that Mr. Singer's folio has neither of them."

Now the fact seems to be this: when Mr. Singer found an emendation in his own corrected folio, he gave the emendation on that authority; and he no where, as far as I know, ever published any of the Perkins emendations as his own. Nor did Mr. Dyce put forth his statements respecting these emendations without authority: both *diseases* for "degrees," and *mirror'd* for "married," are stated by Mr. Singer to be in his corrected folio, Mr. Collier's rash contradiction notwithstanding.[43]

As to the value of these two emendations and several others which Mr. Collier has promoted to the rank of stalking-horses, I shall have much to say in support of my opinion that they are all inadmissible, and nearly all *primâ facie* bad. Mr. Collier not unnaturally regards these and many others with admiration. "If I forged them," he urges,

---

[42] Reply, p 65.

[43] See Singer's Shakespeare Vindicated, pp. 112 and 198: at the same time, I must be allowed to express my surprise that the public have not heard anything of this corrected folio since Mr. Singer's death, though his large and valuable library has been brought to the hammer.

" the least they [his opponents] can do is to give me credit for them."[a] But unfortunately this wide concession can hardly be granted, inasmuch as the great bulk of them belong to the various editors and commentators of Shakspere, both old and new. Those that Mr. Collier has a title to he will certainly have the credit of. They will be found at pp. 104 and 195 of this work. As to these, Mr. Perkins might have used towards Mr. Collier the words of the late Earl of Ellesmere, when his Lordship forced the Bridgewater manuscripts upon him: " They are as much yours as mine; consider and treat them as your own."

---

[a] Reply, p. 32.

CHAPTER VII.

THE PERKINS FOLIO.—PHILOLOGICAL TESTS.

Test-words and test-phrases.

So soon as the manuscript corrections of Mr. Collier's folio, 1632, were promulgated, verbal critics cast about for such intrinsic indications of genuineness or spuriousness as those corrections might present. The obvious method of testing the genuineness of the corrections was to select a word or phrase which had the appearance of being modern in sense, or idiom, and by an induction of instances in which the word is employed by writers of the last two centuries to prove, or at least to attempt to prove, the negative, that such word or phrase was not in use at all, or in a particular sense, till a certain period; and of course if that period were subsequent to the ostensible date of the manuscript notes, the "old corrector" would be degraded into a modern simulator.

The test-word *its* applied to the Ireland forgeries.

Nothing is so slippery as the proof of a negative. In the case of the fabrications of Chatterton, as in those of the Irelands, the spelling alone ought to have been sufficient evidence of fraud; but in the absence of a knowledge of obsolete orthography, the frequent recurrence of *yts* or *its* ought still to have been conclusive evidence of the spuriousness of the manuscripts. In this case the negative was susceptible of proof, and has since been proved. It is this: the genitive *its* does not occur in English literature till 1622. The first folio of Shakspere is the earliest *dated* printed book in which the word is found. Thus:—

> "How sometimes Nature will betray *it's* folly?
> *It's* tendernesse? and make it selfe a Pastime
> To harder bosomes?"—*Winter's Tale*, act i. sc. 2.

Dean Trench greatly understates the fact when he says he believes it occurs but three times in all Shakspere.[1] Pemble, who died in the year 1623, employs the word in his works, 1635, p. 171, "If faith alone by *its* own virtue and force," &c. if we may trust the fidelity of the editor. In all the printed books that have been searched having a date prior to 1622, and they are legion, *his, her, hit* or *it*, are employed in the sense of the genitive *its*.[2] Now in *Vortigern and Rowena*, *its* occurs *four* times, in act i. alone; viz. "*its* master-piece," "*its* nourisher," "*its* golden rays," and "*its* instinct;" and neither *his, her, hit*, or *it*, in the sense of the genitive *its*, ever occurs at all. *Its* then is a test-word that conclusively proves that the Ireland manuscript was of a later date than 1623, a conclusion sufficient to prove it a forgery of the last century. But though

---

[1] English Past and Present, 1855, p. 91.

[2] I am aware that the dateless quarto of Hamlet, in the line,

"It lifted up *it* head,"—(Act i. sc. 2.)

has *its* for the second "it." But before that case can be cited against my position it must be proved that the quarto in question was printed before 1622, which I do not believe. It is generally assigned to the date 1607, on the strength of an entry in the books of the Stationers' Company, which seems to me to refer to the missing quarto of 1609.

Other tests of the Ireland Forgeries.

this point was missed in the case of the Ireland forgeries, yet others quite as conclusive were seized upon. Malone had a test-word or test-phrase for nearly every document he examined. Thus, in a "Deed of Gift to William Henry Ireland" is a narrative of a water adventure in which the drunken watermen "upsette" the barge. Of this word Malone says, "it has crept into our language, I think, within these few years, but certainly within this century;"[3] *Rolls and tea, brynge forward,* and many others, were similarly employed by him as instruments for the detection of forgery.

A test-phrase for the Uranius forgery.

In like manner might the scholars of Berlin have found conclusive evidence of the spuriousness of the palimpsest of Uranius, to which I have already adverted; for the manuscript contained the phrase *κατ' ἐμὴν ἰδέαν,* which, in the intended sense of "according to my idea,"[4] does not occur in any Greek writer of the age of Uranius, or of any earlier time. But, strange as it may seem, the phrase did not arouse the suspicions of those scholars.[5]

Now it was proposed to do by the manuscript notes in the Perkins Folio just what in these cases had or should have been attempted.

---

[3] Inquiry, 1796, p. 219.

[4] That is, ὡς ἔμοιγε δοκεῖ. Oddly enough the word *idea* was a test-word selected by Malone for proving the modern origin of the verses to Queen Elizabeth (one of the Ireland forgeries) where the line occurs—

"No words the bright *idea* can pourtraye."

Inquiry, 1796, p. 100, *note*.

[5] The Athenæum, Feb. 16, 1856.

Mr. Singer's test-word.

The late Mr. Singer once thought he had found a satisfactory test-word in *wheedling*, into which the manuscript corrector unwarrantably alters "wheeling," in *Othello*, act i. sc. 1:—

> "Tying her duty, wit and fortunes
> To an extravagant and *wheeling* stranger
> Of here and everywhere:"[6]

but, as Mr. Collier cautiously observes of this and some other words, "it is not impossible, * * * that they were in earlier use than our lexicographers represent."[7] In fact Samuel Butler employs it—[8]

> "His business was to pump and *wheedle*,"
> P. ii. c. iii. l. 385.

and,

> "Which ralliers in their wit or drink
> Do rather *wheedle* with than think."
> P. iii. c. i. l. 759-60.

A book, called *The Art of Wheedling or Insinuation*, was published in 1679; and I believe it will be found that the verb *to wheedle* occurs in works published long anterior to these.

Mr. Staunton's test-word.

Another attempt to apply a test-word to the manuscript corrections was made by Mr. Staunton. He long ago suggested to me that the emendation of *thirst*, *vice* "first," in *Coriolanus*, act ii. sc. 1,[9] was indicative of a recent origin of the manuscript corrections. This criticism rests on these assump-

---

[6] Notes and Emendations, 1st ed. p. 449; 2nd ed. p. 467.—The Text of Shakspere Vindicated, 1853, p. 279.

[7] Introduction to 1st ed. of Notes and Emendations, *note*.

[8] Hudibras, 1663.

[9] Notes and Emendations, 1st ed. p. 351; 2nd ed. p. 355.

tions :—1st, that "complaint" in the sense of *malady*, (*i. e.* the medical sense) was not in use till after the middle of the eighteenth century; and 2ndly, that the phrase "said to be something imperfect in favouring the *thirst* COMPLAINT," would be nonsense, unless "complaint" were there employed in the medical sense. Now I think the latter position indisputable; but I have not examined a sufficiently large number of instances to arrive at any decided opinion on the former point. However it is not improbable that this test-word may ultimately be found to be of great value in the determination of the question of the genuineness of the manuscript notes of the disputed folio.

Mr. Halliwell remarks[10] that the word *drench*, which the "old corrector" substitutes for "dregs" in a passage in *The Tempest*, act ii. sc. 2, Mr. Halliwell's test-word.

"till the *dregs* of the storm be past."

"appears to be *more modern* than Shakespeare's time." Unless it can be shewn that it is more modern than the second folio, it will be of no use as a test-word.

Mr. Dyce[11] has a similar argument on the "old corrector's" alteration of the line, Mr. Dyce's test-word.

"This *unheard* sauciness and boyish troops,"
King John, act v. sc. 2.

---

[10] Observations on some of the Manuscript Emendations, &c. 1853, p. 8.

[11] Strictures on Mr. Collier's New Edition of Shakspere, pp. 97-98.

The "old corrector"[11] substitutes *of* for "and," apparently under the impression that "unheard" meant *unheard-of!* The line then would mean—*the King does not fear harm from this unheard-of sauciness of troops composed of mere boys.* This "old corrector," then, was not old enough to know that in Shakspere's day, and even later, "unheard" was merely a mode of spelling *unhair'd.* "Unhair'd sauciness," then, does not require the conjunction, which "*unheard-of* sauciness" does.

Various other tests.

Again: those who accept either Mr. Staunton's reading,[12] or Johnson's first interpretation of the soldier's speech in *Timon of Athens,* act v. sc. 4, and especially of the two lines:—

> "Timon is dead, who hath outstretched his span,
> Some beast read this; there does not live a man."—

will doubtless found an argument against the antiquity of the Perkins Folio, upon the substitution of Warburton's *rear'd,* for "read."[14] For myself I entertain no doubts that, sooner or later, this argument will be conclusive against the antiquity of the manuscript notes. But until the leading critics are unanimous in accepting the old text, the substitution of

---

[11] Notes and Emendations, 1st and 2nd ed. p. 210.

[12] Edition of Shakspere, vol. ii. p. 503.

[14] Notes and Emendations, 1st ed. p. 304; 2nd ed. p. 405. Mr. Dyce, I trust, will be the last editor to adopt that most execrable suggestion. From Mr. Dyce's note, I can hardly think the alteration satisfactory even to himself.

course proves nothing to the public against the antiquity of this alteration.

Again: the "old corrector's" substitution of *hills* for "dies," in the following passage from *As you like it*, act iii. sc. 5,—

"Will you sterner be
Than he that *dies and lives* by bloody drops?"[14]

looks very much as if he, like Mr. Collier of 1844, did not know that "dies and lives" was a phrase of common use in the sixteenth and seventeenth centuries, in the sense of, "*subsists from the cradle to the grave*;"[15] but Mr. Collier of 1858 still tenaciously clings to his eminently "droll" emendation of *dines*, *vice* "dies."

Again: in a well known passage in 2 *Hen. IV.* act iv. sc. 1, the "old corrector" has substituted *report of war* for "point of war," apparently in profound ignorance that a point of war meant, and, indeed, still means, a strain of martial music played on the trumpet or the drum.[17]

Even these examples, and I could give many others (especially from Mr. Dyce's *Strictures*, *passim*), form an important array of tests which the "old corrector" has not passed, and *by some of which he is condemned*. And yet, in the face of these, which (with one exception) I brought together in the most

[14] Notes and Emendations, 1st and 2nd ed. p. 134.
[15] Notes and Queries, 1st Series, vol. vii. p. 542.
[17] Staunton's Shakespeare, vol. i. p. 603.

prominent form in my *Shakspeare Fabrications*,[18] the writer in "The Edinburgh Review" remarks that it "is no common testimony to his [the supposed forger's] strange ingenuity," that he "has escaped the ordeal of test-words:" *i. e.* supposing that the one which I have yet to mention should turn out to be as great a failure as that reviewer and the bell-wether whom he follows have conceived it to be.

Admirative comments in the Edinburgh and Saturday Reviews.

A writer, who blunders with a pitiable fatality, in "The Saturday Review,"[19] expresses the same view, in still stronger terms:—

> "Considering the *reckless* profusion with which the emendations of all descriptions, from the insertion of new lines down to mere corrections of the punctuation and stage directions, are lavished, this failure to detect intrinsic proof of fraud, in the shape of literary errors and anachronisms, after the most rigorous scrutiny, is evidence of no slight kind in favour of the genuineness of the volume."

This is the mere effusion of ignorance. A cursory perusal of chap. I. of my *Shakspeare Fabrications*, would have saved this writer from committing himself to such a statement.

Mr. Brae's test-word.

One of the earliest attempts to prove the modern origin of the manuscript notes of the Perkins Folio by means of a test-word was made by Mr. A. E. Brae of Leeds. His test-word was communicated to the editor of "Notes and Queries" and myself in 1853, and I made it public in my *Shakspeare Fabrications*.

Assailed by the Reviews.

Since then it has been ignorantly and wantonly

[18] Chap. i. [19] April 21, 1860.

assailed by every review that has taken cognizance of the Collier controversy, with the single exception of "The Literary Gazette." It is, perhaps, to the credit of certain of these journalists that they did not allow their interests to interfere with their conscientiousness in shewing no quarter to this test-word. Indeed I do not know whether my coadjutors were not more severe upon the unfortunate monosyllable than my opponents. A little more caution however was to have been expected. The test has survived their onslaughts, and is still more vigorous than ever.

In *Coriolanus*, act iv. sc. 7, the folio gives us the following passage:— The text in which it occurs.

"So our virtue
Lie in the interpretation of the time,
And power, unto itself most commendable,
Hath not a tomb so evident as a chair
T' extol what it hath done."

In the corrected folio, 1632,[30] the passage stands thus:— The Perkins gloss.

"So our *virtues*
Live in th' interpretation of the time,
And power, *in* itself most commendable,
Hath not a tomb so evident as a *cheer*
T' extol what it hath done."

Mr. R. Grant White was so enamoured of the emendation of *cheer*, for "chair," that he applied himself to out-perkins Perkins, and proposed to read the line in which that change was made— Mr. R. G. White's gloss.

"Hath not a tomb so *eloquent* as a *cheer*."

[30] Notes and Emendations, 1st ed. p. 361; 2nd ed. p. 366.

Mr. R. Garnett's gloss.

But Mr. Richard Garnett[21] proposes to read *tongue* for "tomb," wondering with the reviewer of "The Athenæum" for August 20th, 1859, how a tomb can extol. Surely it is the *chair* which is given to extol what the man of power and virtue has done! I should not wonder if some future Perkins should adopt all three suggestions, and instead of

"Hath not a tomb so evident as a chair,"

read,

"Hath not a *tongue* so *eloquent* as a *cheer!*"

Meaning of the Perkins gloss.

I apprehend no intelligent person who reads the passage, as corrected by Perkins, will doubt for an instant that *a cheer* is there intended to be understood in the sense of *a shout of applause*. Among the many reviewers who have assailed my criticism, I have met with only one who did not tacitly assume this point. One, indeed,[22] ventured to say that *a cheer* might mean *countenance or bearing*, in the passage in question. But the statement is characterized by nothing but headlong blindness, and does not merit serious refutation.

It struck Mr. Brae, upon reading the passage,

"Hath not a tomb so evident as a *cheer*
To extol . . . . . ".

that the word *cheer* was necessarily employed in a modern sense, and immediately undertook a close examination of the chronology of the words *cheer*

[21] The Athenæum, Oct. 15th, 1859.
[22] The Atlas, Sept. 10th, 1859.

and *cheers*, the result of which with some of the details of the investigation he communicated to me. That result was that *a cheer*, in the sense of *a shout of applause*, was not in use till the present century, and that consequently it is a test-word which proves the manuscript notes of the Perkins Folio to be of recent origin. Nothing that has since been written upon the subject has in the slightest degree invalidated the soundness of this criticism.

Distinction between *three cheers* and *a cheer*.

In the first place I must call attention to the distinction between the use of *three cheers*, and *a cheer*, in the sense of an audible expression of applause. Supposing that it could be shewn that the phrase "three" cheers was employed to express shouts of applause before A.D. 1750, *and which I challenge the world of letters to prove*, it might still happen that *a cheer* was not so employed until A.D. 1800, or thereabouts, *which I challenge the world of letters to disprove*. To confound *three-cheers* with *a cheer*, would be as ignorant a proceeding as to confound the phrases "manning the yards,"[n] and "manning a yard." Before 1750, I find that *three cheers* is a conventional phrase employed by sailors to express a naval salute. On the contrary, *a cheer* did not mean anything of the kind; nor do I believe that any such a term was used by sailors till it became a land expression for a shout of applause; and that it did not do till the present century.

[n] A nautical salute.

The three archaic meanings of *cheer.*

The archaic meanings of *cheer* (subs.) are—

1. Countenance, bearing.

e. g. "Which publique death (receiv'd with such *a cheare*,
As not a sigh, a looke, a shrink bewrayes
The least felt touch of a degenerous[34] feare)
Gave life to Envie, to his courage prayse,"
Samuel Daniel's *Civill Warres*, st. 57.
(Works, 1602, fol. 8).

2. Comfort, cheerfulness.

e. g. "The pretty Lark, climbing the Welkin cleer,
Chaunts with *a cheer*,[35] Here peer—I neer my deer."

"Or, if they sing, 'tis with so dull *a cheer*
That leaves look pale, dreading the winter's near."
Shakspeare's *Sonnets*, XCVII.

"And when shee saw him there, shee sowned three times, * * * so when she might speake, shee * * * said, 'yee mervaile, fair ladies, why I make this *cheere*.'"
The Historie of King Arthur, iii. p. 337 (1858).

"Who forth proceeding with sad, sober *cheare*,"
Faerie Queen, I. Canto xii. v. 21.

3. Sustenance, entertainment.

e. g. "You do not give the *cheer*;"
Macbeth, act iii. sc. 4.

The archaic meaning of *three cheers.*

There is but one archaic meaning of *three cheers*, viz. *a naval salute.*

---

[34] *Gigenerous* in the original.

[35] With *a cheer*; i.e. *with a gladsome energy*, or as we now say, *with a will.*

In my former work[96] I erred not on the side of expansion but on that of restriction. I asserted for *a cheer* what was true only of *three cheers*, viz. that the phrase was first used by sailors in the time of Queen Ann; not indeed in the sense of an acclamation of applause, but one of encouragement, or salutation—in other words *a salute*. This part of my book was quoted by its reviewer in "The Athenæum" of August 20th, 1859; yet in the face of my own too conceding qualification a writer in "The Athenæum" of Feb. 18th, 1860, quotes from a work called "*The Diary of Henry Teonge*, Chaplain on board His Majesty's Ships Assistance, Bristol, and Royal Oak, anno 1675 to 1679," an example in 1675 of *three cheers*, as a naval salute; and strangely exhibits the extract quoted as a refutation of my criticism. Clearly, if that extract refuted my position, my own confession[97] did so far more conclusively. Even if

The Athenæum commits a blunder.

Example from *Teonge's Diary*.

Reply.

[96] In my *Shakspeare Fabrications* (p. 11), I confessed that *a cheer* did mean something audible "before it acquired the admirative sense." In this I committed an error. I should have said "*three cheers* meant something audible before even *a cheer* acquired the admirative sense." I continued, "There is no doubt the first use of *a cheer* in that sense was a nautical use." This was a part of the same error. I should have said, "There is no doubt the first use of *three cheers* was a nautical use." I added, "In the time of Queen Ann sailors began to use the term with a restricted meaning, viz. an acclamation of mutual encouragement; but NOT *of admirative applause*." I should have said, "an acclamation of mutual encouragement or salutation, but not of admirative applause."

[97] The Shakspeare Fabrications, p. 11.

"the time of Queen Ann," were an expression to be interpreted literally, the period I indicated began some fourteen years anterior to Teonge's first voyage. If, on the other hand, the phrase be taken to mean "the reign of Queen Ann," then, the answer is, that if the phrase 3-*cheares* could upset the test (*a cheer*) *it would do it as effectually if current in Queen Ann's time, as twenty years sooner.* Thus, in either case, to all intents and purposes, my position is as effectually refuted *by my own admission*, as by the example adduced by "The Athenæum," *if refuted at all.* In point of fact then, this now famous citation of the nautical use of *three cheers*, in the *Diary* of that quaint, and punch-drinking chaplain, was a mare's-nest, the discovery of which has been proclaimed with flourish of trumpets by the editor of "Notes and Queries," and by the writers in "The Edinburgh Review" and "The Saturday Review." *Teonge's Diary*, in the first place, does not contain more than one example of the use of *cheer*, (subs.) and there it is used in the sense of *countenance or bearing.*[28] Secondly, it contains, not merely eight, (as "The Athenæum" has it), but *twelve* examples of the use of *three cheers.* And to prevent the possibility of mistake I will cite them all.

All the remaining instances of

"21 June, 1675.

"By 6 in the morning all our ladys are sent on shoare in our pinnace; whose weeping eys bedewed the very sids of the ship,

[28] The only phrase in which *cheer* occurs there is the following, "Lament, lament with dolefull *cheare*," *Teonge's Diary*, p. 64. In "The Saturday Review," (Ap. 21, 1860), it is positively stated *a cheer* in the sense of a cry of applause, "is found several times in a Diary written between 1675 and 1679."!

as they went over into the boate, and seemed to have chosen (might they have had their will) rather to have stuck to the syde of the ship like the barnacles, or shell-fish, then to have parted from us. But they were no sooner out of sight but they were more merry; and I could tell with whom too, were I so minded. *three cheers in Teonge's Diary.*

As soone as the boate was put off from the ship, wee honour their departure with 3 *cheares*, 7 gunns, and our trumpetts sounding."[29]

This is the example cited by "The Athenæum;"[30] with the exception that the writer omitted the preamble, whereby he made it appear — Mr. Collier would say "unintentionally of course" — that the "3-cheares" were given to extol the deeds of some departing crew: instead of which, that salute was given to *animate* a boat-load of weeping wives and sweethearts. Nor need the word "honour," as used here, excite any doubt of the soundness of my criticism: for—

1st. It is *playfully* used of a grand naval salute —*playfully* given by the captain and his crew to a set of wailing women—to divert the grief of the men, and to amuse and comfort "our mornefull ladys."

2nd. *Honour* does not necessarily bear a *plausive* sense:—is it not an every day conventionality meaning nothing? Does not a lord honour his tenant by shaking hands with him? Does not a candidate thus honour a voter? Does not a writer feel honoured by

---

[29] Teonge's Diary, p. 14.

[30] Feb. 18, 1860.

addressing his correspondent? And is there the slightest approach in any of these cases to applause for deeds performed?

The following are the remaining eleven instances:

6th August, 1675.

The Sattee cuming up to us about 11 of the clock, the Syppio and the Thomas and William (boath bound for Scanderoond) com under our starne, and boath salute us; the first with 3 *cheares* and 7 gunns, whom wee thank with 5; the other with 5 gunns wee thank with 3; and so all part.—p. 51.

8th August, 1675.

Here wee find only on of our English shipps crusing about, viz. the Newcastle, a 4th rate frigott; whom we salute with 3 *cheares*, and they answer in a like manner.—p. 51.

6th December, 1675.

All the Alopeenes and Captaines dined on board us; were extreamly merry, wishing us thousands of good wishes, and drinking our healths over and over againe. At 4 in the afternoone they all went off: wee gave them 3 *cheares*, and 11 gunns; every on of them haveing dranke Snt. George in a rummar as he went over the ship syd; so wee part.—p. 101.

8th March, 1675-6.

At 8 a clock our ship takes leave of Sir John,[a] and salutes him with 11 gunns and 3 *cheares*; and he nobly saluts us with as many: wee returne him thanks with 5, and so part;—p. 144.

20th April, 1676.

The Gaw, and the Greate Bashaw cam to see our ship; whom wee salute with 5 gunns and 3 *cheares*.—p. 151.

24th June, 1678.

This day Capt. Tho. Langston and his Cornett cam to see our Capt. from Canterbury; and wee were very merry. They went on shoare about 7; and at their going off wee gave them 3 *cheares*, and 7 gunns.—p. 248.

---

[a] Sir John Narborough.

17-18th July, 1678.

I made my scabbard new. The sam day the Lord Strandford and his lady, and her sister, and severall others, cam from Sandowne Castle on board us. At their departure we gave them 3 *cheares* and 9 guuns.—p. 245.

15th November, 1678.

The fleete proves to be our Newfound Land fleete: the Woollidge their convoy; whoe gave us 3 *cheares* and 5 gunns. Wee gave the sam;—p. 264.

16th January, 1678-9.

"every Captaine departed from his old ship, and was received into his new ship, with 3 *cheares*, and drumms beating, and trumpetts sounding."—p. 275.

23rd March, 1678-9.

About 3 the Woolwich and her 5 merchants com and joyne with us; so that now wee doe not feare all the pickaroons in Turca. Shee cam to our starne, and wee saluted her with 7 guns and 3 *cheares*, shee did the same; we gave her 3 more, she did the same; we thanked them with on more, she did so too; and so we sayle together.—p. 293.

23rd April [!], 1679.

This day cam the Governor and many more brave fellows on board us to see our ship. At their departure wee gave them 3 *cheares* and 15 gunns.—p. 301.

Remarks on these examples.

Now it will be obvious to every impartial mind that in each of these twelve examples the expression, 3 *cheares*, has nothing to do with applause. It is a mere naval salute; and as such it is significant from being addressed to animated objects. It may countenance, inspirit, encourage or comfort, in a word, *cheer* the souls to whom it is addressed; but 3 *cheers* to extol deeds done is literally *preposterous*, and was never read or heard of till the latter half of the last century.

Origin of the modern use of *cheer*.

The modern use of *cheer*, as a substantive, certainly originated from the practice among sailors of saluting with shouting repeated three distinct times; and this being always friendly and encouraging came to be known by the conventional name of *three cheers*.

Résumé of the facts.

My positions then are these:—that up to about 1800 this threefold cry was not called "cheers" unless it was repeated thrice; that in a conventional form it was then known as "three cheers;" and that up to about 1750 this phrase was not used to signify three shouts on *terrâ firmâ*, or by landsmen.

To cheer in England, and *Saluer de la voix* in France, meant to utter *three* shouts by way of salutation.

"Saluer de la voix . to salute with three cheers, &c."—Falconer's French Appendix to his Sea Dictionary, (a new edition, corrected, &c., 1789.)

"To cheer . To salute a ship en passant by the people all coming upon Deck and *huzzaing three* times: it also implies encourage or animate."—British Mariner's Vocabulary of Sea Phrases. Moore. 1801.

The use of *huzza*.

Here we have the term *huzzaing*. Now I contend that before 1750, what we now call *a cheer* was called, on land, *a huzza*. I cannot absolutely prove this, but a large induction which I have made has convinced me that such is the fact.

Here are a few instructive examples from the reports of our wars with France in 1743.

"Our Lines halted half Way to the Enemy to give the

Soldiers Time to breathe; and having given a general *shout or Huzza*, marched on to the Enemy with great Alacrity."—*Gentleman's Mag. July*, 1743, p. 383.

"The only *Huzza* the French gave was at their Retreat, and that but a feint one. Our Army gave such *shouts* before we were engaged," &c.—*Ibid.* p. 386.

"Then the Foot gave an *Huzza*, and fir'd very fast; but our Men fir'd too fast for them, and soon made them retreat, and then gave another *Huzza* and fired."—*Ibid.* p. 387.

There is also an account of an exploit, the retaking of the standard at the battle of Dettingen, related in the same volume[32] in these words:—

"Our brave dragoon instantly formed a design of retaking it—made furiously towards the gens d'arms, and, presenting his pistol, shot him through the Head. The standard happened to fall into his arms—upon which he clapped it between his legs and rode as fast as he could through the ranks of the Enemy, in doing which he received five wounds in the face, head, and neck, two balls lodged in his back, three went through his hat, and he rejoined his regiment in a very weak condition, as may be imagined, who gave him *three huzzas* on his arrival."

If the word "cheers" had then been in use on *terrâ firmâ* in a plausive sense, where would it have been so likely to be known and employed, as in the English army composed, as it is, of men of all grades and pursuits, and where so likely to have been applied as to an exploit so gallant, and so notorious, performed in the face of the whole army?

But by 1769, I find "three cheers" in use on land; thus in the Report of the Shakspere Jubilee[33]

The use of *three cheers* on land in 1769.

[32] October, 1743, p. 552. [33] 11th Sept. 1769.

in the "Gentleman's Magazine" for 1769, p. 422, we read,—

"and Mr. Garrick, (whose behaviour exhibited the greatest politeness with the truest liveliness and hilarity) [drank] another [bumper] to the memory of the Bard, to which was subjoined *three cheers*, at the instance of your humble servant."

Now the question here is, in what sense was this expression, "three cheers," used? Was it an acclamation of applause? I will not take upon myself to determine such a refinement of philology: nor is it expedient. I do not wish to be dogmatic; but I am convinced that the expression *three cheers* will not be found in use on land before 1750. In what sense it was used after that date up to 1800 is of no manner of consequence. The earliest use I have found of *a cheer* in the nautical sense is in Campbell's *Battle of the Baltic*, which I think was first published in 1800. In this we read,[34]—

Campbell's mis-use of *a cheer*.

"Again! again! again!
And the havoc did not slack,
Till *a* feeble *cheer* the Dane
To our cheering sent us back;—"

But I cannot find that *a cheer* was employed in the modern sense of a shout of applause till some time after the beginning of this century.

In a case like this the most that can be done is to raise a strong probability for the alleged chronology of the word or phrase which is the subject of

[34] Stanza iv.

the criticism. It is then open to any opponents to refute the position if they can, by the simple process of producing an instance of the word or phrase before the presumed date of its introduction. We have seen how the writer in "The Athenæum" has attempted to do this by the present test-word and failed. Let us now see how other periodicals have dealt with the question.

A weekly paper called "The Bulletin" came out in 1859. It did not attain an extensive circulation, nor, judging from the few numbers which I have seen, did it deserve one. The number for June 11th of that year contained an article on the Perkins Folio. The writer pretended to prove that the manuscript notes were a modern fabrication, on the single ground that in *Coriolanus*, act 2, sc. 1, in the passage,— The article in The Bulletin.

"Your prattling nurse
Into a rapture lets her baby cry
While she *chats* him;"

the corrector had superseded "chats" by *cheers*. The writer in "The Bulletin" argued thus:—

"The verb 'to cheer,' in the amended passage, is used in its modern sense of hurrahing or shouting approvingly. Now in Shakspeare's time, and for 150 years afterwards—we believe we might state a longer period—the word had no such signification, and therefore it is evident that the 'old corrector's' alteration is a modern deception."

On July 5th, of the same year, *i. e.* three days after Mr. Hamilton's first letter had appeared in "The Times," a long extract from "The Bulletin" article was re-published in "The Times," being pre- Letter signed "Looker-on" in The Times.

faced by a letter from a "Looker-on," beginning thus, "Let credit be given where credit is due," and claiming for the writer in "The Bulletin" the credit of being the first to prove that the manuscript notes of the Perkins Folio are modern fabrications.

Considering that "The Times" had inserted "Looker-on's" letter, and the extract from "The Bulletin" from ignorance or precipitancy, I wrote to the editor of "The Times" a short letter, temperately pointing out that "Looker-on's" claim on behalf of the writer in "The Bulletin" was founded on a mistake; that the word *cheer*, was indeed an excellent test-word, and did occur in manuscript on the margin of *Coriolanus* in the Perkins Folio; but that the word was the *noun singular*, not the verb; and that the passage on which it was foisted by the "old corrector" was one in the ivth act and 7th scene of that play. Moreover I learn that a gentleman of the highest critical attainments, unknown to me addressed a letter to "The Times" in reply to "Looker-on's" letter, pointing out, and proving that the verb *to cheer* was used in Shakspere's day in the sense of "hurrahing or shouting approvingly." Neither of these letters were inserted in "The Times."

The Times suppresses the truth.

From this suppression of the truth it became evident that the writer of the article in "The Bulletin," "Looker-on," and the staff of "The Times," had some common interest, which rendered it highly inexpedient that "The Bulletin" article should be refuted.

At this time the proof sheets of my little book on *The Shakspeare Fabrications* were going through my hands; but I took no notice of "The Bulletin," deeming that its mis-statements might be left to oblivion, or, as it might happen, to refutation by those who attributed to the paper a greater importance than I did.

"The Bulletin" itself expired shortly afterwards; but its mis-statements were destined to survive in the pages of "Fraser's Magazine." Before adverting to this part of the story, it is necessary that I should state exactly the posture of the question at the time of the publication of my little book.

The statements of "The Bulletin" are these:—

"The verb 'to cheer' in the amended passage, is used in its modern sense of hurrahing or shouting approvingly. Now in Shakspeare's time, and for 150 years afterwards—we believe we might state a longer period—the word had no such signification."

The statements of The Bulletin refuted.

The first statement is "begged." If "to cheer," in the passage "While she *cheers* him," be taken in the sense of *to enliven*, the sense is perfect, and *to cheer* is used in an archaic sense. The second statement is utterly untrue. To *cheer* in Shakspere's day was used in the "sense of hurrahing or shouting approvingly." Thus, in Phaer's translation of the *Æneid*, the words, "Excipiunt plausu pavidos,"[35] is rendered

"The Trojans them did *chere*—"

and this book was first published in 1558. So that

[35] Æneid. lib. v. l. 575.

"The Bulletin" article, and "Looker-on's" letter go to what our transatlantic cousins descriptively call "almighty smash."

Mr. Singer's mistake.

The late Mr. Singer, in his *Shakespeare Vindicated*, 1853, p. 214, ventures to say of the emendation *cheers, vice* "chats," that

> "it savours too much of recent times. * * * *Cheers* is never used by Shakspeare in the sense of *applauding*."

Doubtless Mr. Singer was right in stating that the verb *to cheer* is not used by Shakspere in the sense of *to applaud*; but he committed an error in saying that "it savours too much of recent times." It was as familiar English in Shakspere's day as in ours.

These are the facts, then, as to the use of the verb *to cheer*, in the sense of *to applaud*, and of the substantive singular *a cheer*, in the sense of *an acclamation of applause*. The former was familiar in Shakspere's day, the latter probably came into use in the present century.

Mr. T. J. Arnold's mistake and awkward explanation.

In "Fraser's Magazine" for January last, in an article on "The Shakspearian Discovery," appeared a note on my *Shakspeare Fabrications*, and in particular on my remarks *in vocem, cheer*. The writer says,

> "Dr. Ingleby * * has been anticipated in his objection as to the modern use of the word *cheer*, by Mr. Singer * * and also by a writer in the *Bulletin*."

Now I have shewn that both these writers make an assertion which is not borne out by facts: the statements of the writer in "The Bulletin" being wholly reversed and disproved. Nor did I anywhere put forth such a statement as that in "The Bulletin" or even that of Mr. Singer. My statements related to another word—not a verb at all—but a noun substantive—with the advantage that my position had not (and has not) been disproved. I accordingly wrote to the editor of "Fraser's Magazine" complaining of the injustice that had been done me, enclosing, for insertion, a letter of simple facts. That letter was not inserted. In the February number of "Fraser's Magazine" the writer of the former article, in a note to a second article on the same subject, makes the *amende* as follows :—

"*To cheer* is, as was mentioned in the note in question, [*i.e.* the note appended to the first article] as old at least as Dryden; Dr. Ingleby shews in his letter that it was used in the time of Shakespeare. *A cheer* is, on the other hand, clearly a word of comparatively recent introduction."

This reads very well: but the verb *to cheer*, in the sense of *to extol or applaud by shouts*, was NOT "mentioned in the note in question, to be as old at least as Dryden." The remark was on the verb *to cheer*, in the *other* sense of *to encourage by shouts*. What I did shew was that *to cheer*, in the sense of *to applaud by shouting*, was used in the time of Shakspere, which has little in common with the statement of the writer of that note.

It is not difficult to understand how the writer in

"The Bulletin" obtained the hint as to *cheer* being a test-word for the manuscript notes of the Perkins Folio. He no doubt had heard of Mr. Brae's test-word, and stumbled on the passage in the *first* act of *Coriolanus*, instead of that in the *fourth* act; made the verb (*to cheer*) the test-word, instead of the noun substantive (*a cheer*), and by consequence, instead of reaping fame, "came to grief." So may such ill-gotten gains ever prosper!

But why did the writer in "Fraser's Magazine" take such pains to make it appear that I had told him nothing new? In the note to the January article he had coupled together two statements. 1st. That I had been anticipated by "The Bulletin." 2nd. That *to cheer*, in the sense of *to encourage by shouts*, was as old as Dryden. These two statements are consistent, even if for Dryden he had written Shakspere. Now in the note to the February article he identified my statement (which I substantiated by proof) that *to cheer*, in the *other* sense of *to applaud by shouts*, was as old as Shakspere, with his own in the former note, without telling his readers in what my statement differed from his: leaving them in fact to infer that I had simply found an earlier date for the verb *to cheer* in the sense of *to encourage by shouts*, and thus leaving the statement, that I had been anticipated, *uninvalidated*. Whereas, what I stated and proved completely invalidated that statement. He thus at once avoided the indignity of retracting his own erroneous statement, and covered the retreat of the mysterious "Bulletin" peddler.

But it must be owned that one important concession is extorted from this writer :—

"Dr. Ingleby is undoubtedly right. * * *A cheer* [in the sense of an audible expression of *admirative applause*, for in no other sense did I ever contend that it was modern] is * * clearly a word of comparatively modern introduction. * * * Certainly there was no intention to detract from the undoubted merit and originality of Dr. Ingleby's argument on the use of the noun."

This is, *at least*, an admission of the correctness of my views on this point.

To the remarks on the "cheer" criticism in "The Athenæum" of February 18th, 1859, I have already fully replied.

Mr. Collier, in his *Reply*, in a note, takes notice of this test-word. He remarks :—[36] Mr. Collier's mistakes.

"that *cheer* was in use as a word of encouragement and approbation early in the reign of Elizabeth, and that the expression *three cheers* is found in *Teonge's Diary* from 1675 to 1679. Yet we are told by the enemies of the Perkins folio that the earliest use of *three cheers* was about 1806! Those who make such unfounded objections come very ill provided to maintain them."

I should think so. But where did Mr. Collier encounter such a statement? I never put forth anything so absurd: nor, as far as I am aware, has the result of my criticism been so mis-stated until subsequently to the publication of Mr. Collier's *Reply*.[37]

---

[36] Page 65.

[37] Thus in "The Athenæum," for April 21st, 1860, a writer

The mistake of the editor of Notes and Queries.

The editor of "Notes and Queries" at last achieves the feat of a leading article on the Shakspere Controversy,[38] where in allusion either to Mr. Brae, or myself, he says:—

"we then knew, as all the world knows now, that the test word "cheer," over which there had been such a prodigious cackling, was no test-word at all; and that, although a certain learned gentleman fancied that he had proved that "cheer, as an audible expression of admirative applause, could not have been used before 1807," it did exist, and had existed sufficiently long to prove the curious ignorance of those who supposed it only to date from the present century."

These assertions are easily made. Why does not Mr. W. J. Thoms publish in his "Notes and Queries" one example of *a cheer* in the specified sense of an earlier date than 1800? I challenge him to do so, or to confess that he "said the thing that was not."

Mr. H. Merivale's mistake.

I must now briefly notice Mr. H. Merivale's remarks in the "Edinburgh Review,"[39] on the test-word "cheer." He writes thus:—

"It was reserved for Dr. Ingleby to attempt the boldest discovery in this line, and to meet with the most signal discomfiture. *His* test-word is 'cheer,' in the modern sense of an applauding and encouraging cry. (Coriolanus, act iv. scene 7, where the corrector substitutes 'cheer' in this sense for 'chair.') This, says Dr. Ingleby, is positively modern:"

---

says that I have "pledged [my] literary credit that the word *cheer* was unknown in our language before 1808."

The "Edinburgh" reviewer (Ap. 1860), if more truthful, is hardly more correct.

[38] Second Series, vol. ix. p. 211. [39] April, 1860.

My answer is short and decisive: that I never attempted to appropriate the discovery of the test-word cheer; the entire merit of that belongs to Mr. Brae: that the test-word is not 'cheer' in the modern sense of an applauding *and encouraging* cry, but in the sense of an applauding cry only: that I never said that the word in the sense of "an applauding and encouraging cry" was modern. This is an admirable specimen of the reckless inaccuracy of reviewers. But that Mr. Herman Merivale's name is a guarantee for his truthfulness, I should conceive that he had studied how he could best misrepresent the real state of the case, and my views on the test-word. He closes his scanty and inaccurate remarks on this subject by citing Mr. Teonge again, evidently in the most childlike ignorance of what Mr. Teonge's testimony really is; and adds:—

"We do not see how this is to be met, unless by adding a new count to the prosecution, and charging that 'Teonge's Diary,' a singular book enough,* is also a forgery of Mr. Collier's."

Without wishing to throw out any doubt as to the genuineness of Teonge's Diary, I am bound to remind my readers that it is not an old printed book; it was published by Mr. Charles Knight in 1825. The manuscript I have never seen. It is most probably genuine. But it certainly cannot carry the same authority as a contemporary *printed* book. I

* Did Mr. Merivale ever see it? I should certainly think not.

am not aware that any question has ever been raised as to its genuineness; but it is perfectly *harmless*, and very entertaining, and for all I know it may owe its immunity to those very features. But, be it genuine or spurious, the use of "3 cheares" therein is quite beside the present question.

CHAPTER VIII.

THE PERKINS FOLIO.—MR. COLLIER'S DEALINGS WITH THE EMENDATIONS.

No direct charge of forgery brought against Mr. Collier.

NEITHER my *Shakspeare Fabrications*, nor yet Mr. Hamilton's *Inquiry*, *directly* charges Mr. Collier with fabricating the manuscript corrections of the Perkins Folio, or those of the Bridgewater Folio. Mr. Hamilton indeed commits himself to the opinion that all the corrections of both folios are by one hand; and in that opinion I sincerely concur. In my former work on the subject I pass a judgment upon the identity of the pencil-writing in the body of the Perkins Folio, with that on the board at the end. I there say:—

"Mr. Collier admits that on the board at the end of the folio he wrote various words, and made several notes, which he never attempted to erase; and he challenges a comparison of the pencil-writing in the body of the folio with those notes. I have compared them; and must say candidly, that a comparison of the two, *if it can support a conclusion* (for inference from handwriting alone is always a doubtful matter), can lead to no other conclusion than that one hand wrote both."[1]

Mr. T. J. Arnold in his second article in "Fraser's Magazine,"[2] appears not to understand what pencillings in the body of the folio I refer to. Now the fact is, that when I wrote the passage which I have just cited, it had not occurred to me that there were *two* handwritings in pencil in the book.[3] "Scrutator," in-

[1] P. 77. [2] Feb. 1860.

[3] There *are* two handwritings in *ink*, viz. the "old corrector's"

deed, finds three such handwritings there; but it is difficult to say what he would not find, if his case required it. I will now be more explicit. I find *three* classes of expressions in pencil:—1st, Corrections of the text, wholly or partially corresponding with ink corrections; 2nd, Apparent corrections of the text, not adopted in ink; 3rd, References to other parts of the folio, and to other books—and other remarks, ticks, lines, &c.

Three classes of pencillings in the Perkins Folio.

The irresistible inference.

If Mr. Collier had been dead and buried 50 years, *i. e.* if we were now in A.D. 1910, I do not think it would have ever entered into the thoughts of reader, critic, commentator or editor, who might use this copy of the second folio, that more than one hand wrote these various pencillings. I further say that all the pencillings of the first class are so obviously in one hand, that any person who doubts it, including "Scrutator" if indeed he does doubt it *bonâ fide*, must be out of his senses. And I further say, that the pencillings in all three classes appear to me to be in one handwriting, and to differ only in the fact that those in class 3, are (like the pencil-writing on the board at the end) plainer, apparently more recent, than those in classes 1 and 2.

Mr. Collier's evil genius.

If Mr. Collier be innocent of the charge of writing the pencillings in classes 1 and 2, it must be allowed that he is the most unlucky among mortals, and that

modern antique, and a genuine handwriting of the last century, in which the *dramatis personæ* of Hen. V. are written. See sheet of facsimiles, no. VI.

he has acted in respect of these pencillings like a man—

> ὅτῳ φρένας
> Θεὸς ἄγει πρὸς ἄταν·

Mr. Collier's denial of the presumed charge of forgery.

He begins his reply to a charge which nobody had directly brought against him, by making allegations which his opponents would be very willing to admit. Here are two of them: 1st, as to the ink corrections—

> "These manuscript notes I never altered, added to, nor diminished."[4]

Granted; but did he make them as they stand? 2nd, as to the pencillings—

> "I declare most positively, in the face of the whole world, that, while the Perkins folio was in my hands, I never saw a pencil-mark in it that I had not made myself, ..."[5]

Nor anybody else—if Mr. Collier had really made them all!

But he does, indeed, very lamely deny both the imputations. He says, speaking of other books:—

> "I have even sometimes resorted in the first instance to pencil, and when next I had a pen and ink at hand, I have written in ink over my own pencillings. * * *
>
> That I did so in the case of the Perkins folio I utterly and absolutely deny;"[6]
>
> "If I wanted to be sure not to forget to look at a particular passage in *Malone*, or in any other commentator, or if I wished to note something that required again to be examined in the folio, I took the ordinary method with a pencil that I always kept at hand; but that I thus added the slightest hint with reference

[4] Reply, p. 19. [5] Reply, p. 24. [6] Reply, p. 20.

to any projected alteration of the language of the poet I deny in the strongest form in which it is possible to clothe a denial."[7]

Verdict on the pencil-writing.

Unfortunately for Mr. Collier, the evidence against him, derived from the writings in the Perkins Folio, is of a very damnatory character; and the similarity between the pencil-writing which Mr. Collier repudiates, and the pencil-writing which he owns, is of a most startling closeness. Indeed, *similarity* is a feeble word to express the resemblance in question.

On this point some of Mr. Frederick G. Netherclift's facsimiles, prefixed to Mr. Hamilton's book, are incompetent to guide opinion. The peculiar character of the handwriting in pencil is not always preserved in the lithograph.[8]

If the reader will here turn to sheet no. V. he

---

[7] Reply, p. 24.

[8] How far it is possible by lithography to simulate the characteristics of handwritings I am not prepared to say. Whether the failure to which I allude in Mr. Frederick G. Netherclift's facsimiles is a fault inseparable from lithography, or whether it is due to a want of fidelity in the tracings, I will not undertake to decide. But this I must say, that having examined all those facsimiles which are on Mr. Hamilton's frontispiece with the originals in the Perkins Folio, by the aid of compasses, I have found that several of them differ from their prototypes, both in the proportions of their parts, and in the inclination of the lines. In particular I will instance the pencil words *Wall* and *aside*, and the ink word *God*. None of these can be called facsimiles without great licentiousness of expression. The word *aside*, and the phrase *us now*, both of which appear in Mr. F. G. Netherclift's sheet, have been facsimiled by Mr. Ashbee (see sheet no. V.) The reader who has access to the originals may judge how far that artist has been suc-

M.S. Notes & Corrections from the Perkins Folio.

(1) Malone XVII 391 says that the ...
printed from a MS

Henry V along the top of page 69.

(3) now

Midsummer Nights Dream: page 150. col. 2.

(4) (aside)

King John _page 6. col. 2.

(2)

On the leaf pasted within the Cover at back.

(5) Exit Anne

Merry Wives of Windsor page 40. col. 2.

(6) Exeunt Ales

Winter's Tale _page 278. col. 2.

(7)

Pro. 'Save your Honor. Going, Stand back!

Measure for Measure _page 67 col. 1

1 & 2 Pencil-notes in Mr. Colliers handwriting
3, 4, 5, 6 & 7 Examples of the 'Old Corrector's' corrections in pencil & ink.

To face p. 174

will observe the *extraordinary* resemblance between Mr. Collier's writing and that of the "old corrector." Here we have a note in pencil by Mr. Collier, compared with several words in faint pencil, which correspond (more or less) with the "old corrector's" manuscript notes in ink. Here too we have the word *aside*, taken from the references written in pencil on the leaf pasted inside the second board of the Perkins Folio, which Mr. Collier acknowledges to have written: and to this I have annexed the word *aside*, taken from a pencil note on the margin of the folio, corresponding with the "old corrector's" manuscript word in ink. Further, on sheet no. IV. we have a facsimile of the G which Mr. Collier wrote in pencil opposite the fifth of the *additional facsimiles*, which he printed for private circulation; and side by side we have no less than seven of the "old corrector's" G's in ink, not written, however, in his usual character.

Internal evidences tending to inculpate Mr. Collier.

We have seen how far Mr. Collier's case is compromised by the internal evidences of the manuscript notes of the Perkins Folio. Let us now inquire whether the corrections, irrespective of the character of any of the writing, in any way connects Mr. Collier with the fabrication of the notes. It must be borne in mind that direct proof is wanting; and

cessful: at any rate the two lines, representing some pencil-writing of Mr. Collier's will probably be found to contain a proportional amount of disparity; so that the two writings may be fairly compared.

M 2

in its absence we must be content with any circumstantial evidence which may be competent to raise a degree of probability, of more or less magnitude, that Mr. Collier was the power that set in motion the machinery, if not comprising within himself the sole agency, by which the fabrication of the notes was effected.

Now it so happens that in four cases, Mr. Collier's conduct has not been that which was to have been expected from a man who was in no way connected with the fabrication. I speak of the late Mr. Singer's emendation of *rother's, vice* "brother's," in *Timon of Athens,* act iv. sc. 3; of the late Mr. W. Sidney Walker's emendation of *infinite cunning, vice* "infuit comming," in *All's well that ends well,* act v. sc. 3; of Mr. Dyce's emendation of *up-trimm'd, vice* "untrimm'd," in *King John,* act iii. sc. 1; and of the stage direction, *Writing,* in *Hamlet,* act i. sc. 4. I will take these four cases *seriatim.*

"brother's" *v. rother's.*

I. Mr. Singer's correction was first published by him in 1842, when it appeared in "The Athenæum" for May 14th of that year. In Mr. Collier's edition of 1841-1844[9] he gives Mr. Singer the full credit of this correction (with a mistake, however, in the reference), and adopts it in his own text. For this disinterested act he afterwards takes credit in a communication to "Notes and Queries."[10] He there reminds Mr. Singer—

[9] Vol. vi. p. 559. [10] 1st Series, vol. vii. p. 216, Feb. 26, 1853.

"that there was no reluctance on my part to give MR. SINGER full credit for a very happy emendation."

For this recognition of Mr. Singer's claim Mr. Collier afterwards indemnifies himself. The emendation being found on the margin of the Perkins Folio, Mr. Collier communicates the fact in his *Notes and Emendations*, 1853,[11] in the following words:—

"Again, for "brother's sides" we have "*rother's* sides" properly substituted;"

Nor in the supplementary *Notes* is there any reference to Mr. Singer.

"infuite comming" *v. infinite cunning.*

II. On April 17th, 1852 (only three weeks after Mr. Collier's last letter in "The Athenæum,") a letter was published in that periodical from Mr. W. N. Lettsom, communicating Mr. W. Sidney Walker's emendation. Now in "The Athenæum" of Jan. 31st, Feb. 7th, and March 27th, 1852, Mr. Collier had already made known what he considered for the purposes of advertisement the most prepossessing exemplars of the manuscript corrections of the Perkins Folio; but *infinite cunning* was not one of them.

On the 29th of May following, a communication from Mr. Collier, dated "May 22, 1852," was published in "Notes and Queries,"[12] where, in reference to a prior article of Mr. Singer's, Mr. Collier asked that gentleman to inform him

---

[11] 1st Ed. p. 392; 2nd Ed. p. 402.

[12] 1st Series, vol. v. p. 509.

"where the proposed emendation, referred to by him in "N. & Q.," vol. v., p. 436., in *All's Well that ends Well*, *infinite cunning* for "infuite comming," of the folio 1623, is to be met with?"

Mr. Collier adds:—

"If it be in the *Athenæum* it has escaped my observation, although I have turned over the pages of that able periodical carefully to find it. I have a particular reason for wishing to trace the suggestion, if I can, to the source where it originated."

No reply from Mr. Singer ever appeared in "Notes and Queries." In fact nothing further transpired on the subject until the appearance of Mr. Collier's *Notes and Emendations* in the month of January following, when the emendation of "infinite cunning" was not mentioned in the introduction as among the examples of sound and self-evident emendation, but was introduced[19] in the following innocent manner:—

"on the evidence of the manuscript-corrector, as well as common sense, we must print the passage hereafter,—

"Her *infinite cunning*, with her modern grace,
Subdued me to her rate."

This appears to be one of the instances in which a gross blunder was occasioned, in part by the mishearing of the old scribe, and in part by the carelessness of the old printer. The sagacity of the late Mr. Walker hit upon this excellent emendation. See Athenæum, 17 April, 1852."

If the importation of this reading into the Perkins Folio were, in fact, made before that book came into Mr. Collier's possession, there are four points which excite my unqualified astonishment.

---

[19] 1st and 2nd Ed. p. 169.

1. That Mr. Collier did not select this as an original specimen of the Perkins emendations—being, as it is, the best, or certainly in the opinion of every qualified person, one of the best that the annotations comprize. Like Mr. Singer's "rother's," (which, however, I am not in the least disposed to adopt,) it has received the stamp of approval from Mr. Dyce and Mr. Staunton, by being unhesitatingly installed in the text of their editions. The late Mr. Singer also spoke of it in terms of unqualified admiration,[14] and adopted it in his latest text. If it should occur to any one that perhaps Mr. Collier did not select this emendation for special and prominent approval, because it had been already suggested in print, I beg to remind such an objector that the emendation of "*ethicks*," *vice* "checks," in the *Taming of the Shrew*, act i. sc. 1, was so selected by Mr. Collier; and yet that it had been introduced into the text of no fewer than *five* editors (the earliest being that of the Rev. J. Rann, 1787),[15] and was independently suggested by Mr. Justice Blackstone.

2. That Mr. Collier himself, using "The Athenæum" for his medium of communication with the public, and naturally expecting communications on the subject of his revelations to appear in that periodical, yet asked Mr. Singer, in "Notes and Queries,"

[14] Notes and Queries, 1st Series, vol. v. p. 556.

[15] Observations on some of the Manuscript Emendations, &c. by J. O. Halliwell, 1853, p. 14.

where the emendation was to be found, because, if in "The Athenæum," it had escaped him!

3. That Mr. Collier did not see that *it was his duty as well as policy even then* to make known his discovery, that the emendation was on the margin of his folio.

4. That when his *Notes and Emendations* did finally appear, not a word in explanation of this extraordinary oversight in his first examination of the folio, or of his subsequent discovery, was to be found; nor was it mentioned in the *Introduction* as an instance of felicitous emendation; but, on the contrary, this emendation, the most important by far in the whole collection, is smuggled into that work in the most diffident manner, and with far less approbation bestowed upon it than is lavished on nine-tenths of the conjectures with which this unhappy book is crammed.

These are the improbabilities with which we have to contend in vindicating Mr. Collier's good faith in this instance.

"untrimm'd" *v. uptrimm'd.*

III. Mr. Dyce's emendation of *uptrimm'd, vice* "untrimm'd," was first divulged by Mr. Singer in "Notes and Queries" for July 3, 1852;[16] and it has been adopted by Mr. Singer and Mr. Staunton. Mr. Dyce of course adopts it in the text of his edition, and in his *Few Notes,*[17] speaks of it with the same mixture of confidence and modesty with which

[16] 1st Series, vol. vi. p. 6. [17] p. 87.

Theobald broached his now famous emendation of *busie-less, vice* "busie lest," in *The Tempest*; yet I must say with the utmost respect for both these critics, that I cannot accept either the one alteration or the other. I believe, with Mr. Staunton's second thoughts, that *untrimmed* was an epithet formerly applied to brides, in technical reference to the fashion of wearing the hair loose over the shoulders. Mr. Dyce's emendation is on the margin of the Perkins Folio. Mr. Collier did not publish it till 1856, when it appeared in his *List of every manuscript note and emendation, &c.*, appended to the *Seven Lectures, &c.*

IV. In "Notes and Queries,"[18] for March 13th, 1852, an article was published, bearing Mr. Brae's well known initials (A. E. B.), and for the first time calling in question the place of the stage direction ("Writing"), which in all modern editions stands opposite the line, — The stage-direction *Writing.*

"At least I'm sure it may be so in Denmark;"

in *Hamlet*, act i. sc. 4. This article is one of the first importance, if it be regarded merely as affecting our judgment on that much disputed point, the character of Hamlet. Coleridge, as is well known, deduced from the "tables" scene, the inference that Hamlet's sanity became first disturbed immediately after the disappearance of the Ghost, and that Hamlet's incipient insanity is manifested in an absurd action: viz. the jotting down of a generalized truth—

("That one may smile and smile and be a villain,")

[18] 1st Series, vol. v. p. 241.

on his material tables, because he had sworn to wipe all such "from the tables of [his] memory," and to retain there only one thing, the Ghost's "commandment."

Now it is obvious, that if Shakspere did not intend Hamlet to jot down the line,

"That one may smile and smile and be a villain,"

but, on the contrary, to "make note of" the Ghost's parting injunction,

"Adieu, adieu, adieu, remember me!"

there is an end of the absurd action, and one ground upon which the hypothesis of Hamlet's insanity has been built, is "swagged."

I mention these matters thus particularly—

1st. Because in the whole course of "Notes and Queries," with one very trifling exception (which is a note signed M.,[10] and is on a subordinate point incidentally touched on in A. E. B.'s article), not a single note or comment on that article has ever been admitted into that periodical.

2nd. Because Hamlet's character has long been regarded by the world, and by critics in particular, as the most interesting of Shakspere's masterpieces; and A. E. B.'s article has so direct a bearing on our judgment thereupon.

Let us, then, distinctly understand A. E. B.'s reading. It is this; the line,—

"That one may smile and smile and be a villain!"

---

[10] Vol. v. p. 285.

is an *admirative comment* on the fact, that, at least in Denmark, there is a man who "murders while he smiles."[30] So in *Cymbeline*, act i. sc. 1, we are presented with the fact that the king's two sons have been stolen, and the "2nd Gentleman's" admirative comment on this is,—

> "That a king's children should be so convey'd,
> So slackly guarded!"

Hamlet's speech is broken from excitement and impulse. He begins to say that he must set "it" down; but does not say what. Then comes his admirative comment on the King's smiling villainy; then the statement of the known instance. "So uncle, there you are!" means, "So uncle, that's your little game, is it!" Then checking himself, he says, "Now to my *word*" (or "words," as the 4to. 1603 has it), *i.e.* the thing which he is to set down.

> "Meet it is I set *it* down." * * *
> "*It* is, 'Adieu, adieu, remember me!'"

A. E. B., accordingly, gives these directions for punctuating the passage:—

> "After "set it down," a full stop; after "and be a villain," a note of admiration; the stage direction "(*writing*)" to be removed two lines lower down."

The passage would then stand thus:—

> "O villain, villain, smiling damned villain!
> My tables! meet it is I set it down.—
> That one may smile and smile and be a villain!

[30] 3 Hen. VI. act iii. sc. 2.

At least I'm sure it may be so in Denmark;
So uncle there you are!—now to my word;
It is 'Adieu, adieu, remember me.' [*Writing*]
[*He kisses the tables.*] I have sworn it."

Now, I repeat, it would be difficult to overrate the importance of this change: and the suggestion is one which involves merely a change of punctuation (for the stage direction is not in any old copy), and is besides recommended by its consistency and beauty.

For a long time I remained unconvinced by A.E. B.'s argument, simply because I could not regard the phrase

"That we may smile and smile, and be a villain."

as an admirative comment. My hesitation, however, has vanished. I now see that the only difference of construction between that and the line

"That a king's children should be so convey'd,"

is, that in the latter, the speaker's wonderment is on a FACT—the fact of the *indignity* of the theft: while in the former the speaker's wonderment is on a POSSIBILITY—the possibility of the *incongruity* of his uncle's character. Therefore the one speaker wonders "that it should be so:" the other "that it may be so."

This remarkable article having been greeted with an honourably distinctive silence, A. E. B. subsequently asked in "Notes and Queries," for Sept. 18, 1852,[11]

---

[11] 1st Series, vol. vi. p. 270.

"In what edition was the stage direction '(writing)' at the conclusion of the Ghost scene in *Hamlet*, first inserted?"

To this question no reply ever appeared. In "Notes and Queries," for Feb. 19, 1853,[22] A. E. B. reverts to the subject of his question, and says:—

"Perhaps Mr. Collier will do me the favour to answer it, particularly as his annotated folio is remarkably rich in "*stage directions.*"

Before taking the liberty of putting the question so directly to Mr. Collier, I awaited an examination of his recently-published volume of selected corrections, in which, however, the point upon which I seek information is not alluded to."

In "Notes and Queries," for Feb. 26, 1853,[23] Mr. Collier writes:—

"Domestic anxieties having unavoidably detained me in this place [Torquay] during the last three or four months, I am necessarily without nearly all my books. My corrected folio, 1632, is one of the very few exceptions; and as I have not the No. of "N. & Q." to which A. E. B. refers, I am unable to reply to his question, simply because I do not remember it.

To whomsoever these initials belong, he is a man of so much acuteness and learning, that although I may deem his conjectures rather subtle and ingenious than solid and expedient, I consider him entitled to all the information in my power. I do not, of course, feel bound to notice all anonymous speculators (literary or pecuniary); but if A. E. B. will be good enough to take the trouble to repeat his interrogatory, I promise him to answer it at once."

Now what is all this about? Surely in Mr. Collier's nursery English this is a "mighty fuss,"

---

[22] 1st Series, vol. vii. p. 178.

[23] 1st Series, vol. vii. p. 216.

about a very slight matter. He writes as if A. E. B. had solicited him to undertake some onerous task, and as if the repetition of the "interrogatory" were itself a very serious tax on A. E. B.'s time and good nature—"if he will be good enough, to take the trouble, to repeat," &c.! But with all Mr. Collier's guarded politeness two things were manifest. 1st, That he wished to depreciate A. E. B.'s abilities as a critic. 2nd, That he meant to put off *sine die* answering an inconvenient question: in a word to provide a means of present delay, and, if necessary, of prospective subterfuge.

A. E. B. having waited two months to give Mr. Collier time to return to his books, wrote to the editor of "Notes and Queries:"—

"I now no longer hesitate to ask the Editor for an opportunity of again *inserting* it [the query], trusting that a sufficient excuse will be found in the importance of the subject, as affecting the fundamental sense of a passage in Shakspeare."

This note was accompanied with a private communication to the editor, expressly desiring that the original query might (in compliance with Mr. Collier's request) be reprinted at the foot of the note. The note duly appeared in "Notes and Queries" for May 7, 1853,[a] *but not in its integrity.* It was, I have no doubt, necessary to make secure the retreat which Mr. Collier seems to have contemplated; and this was now done by not repeating the original

---

[a] 1st Series, vol. vii. p. 449.

query; and accordingly, the words "inserting it" were supplanted by the words "referring to it." Truly Mr. Collier had a friend in need in the editor of "Notes and Queries." The editorial shears may at times perform the feats of a magician's wand.

In August, 1853, in reply to a remark of Mr. Collier's in "Notes and Queries,"[35] I wrote to him, plainly charging him with having forfeited his plight to "a well-known anonymous correspondent" in "Notes and Queries."

But this champion of the little band, who had from the first assailed the Perkins imposition, had strangely faded from Mr. Collier's memory. In his rejoinder, dated August 10, 1853, he writes,—

"I am not aware that I "ever forfeited my plight" to any correspondent, anonymous or avowed; but my memory may fail me."

What a convenient memory is this of Mr. Collier's! He had declared, as we have seen, almost in the same words, only six months before, when replying to this very "anonymous correspondent," that he does not answer his query "simply because *I do not remember it*;" and yet, when the same memory is applied to the Coleridge Lectures, it recalls without effort, and without hesitation, the minutest details across a vast of forty years! It must not be lost sight of in this inquiry, that only three months before Mr. Collier's letter to me, when

---

[35] 1st Series, vol. viii. p. 73.

the *second appeal*, garbled as it was, did appear, *his name, in large type*, appears thrice on two independent pages of the same number of "Notes and Queries," in which there is a paper from himself.

However, the fact is, that Mr. Collier did profit by the subterfuge thus furnished him, and never did reply to A. E. B.'s query.

This was a short-sighted policy. In December, 1853, I went to the British Museum to make some collations of *Hamlet* quartos, and I availed myself of the occasion to search the various editions of that play for the first appearance of the stage-direction "(writing);" and it came to pass that, working upwards, I first came upon it in Rowe's edition, 1709. That Rowe should have been the first to introduce it, is a proof that it rests not upon any nice critical appreciation of the character of Hamlet. Rowe was a very small critic, and was not a man to originate such a reading, unless from ignorance; but that his edition is the first in which this stage-direction appears is, I doubt not, the very reason which rendered the question of A. E. B. so inconvenient to answer. Now it was evident, that if after all it should turn out that it was so introduced, it would add another strong suspicion as to the modern fabrication of the Perkins annotations.

But the fact was still more suspicious than the simple existence of the stage-direction could have been.

On June 4th, 1859, I went to the British Museum, for the purpose of examining the Perkins Folio. Among a vast number of passages which I examined, I turned to the "tables" scene in *Hamlet*, expecting to find the stage-direction, "(writing)" opposite the line,

"At least I'm sure it may be so in Denmark."

but there was no such manuscript note to be found anywhere. I then held up the leaf against the light, but could not in that manner perceive an erasure. I then examined the right-hand margin by reflected light, and fancied there was an appearance as of an erasure skilfully effected. I appealed to Mr. Staunton, and also to Mr. Ward of the Department of Manuscripts; but neither of these gentlemen could see any erasure. At this time Sir Frederic Madden had left, so I postponed further examination of the supposed erasure till my next visit.

On the 6th of that month I again visited the Department of Manuscripts, and pointed out to Sir Frederic Madden the place where I suspected there had been an erasure. He saw it at once; and on my telling him what word I suspected to have been once there, he said that he could even then see a W, or at least faint traces of where that letter had been. At my request he then applied to the suspected place the hydro-sulphate of ammonia; and even before it was dry, the letters *Wri* became visible! Yet the acid took so little effect, that Sir Frederic Madden immediately said there could not be much iron in the ink in which the word had been written. When the place had become dry, the entire word *Writing* was faintly legible. Subsequently all had faded but *Wri g*, and now *Wri* is all that can be made out.

It is most instructive to review the real state of this case.

1. The original query was proposed in the same number of "Notes and Queries," with and within a page or two of a paper by Mr. Singer, *which was responded to by Mr. Collier within the week:* hence his attention was particularly engaged upon the identical number of which he afterwards pleads entire forgetfulness.

2. At the same time, Mr. Collier was such an attentive reader of "Notes and Queries," that not even casual remarks escaped reply from him. Thus we find him on the 20th of November commenting upon the incidental mention by Mr. Singer (only the week before) of an emendation made by him twenty-five years previously; but when asked, directly and by name, on the following 19th of February, to answer the query proposed four months before, Mr. Collier pleads inability to do so, because he has not with him the number containing it! He also pleads that domestic anxieties have detained him in Torquay *three or four months*, the latter being precisely the interval from the first proposal of the query, although we have seen him in the interim correcting proofs for the press, and needlessly commenting within the week upon matters not so obviously connected with his forthcoming volume.

3. Now, supposing Mr. Collier's excuse literally true, would it not have been infinitely easier to obtain the back number by return of post, than to ask the querist, in a roundabout way, through the pages of "Notes and Queries," *to "be good enough to take the trouble to repeat his interrogatory"?* Such a demand, even supposing it *bonâ fide*, must have appeared to any person of ordinary sense too absurd and preposterous to notice!

4. Nevertheless, the querist, although doubtless amused with the shuffle of the request, did at length comply with it, first having given Mr. Collier three months to refer to the original query, had he chosen to do so. Then, as a last resource, he did "take the trouble to repeat his interrogatory," at least he intended the editor of "Notes and Queries," or one of his printers' assistants to take that slight trouble; but, to his great surprise, his note was altered by the editor, and his renewed appeal to Mr. Collier, so altered, was published in "Notes and Queries" of May 7, 1853, without a heading, and without being accompanied, as requested, by a reprint of the original query: such treatment being *significant*, when it is recollected that the editor of that periodical was and still is the declared partisan of Mr. Collier!

Fifthly: This last appeal was never responded to by Mr. Collier, although he had said that

"if A. E. B. would be good enough to take the trouble to repeat his interrogatory, I promise to answer it at once."

And A. E. B.'s article, his original and both his repeated queries, as well as the notes of Mr. Collier and "M." were excluded from their legitimate place in the General Index to the first twelve volumes of "Notes and Queries;" notwithstanding the fact that I took the trouble to point out to the editor the omission of one from its proper division in the Index to vol. v., and the mistake in the entry of another in the Index to vol. vi., at the time that I contributed a list of omissions towards the completion of the General Index.

Finally, The stage direction which would have told such tales has been skilfully erased!

All these four cases were made public in my *Shakspeare Fabrications*, yet, up to this present time, Mr. Collier has vouchsafed no reply to the *primâ facie* case which is implied in them. This is my apology, if apology be needed, for again bringing them before the public. They still challenge examination and reply.

"Wonderful sympathy" between Mr. Collier and the "old corrector."

Another circumstance which, it is conceived, should have its weight in the question of Mr. Collier's *bona fides*, is that of which Mr. Singer made a point in his *Text of Shakespeare Vindicated*,* viz. that there is a "wonderful sympathy" between Mr. Collier and the "old corrector," shewn by the number of Mr. Collier's original suggestions which have found their way into the Perkins Folio. Whether that number is sufficiently great to justify the expression, "won-

* Page 146.

derful sympathy," is a matter of opinion. I think it is: and though it cannot be said that a large number of such coincidences necessarily inculpates Mr. Collier, yet it may well be sufficiently large to raise a strong probability either that Mr. Collier's suggestions are not independent of the "old corrector's" emendations, or that the "old corrector's" emendations are not independent of Mr. Collier's suggestions. It must be presumed that the following list does not include any cases of coincidence between the Perkins notes and those original suggestions of Mr. Collier's, in which he had, apparently unknown to himself, been anticipated by other editors or critics. Such cases are very numerous: for instance—

Mr. Collier's emendations, apparently original, but not new.

MEASURE FOR MEASURE.

Act iii. sc. 2. "What say'st thou, trot"—*troth*, Collier, ed. 1844, vol. ii. p. 59.

TWELFTH NIGHT.

Act v. sc. 1. "*Then* cam'st in smiling"—*Thou*, Collier, ib. vol. i. p. cclxxxvi.

In neither of these cases does Mr. Collier make any allusion to Jackson; and yet in both he is anticipated by that dreary old printer; and both are on the margins of the Perkins Folio. See also Collier's ed. 1841-1844, vol. i. p. 69; vol. ii. pp. 57, 74, 81, 129, 139, 142, 149, 208, 209, 215, 227, &c.; vol. iii. pp. 63, 373, &c.; so also vol. vii. pp. 277, 411, 582, &c.; and vol. viii. p. 74, and other places too numerous to mention; where the original suggestions of Mr. Collier, which have been forestalled by other writers,[n] jump with the emendations of the Perkins Folio.

Nor does the ensuing list comprize the suggestions of that mysterious personage the Rev. Mr. Barry, as contained in the notes to Mr. Collier's edition of 1841-1844; and which in several places I have found to tally with the Perkins corrections. This is making a large deduction from the total number of coincidences between Mr. Collier's original suggestions, and the "old corrector's" manuscript emendations, which would certainly amount in the gross to more than sixty. After making the deductions I have indicated, the following is the remainder.

Mr. Collier's emendations original and new.

Mr. Collier's readings which are both original and new.

Folio text.	Perkins reading.	Collier's Ed. 1844.
MEASURE FOR MEASURE.		
Act iv. sc. 2.—That wounds th' *unsisting* postern	*resisting*	ii. 73
COMEDY OF ERRORS.		
Act. i. sc. 1.—To seek thy *help* by beneficial help	*hope*	ii. 118
Act v. sc. 1.—And thereupon these errors *are* arose	*all*	ii. 177

[n] Among these are emendations of Lord Chedworth, Rowe, Warburton, Pope, Johnson, Mason, Theobald, and others; but we do not find in Mr. Collier's notes the slightest hint that these commentators and editors had forestalled him, any more than in Mr. Perkins' margins we are led to suppose that those very emendations had been proposed by Mr. Collier.

Folio text.	Perkins reading.	Collier's Ed. 1844.
LOVE'S LABOUR'S LOST.		
Act v. sc. 1.—Do you not educate your youth at the *charge* house	*large*	ii. 348
MIDSUMMER NIGHT'S DREAM.		
Act iii. sc. 1.—The flowers *of* odious savours sweet	*have*	ii. 421
Act iii. sc. 2.—This *princess* of pure white	*impress*	ii. 431
TAMING OF THE SHREW.		
Act v. sc. 2.—When the raging war is *come*	*gone*	iii. 194
WINTER'S TALE.		
Act ii. sc. 1.—I would *land-damn* him	*lamback*	iii. 450
Act iv. sc. 2.—Doth set my *pugging* tooth on edge	*prigging*	iii. 488
KING JOHN.		
Act iii. sc. 3.—Sound on into the drowsy *race* of night	*ears*	iv. 53
RICHARD II.		
Act v. sc. 5.—Now, *sir*, the sound	*for*	iv. 211
HEN. V.		
Act i. sc. 2.—To *tame* and havoc	*tear*	iv. 476
1 HEN. VI.		
Act v. sc. 3.—*Mad* natural graces	*Mid*	v. 95
2 HEN. VI.		
Act iii. sc. 1.—For he's inclin'd as is the ravenous *wolves*	*wolf*	v. 153
CORIOLANUS.		
Act i. sc. 3.—At Grecian sword *contenning*	*contemning*	vi. 154
ROMEO AND JULIET.		
Act ii. sc. 2.—The lazy *puffing* clouds	*passing*	vi. 407

Folio text.	Perkins reading.	Collier's Ed. 1844.
HAMLET.		
Act i. sc. 3.—*Roaming* it thus	*Running*	vii. 216

Mr. Collier's suggestions carried out by Mr. Perkins.

Besides these *seventeen* literal coincidences there are several remarkable suggestions of misprints, upon which emendations are actually made in the Perkins Folio. I give one of these as a sample of what I mean:—

In *Macbeth*, act v. sc. 3, Macbeth says to the doctor,

"Canst thou not minister to a mind diseas'd,
Pluck from the memory a rooted sorrow,
Raze out the written troubles of the brain,
And with some sweet oblivious antidote
Cleanse the stuff'd bosom of that perilous stuff
Which weighs upon the heart?"

Propositions for the remedy of a supposed defect in the fifth line (viz. the tame and senseless repetition of the word *stuff*), I believe, invariably turned upon an alteration of the word *stuff'd*, till Mr. Collier, in his edition, 1844, vol. vii. p. 177, well says that, "The error, if any, rather lies in the last word of the line." This was certainly a new and I think important light. The "old corrector" has profited by it. He reads,—

"Cleanse the stuff'd bosom of that perilous *grief*
Which weighs upon the heart."

I am so heterodox as to think this a fine reading. I do so, 1st, because it restores perfect sense and beauty to what I believe to be a vile corruption.

2nd. Because "*stuff*" is an easy misprint for grieff, or griefe, in old writing.

3rd. Because *grief*, in the language of the old medical writers, did weigh on the heart, and stuff the bosom.[26]

I must further add, that besides the emendations of Mr. Collier given in the foregoing list, I find in the notes to his edition of 1841-1844, about forty-five original readings of which not one is to be found in the *List of every manuscript note and emendation*, &c. (1856). But I am far from being satisfied but that some of them are not on the margins of the Perkins Folio.

The short-hand in the Perkins Folio.

The last point to which I will call attention in this chapter is the presence of words written in short-hand, in pencil, on the margin of the Perkins

---

[26] See, for instance, the following passage in Daniel's *Queen's Arcadia*, (1606), act iii. sc. 2:—

"that layes upon my *heart*,
This heavy loade *that weighs it downe with griefe*."

Ex. Ibid.: act iv. sc. 1;

"perhaps it pleas'd her then
To cast me up in this way of [*i.e.* off] her mouth
From of [*i.e.* off] *her heart, least it might stuffe the same*."

Grief is sickness, malady: when Mr. Dyce then, asks (*Few Notes*, &c. p. 132), if the manuscript corrector's alteration does not introduce a great impropriety of expression—"CLEANSE the bosom of GRIEF?" the answer is plain; certainly not: for he evidently does not mean cleanse the bosom of *grief*, but of *a* grief—*i. e.* a sickness.

Folio. Mr. M. Levy has made known in the pages of "The Literary Gazette,"[29] the fact that in *Coriolanus,* act v. sc. 2, under the words, "Nay, but fellow, fellow," the stage-direction "struggles, or instead noise," is written in pencil in the short-hand of John Palmer's system (which is called an improvement on that of John Byrom), first published in 1774. We have already seen[30] that Mr. Collier was taught short-hand by his father, and it is to say the least a very suspicious circumstance that Mr. Collier refuses to say what system of short-hand he has been accustomed to use. Certainly if Mr. Collier's system should turn out to be that published by Palmer in 1774, we should have a new circumstance in this case, which would be of itself enough to create the strongest suspicions of foul play on Mr. Collier's part; and taken with the other evidence set forth in this chapter would be sufficient to convict him of the forgery of all the manuscript notes in the Perkins Folio.

---

[29] March 17, 1860. [30] See p. 184 of this work.

CHAPTER IX.

THE PERKINS FOLIO.—VALUE OF THE EMENDATIONS.

Mr. Collier's claim of originality for the "old corrector."

I HAVE already, more than once, in reply to Mr. Collier's statements about and claims for his "old corrector," reminded (or informed) my readers that his assumption of the novelty, to say nothing of the excellence (which I reserve for discussion), of the emendations in the Perkins Folio is not borne out by facts.

His own oversights partially accounted for.

Mr. Halliwell[1] accounts for Mr. Collier ignoring in so very many cases coincident criticisms, on the general ground that he,

> "compiling his volume of Notes with unusual rapidity, and under circumstances which rendered access to many books exceedingly inconvenient, * * * overlooked numerous early parallel conjectures;"

But Mr. Halliwell rightly remarks, that it is not so obvious why Mr. Collier should so often

> "have ignored coincident suggestions on the very page of his own edition to which he was referring."

[1] Observations on some of the Manuscript Emendations, &c. 1853, p. 13.

The difficulty of collation.

Collation is the process which brings these defaults to light; hitherto Mr. Collier has enjoyed an immunity from detection, in a vast number of cases, for a very obvious reason. The fact is, that collation is a very irksome task, and few who profess to perform it, ever do. I have very little faith in the professions of editors that they have re-collated the old copies: for, first, I am assured that few even go through the form of collation, but trust to their *Jennens*, and other works of the kind: and, secondly, I am confident that few of those who do collate bestow upon the operation the time and methodical pains, necessary to insure the two qualities which alone give a collation any value, viz. *exactness* and *completeness*. I have, for instance, verified Mr. Collier's collations of *Hamlet*, in the quarto 1603, and the folio 1632; and as to parts of the play, I have compared his collations with several other early quartos, and I can positively say that his collations are not to be relied upon. I am not sure that all men have the ability to collate; but I am sure that no man can collate correctly without special training.

How to determine the question of the old corrector's originality.

Now, in determining the question of the originality of the "old corrector," even in a single play, one has to perform the operation of making out a list of all the manuscript emendations of that play in the Perkins Folio (for none of Mr. Collier's lists can be relied upon), and then that of collating the list so formed with the leading editions and commentaries. Who would not shrink from such a labour? Mr.

Staunton himself did not go through this toil in preparing his collations for Mr. Hamilton's *Inquiry*. It is true that these gentlemen did make an exhaustive list of the manuscript emendations in *Hamlet*. They could hardly have chosen a more thickly annotated play. It is also true that Mr. Staunton collated this list with one of the *Variorum* editions, and with *Jennens*; and probably verified many of the collations by reference to particular editions and commentaries. This indeed could have been on slight labour. But it was not enough to insure perfection: the collations in Mr. Hamilton's *Inquiry*,[2] are not perfect. For instance, the lines

Mr. Staunton's table of the MS. alterations in *Hamlet*.

"No Faiery talkes, &c."[3]

and

"Roaming it thus, &c."[4]

in the first of which the "old corrector" cancels the "I;" and in the second, for "Roaming," substitutes *Running*, are passed over without reference to any old or modern edition. Now the fact is that the first correction is found in all the early quartos, and the second is an original emendation of Mr. Collier's, and is in the text of his edition 1841-1844.[5]

But let us suppose that we have at last a play, corrected by Perkins, collated with every known

The value of statistics of quantity.

[2] Page 34. [3] Page 35. [4] Page 37.

[5] The presumed absence of any coincidence in the collations of this play between the "old corrector" and any modern critic, has been made a point of by Mr. Merivale in "The Edinburgh Review, April, 1860."

edition and commentary. How much forwarder are we in determining the amount of originality in the "old corrector?" Does change merely for change's sake, do wanton alterations made with the single object of displaying a vast quantity of marginal readings, prove the possession of any original powers of verbal criticism? Certainly not. Any fool can mar Shakspere's text; and because he may have overlaid the text with an immense number of readings, by the exercise of unintelligent comparison, he is not to be credited with original genius. On the contrary, if we find that he has marred 99 readings for one he has amended, the inference is that he stole that one emendation, and that the 99 blunders or wanton changes are his own. What then, after all, is the use of a table of collations of the "old corrector's" labours, shewing how many readings have been traced to known sources, and how many appear to be novelties? Supposing two-thirds of the changes are new, what is the inference? Is it not plain that any available inference depends not merely on the statistics of quantity, but on the *value* of those changes with which he is credited. No mere preponderance of quantity can prove him to have possessed originality in the proper sense of that word. For instance, we read in *Love's Labour's Lost*, act iii. sc. 1,

"No salve in the male, sir."

The "old corrector" changes "the male" into *them all*, as Tyrwhitt did. Supposing he did not get this reading from Tyrwhitt, it certainly does not prove that the "old corrector" possessed any extraordinary intelligence. But it does prove him to have been as ignorant as Tyrwhitt must have been (when he made this alteration) of the meaning of a *male*—viz. *a wallet for herbs.*[6] This is an unusually favourable specimen of the manuscript corrections. The result of a lengthy examination which I have made of them is, that the majority shew less intelligence than the preceding; and that, if we exclude additions to the text made for the purpose of eking out lines, furnishing rhymes, and modernizing words, which in truth make up the vast bulk of them, their prevailing characteristic is that of altering (often in the most clumsy and stupid manner) phrases, the sense of which is perhaps not very obvious, so as to invest them with *an obvious senseless meaning;* and this by the process of changing words in the text into others but little or not at all like them, and adding to them *ad libitum* such letters or words as are necessary to piece out the new sentences. Here is an example of what I mean. How many hundred more might I not adduce!

> "So you to study now it is too late,
> That were to climb o'er th' house t' unlock the gate."

The "old corrector" cobbles this into,

> "So you *by* study now it is too late,
> Climb o'er the house-*top to* unlock the gate."

[6] See Collier, Coleridge and Shakespeare, pp. 70-76.

To inquire what felicity or appropriateness is in such an alteration, would be a mere waste of time: but to inquire how such changes prove originality in Mr. Perkins (except indeed original vulgarity and wantonness) is most instructive: for we thereby learn that no statistics of quantity can establish his claim to originality, in the proper sense of that word: and that the "old corrector" did not emendate as conscientious critics do, but laboured only to make a display of quantity, "as though he had foreseen the use that might afterwards be made of it."[1]

Conjectural experiment on the text of Shakspere.

Now, supposing that we have evidence that he worked with this motive: let us inquire what facilities the text of Shakspere provides for a miscreant so disposed. In point of fact I have, just by way of experiment, put myself in his shoes; and I find that without the exercise of much intelligence, by a mere verbal comparison and an observance of grammar, it is possible to turn out emendations, as good as the average of the "old corrector's," as fast as my late friend Mr. Cross turned out his *acari*. The following table exhibits the result:—

TEXT.	CORRECTION.
	Tempest.
It should the good ship so have swallowed, and The *freighting* souls within her. (Act I. sc. 2.)	It should the good ship so have swallowed, and *The frightened* souls within her.
One midnight *Fated* for the purpose, (Ibid.)	One midnight *Suited* for the purpose.

[1] Collier, Coleridge and Shakespeare, p. 45.

TEXT.	CORRECTION.
Two Gentlemen of Verona.	
If so, I pray thee, breathe it in mine ear, *As* ending anthem of my endless dolour. (Act III. sc. 1.)	If so, I pray thee, breathe it in mine ear,— *An* ending anthem of my endless dolour.
As you Like it.	
* *Good* my complexion! (Act III. sc. 2.)	*Hood* my complexion!
Winter's Tale.	
Make't thy question, and go *rot!* (Act II. sc. 1.)	Make't thy question, and go, *do't!*
Apollo's *angry;* and the heavens themselves Do strike at my injustice. (Act III. sc. 2.)	Apollo's *augury* and the heavens themselves Do strike at my injustice.
King John.	
Bedlam, have done. (Act II. sc. 1.)	*Beldame*, have done.
Creatures *of note* for mercy-lacking uses. (Act IV. sc. 1.)	Creatures *so naught* for mercy-lacking uses.
I K. Hen. IV.	
Why, thou whoreson, impudent, *embossed* rascal, (Act III. sc. 3.)	Why, thou whoreson, impudent, *deboshed* rascal,
II K. Hen. IV.	
That ever in the *haunch* of winter sings (Act IV. sc. 4.)	That ever in the *choir** of winter sings
Like a rich armour worn in heat of day, That *scalds* with safety. (Act IV. sc. 4.)	Like a rich armour worn in heat of day, That *scathes* with safety.
K. Hen. VIII.	
that their very labour Was to them as a *painting.* (Act I. sc. 1.)	that their very labour Was to them as a *panting.*
• In faith, for little England You'd venture an *emballing*: (Act II. sc. 3.)	In faith, for little England You'd venture an *ennobling.*

* The reader may suppose this to have been written partly on an erasure where an erased word (say, *chaunt* or *haunts*) is still legible! The Perkins Folio has very many such indications of *μετάνοια*. If such "second thoughts are best," "bad is the best."

Text.	Correction.
Troïlus and Cressida.	
And appetite, an universal wolf * * * * Must make perforce an universal prey, And *last* eat up himself. (Act I. sc. 3.)	And appetite, an universal wolf * * * * Must make perforce an universal prey, And *lust* eat up himself.
The *fool* slides o'er the ice that you should break. (Act III. sc. 3.)	The *foot* slides o'er the ice that you should break.
Timon of Athens.	
but moves itself In a *wide sea of wax:* (Act I. sc. 1.)	but moves itself In a *wide-waving* sea:
Leaving no *tract* behind. (Ibid.)	Leaving no *track* behind.
*But only *painted*, like his *varnish'd* friends? (Act IV. sc. 2.)	But only *transient* like his *vanish'd* friends?
Romeo and Juliet.	
but the kind prince, Taking thy part, hath rush'd aside the law. (Act III. sc. 3.)	but the kind prince, Taking thy part, hath *pushed* aside the law.
Julius Cæsar.	
O *then* by day Where wilt *thou* find a *cavern* dark enough To mask thy monstrous visage? (Act II. sc. 1.)	O where by day Wilt find a *craven visard* dark enough To mask thy monstrous visage?
Brutus. Kneel not gentle Portia. *Portia.* I should not *need*, if you were gentle Brutus. (Act II. sc. 1.)	*Brutus.* Kneel not gentle Portia. *Portia.* I should not *kneel*, if you were gentle, Brutus.
To *keep* with you at meals, comfort your bed, (Act II. sc. 1.)	To *help* your meals, *consort* with you at bed.
Macbeth.	
But float upon a wild and violent sea *Each* way *and* move (Act IV. sc. 2.)	But float upon a wild and violent sea *Which* way *we* move.
Profit *again* should hardly draw me *here*. (Act V. sc. 4.)	Profit *or gain* should hardly draw me *near*.
Hamlet.	
though I am native here, And to the *manner* born, it is a custom (Act I. sc. 4.)	though I am native here, And to the *manor* born, it is a custom
And for the day confin'd *to fast in* fires, (Act I. sc. 4.)	And for the day confined *fast to* fires
Nay, 'tis *twice* two months, my lord. (Act III. sc. 2.)	Nay, 'tis *quite* two months, my lord.
O my offence is rank, it smells to heaven, It hath the primal eldest curse upon't, (Act III. sc. 3.)	O my offence is rank, it smells to heaven, *And earth doth still cry out upon my fact;* It hath the primal eldest curse upon't,
* If it be so Laertes, *As* how should it be so? How otherwise?— (Act IV. sc. 1.)	If it be so Laertes,— How should it *not* be so? How otherwise?—

Text.	Correction.
Othello.	
(as it is a most pregnant and *unforced* position,) (Act II. sc. 1.)	(as it is a most pregnant and *enforced* position,)
And *shut* myself *up in* some other course, (Act III. sc. 4)	And *shunt* myself *upon* some other course,
O balmy breath, that dost almost persuade Justice to break her *sword*. (Act V. sc. 1.)	O balmy breath, that dost almost persuade Justice to break her *word*.
Anthony and Cleopatra.	
What of death too, That rids our dogs of *languish*? (Act V. sc. 2.)	What of death too, That rids our *days* of *anguish*?
Cymbeline.	
find The ooze, to shew what coast thy sluggish *crare* Might easiliest harbour in? (Act IV. sc. 2.)	find The ooze, to shew what coast thy sluggish *craft* Might easiliest harbour in?
bring thee all this; Yea and *furr'd* moss besides, when flowers are *none*, (Act IV. sc. 2.)	bring thee all this; Yea and *fetch* moss besides, when flowers are *gone*.
* having found the back-door open Of the unguarded *hearts*, Heavens, how they wound! (Act V. sc. 3.)	having found the back-door open Of the unguarded *harts*, Heavens, how they wound!
You good gods, give me The *penitent* instrument to pick that bolt, (Act V. sc. 4.)	You good gods, give me The *penetrant* instrument to pick that bolt,
Sonnet LXXVI. ***(Allusion to tobacco!)***	
Why write I still all one, ever the same, And *keep* invention in a noted weed?	Why write I still all one, ever the same, And *steep* invention in a noted weed?[*]

All these alterations belong to only one class of corrections, and that class contains a very small proportion of the manuscript emendations in the Perkins Folio. Yet those are just the changes which require some amount of ingenuity—little as

[*] Two I have struck out of my list, which I had discovered in the Perkins Folio. Perhaps it may not be superfluous to remind my readers that in order to perceive the plausibility of some of the foregoing "corrections," it is necessary to read and study the context which I have no room for here. I allude especially to those to which an asterisk (*) is prefixed.

it may be. It may be judged then, how little sagacity has to do with the perpetration of the residue of the manuscript emendations, which are the great majority. To shew this more plainly, I propose to divide the manuscript emendations of the Perkins Folio into classes.

Classification of the manuscript alterations.

I. Alterations of words supposed to have been misprinted. Here is a wide and legitimate sphere of conjectural criticism. There are but two considerations that give a conjecture a value as a probable restoration, viz. (α) Similarity in the conjectured word to the trace of the misprint, and (β) Thorough fitness in the conjectured word to satisfy the utmost requirement of the passage.

Example:—it will not *cool my* nature.

Twelfth Night, act i. sc. 3.

Correction by Theobald:—it will not *curl by* nature.

II. Insertions of words or phrases supposed to have been omitted by mistake. Here is a smaller, but still a legitimate sphere of conjectural criticism; as in so many cases, in which a word is omitted, the context supplies abundant evidence of the nature of the omission. But no editor ought to admit such conjectures into his text, except where the evidence in their favour is overwhelming. In general they should be relegated to the notes: since from the nature of the case it is but seldom that the evidence is sufficient; and the more numerous the wanting words are, the less is the probability that the lost phrase will be supplied *verbatim*, and the less there is to guide conjecture in that wider exercise of ingenuity. Accordingly, conjecture here is apt to sink into a mere exercise of ingenuity; and its happiest efforts are often clouded with doubt.

Example :—*Item*, She is not to be fasting,

Two Gentlemen of Verona, act iii. sc. 1.

Correction by Rowe: *Item*, She is not to be *kissed* fasting,

III. Omissions of words supposed to have been inserted by mistake. Here again is a very limited but legitimate sphere of conjectural criticism. It is only where a word has been repeated, as if caught by the compositor from a contiguous or proximate word (as from a word in the same, or in a next higher or lower line), that its omission would be justifiable, and then only with a view to eliminate some obvious corruption of the text.

Examples :—King, father, royal Dane: oh *oh* answer me.

Hamlet, act i. sc. 4.

Corrected by Rowe from the 4tos. :—

King, father, royal Dane: oh answer me.

One *chief* speech in it I chiefly remember.

Ibid. act ii. sc. 2.

Corrected by Rowe from the 4tos. :—

One speech in it I chiefly remember.

IV. Transpositions; substitutions of the plural for the singular, or *vice versâ*; alterations in the tense of a verb by the simple addition or omission of a letter (as s or d); and other such simple, but *material* changes of the text.

V. Changes of punctuation and spelling.

VI. Insertions of or changes in stage-directions, names of speakers, and divisions into acts and scenes.

The manuscript alterations of the Perkins Folio being divided into these classes, it is found that class I. contains the greatest number of changes, General results.

and class III. the least. It is also found that class I. is for the most part filled with substitutions of words or phrases for others not understood by the "old corrector," or reckoned obsolete by him, and so liable to be not understood by readers; and that class II. is filled with additions to the text which are altogether uncalled for, and could only have been inserted for the purpose of mending (according to the "old corrector's" notions of improvement) the poet's measure, and introducing a foot or a rhyme where in all probability none was designed. In a word—that in classes I. and II. the "old corrector" is not playing the editor but the censor, and a very ignorant and tasteless censor he is.

The system of classification applied to the manuscript alterations in Hamlet.

I will now take the play of *Hamlet*, and distribute the manuscript readings as they are given in the table at p. 34 of Mr. Hamilton's *Inquiry* into these six classes.

I will simply premise that in class I. I have given the printed reading of the folio 1632 in the first column; the Perkins gloss in the second column; and the names of editors and commentators who have anticipated the Perkins reading in the third column. Where the names of two or more editors or commentators are given, it is to be presumed that they independently suggested the reading opposite which their names stand. The pairs of alterations which are printed in italics are synonymous. Throughout the six classes I have indicated those manuscript alterations which have been more or less obliterated from the Perkins Folio by an asterisk (*).

Hamlet.

CLASS I.

Folio 1632.	Perkins.	Commentator or editor.
now [struck]	new [struck]	Steevens
*beating	tolling	
*[seiz'd] on	[seiz'd] in	
*return'd	remain'd	
*design'd	then sign'd	
foreknowing	*foreknowledge*	
beare	bathe	
*his	this	
nightly	*nightlike*	
*beteene	let e'en	Theobald
who?	whom	Johnson
bestill'd	bechill'd	
his [temple]	the [temple]	Hanmer
watchmen	watchman	
cheff	choise	Steevens
Roaming	Running	Collier
bonds	bawds	Theobald
slander	squander	
sonnet	summit	Rowe
your soveraignty of	you of your soveraign	
*fast in	lasting	Heath
despatcht	despoiled	
hurling	hurting	
four	for	Hanmer
sallets	salt	Pope
*received	conceived	
passion in	passionate	[Hanmer and Capell read *passioned.*]
oppression	transgression	
becke	backe	
pratling	painting	[Theobald reads *paintings*]

Folio 1632.	Perkins.	Commentator or editor.
his [guard]	a [guard]	Jennens
a [suite]	no [suite]	
cart	carr	Rowe
*seasons	poisons	
it now	her vow	
hesitate	must take	Theobald
rac'd	rais'd	Steevens
my [affair]	the [affair]	
prize	purse	
silence	sconce	Hanmer and Warburton
set	send	
step	stoop	
time	fume	
set	see	
hops	hopes	Johnson
Lord	*King*	
goe to thy [death-bed]	gone to his [death-bed]	
of [all Christian souls]	*on* [all Christian souls]	Johnson
stood	sole	
his [envy]	hir [envy]	
deduced	*reduced*	
Yaugan	You'	
sage	sad	
spleenative	*splenatick*	
and [Dog]	the [Dog]	Theobald
be [rashness]	to [rashness]	
know	owne	
paulo	faile	Pope
Assis	Asses	Johnson
sement	sequell	(4tos. read sequent.)
*he throw	be thrown	
same	scene	
63	41	22

In this class there are also ninety corrections which have been derived from the old copies. Mr. H. Merivale, in "The Edinburgh Review,"[10] complained of Mr. Hamilton for having selected a play for examination which exists in so many early quarto editions:[11] inasmuch as even supposing that the "old corrector" did derive his readings from manuscript or conjecture, those readings, if right, must have often coincided with the early quartos: and the greater might be the number of quartos with various readings, the greater amount of coincidence would result. By separating those readings which agree with the readings of the old copies, this objection is obviated.

CLASS II.

4to. 1604.	The perfume and suppliance of a minute No more.
fo. 1632.	The suppliance of a minute; No more.
Perkins.	The suppliance of a minute; *but* no more.
4to. 1604. and fo. 1632.	And hath given countenance to his speech,
Perkins.*	And hath given (qu. giv'n) countenance to *it in* his speech,
4to. 1604.	Looke too't I charge you, come your wayes.
fo. 1632.	Look too't, I charge you; come your way.
Perkins.	Look too't, I charge you; *so now* come your way.
4to. 1604.	O most pernicious woman.
fo. 1632.	Oh most pernicious woman!
Perkins.	Oh most pernicious *and perfidious* woman!

---

[10] April, 1860.

[11] He modestly says *three*. There are in fact *five* quarto editions published before 1612, if we count the missing 4to. of 1609, and do not count the dateless 4to.

4to. 1604.	To keepe those many many bodies safe
fo. 1632.	To keepe those many bodies safe
Perkins.	To keepe those *verie* many bodies safe
4to. 1604.	a certaine convocation of politique wormes
fo. 1632.	a certaine convocation of wormes
Perkins.	a certaine convocation of *palated* wormes.
4to. 1604.	Woo't weepe, woo't fight, woo't fast, woo't teare thy selfe
fo. 1632.	Woo't weepe? woo't fight? woo't teare thy selfe?
Perkins.	Woo't weepe? woo't fight? woo't *storme or* teare thy selfe?
4to. 1604.	Ile doo't, doost come heere to whine?
fo. 1632.	Ile doo't. Dost thou come here to whine;
Perkins.	Ile doo't *Ile doo't*. Dost thou come here to whine;
4to. 1604.	Tis dangerous when the baser nature comes
fo. 1632.	Tis dangerous when baser nature comes
Perkins.	Tis dangerous when *a* baser nature comes.
4to. 1604.	Heere *Hamlet* take my napkin rub thy browes,
fo. 1632.	Here's a Napkin, rub thy browes,
Perkins.	Here is a Napkin, rub thy browes *my sonne*,
4to. 1604.	Is strict in his arrest, ô I could tell you,
fo. 1632.	Is strick't in this Arrest) oh I could tell you,
Perkins.*	Is strick't in this Arrest) oh I could tell you *all*,

In this class there are also eighteen corrections derived from the old copies. All, but one, of the specified eleven additions were obviously made to eke out the measure of the heroic lines. The last (*all*) was intended to perfect the line,

Had I but time, oh I could tell you,

the "old corrector" having struck through the portions of lines included in the parenthesis,

(as this fell sergeant, death,
Is strict in this Arrest,)

CLASS III.

4to. 1604.	*Hora.* Haile to your Lordship. *Ham.* I am glad to see you well;
fo. 1632.	*Hora.* Haile to your Lordship. *Ham.* I am glad to see you *well:*
Perkins.	*Hora.* Hail to your Lordship *Ham.* I am glad to see you:
4to. 1604.	And shall I coupple hell, ô fie, hold, hold my hart,
fo. 1632.	And shall I couple hell? Oh fie: hold *my* heart;
Perkins.	And shall I couple hell? O fie: hold heart;
4to. 1604.	Why what an Asse am I, this is most brave,
fo. 1632.	Who? what an Asse am I? *I sure,* this is most brave,
Perkins.	Why what an Asse am I, this is most brave,

In this class there are also nine corrections derived from the old copies.

The contents of the other three classes I shall not specify, but only the number of alterations in each. The six classes, accordingly, thus stand:—

CLASS.	No. of changes.
I.	153
II.	29
III.	12
IV.	33
V.	99
VI.	94
	420

There are, also, half a dozen anomalous glosses, not included in these classes.

I do not propose to weary the reader with an analysis of all these alterations. Not one of those to which the name of no editor or commentator is appended has been received into any edition of Shakspere, with the exception of two of Mr. Collier's editions, where of course many of them will be found advocated and explained by their admiring sponsor.

I shall, however, examine at length some of those emendations of the Perkins Folio, on which Mr. Collier has, as it were, rested the credit of his "old corrector."

Many of the glosses in class I. appear to have been arrived at by a legitimate, though very infelicitous and not very intelligent exercise of conjecture.

The design of Chapter III. of *The Shakspeare Fabrications.*

In the third chapter of my former work I pointed out several instances in which the "old corrector's" emendations appeared to me to have been manufactured by an ingenious use of parallel passages in Shakspere. My object was to raise a presumption against the corrector having obtained them from any authoritative source, in opposition to those who, judging of the critical powers of others by their own, had pronounced the emendations such as no critical sagacity could have arrived at.

Charges of The Literary Gazette and Saturday Review.

In this course I was taken to task by writers in "The Literary Gazette" and "The Saturday Review." The reviewer of "The Literary Gazette"[11] reminds me

"that there is no style of emendation so trustworthy as that which is derived exclusively from an author himself. To explain Shakspeare by Shakspeare is only acting on a maxim of which we should have expected no classical scholar to forget the value."

[11] Sept. 17, 1859.

This remark would have been in point, and of value, if I had exposed the process of manufacture of the Perkins emendations with the object of disproving them. But my object was to shew that, were they good or bad, right or wrong, they were to be referred to conjectural criticism, and consequently that there was no need to suppose that the "old corrector" had (as Mr. Collier and others believed) access to manuscript or better copies than we possess. Indeed I expressly endorsed one of the emendations which I considered to have been so arrived at, believing it to be a restoration of the text of Shakspere.

Reply to Literary Gazette.

The writer in the "Saturday Review"[13] makes a similar observation. He says,

"Dr. Ingleby undertakes to show the "process" by which some of the more important emendations have been "manufactured." But he succeeds only in showing that they are supported by very subtle analogies of expression in other passages of Shakspeare. Did it not occur to him that if the emendations were true they would be Shakspeare's, and that Shakspeare would write like himself?"

It certainly did not escape me that if the emendations were real restorations (or "true," as the reviewer oddly phrases it), they would be Shakspere's! But though Shakspere sometimes wrote like himself *in the same play*, I am convinced that his richness of thought and "infinite variety" of expression was such, that an emendation in one play, arrived at by the consideration of a parallel passage

Reply to The Saturday Review.

[13] April 21, 1860.

in another, is far from being a reliable means of restoring the corrupted word or phrase.

The new line in *Winter's Tale.*

Among the various examples I adduced in illustration of my position, were two of the ten or eleven "lost lines," for the recovery of which Mr. Collier invokes the gratitude of his generation.[14] One of these was inserted in *Winter's Tale,* act v. sc. 3. Leontes, who is standing with Perdita, Antigonus, Paulina and others before the statue of Hermione, says,

"Do not draw the curtain.
Paulina. No longer shall you gaze on't; lest your fancy
May *think anon* it moves.
Leontes. Let be, let be.
Would I were dead, but that *methinks already* —"

* * * *

"And then he broke the sentence in his heart
Abruptly, as a man upon his tongue
May break it, when his passion masters him."[15]

Had he finished what he had begun he would doubtless have said,

"Let be, let be.
Would I were dead, but that methinks already
It does move."

---

[14] "Truly," as the reviewer in "Blackwood's Magazine," (August, 1853), well says, "we must be thankful for small mercies! Mr. Collier may be assured that the very thing which Leontes says most strongly, by implication in this speech is, that he is *not* stone looking upon stone."

In amusing contrast to this intelligent note, a wiseacre in "The North American Review," (April, 1854), gravely tells us that "it would almost argue insanity to doubt [the] genuineness" of the new line!

[15] Idylls of the King, p. 47.

Plainly *methinks already* is antithetical to *think anon.* Though we have here an example of *aposiopesis*, yet the context clearly shews what Leontes *intended* to have said when he began,

"Would I were dead, but that methinks already—"

where his very thoughts were broken off by his emotion. If Shakspere had supplied the missing words, as he might very well have done without interfering with the music of the lines, we should rather have been losers than gainers. We should have lost one of the sublimest instances of implied passion, in all Shakspere.

We can fancy, then, in what a state of dulness the perceptions of the "old corrector" must have been when it occurred to him to interpolate the line,

"I am but dead stone looking upon stone."

The passage accordingly stands thus:—

"Let be, let be.
Would I were dead, but that methinks already
I am but dead stone looking upon stone.
What was he that did make it?" &c.

Mr. Staunton's remarks[16] on this piece of tawdry are so excellent, that I shall offer no apology for quoting them at length. Mr. Staunton's note.

"To a reader of taste and sensibility, the art by which the emotions of Leontes are developed in this situation, from the moment when with an apparent feeling of disappointment he first beholds the "so much wrinkled" statue, and gradually becomes impressed, amazed, enthralled, till at length, borne along by a wild, tumultuous throng of indefinable sensations, he

[16] Edition, vol. iii. p. 250.

reaches that grand climax where, in delirious rapture, he clasps the figure to his bosom and faintly murmurs,—

"O, she's warm!"

must appear consummate. Mr. Collier and his annotator, however, are not satisfied. To them the eloquent abruption,—

"—but that, methinks, already—
What was he that did make it?"

is but a blot, and so, to add "to the force and clearness of the speech of *Leontes*," they stem the torrent of his passion in midstream and make him drivel out,—

"Would I were dead, but that, methinks, already
I am but dead, stone looking upon stone."!

Can anything be viler? Conceive Leontes whimpering of himself as "dead," just when the thick pulsation of his heart could have been heard! and speaking of the statue as a "stone" at the very moment when, to his imagination, it was flesh and blood! Was it thus Shakspeare wrought? The insertion of such a line in such a place is absolutely monstrous, and implies, both in the forger and the utterer, an entire incompetence to appreciate the finer touches of his genius. But it does more, for it betrays the most discreditable ignorance of the current phraseology of the poet's time. When *Leontes* says,—

"Would I were dead, but that methinks, already—"

Mr. Collier's annotator, and Mr. Collier, and all the advocates of the intercalated line, assume him to mean,—"I should desire to die, only that I am already dead or holding converse with the dead;" whereas, in fact, the expression, "*Would I were dead*," &c. is neither more nor less than an imprecation, equivalent to—"*Would I may die*," &c.; and the King's real meaning, in reference to Paulina's remark, that he will think *anon* it moves, is "May I die, if I do not think it moves *already*." In proof of this, take the following examples, which might easily be multiplied a hundred-fold, of similar forms of speech:—

"——and, *would I might be dead*,
If I in thought—" &c.

The Two Gentlemen of Verona, Act IV. Sc. 4.

"*Would I had no being,*
If this salute my blood a jot."
Henry VIII. Act II., Sc. 3.

"*The gods rebuke me, but* it is a tidings
To wash the eyes of kings."
Antony and Cleopatra, Act V., Sc. 1.

"*Would I with thunder presently might die*
So I might speak."
Summer's Last Will and Testament.

"——*Let me suffer death*
If in my apprehension—" &c.
BEAUMONT *and* FLETCHER's *Play of the "Night-Walker,"* Act III., Sc. 6.

"*Would I were dead,*" &c.
"If I do know," &c.
BEN JONSON's *Tale of a Tub*, Act II., Sc. 1."

The "old corrector," then, committed here three blunders.

The "old corrector's" three blunders in one.

1st, He mistook the phrase, "Would I were dead, but that methinks," &c. for a wish for death; whereas it was a common adjuration, like the Jewish form, "God do so to me and more also if I do not think, &c."

2ndly, Thus mistaking the adjuration, "Would I were dead," he entirely overlooked the obvious reference of "You'll *think anon*," to "Me*thinks already*."

3rdly, He failed to observe that it is at this moment that Leontes begins to believe that the statue is living flesh and blood; wherefore he makes Leontes speak of it as "dead stone."

The result of his abominable patchwork is, in fact,

susceptible of only one meaning, viz. God is my witness that methinks I am already only dead!

And this is the restoration which Mr. Collier tells us we may be thankful for.[13]

Mr. Dyce's notes.

However strange it may appear, it is nevertheless a fact that Mr. Dyce once thought the line supplied by the "old corrector," "Shakspearian:" but it is infinitely more astonishing to learn that he now thinks it "too Shakspearian!" Surely Mr. Dyce is quite wrong in implying that Shakspere, "whose variety of expression was inexhaustible," would not have repeated himself. If one generalized truth in Shakesperian criticism be more certain and unexceptionable than another, it is this—that in the same play Shakspere frequently repeats the same expression, especially if it be an unwonted one with him. Thus, "hest" occurs many times in the *Tempest*; "father" or "mother," used in a symbolical sense, several times in *Cymbeline*; "comfort," in the sense of *strengthen*, several times in *Winter's Tale*; "shows," in the sense of *apparel*, and "assay," in the sense of *rescue* or *onset*, occur frequently in *Hamlet*, and so on.

The fact is that Mr. Dyce, like Mr. Collier, does not seem to have been aware of the phrase, "would I were dead," being an adjuration, and nothing more. Had he known this, he would hardly have found anything Shaksperian in the new line. I believe that

[13] Notes and Emendations, 1st and 2nd Ed. p. 197.

[14] Few Notes, p. 81, and Strictures, p. 88.

Mr. Dyce is perfectly correct in his version of the process of manufacture of this precious "restoration." The "old corrector" observed, that Leontes has previously said,—

"*Does not the stone rebuke me*
For being more stone than it? O royal piece,
There's magic in thy majesty, which has
My evils conjur'd to remembrance, and
From thy admiring daughter took the spirits,
Standing like stone with thee."

And from the lines in italic type he readily manufactured the line,—

"I am but dead stone looking upon stone,"

and the line which it supplanted,—

"I am but dead looking upon dead stone."[15]

The new line in *Coriolanus.*

Another of these miraculously felicitous lines was inserted in *Coriolanus*, act iii. sc. 2. Here Volumnia entreats the hero in these words,—

"Pray be counsell'd;
I have a heart as little apt as yours,
But yet a brain, that leads my use of anger
To better vantage."

There is an obvious hitch here. "Apt" it is true might be strained to bear the sense of *pliable*. But the difficulty is in the words "my use of anger." This should have reference to something preceding; which is not the case, since the attempts to bend the wills of obstinate people, ("headstrong wills"[16])

---

[15] See p. 89.

[16] So the late Mr. W. Sidney Walker reads the passage in Measure for Measure, act i. sc. 4.

does not of necessity, or by implication, provoke their anger. Mr. Staunton very ingeniously proposes to substitute *of mettle* for "as little." "A heart of apt mettle," is indeed sense: but "mettle" is *temper*, and is therefore not equivalent to "anger."

So the difficulty still remains. The "old corrector" evades it by interpolating a line; and a most ingenious one it is. Let us review the process by which it must have been manufactured.

"Use of anger" or "anger" would, in all probability have occurred in the lost line, if there had been one; for Volumnia employs the phrase "use of anger" apparently in *apposition* to a foregoing phrase of the same purport. To illustrate this, let us consult the following passage in the *Merchant of Venice*, act iii. sc. 2:—

"Yet look, how far
The substance of my praise doth wrong this shadow
In underprizing it, so far this shadow
Doth limp behind the substance."

Here is a like *apposition*. Now let us suppose that the line,

"The substance of my praise doth wrong *this shadow*"

had been omitted by the compositor; and that, in consequence of the recurrence of "his shadow," in the next line, which he duly printed, he did not perceive the omission of which he had been guilty. The passage then would stand thus:—

"Yet look, how far
In underprizing it, so far this shadow
Doth limp behind the substance."

Every intelligent reader would perceive that something had been omitted here. Some critics would convert "so" into *how*, (*more* Rowe and cobblers like him;) but I apprehend a critic of a little more than ordinary skill, even if he did not succeed in recovering the lost line, would readily manufacture one extremely like it.

He could not fail to perceive, 1st, that the line lost is substantially this:—

"*My estimate of this shadow wrongs it;*"

and, 2ndly, that "this shadow," must end the line, to account for the misprint having escaped correction. He would then reconstruct the line—perhaps thus:—

"*My estimate of it wrongs this shadow;*"

or rhythmically,

"*The purport of my censure wrongs this shadow.*"

By a very felicitous conjecture, guided by a not unusual Shaksperian antithesis, he might be led to put *substance* for "purport;" and his ear might lead him to put a monosyllable for "censure," followed by *doth*—and he would recover the lost line.

I grant that this would, under all the circumstances, be an unlikely result; and that inasmuch as satisfactory verification is impossible, conjectural criticism cannot be allowed the license of guessing at lost lines, except for the purpose of illustration and exposition.

The "old corrector" observed this method of conjecture in the passage in *Coriolanus*—"As little apt as yours." To do what? he asked: To forego the use of anger, under provocation.

He would thus easily arrive at the line,

"To brook control without the use of anger;"

or,

"To brook reproof without the use of anger;"

"use of anger," in either case closing the line, in order to account for the compositor overlooking the misprint. But neither of these lines can be what Shakspere wrote: "without the *use* of anger," is quite unshaksperian. Coriolanus' demeanour was not *a use* with a view to a *vantage* of some sort, but the natural effect of anger not repressed, behaved or regulated under the purpose of volition. It was this defect in Coriolanus that Brutus urged the people to take advantage of:—[17]

"You should have ta'en *the advantage of his choler*,
And pass him unelected."

Again,

"If, as his nature is, he fall in rage
With their refusal, both observe and answer
The vantage of his anger."

I should therefore prefer to read,

Vol. "I have a heart as little apt as yours
To brook reproof, and not bewray my anger,
But yet a brain that leads my use of anger
To better vantage."

While, therefore, I have shewn how the "old corrector" manufactured his line, I have assigned

---

[17] Act ii. sc. 3.

valid reasons why the line which he manufactured could not have been written by Shakspere.

As I have said; these two examples were given in my former work: but they have received a more matured and more extensive consideration in these pages. These have been repeated, simply because they are the two most remarkable of the *entire lines* derived from the Perkins Folio. I shall not avail myself of any other examples, shewing the process of manufacture of emendations, which have already appeared in my *Shakspeare Fabrications*.

I will now proceed to consider some of the emendations on which Mr. Collier has staked the "old corrector's" credit; and which he has made his *chevaux de bataille* in his *Reply*, p. 64, as well as in the Introduction to his *Notes and Emendations*. I shall shew conclusively that these have been conjecturally arrived at, and are besides totally unworthy of adoption.

In the *Merchant of Venice*, act iv. sc. 1, Shylock is enumerating the involuntary affections resulting from the presence of odious objects:— "Woollen," v. *bollen.*

"Some men there are love not a gaping pig;
Some, that are mad if they behold a cat;
And others, when the bag-pipe *sings i' the nose*
Cannot contain their urine: for affection,
Master of passion, sways it to the mood
Of what it likes or loathes. Now, for your answer—
As there is no firm reason to be render'd,
Why he cannot abide a gaping pig;
Why he, a harmless necessary cat;
Why he, a *woollen* bag-pipe, &c."

So the folio. The "old corrector" reads *bollen* for "woollen," a word which he might have obtained from his Bible; but at any rate, as a reader of Shakspere's poems, he could not have failed to have associated the passage under consideration with one in *The Rape of Lucrece.*

"Here one, being throng'd, bears back, all *boll'n* and red."

Mr. Dyce's note.

Mr. Dyce adopts *bollen, vice* "woollen," in preference to Steevens' *swollen;* and is as firmly convinced as I am that "woollen" is a corruption. The reason Mr. Dyce well explains to be,

"that Shylock *does not intend the most distant allusion to the material which either composed or covered the bag-pipe;*"

Monck Mason's note.

and he quotes Monck Mason's note,

"it is to be observed, that it is not by the sight of the bagpipe that the persons alluded to are affected, but by the sound."

How, in the face of this remark, Mr. Dyce can have adopted the "old corrector's" *bollen* surpasses my ability to understand.[18] If, as is evident, it is the

[18] The physical fact referred to in the text of the *Merchant of Venice*, is a frequent subject of remark with Elizabethan writers. Thus, in *The Optick Glasse of Humors*, 1607, folio 70, we read, "*Julius Scalliger* relates a mery tale of a certaine man of good esteeme, that sitting at the table at meate if he chaunc'd to heare the lute plaid upon, tooke such a conceit at the sound or something else that he could not hould his urine, but was constrained eft to" * * * the catastrophe being

sight of the pig or the cat that affects some men, and the *sound* of the bag-pipe as it "sings i' the nose," that affects others, surely Capell's suggestion must at least be near the trace of the lost word, viz. *wauling*. Mr. Brae and myself independently proposed the same reading, neither being aware of having been anticipated by Capell. But Mr. Brae did not rest satisfied with *wauling*; five years consideration enabled that excellent critic to make it edge nearer to the existing misprint by taking *waul* in the shape of a passive participle in en, i.e. *waulen*, or *waullen*—or even *wollen*, which would almost coincide with the existing word. The bag-pipe being inanimate cannot, strictly speaking, *waul*, but to sound at all it must be *made to waul*. It is therefore heard *waulen*, rather than *wauling*. Similarly, "fallen" is a neuter verb with a participial construction; and it is also similar in *sound*.

Capell's emendation.

Mr. Brae's reading.

I am not yet convinced of the expediency of this after-refinement upon *wauling*, and should think *waulin'* a perfectly satisfactory emendation; in comparison with which *swollen* and *bollen* are very bad.

---

somewhat too graphically and broadly described for modern "ears polite." So in *Every Man in his Humour*, act iv. sc. 1, E. Knowell asks,—

"What ails thy brother? Can he not hold his water at reading a ballad?

Wellbred. O, no; a rhyme to him is worse than cheese, or a bagpipe:"

Probably Mr. Dyce, as a Scotsman, scouted Capell's suggestion, on the ground of its being somewhat uncomplimentary to the "martial noise" of his fatherland. However that may be, it is the most expressive epithet that could be found for that most distressing sound, wherein to find music or take pleasure one must surely have first acquired a very peculiar taste and very considerable nerve.

"Degrees" *v. diseases.*

In 2 *Hen. IV.* act i. sc. 2, Falstaff is deploring his being victimised at once by the want of money and the "evils" of age and youth. He says,

"A man can no more separate age and covetousness than he can part with young limbs and lechery: but the gout galls the one, and the pox pinches the other; and so both the *degrees* prevent my curses."

In both the Perkins Folio and Mr. Singer's corrected folio, "degrees" is superseded by *diseases.* That both correctors obtained this from the following speech of Falstaff is evident:

"I can get no remedy against this consumption of the purse: borrowing only lingers and lingers it out,[*] but the *disease* is incurable. * * * A pox of this gout! a gout of this pox! for the one or the other pinches my great toe. It is no matter if I do halt; I have the wars for my colour, and my pension shall seem the more reasonable. A good wit will make use of anything: I will turn *diseases* to commodity."

Hence it might be very plausibly inferred that these

---

[*] This passage shews that Mr. J. Hayward is in error in supposing that the verb *to linger* is not transitive. See his *Translation of Faust*, 4th ed. 1847, Preface, p. xvii.

are the "diseases" which "prevent," or go before, Falstaff's curses.

Plausible as this emendation unquestionably is, it by no means clears the passage; and is besides totally devoid of the characteristic humour of Falstaff.

In *Troïlus and Cressida*, act iii. sc. 3, in a speech of Achilles, the Perkins Folio has a correction which has been adopted by all modern editors. The hero says, "Married" *v. mirror'd.*

> "The beauty, that is borne here in the face
> The bearer knows not, but[20] commends itself
> To others' eyes: nor doth the eye itself
> (That most pure spirit of sense) behold itself,
> Not going from itself; but eye to eye oppos'd
> Salutes each other with each other's form.
> For speculation turns not to itself,
> Till it hath travell'd, and is *married* there,
> Where it may see itself."

Here the Perkins corrector substitutes *mirror'd* for "married;" and Mr. Singer's corrected folio has the same emendation.

I have no doubt both correctors obtained the hint for this alteration from *Julius Cæsar*, act i. sc. 2, where Cassius asks:—

> "Tell me, good Brutus, can you see your face?
> *Brutus.* No, Cassius; for the eye sees not itself,
> But by reflexion by some other things.
> *Cassius.* 'Tis just:
> And it is very much lamented, Brutus,

---

[20] Understand *it*, immediately before "commends."

> That you have no such *mirrors* as will turn
> Your hidden worthiness into your eye,
> That you might see your shadow."

Mirror'd for "married," is just one of those emendations which beguile the judgment, lull criticism, and enlist our love of the surprizing and ingenious. But it is not sound. It is so *plausible* that were it the original word of the text, no one could find fault with it: but it is otherwise when it is an alien challenging admission, to the exclusion of the present occupant: we must not then be dazzled by plausibility; we must probe it beneath the surface, and only admit it on two conditions:—1. The supplanted word must be incapable of good interpretation. 2. The substitute must be free from all chance of favouring *misinterpretation* of that which it seems to improve. Now, in the present case, I do not think that either of these conditions is fulfilled by *mirror'd*. The question turns upon this, Is the reflexion meant to be *figurative* or *real?* Now in the passage I have quoted from *Julius Cæsar*, the word "reflexion" is certainly used in its physical or moral sense:

> "the eye sees not itself
> But by *reflexion*,"

There *mirrors* is used figuratively. But in the passage in *Troïlus and Cressida* no *optical* reflexion is described upon which a figurative use of *mirror'd* could be founded: the eye is not here described as seeing itself by reflexion; but it

> "Commends itself to *others'* eyes."

and

"eye to eye opposed
Salutes *each other* with *each other's* form."

So that there are two pair of eyes regarding *each other*. Whereas if the notion were that of optical reflexion, it would be the eye's *own form* that would salute it, and not *another's*. Therefore I say that inasmuch as the eye arrives at a knowledge of its own form by seeing a *fellow* eye, the original expression "*married*," i. e. *fellowed*, is more in harmony with the context than the Perkins emendation.

Suum cuique. It is due to Mr. Brae, to say, that until I had received his defence of the original text I was ensnared by this specious and most ingenious emendation. The defence I have given is substantially his own.

In *Coriolanus*, act iii. sc. 1, the hero says,

"Bosome multiplied" *v. bisson multitude.*

"They [the people] know, the corn
Was not our[21] recompense, resting well assur'd
They ne'er did service for 't: being press'd to the war,
Even when the navel of the state was touch'd,
They would not thread the gates: this kind of service
Did not deserve corn gratis: being i' the war,
Their mutinies and revolts, wherein they show'd
Most valour, spoke not for them: the accusation
Which they have often made against the senate,
All cause unborn, could never be the native[22]
Of our so frank donation. Well, what then?
How shall this *bosom multiplied* digest
The senate's courtesy?"

---

[21] Query, *for*, *vice* "our."

[22] For "native," Monck Mason reads *motive*.

In the folio "bosom" is spelled *bosome*. For "bosom multiplied," the "old corrector" reads *bisson multitude*. On this emendation being communicated by Mr. Collier to "The Athenæum,"[23] the late Mr. Singer immediately gave in his adhesion to it.[24]

Mr. Singer's adoption of the Perkins reading.

Mr. Halliwell,[25] speaking of this reading, says,—

Mr. Halliwell's adoption.

"This, more than any other, gives hopes of important results; and it does something more than this: it opens a reasonable expectation that the MS. corrector had, in some cases, recollection of the passages as they were delivered in representation. Once establish a probability of this, and although many of the corrections must still be looked upon as conjectural, the volume will be of high value. The correction "*bisson multitude*" seems to me to be clearly one of those alterations that no conjectural ingenuity could have suggested."

This is certainly a curious note. Surely the correction in question was an obvious one: for this reason; previously, in the same play,[26] Menenius has said to the tribunes,

"What harm can your *bisson* conspectuities glean out of this character, if I be known well enough too!"

In the folio "bisson" here is spelled *beesome*. *Beesome* has been corrected into "bisson" by the editors. With this example under the nose of a critic, he could not fail to suggest the application of

[23] March 27th, 1852.

[24] Notes and Queries, 1st Series, vol. v. p. 480.

[25] Notes and Queries, 1st Series, vol. v. p. 484.

[26] Act ii. sc. 1.

the same correction to "Bosome multiplied," and when once "bosome" had been turned into *bisson*, it would be the next thing to impossible to avoid perceiving the plausibility of changing "multiplied" into *multitude*; and the "old corrector's" emendation is arrived at by a pure conjectural process.

The publication of Mr. Singer's and Mr. Halliwell's adhesion to this remarkable emendation at once called Mr. Brae into the field. It would be impossible for me to give the reader of this work an adequate notion of the power of A. E. B.'s paper in "Notes and Queries,"[27] without copious extracts from it: so I prefer giving *in extenso* the *five* grounds on which he rejected *bisson multitude*.

A. E. B.'s defence of the text.

"1. Because the apologue of the "belly and the members," in the first scene, gives its tone to the prevailing metaphor throughout the whole play. Hence the frequent recurrence of such images as "the many-headed multitude," "the beast with many heads butts me away," "the horn and noise of the monster," "the *tongues* of the *common mouth*," &c.; and hence a strong probability that, in any given place, the same metaphor will prevail.

2. Because in *Coriolanus* there are three several expressions having a remarkable resemblance in common, viz.:

"multiplying spawn,"
"multitudinous tongue,"
"bosom multiplied,"

and the concurrence of these three is strongly presumptive of the authenticity of any one of them.

3. Because, in the speech wherein *bosom multiplied* occurs—

[27] 1st Series, vol. vi. p. 20.

the matter in discussion being the policy of having given corn to the people *gratis*—when *Coriolanus* exclaims, "Whoever gave that counsel, *nourished* disobedience, *fed* the ruin of the State;" these two words of themselves, seem intended to be metaphorical to the subject: but when he goes on to inquire, "how shall this bosom multiplied *digest* the senate's courtesy," it becomes manifest that *digest* continues the metaphor which *nourished* and *fed* had begun. And if, in addition, it can be shown that *bosom* was commonly used as *the seat of digestion*, then the inference appears to be irresistible, that *bosom multiplied* is a phrase expressly introduced *to complete the metaphor*. Now, that *bosom* was so used, and by Shakspeare, is easily proved. Here is one example, from the Second Part of *Henry IV.* act i. sc. 3.

"Thou beastly feeder
. . . . . disgorge thy glutton bosom."

But I shall go still further: I assert that Shakspeare nowhere has used *digest* in the purely mental sense; that is, without some reference, real or figurative, to the animal function of the stomach. Certainly there is one *seeming* exception; but even that, when examined into, arises from a palpable misinterpretation, which, when corrected, returns with redoubled force in favour of the assertion. I refer to the apologue of "the belly and the members," already alluded to, in which the following passage is, in all the editions, as far as I am aware, pointed in this way:

"The senators of Rome are this good belly,
And you the mutinous members: For examine
Their counsels and their cares; digest things rightly,
Touching the weal o' the common; you shall find
No public benefit, which you receive,
But it proceeds, or comes, from them to you,
And no way from yourselves."

If this reading were correct, it would doubtless afford an example of the use of *digest* in the abstract sense; but it is in reality a gross misprision of the true meaning of the passage, and is only another proof of how far we are still from possessing a correctly printed edition of Shakspeare. The proper punctuation would be this:

"The senators of Rome are this good belly,
And you the mutinous members!—For examine—
Their counsels, and *their* cares *digest* things rightly
Touching the weal o' the common!—You shall find"—&c.

"*For examine*" is introduced merely to diversify the discourse, and to fix the attention of the listeners;[36] it might be wholly omitted without injury to the sense: but in the passage as it now stands, *examine* is made an effective verb, having for its objects the counsels and cares of the senators; while *digest* is made auxiliary to and synonymous with *examine*, and, like it, is in the imperative mood, as though addressed to the people, instead of being, as it ought to be, in the indicative, with *counsels* and *cares* for its agents. It is a curious instance of how completely the true sense of a passage may be disturbed by the misapplication of a few commas.

Digest, therefore, in this passage, as elsewhere, is in direct allusion to the animal function. The very essence and pith of the parable of "the belly and the members" is to place in opposition the *digestive* function of the belly with the more active offices of the members; and the application of the parable is, that "*the senators* are this good belly," *their* counsels and *their* cares *digest* for the general good, and distribute the resulting benefits throughout the whole community. This is the true reading; and no person who duly considers it, or who has compared it with the original in Plutarch, but must be satisfied that it is so.

4. Because, since *digest* is thus shown to have been invariably used by Shakspeare with reference to the animal function,

[36] Like the expression just above,
"if you do remember,—
I send it through the rivers of your blood," &c.
(C. M. I.)

bosom multiplied, having close relation with that function, is in strict analogy with the prevailing metaphor of the play; while, on the other hand, *bisson multitude* has no relation with it at all; and therefore, had the latter been the genuine expression, it would have been associated, not with *digest*, but with some verb bearing more reference to the function of sight,[29] than to that of deglutition and concoction.

5. Because I cannot perceive why there should be any greater difficulty in the metaphorical allusion to *the bosom multiplied digesting the senate's courtesy*, than *to the multitudinous tongue licking the sweet which is their poison*. There is, in fact, such a close metaphorical resemblance between the two expressions, that one can scarcely be doubted so long as the other is received as genuine."

The effect of this masterly note on Mr. Singer, Mr. Halliwell, and Mr. Dyce, was very different.

Mr. Singer's "fatal objection"

Mr. Singer,[30] at once urges a "fatal objection," to A. E. B.'s reading,

"The accusation
Which *they* have often made against the senate,
* * * * * *
How shall this *bosome multiplied* digest
The senate's courtesy? Let deeds express
What's like to be *their* words:"

"the context," he says, "requires a plural noun."

answered and obviated.

To which A. E. B. replies[31] by quoting from the same scene,[32]

"at once pluck out
The *multitudineus tongue*, let *them* not lick
The sweet which is *their* poison:

[29] "Bisson" is the A. S. *Bisen*, blind. (C. M. I.)
[30] Notes and Queries, 1st Series, vol. vi. p. 85.
[31] Notes and Queries, 1st Series, vol. vi. p. 154.
[32] Coriolanus, act iii. sc. 1.

and remarks, that "the dominant antecedents throughout the whole speech to such words as *they, them, their*, &c., is *the people*," in this question of Brutus, which occurs a few lines previously:

> "Why, shall the people give
> One that speaks thus, their voice?"

Mr. Singer then surrendered at discretion, and in his new edition printed "bosom multiplied." Mr. Singer surrenders.

Mr. Halliwell, more cautious, brought forward no objections, fatal or otherwise, but took time to consider. In his *Observations on some of the Manuscript Emendations*, &c. 1853,[a] he confesses that his previous conviction (that the emendation in question had been derived from purer sources than we now possess) Mr. Halliwell's caution.

> "was greatly disturbed by an interesting article on the passage by 'A. E. B.' (in the *Notes and Queries*), and further reading has furnished reasons that justify the gravest doubts as to the propriety of its reception."

On the other hand, in charming contrast to these two recantations, Mr. Dyce adopts with praise the emendation, *bisson multitude*, and in a note on the phrase, "digest things rightly," remarks that Mr. Dyce's adoption.

> "a writer in *Notes and Queries*, vol. vi. 27, defending the gross corruption of the folio in act iii. sc. 1, "Bosome-multiplied," rests a portion of his very weak argument on the present passage."

---

[a] Page 15.

Mr. Staunton's final decision.

Mr. Staunton inserted the new reading in his edition, but he did so with some hesitation: and he informs me that he is now convinced that the old reading ought not to be disturbed.

CHAPTER X.

The Bridgewater Manuscripts.

The manuscripts, whose genuineness has been either disallowed or simply called in question by professional palæographists and record-readers, consist of (α) six documents which have been collected into one volume (and this for facility of reference I shall call the *Shakspere Volume*); and (β) some accounts of rewards and payments to persons of the Queen's Household and to Players during Queen Elizabeth's stay at Harefield, which occur in a volume of Household Expences in the handwriting of Sir Arthur Maynwaringe. Besides these there are other documents which demand investigation; but I shall confine myself for the present to the two classes which I have specified.

All the documents in these classes (in number seven) were brought to light by Mr. Collier. That gentleman has, in various works, published the narrative of their discovery. The following extract is from his *New Facts*, 1835, p. 6:—

Mr. Collier was the discoverer and sponsor of the MSS.

"I should begin by stating that the most interesting of them are derived from the Manuscripts of Lord Ellesmere, whose name is of course well known to every reader of our history, as Keeper of the Great Seal to Queen Elizabeth, and Lord Chancellor to James I. They are preserved at Bridgewater House; and Lord Francis Egerton gave me instant and unrestrained access to them, with permission to make use of any literary or historical information I could discover. The Rev. H. J. Todd had been there before me, and had classed some of the documents and correspondence; but large bundles of papers, ranging in point of date between 1581, when Lord Ellesmere was made Solicitor General, and 1616, when he retired from the office of Lord Chancellor, remained unexplored, and it was evident that many of them had never been opened from the time when, perhaps, his own hands tied them together.

Among these, in a most unpromising heap, chiefly of legal documents, I met with most of the new facts respecting Shakespeare, which are the occasion of my present letter."

Mr. Collier gives a more circumstantial account of the discovery of the documents in question, in his *Reply*.[1]

"I admit without reserve, that the weakest part of my case relates to the finding of Shakespeare documents among the late Earl of Ellesmere's MSS. at Bridgewater House. And why is it the weakest part of my case? For this sole reason, that I never could have had any direct corroboration of my own testimony as to the discovery of them: nobody was with me at the precise moment, although the noble owner of the papers had been in the room only a few minutes before. * * *

I never suspected the papers to be anything but what they purported to be, and the moment I discovered them and had hastily read them over, I carried them to the Earl of Ellesmere (then Lord Francis Leveson Gower) and read them to him. At his Lordship's instance I copied them, and left both originals and copies with his Lordship. Going again to Bridgewater House (I think it must have been on the very next day, for I was all eagerness to pursue my search) I overtook his Lordship about to

[1] Page 34.

enter the door, having just alighted from his horse. He told me that he had seen Mr. Murray, the publisher, who offered to give me £50 or £100 (I believe the smaller to have been the sum) if I would put the documents into shape and write an Introduction to them. I declined the proposal at once, saying that I could not consent to make money out of his Lordship's property. Lord Ellesmere appeared a little surprized at my hypersqeamishness, and replied, with his habitual generosity, that the documents were as much mine as his, for though I had found them in his house, but for me, they might never have been discovered till doomsday. * * *

* * * From Bridgewater House I took all the papers, originals and transcripts, to Rodd's, the bookseller, where we examined them carefully; and although I at first agreed that he should sell some copies of them when printed, I afterwards (upon my own principle, as stated to Lord Ellesmere) altered my resolution, and only a few *New Facts* were passed over Rodd's counter to his customers."

The six manuscripts in the Shakspere Volume, are :— Table of the MSS. in the Shakspere Volume.

I. A statement of the value of the shares of Shakespeare and others in the Blackfriars property, upon avoiding the Playhouse. (n. d.)

II. A letter addressed to Sir Thomas Egerton, signed "S. Danyell." (n. d.)

III. A Memorial of the Blackfriars Players, to the Privy Council. (Nov. 1589.)

IV. A Report by two Chief Justices on the right of citizens within the precinct of the White and Black Friars to exemption from certain charges. (Jan. 27th, 1579.)

V. A Warrant appointing Robert Daborne, William Shakespeare, and others, instructors of the

Children of the Revels to Queen Elizabeth. (Jan. 4th, 1609.)

VI. A letter to Sir Thomas Egerton signed H. S. (n. d.) "*vera copia.*"

The four palæographical examinations.

The first palæographical examination of these six documents was made by the Rev. Jos. Hunter, and Mr. W. H. Black, formerly Assistant Keeper of Her Majesty's Public Records; but neither of these most competent judges have publicly expressed any opinion on the genuineness or spuriousness of the manuscripts. Mr. Halliwell subsequently examined them, and, though prepossessed in favour of the genuineness of one of them (the H. S. letter), came to the conclusion that nos. I., III., V. and VI. are spurious, and that in particular no. V. is an obvious forgery. Mr. Halliwell's views on these manuscripts were made known in 1853, in three forms: 1st, The first volume of his folio *Shakespeare*, p. 185; and 2ndly, *Curiosities of Modern Shakesperian Criticism*, 1853, in which, at p. 20, is a report of the remarks on the Bridgewater House manuscripts which had been already published in the folio Shakspere; while, 3rdly, in his *Observations on the Shaksperian Forgeries at Bridgewater House*, 1853, he committed Mr. W. H. Black to the opinion that the H. S. letter,

"even as seen in the facsimile, is open to great suspicion;"

and gave his own opinion in these words:—

"I have examined *all* the documents, and will pledge myself to the opinion that they are fabrications."[2]

I apprehend, however, that this remark was not in-

[2] Page 1.

tended to apply to all the six manuscripts, but to certain of them, which only Mr. Halliwell had inspected.

Another palæographic examination of these six documents was made in 1859, by Sir F. Madden and Mr. N. E. S. A. Hamilton. The conclusion those gentlemen arrived at was, that no. IV. was genuine; but that the other five manuscripts were spurious, and probably forgeries (in contradistinction to copies of genuine manuscripts) executed by one scribe. These views were published by Mr. Hamilton in his *Inquiry*, 1860, p. 82.

These manuscripts at Bridgewater House have been subsequently examined by several skilled Record Readers, viz. Mr. Richard Gairdner and Mr. W. B. D. D. Turnbull on one occasion, and by Professor Brewer and Mr. T. Duffus Hardy[3] on another occasion; and every one of these gentlemen entertains the opinion that all the documents in the Shakspere Volume, with the exception of no. IV., are forgeries, as well as the other manuscript at Bridgewater House of which I shall hereafter give an account; and Professor Brewer is understood to have come to the conclusion that no. IV. is also spurious; while the other palæographists mentioned simply doubt its genuineness, and Sir F. Madden and Mr. Hamilton are convinced that it is genuine.

---

[3] The reader may consult Mr. Hardy's pamphlet, entitled *A Review of the Present State of the Shakespearian Controversy*, 1860, (pp. 54—60), for that gentleman's opinions on these six documents *seriatim*.

Let us take the six documents seriatim.

I. The valuation of shares in the Blackfriars property.

I. This is *verbatim* as follows:—

For avoiding of the playhouse in the Blacke Friers.

Impr.	Richard Burbidge owith the Fee and is alsoe a sharer therein His interest he rateth at the grosse summe of 1000li for the Fee and for his foure Shares the summe of 933li 6s 8d	1933li 6s 8d
Item	Laz Fletcher owith 3 shares wch he rateth at 700li that is at 7 yeares purchase for eche share or 33li 6s 8d one yeare wth an other	700li
Item	W. Shakspeare asketh for the wardrobe and properties of the same playhouse 500li and for his 4 shares the same as his fellowes Burbidge and Fletcher 933li 6s 8d	1433li 6s 8d
Item	Heminges and Condell eche 2 shares	933li 6s 8d
Item	Joseph Taylor one share and an halfe	350li
Item	Lowing one share and an halfe	350li
Item	foure more playeres wth one halfe share vnto eche of them	466li 13s 4d
	Sumā totalis	6166 13 4

Moreover the hired men of the companie demaund some recompence for their greate losse and the Widowes and Orphanes of players who are paide by the sharers at divers rates & proporcōns soe as in the whole it will coste the Lo. Mayor and Citizens at the least 7000li

This document, as it appears to me, contains internal evidence of its spuriousness. It is, to me, quite incredible that the value of the goodwill, wardrobe, and properties of the Blackfriars theatre should be worth so large a sum as £6166. 13*s* 4*d*, which at the present day would be equal to between £30,000 and £40,000. It is proportionally incredible that the wardrobe and properties could be worth

I

Forged Statement of the Value of the Shares of Richard Burbage, Lawrence Fletcher, William Shakespeare, Heminge & Condell, in the Blackfriars Property, upon avoiding the Playhouse.

ffor avoiding of the playhouse in
the Blacke ffriers

Impr. Richard Burbidge owith the ffee and is alsoe a sharer therein his interest he rateth at the grosse summe of 1000li for the ffee and for his foure shares the summe of 933li 6s 8d	1933li. 6s 8d
Item Laz ffletcher owith 3 shares wch he rateth at 700li that is at 7 yeares purchase for eche share or 33li. 6s. 8d one yeare wth an other	700li
Item W. Shakspeare asketh for the wardrobe and properties of the same playhouse 500li and for his 4 shares the same as his fellowes Burbidge and ffletcher 933li 6s 8d	1433li. 6s. 8d
Item Heminges and Condell eche 2 shares	933li. 6s. 8d
Item Joseph Taylor one share and an halfe	350li.
Item Lowing one share and an halfe	350li.
Item foure more playeres wth one halfe share unto eche of them	466li. 13s. 4d
Suma totalis	6166. 13. 4

Moreover the hired men of the companie demaund some recompence for
their greate losse and the widowes and
Orphanes of players who are paide by
the sharers at divers rates & proportions
soe as in the whole it will coste the Lo.
Mayor and Citizens at the least 7000li

To face p. 246

Ashbee & Dangerfield, Lithog.
22 Bedford Street Covent Garden.

£500, which would be now represented by a sum of between £5000 and £6000!

As to the manuscript itself, the paper is of a later date than the time to which the document professes to belong; and the supposition of its being an early copy of a genuine original manuscript, involves a very improbable presumption, that at so early a date, documents of this kind were considered as of sufficient interest, in a literary point of view, to be copied for preservation. For no other purpose can we suppose such a copy to have been made. But the character of the writing is decisive on the question of genuineness. To the practised eye it betrays its spuriousness at a glance.

II. This is *verbatim* as follows:—

II. The letter to Sir T. Egerton signed S. Danyell.

To the Right honorable Sir Thomas Egerton Knight Lord Keeper of the great Seale of England

I will not indeavour Right Honorable to thanke you in words for this new great and vnlookt for fauor showne vnto me whereby I am bound to you for ever & hope one day with true harte and simple skill to proue that I am not vnmindfull. Most earnestly doe I wishe I could praise as your Honour has knowne to deserue for then should I like my maister Spencer whose memorie your Honor cherisheth leaue behinde me some worthie worke to be treasured by posteritie. What my pore muse could performe in haste is here set downe and though it be farre below what other poets and better pennes have written it commeth from a gratefull harte and therefore maye be accepted. I shall now be able to liue free from those cares and troubles that hetherto haue been my continuall and wearisome companions. But a little time is paste since I was called vpon to thanke yor Honor for my brothers advancement and nowe I thanke you for my owne wth double kindnes will alwaies receive double gratefullnes at both our handes. I cannot but knowe that I am lesse deseruing then some that sued by other of the nobilitie vnto her Matie for this roome if M. Drayton my good friend had bene chosen I should not have murmured for sure I am he wold have filled it most excellentlie but it seemeth to myne humble iudgement that one which is the authour of playes now daylie presented on the publick stages of London and the possessor of no small gaines and moreover himself an actor in the kinges companie of Commedians could not with reason pretend to be m^{r} of the Queenes Maties Reuelles for asmuchas he wold sometimes be asked to approue and allowe of his owne writings. Therfore he and more of like qualitie can not iustly be disappointed because through yor Honors gracious interposition the chance was haply myne. I owe this and all else to yor Honor and if euer I haue time and abilitie to finishe anie noble vndertaking as god graunt one daye I shall the worke will rather be yor Honors then myne God maketh a poet but his creation wold be in vaine if patrones did not make him to liue Yo^{r} Honor hath ever showne yor selfe the friend of desert and pitty it were if this should be the first exception to the rule It shall not be whiles my poore witt and strength doe remaine to me though the verses wch I nowe sende be indeede noe proofe of myne abilitie I onely intreat yor Honor to accept the same the rather as an earnest of my good will then as an example of my good deede In all things I am yor Honors

Most bounden in dutie and
obseruance
S Danyell[4]

---

[4] Mr. Collier, in his *New Facts*, p. 49, gives the signature as "Samuel Danyell;" and in the twenty-second line above the signature he gives "who" instead of "which" [written at length, not "w^{ch}"]. These, and some *seventy* other less material variations suggest the question whether Mr. Collier did not use some other draft of the letter for his *New Facts*. A few errors of spelling will probably be found in the middle of my transcript, in consequence of the original being inaccessible to me when this sheet was revised.

II

Forged Letter addressed to Sir Thomas Egerton and subscribed S. Danyell.

To the Right honorable Sir Thomas Egerton Knight Lord keeper of the great Seale of England.

I will not indeavour Right honorable to thanke you in words for this newe great and unlookt for favour showne unto me whereby I am bound to you for ever though one day will true harte and simple skill to prove that I am not unmindfull. Most earnestly each wishe

. . . . .

Yor honour hath ever showne yor selfe the frende of letters and pitty of learning. if this poeme be the first exception to the rule it shall not be whiles my poore witt and strength doe remaine to me though the verses which I nowe sende be indeede noe proofe of suche abilitie I onely intreat yor honor to accept the same the rather as an earnest of my good will then as an example of my good deede In all things I am yor honors

Most bounden in dutie and
observance

S. Danyell.

To face p. 240

Forged Petition of Thomas Pope, Richard Burbage, John Hemings, Augustine Phillips, William Shakespeare, William Kempe, William Slye, Nicholas Tooley, and others, to the Lords of the Privy Council.

To the right honorable the LL of her Maties most honorable privie Counsell

The humble petition of Thomas Pope Richard Burbadge John Hemings Augustine Phillips W
Shakespeare William Kempe William Slye Nicholas Tooley and others servaunts to the right honorable the L. Chamberlain
to her Matie — Sheweth most humbly that yor petitioners are owners and players of the private house or theater in the pre
and libertie of the Blackfriers wch hath beene for manie yeares used and occupied for the playing of tragedies commedies h
enterludes and playes That the same by reason of having beene soe long built hath fallen into great decaye and that beside
reparation thereof it hath beene found necessarie to make the same more convenient for the entertainment of auditories comm
thereto That to this end yor petitioners have all and eche of them putt downe sommes of money according to their shares in the sa
theater and wch they have justly and honestlie gained by the exercise of their qualitie of Stage players but that certaine persons (so
them of honour) inhabitants of the precinct and libertie of the Blackfriers have as yor petitioners are informed besought yor hono
LLs not to permitt the saide private house anie longer to remaine open but hereafter to be shutt upp and closed to the manife
great injurie of yor petitioners who have no other meanes whereby to maintaine their wives and families but by the exercise
their qualitie as they have heretofore done. Furthermore that in the summer season yor petitioners are able to playe at t
newe built house on the Bankside calld the Globe but that in the winter they are compelled to come to the Blackfriers
yor honorable LLs give consent unto that wch is prayde against yor petitioners they will not onely while the winter endureth los
meanes whereby they nowe support them selves and their families but be unable to practise them selves in anie playes or e
when calde upon to performe for the recreation and solace of her Matie and her honorable Court as they have beene heretofo
accustomed. The humble prayer of yor petitioners therefore is that yor honble LLs will grant permission to finishe th
reparations and alterations they have begunne and as yor petitioners have hitherto beene well ordered in their behavio
and just in their dealings that yor honorable LLs will not inhibit them from acting at their above named private hous
the precinct and libertie of the Blackfriers and yor petitioners as in dutie most bounden will ever praye for the encre
honour and happinesse of yor honorable LLs.

Two MS. additions in the Perkins Folio.

Par. Go to I say I have found thee: no more
I have found thee, a witty foole.

All's well that ends well. page 239 col. 2.

layed it downe
before Leonte

Winters Tale. page 284 co

III.

Forged Memorial or Certificate of the Blackfriars Players.

These are to certifie yor right honorable LL that her Ma^{ts} poore playeres James Burbidge Richard Burbidge John Laneham
Thomas Greene Robert Wilson John Taylor Anth. Wadeson Thomas Pope George Peele Augustine Phillippes Nicholas Towley
William Shakespeare William Kempe William Johnson Baptiste Goodale and Robert Armyn being all of them sharers in
the blacke Fryers playehouse have never given cause of displeasure in that they have brought into their playes maters
of State and Religion unfitt to be handled by them or to be presented before lewde spectators neither hath anie complainte in that
kinde ever beene preferrde against them or anie of them Wherefore they truste moste humblie in yor LL consideration
of their former good behaviour beinge at all tymes readie and willing to yeelde obedience to anie command whatsoever yor LL in yor wisdome maye thinke in such case meete &c.
Nov. 1589.

This, according to Mr. Halliwell, is a late copy. If it be such, no original is known to be extant. Sir Frederic Madden and Mr. Hamilton consider it to be, like the last, not a copy, but a "manifest forgery." The handwriting, they consider, is not a genuine hand of any known period.

III. The Certificate of the Black-friarsPlayers.

III. This is *verbatim* as follows:—

These are to sertifie yor right honorable Ll that her Matie poore playeres James Burbidge Richard Burbidge John Laneham Thomas Greene Robert Wilson John Taylor Anth. Wadeson Thomas Pope George Peele Augustine Phillippes Nicholas Towley William Shakespeare William Kempe William Johnson Baptiste Goodale and Robert Armyn being all of them sharers in the blacke Fryers playehouse have neuer giuen cause of displeasure in that they haue brought into their playes maters of state and Religion vnfitt to be handled by them or to be presented before lewde spectators neither hath anie complainte in that kinde ever beene preferred against them or anie of them Wherefore they truste moste humblie in yor Ll consideracōn of their former good behauiour beingo at all tymes readie and willing to yeelde obedience to anie cōmaund whatsoever yor Ll in yor wisedome maye thinke in such case meete, &c.

Nov., 1589.

Mr. Halliwell says of this,[5]—

"The most important of all, the certificate from the players of the Blackfriars' Theatre to the Privy Council in 1589, instead of being either the original or a contemporary copy, is evidently at best merely a late transcript, if it be not altogether a recent fabrication.

The question naturally arises, for what purpose could a document of this description have been copied in the seventeenth

[5] Curiosities, &c. p. 22.

century, presuming it to belong to so early a period? It is comparatively of recent times that the slightest literary interest has been taken in the history of our early theatres, or even in the biography of Shakespeare; and, unless it was apparent that papers of this kind were transcribed for some legal or other special purpose, there should be great hesitation in accepting the evidence of any other but contemporary authority. The suspicious appearance of this certificate is of itself sufficient to justify great difficulties in its reception;"

There is one point connected with this certificate or memorial; viz. that it is *exactly* in the same hand that wrote the manuscript notes of the Perkins Folio. Mr. Hamilton, indeed, has mentioned this in general terms; but let any one compare the facsimile of it (on sheet no. X) with the facsimiles of two of the longer pieces of ink-writing in the Perkins Folio, on the same sheet; and he will surely entertain no doubt that one hand wrote both.

IV. A Report by two Chief Justices on the right of residents within the precincts of the White and Black Friars to certain exemptions.

IV. This is *verbatim* as follows:—

The opinions of the two Chief Justices of either bench concerning the Jurisdiccon authoritie and libties claymed by the Cittizens of London within the precincte of the late dissolved houses of the white and black Fryers of London delivered the xxvii[th] of Januarie 1579.

Imprimis it appeareth to us as well by good evidence old presidents and other good prooffes that the soile of the said Fryers is scituated within the precincte of the Cittie of London.

And that all fynes recoveries and other recordes for assurance of landes and Tenements in the said Fryers doe allwaies passe within the Cittie.

That all robberies murders fellonies forcible entries breaches of peace and all other matters of the Crowne comitted or

IV.

Genuine contemporary copy of opinion of two Chief Justices on the right of citizens within the precinct of the White and Black Friars to exemption from certain charges

The opinions of the two Chiefe Justices of either benche concerning the Jurisdiction authoritie and liberties clamed by the Cittizens of London within the precincte of the late dissolued howses of the white and blacke ffryers of London deliuered the [illegible] of Januarie 157[illegible].

Inprimis it appeareth to us as well by good evidence olde presidents and other good proffes that the soile of the said ffryers is situated within the precincte of the Cittie of London.

And that all fynes recoveries and other recordes for assurance of landes and Tenementes in the said ffryers doe allwaies passe within the Cittie.

That all robberies murders felonies forcible entries breaches of peace and all other matters of the Crowne committed or don within the precincte of the said ffryers oughte to be enquired of and determined within the Citty of London.

That all locall actions trespasses and causes rising or growing in the said precincte of the said ffryers oughte to be enquired and tried in the Citty of London.

That the enquest of wardmote may and oughte to enquire of disorders and abuses in the ffryers as in the rest of the Cittie.

Item that all arrestes attachementes summons distresses and serving of any proces of lawe within the said precincte and of and upon any howse or person or inhabiting within the same shalbe executed by the officers and ministers of the Citty of London as in other places within the said Citty are usually executed.

Item that the Lo: Mayor and Sheriffes of London for the tyme being may use and exercise within the said precinctes iurisdictions and corrections of weightes and measures assize of bread ale and wyne as in other places within the said Cittie of London.

Neverthelesse we thinke that forasmuch as we finde that allwaies in tymes past when the said two howses of the ffryers had their being the Inhabitantes of the same have had and enioyed these liberties and privileges following viz: To be free of and from all taxes and fifteenes, all charges of scott and lott, and of watche and warde, the offices of Constables Scavingers and such like offices of charge of the Citty (other then the charges of paving and clensing of the lanes and waies within the said precinctes) That the same shalbe enioyed and contynued by them as it hath ben heretofore used by them.

Christopher Wraye.
James Dyer.

INDORSE.

The opinions of the 2 chief Justices.

or don within the precincte of the said Fryers oughte to be enquired of and determined within the Citty of London.

That all locall offences trespasses and causes rising or growing in the saide precincte of the said Fryers oughte to be enquired and tried in yᵉ Citty of London.

That the enquests of wardmote may and oughte to enquire of disorders and abuses in the Fryers as in the rest of the Cittie.

Itm̃ that all arrests attachemᵗˢ suṁons distresses and serving of any proces of lawe within the said precincte and of and upon any howse or person inhabiting within the same shalbe executed by the officers and mynisters of the Citty of London as in other places within the said Citty are usually executed.

Itm̃ that the Lo: Mayor and Sherrieffes of London for the tyme being maye use and exercise within the said precinctes iurisdiccōns and correccōns of weightes and measures assize of bread ale and wyne as in other places within the said Cittie of London.

Nevertheless wee think that forasmuch as wee find that allwaies in tymes past when the said two houses of the Fryers had their being the Inhabitants of the same have had and enioyed their liberties and priviledges following vizᵗ To be free of and from all taxes and fifteenes, all chardges of scott and lott, and of watch and warde, All offices of Constables Scavingers and such like offices of chardge of the Citty (other then the chardges of paving and clensing of the lands and waies within the said precinctes) That the same shalbe enioyed and contynued by them as it hath byn heretofore used by them.

CHRISTOPHER WRAYE
JAMES DYER.

Mr. Halliwell passed no particular opinion on this document: nor does it even appear that he ever saw it. Sir F. Madden and Mr. N. E. S. A. Hamilton in last November considered it genuine. Professor Brewer and Mr. T. Duffus Hardy examined it last spring; and while Professor Brewer considers it spurious, Mr. Hardy merely says that "its genuineness seems questionable." But lately Sir Frederic Madden has again, at my request, subjected the document to a second and more careful scrutiny, and he informs me that it is his "*decided* opinion that no. IV. is *perfectly genuine*," and that he "can perceive no cause whatever to doubt its genuineness." Still it is obvious, however, on the face of it, that it is not the original document, but a (contemporary) copy.

V. The Warrant appointing Daborne, Shakspere and others, instructors of the Children of the Revels.

V. This is *verbatim* as follows:—

Right trustie and wellbeloved &c James &c To all Mayors, Sheriffes, Justices of the peace &c Whereas the Queene our dearest wife hath for her pleasure and recreacōn appointed her seruauntes Robert Daborne &c to prouide and bring vppe a conuenient nomber of children who shalbe called the children of her Ma[tes] reuelles Knowe yee that We haue appointed and authorized and by these presentes doe appoint and authorize the saide Robert Daborne Willm̄ Shakespeare Nathaniel Field and Edward Kirkham from time to time to prouide and bring vpp a conuenient nomber of children and them to instruct and exercise in the qualitie of playing Tragedies Comedies &c by the name of the children of the reuelles to the Queene within the blacke Fryers in our Cittie of London and els where within our realme of England. Wherefore we will and commaund you and everie of you to permitte her said seruauntes to keepe a conuenient nomber of children by the name of the children of the reuelles to the Queene and them to exercise in

V

Forged Warrant appointing Robert Daborne, William Shakespeare, Nathaniel Field, & Edward Kirkham, Instructors of the Children of the Revels to Queen Elizabeth.

Right trustie and welbeloued &c James &c To all Mayors Sheriffes
Justices of the peace &c Whereas the Queene our dearest wife hath for
her pleasure and recreation appointed her seruauntes Robert Daborne &c
to provide and bring uppe a conuenient nomber of children who shalbe
called the children of her Matis reuelles Knowe yee that We haue appointed
and authorized and by these presentes doe appoint and authorize the saide
Robert Daborne Willm Shakespeare Nathaniel ffield & Edward Kirkham from
time to time to provide and bring upp a conuenient nomber of children and
them to instruct and exercise in the qualitie of playing Tragedies Comedies &c
by the name of the children of the reuelles to the Queene within the blacke
ffryers in our Cittie of london & els where within our realme of England.
Wherefore we will and commaund you and euerie of you to permitte her
said seruauntes to keepe a conuenient nomber of children by the name of the
children of the reuelles to the Queene and them to exercise in the qualitie of
playing according to our Royall pleasure Provided allwayes that noe playes &c
shalbe by them presented but such playes &c as haue receiued the aprobation
and allowance of our Maister of the Reuelles for the tyme being And
these our lres shalbe yor sufficient warrant in this behalfe In Witnesse
whereof &c, 4o die Janu 1609

Bl ffr and globe
Wh ffr and parishe garden } All in & neere
Curton and fortune } london
hope and Swanne

Rendo ponortie
Widdowes mite
Antonio Kinsmen
Triumph of truth
Touchstone
Mirror of life
Grissell
Engl tragedie
ffalse ffriendes
hate and loue
Taming of S
K. Edw 2

Stayed

the qualitie of playing acording to our Royall pleasure Prouided allwayes that noe playes &c shalbe by them presented but such playes &c as haue receiued the aprobacōn and allowance of our Maister of the Reuelles for the tyme being And these our lres shalbe yor sufficient warraunt in this behalfe In Witnesse whereof &c 4° die Jan^ry. 1609

Bl Fr and globe Wh Fr and parishe garden Curten and fortune Hope and Swanne	All in & neere London

Proude pouertie
Widdowes mite
Antonio kinsmen
Triumph of truth
Touchstone
Mirror of life
Grissell
Engl tragedie
False Friendes
Hate and loue
Taming of S
K. Edw 2

Stayed

Of this Mr. Halliwell gives the following account:—[6]

Mr. Halliwell's opinion on the Daborne Warrant.

"This document is styled by Mr. Collier 'a draft either for a Patent or a Privy Seal.' It is not a draft, for the lines are written book-wise, and it is also dated; neither is it a copy of a patent, as appears from the direction, 'Right trustie & welbeloved;' but, if genuine, it must be considered an abridged transcript of a warrant, under the sign-manual and signet, for

[6] Curiosities, p. 22.

a patent to be issued. Now if it be shewn that the letters patent to 'Daborne and others' were granted on the same day on which Lord Ellesmere's paper is dated; and if it be further proved that the contents of the latter are altogether inconsistent with the circumstances detailed in the real patent, it will, I think, be conceded that no genuine draft or transcript, of the nature of that printed by Mr. Collier, can possibly exist.

It appears that the following note occurs in an entry-book of patents that passed the Great Seal while it was in the hands of Lord Ellesmere in 7 James I.:—'A Warrant for Robert Daborne and others, the Queenes Servants, to bring up and practice Children in Plaies by the name of the Children of the Queen's Revells, for the pleasure of her Majestie, 4° Januarii, anno septimo Jacobi.' This entry may have suggested the fabrication, the date of the questionable MS. corresponding with that here given; though it is capable of proof that, if it were authentic, it must have been dated previously, for the books of the Signet Office show that the authority for Daborne's warrant was obtained by the influence of Sir Thomas Munson in the previous December, and they also inform us that it was granted 'to Robert Daborne, and other Servauntes to the Queene, from time to time to provide and bring up a convenient nomber of children to practize in the quality of playing, by the name of the Children of the Revells to the Queene, *in the White Fryers, London*, or any other convenient place where he shall thinke fit.' The enrolment of the instrument, which was issued in the form of letters patent under the Great Seal, recites, 'Whereas the Quene, our deerest wyfe, hathe for hir pleasure and recreacion, when shee shall thinke it fitt to have any playes or shewes, appoynted hir servantes Robert Daborne, Phillipe Rosseter, John Tarbock, Richard Jones, and Robert Browne, to provide and bring upp a convenient number of children, whoe shalbe called Children of hir Revelles, Know ye that wee have appoynted and authorised, and by theis presentes do authorize and appoynte the saide

Robert Daborne, &c., from tyme to tyme, to provide, keepe, and bring upp a convenient nomber of children, and them to practice and exercise in the quality of playing, by the name of Children of the Revells to the Queene, within the White Fryers in the suburbs of the Citty of London, or in any other convenyent place where they shall thinke fitt for that purpose.' This patent is dated January 4th, 7 Jac. I., 1609-10, so that any draft, or projected warrant, exhibiting other names than the above, could not possibly have had this exact date. It will be observed that the names, with the exception of that of Daborne, are entirely different in the two documents, and this company of children was to play at the Whitefriars, not at the Blackfriars. The fabricator seems to have relied on the supposition that the entry relative to "Daborne and others" referred to the latter theatre; and consequently inserted the name of Edward Kirkham, who is known to have been one of the instructors of the children of the Revels at the Blackfriars in the year 1604. There is, in fact, no reasonable supposition on which the Ellesmere paper can be regarded as authentic. Had no date been attached to it, it might have been said that the whole related merely to some contemplated arrangement which was afterwards altered; although even in that case, the form of the copy would alone have been a serious reason against its reception. In its present state, it is clearly impossible to reconcile it with the contents of the enrolment just quoted. Fortunately for the interests of truth, indications of forgery are detected in trifling circumstances that are almost invariably neglected by the inventor, however ingeniously the deception be contrived. Were it not for this, the search for historical truth would yield results sufficiently uncertain to deter the most enthusiastic enquirer from pursuing the investigation."

Mr. Hamilton calls the Daborne warrant such a "manifest forgery,"

"that it seems incredible how [it] could have cheated Mr.

Collier's observation, even under the circumstances of excitement described by him as consequent upon [its] discovery.'[7]

Mr. Hamilton remarks, what must be plain to every one who compares the facsimile of the Daborne warrant with those of the manuscript emendations in the Perkins Folio, that the same hand that wrote the one wrote the other. In particular, the letters E, S, J, and C, are formed in the same peculiar pseudo-antique manner in both these fabrications. The fact is that the scribe, in posting up the corrections in the Perkins Folio, sometimes allowed his hand to degenerate from the character of no. III. of the Shakspere Volume, to the less artificial hand of no. V.

It has been very recently discovered by a law-writer, with whose name I am not acquainted, that this document has a gilt edge, which is a most suspicious circumstance; and Sir F. Madden has since found that the leaf has been cut from some book, the marks of the penknife used for that purpose being still visible. It is not improbable that it will ultimately be discovered from what book in the Library at Bridgewater House this folio fly-leaf has been taken.

The Letter to Sir. T. Egerton signed H. S.

VI. This is *verbatim* as follows:—

My verie honored Lo the manie good offices I haue receiued at yor Lps handes wh^ch ought to make me backward in asking further fauors onely imbouldeneth me to require more in the same kinde. Yo^r Lp wilbe warned howe hereafter you graunt anie sute seeing it draweth on more and greater demaunds

[7] Inquiry, p. 82.

VI.

Forged "Copia vera" of a spurious letter without address attributed by Mr Collier to Lord Southampton

My verie honored Lo. The manie good offices I haue
receiued at yor Lops handes wch ought to make me backward
in asking further fauor, onely imboldeneth me to require more
in the same kinde. Yor L. will be warned howe hereafter you
graunt anie sute, seeing it draweth on more and greater demaunds
this wch now presseth is to request yor Lo. in all you can to be
good to the poore players of the blacke Fryers who call them
selues by authoritie the Servauntes of his Matie and aske for
the protection of their most gracious maister and Soveraigne in
this the tyme of there troble. They are threatened by the Lo.
Maior and Aldermen of London never friendly to their calling wth
the distruction of their meanes of livelihood by the pulling downe of
their plaiehouse wch is a private theatre and hath never given
occasion of anger by anie disorders. These bearers are two of
the chiefe of the companie one of them by name Richard Burbidge
who humblie sueth for yor Lops kinde helpe for that he is a man
famous as our english Roscius one who fitteth the action to the
worde and the worde to the action most admirablie. By the
exercise of his qualitie industry and good behaviour he hath
become possessed of the Blacke Fryers playhouse wch hath
bene imployed for playes sithence it was builded by his
Father now nere 50 yeres agone. The other is a man no
whitt lesse deserving favor and my especiall friende till of late
an actor of good account in the companie now a sharer in the
same and writer of some of our best english playes wch as your
Lo. knoweth were most singularly liked of Quene Elizabeth when
the companie was called uppon to performe before her Matie
at Court at Christmas and Shrovetide. His most gracious
Matie King James alsoe since his coming to the crowne hath
extended his royall favour to the companie in divers waies and
at sundrie tymes. This other hath to name William Shakespeare
and they are both of one countie and indeede allmost of one
towne both are right famous in their qualities though it longeth
not of yor Lo. gravitie and wisdome to resort unto the places
where they are wont to delight the publique eare. Their trust
and sute nowe is not to bee molested in their waye of life
whereby they maintaine them selves and their wives and
families (being both maried and of good reputacion) as well as
the widowes and orphanes of some of their dead fellows. Yor
Lo. most bounden at com.

H S

Copia vera

Ashbee & Tuckett, Lithographers

this wch now presseth is to request yor Lp in all you can to be good to the poore players of the blacke Fryers who call them selues by authoritie the Seruantes of his Matie and aske for the proteccōn of their most gracious maister and Soueraigne in this the tyme of there troble. They are threatened by the Lo Maior and Aldermen of London never friendly to their calling wth the distruccōn of their meanes of liuelihood by the pulling downe of their plaiehouse wch is a priuate theatre and hath never giuen ocasion of anger by anie disorders. These bearers are two of the chiefe of the companie one of them by name Richard Burbidge who humblie sueth for yor Lps kinde helpe for that he is a man famous as our english Roscius one who fitteth the action to the worde and the word to the action most admira.ly. By the exercise of his qualitie industry and good behaviour he hath become possessed of the Blacke Fryers playhouse wch hath bene imployed for playes sithence it was builded by his Father now nere 50 yeres agone. The other is a man no whitt lesse deseruing fauor and my especial friende till of late an actor of good account in the companie now a sharer in the same and writer of some of our best english playes wch as your Lp knoweth were most singulerly liked of Quene Elizabeth when the cumpanie was called vppon to performe before her Matie at Court at Christmas and Shrove tide His most gracious Matie King James alsoe since his coming to the crowne hath extended his Royall fauour to the companie in diuers waies and at sundrie tymes This other hath to name William Shakespeare and they are both of one countie and indeede allmost of one towne both are right famous in their qualities though it longeth not of yor Lo grauitie and wisdome to resort vnto the places where they are wont to delight the publique eare. Their trust and sute nowe is not to bee molested in their waye of life whereby they maintaine them selues and their wiues and families (being both maried and of good reputacōn) as well as the widowes and orphanes of some of their dead fellows. Yo^{r} Lo. most bounden at com̄

H. S.

Copia vera.

Mr. Halliwell has the following remarks on this letter and no. I.[8]

"Although the caligraphy is of a highly skilful character, and judging solely from a fac-simile of the letter, I should certainly have accepted it as genuine, yet an examination of the original leads to a different judgment, the paper and ink not appearing to belong to so early a date. It is a suspicious circumstance that both these documents are written in an unusually large character on folio leaves of paper, *by the same hand*, and are evidently not contemporaneous copies. Again may the question be asked, Why should transcripts of such papers have been made after the period to which the originals are supposed to refer? It is also curious that copies only of these important records should be preserved;"

Mr. Hamilton, while admitting[9] that the H. S. letter "manifests some dexterity of execution," unhesitatingly pronounces it a forgery, an opinion in which Sir F. Madden very strongly concurs. I must confess that the *matter* of the letter would have made me doubt its authenticity long before I received any suspicion of its genuineness from the *writing*. We shall find, however, that all doubt is removed by the very striking resemblance between no. VI. and one of the Dulwich manuscripts. Sir F. Madden, like Mr. Halliwell, is strongly of opinion that the same hand wrote nos. I. and VI. This may indeed be the case: but the latter is far better executed than the former.

Mr. Collier's replies respecting the H. S. Letter.

Mr. Collier denies having forged any of the six documents in the Shakspere Volume. He says,[10]

---

[8] Curiosities, &c. p. 24. [9] Inquiry, p. 82. [10] Reply, p. 44.

"While, therefore, I freely acknowledge the finding of those documents, the forgery of them I as firmly deny."

His other replies to the charges of Mr. Halliwell and Mr. Hamilton are as brief, and touch particularly only one of the Bridgewater manuscripts in the Shakspere Volume, viz. no. VI. On the subject of that Mr. Collier has been more communicative than of any of the others. Suspicions of its genuineness had crossed the minds of several persons, even before Mr. Joseph Netherclift had facsimilied it; Mr. Rodd, as I have good means of knowing, suspected it to be a fabrication, and was not disposed to accept Mr. Collier's account of its discovery. These rumours must have reached Mr. Collier himself, and it is probable that he spoke to Mr. Joseph Netherclift of the prejudice which existed in some minds against the genuineness of the H. S. letter: for we learn from Mr. Collier, that Mr. Joseph Netherclift, before making any tracing of the manuscript, offered his testimony on Mr. Collier's side, in these words:—

"If at any time you happen to want a witness that it is a genuine document, I will be that witness."[11]

And Mr. Joseph Netherclift has already partly redeemed his promise. He has shewn himself quite ready to encounter the terrors of professional browbeating in Mr. Collier's behalf, and has, in a truly Roman spirit, sacrificed the ties of kindred at the shrine of his *patron saint.*[12]

---

[11] Reply, p. 40.

[12] See Mr. Netherclift's letter to The Athenæum of Feb. 25, 1860.

The rest of Mr. Collier's remarks on the H. S. letter relates to certain opinions expressed by Messrs. Halliwell and Dyce. Critics who pretend to judge of the genuineness of manuscripts by facsimiles, without consulting the originals, have only themselves to thank for the odium of having encouraged the reception of forged documents, and for the just severity with which Mr. Collier complains of his having been misled by their precipitation.[13] The opinions of these gentlemen were absolute and unequivocal. Mr. Dyce, in a letter to Mr. Collier, says,

> "The facsimile has certainly removed from my mind all doubts about the genuineness of the letter."

Mr. Halliwell says,[14]

> "the fac-simile of that portion of it relating to Shakespeare, which the reader will find at the commencement of this volume, will suffice to convince any one acquainted with such matters that it is a genuine manuscript of the period. No forgery of so long a document could present so perfect a continuity of design; yet it is right to state that grave doubts have been thrown on its authenticity. A portion of the fac-simile will exhibit on examination a peculiarity few supposititious documents would afford, part of the imperfectly formed letter *h* in the word *Shakspeare* appearing by a slip of the pen in the letter *f* immediately beneath it."[15]

---

[13] Reply, pp. 41-42.

[14] Life of Shakespeare, 1848, p. 224.

[15] In the Preface (p. xiii), speaking of "the illustrations and facsimiles," Mr. Halliwell tells us, "Nothing has been copied which will not bear the test of the strictest examination," and

Mr. Collier writes:[16]

"Mr. Halliwell then refers to Mr. Wright, who also had seen the original, as a highly competent judge of such matters, a point few will dispute; and he subjoins in a note, "In the Library of the Society of Antiquaries, No. 201, Art. 3, is preserved 'a copye of the comysion of sewers in the countye of Kent,' marked as *vera copia*, and singularly enough written apparently by the same hand that copied the letter of H. S.""

I have taken the trouble to examine this copy commission, and must beg to differ *toto cœlo* with Mr. Halliwell on this point. There appears to me to be no more resemblance between the writing of the H. S. letter and that of the copy commission, than between either of these, and any other document of the period written in the same character.

(β.) The volume of the accounts of Sir Thomas Egerton's Household Expences is, with the exception I am about to mention, entirely in the fine handwriting of Sir Arthur Maynwaringe, and every statement of accounts is signed by him. In the middle of this volume has been foisted a sheet of alleged payments to officers of the Queen's household and players, bearing the signature of "Arthur Maynwaringe." The following is a *verbatim* copy:—

Statement of account of rewards and payments for entertaining Queen Elizabeth at Harefield, signed "Arth. Maynwaringe."

(p. xiv), that "nothing of the material [*sic*] which is not unquestionably genuine is here perpetuated." It is amusing to find that the first facsimile is from the H. S. Letter!

[16] Reply, p. 48.

Date	Item	Amount	Total
30 Julye 1602	Receyvid of yor Lop at yorkehowse — v c li —	} v c liiii li vi s	
3 August 1602	Receyvid of yor lop at Harefield — liiii li vi s		
	Whereof Disbursed by yor Lops apoyntment as by bills and by my booke ^more^ particularlye apeareth		
3 August 1602	Deliuered to mr Steward at Harefield ———	cc li	
	Rewardes; to seuerall offices in her mats house and to particuler persons there ———	lxvi li xii s iiii d	
6 August 1602	Rewardes; to the vaulters players and dauncers Of this x li to Burbidges players for Othello—	lxiiii li xviii s x d	
	Rewarde; to mr Lyllyes man wch brought ye lotte-rye boxe to Harefield: and mr Andr Leigh ——	x s	
	Rewardes; to Tentkeepers ———	xl s	
10 August 1602	Payde; to mercers, ye Imbroderer, silkeman and the Queenes taylor ———	lxxv li xv s	280 li 6 s 2 d
	payde; to the Goldsmith part for ye Anchor and for other matters ———	viii li	
	payde; to the Goldsmith for badges ———	xxix li iii s	
	payde; to the lynnan Draper for broune canvas part of wch was not vsed ———	xvii li v s	
	payde; to ye London Butler for hyre of Damaske & Dyaper and knyves	xv li vii s	
	payde; for ye caryage of ye Turkye carpetts from Harfield to mr Garwayes howse	v s	
	Rewarde; to mr Garway his men for removing of the same ———	x s	
	Soe remayneth due to yor Lop in my handes vpon this accompt this 20: August 1602 the somme of	lxxii li xix s x d	
	Arth Maynwaringe		
20 August 1602	Payd more by me for Lotterie guiftes as by my booke and by bill also speareth; beinge paide to mr Stewarde	18 li — 2 s — 9 d	
	Soe remayneth now due to yor Lop in my hands vpon this accompt this said 20 August 1602, the somme of	54 li — 17 s — 1 d	
	Arth Maynwaringe		

The paper is endorsed thus:

Maynwaringes accompt.
Alone for Disbursment
about Harfield.
1602.

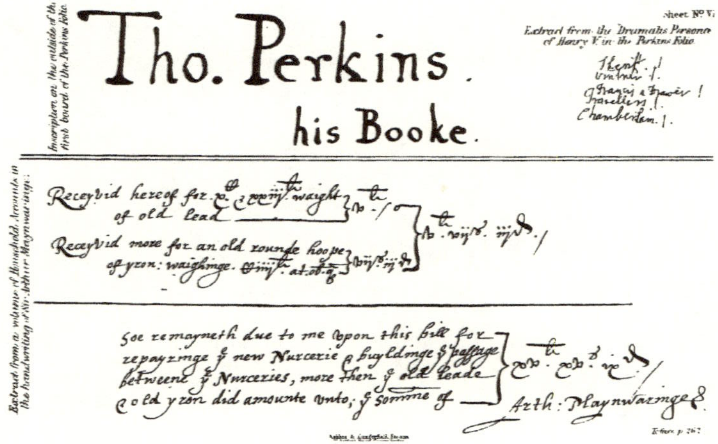

Sheet No. VI.
Extract from the Dramatis Personæ of Henry V in the Perkins Folio.
Inscription on the outside of the first board of the Perkins Folio.
Tho. Perkins.
his Booke.
Receyvid hereof for ... waight of old lead
Receyvid more for an old rounde hoope of yron: waighinge ...
Extract from a volume of Household Accounts in the handwriting of Sir Arthur Maynwaringe.
Soe remayneth due to me vpon this bill for repayringe the new Nurcerie & buyldinge the passage betweene the Nurceries, more then the old leade & old yron did amounte unto; the somme of
Arth: Maynwaringe.
To face p. 267

VII.

Forged Statement of account of rewards and payments for entertaining Queen Elizabeth at Harefield, in 1602: signed "Arth. Maynwaringe."

30 Julye 1602. Receyvid of yor Lop at yorkehowse — v^c li } v^c lxiiij li vj s
3 August 1602. Receyvid of yor Lop at Harefield — lxiiij li vj s }

Whereof Disbursed by yor Lops apoyntment as by bills and by my booke more particularlye apeareth

3 August 1602 Delivered to mr Steward at Harefield — iij^c li

Rewardes; to severall offices in her mats howse and to particuler persons there — } lxvj li xiij s iiij d

6 August 1602 Rewardes; to the vaulters players & daunceers Of this x li to Burbidges players for Othello — } lxiiij li xviij s x d

Rewarde; to mr Lyllyes man wch brought ye lottarye boxe to Harefield; p mr Andr Leigh — } x s

Rewardes; to Tentkeepers — xl s

10 August 1602 payde; to mercers, ye Imbroderer, silkeman and the Queenes taylor — } lxxx li xv s

payde; to the Goldsmith part for ye Anchor and for other matters — } viij li

payde; to the Goldsmith for badges — xxix li iiij s

payde; to the lynnen Draper for broune canvas part of wch was not used — xvij li v s

payde; to ye london Butler for hyre of Damaske & Drapes and knyves — } xv li vij s

payde; for ye caryage of ye Turkye carpetts from Harfield to mr Garwayes howse } v s

Rewarde; to mr Garwaye his men for removing of the same — x s

280 li
68 s 2 d

Soe remayneth due to yor Lop in my handes upon this accompt this 20: August 1602 the somme of } lxxij li xix s x d

Arth Maynwaringe

20 August 1602 Payd more by me for Lotterie guiftes as by my booke and by bill also apeareth; beinge paid to mr Stewarde — } 18 li — 2 s — 9 d

Soe remayneth now due to yor Lop in my hands upon this accompt this said 20. August 1602. the somme of } 54 li — 17 s — 1 d

Arth Maynwaringe

INDORSE

Maynwaringes accompt.
Alone for Disbursment
about Harfield.
1602.

This document was first communicated by Mr. Collier, in his *New Particulars*.[17] He there says,

"I have found proof that Othello was written, not in 1604, according to Malone's Chronology, (Shakesp. by Boswell, iii, 401,) but certainly as early as 1602. In the month of August, of that year, it was played by the company usually performing at the Blackfriars theatre in the winter, and at the Globe in the spring, summer, and autumn.

This important fact I learn from the detailed accounts preserved at Bridgewater House, in the handwriting of Sir Arthur Mainwaring, of the expences incurred by Sir Thomas Egerton, afterwards Lord Ellesmere, in entertaining Queen Elizabeth and her Court for three days at Harefield. * * *

It is indisputable, from this evidence, that Othello was acted at Harefield in 1602: consequently, Malone's conjecture of 1604, as the date of its composition, must be wrong."[18]

In his *Reply*,[19] Mr. Collier says,

"My object [in conversing with the Rev. H. J. Todd] was to gain from him some information respecting the MS. where the performance of "Othello" before the Queen at Sir Thomas Egerton's was mentioned. Mr. Todd was very deaf, and I could learn no more from him than that he knew that such a circumstance was mentioned in some MS. In fact, part of the direction of a letter to the Rev. Mr. Todd remained between the leaves to keep the place, when I saw the book."

To say the least, this method of explanation which the reader will find resorted to by Mr. Collier in the case of one of the Dulwich manuscripts is the most unsatisfactory conceivable and is necessarily fraught with suspicion. It is just as if a witness were called for the defence, in a suit; and on his being com-

---

[17] Page 57. [18] Page 59. [19] Page 35, note.

mitted for perjury, the defendant were to complain of that committal, on the ground that "Mrs. Harris" had a high opinion of the witness's character.

Palæographic Examinations.

The genuineness of this page of accounts was not publicly impugned until the publication of Mr. Hardy's pamphlet.[20] Last spring however an experiment was made on the suspected document. Several of the statements of account in the volume, and the suspected one also, were laid before Mr. Richard Gairdner, Assistant Keeper of Public Records, Mr. W. B. D. D. Turnbull, an accomplished *amateur* in palæography, and Mr. N. E. S. A. Hamilton, papers being placed over all the writing except the signatures. Each of these three palæographists in succession examined the signatures, and each *independently* selected that which is at the foot of the disputed page of accounts, and pronounced it a forgery! Sir F. Madden has also very recently examined these accounts, at my request, and he pronounces them "a shameful forgery." Of the correctness of this conclusion the reader may form an opinion by comparing the facsimile of the impugned document with that which I have had made of some of the genuine writing and of a genuine signature of Sir Arthur Maynwaringe.

The ink chemically tested.

This forgery is not written in ordinary ink. The constituents of the colouring matter in this case are probably similar to that of the Perkins Folio. On applying the hydrosulphate of ammonia to one of the

[20] See Mr. Hardy's *Review*, p. 60.

forged signatures the colour remained unaffected: whence it follows that the colouring matter contains no iron. On the other hand, on the application of the same chemical to some genuine writing of Sir Arthur Maynwaringe's the black of the ink in which it is written was considerably intensified, a result which proves that its colour, like that of all common inks, is due to the presence of iron.

Identity of the handwritings of the Perkins notes, and of four MSS.

The writing of this forgery is, in all probability, by the same hand as the manuscript notes of the Perkins Folio, the Certificate of the Blackfriars Players, the Petition of the Blackfriars Players, and the Daborne Warrant.

CHAPTER XI.

The Dulwich Manuscripts.

The Library of Dulwich College contains a considerable number of manuscripts of very questionable genuineness, and not a few which, having been subjected to palæographical examination, have been condemned as forgeries. Those which I propose to consider in the present chapter may be thus enumerated:—

I. Some verses addressed to Edward Alleyn, (n.d.)

II. A list of players appended to a letter of the Council to the Lord Mayor, (n. d.)

III. A letter addressed to Henslowe, signed John Marston, (n. d.)

IV. A Complaint or Memorial from certain inhabitants of the liberty of Southwark, (July, 1596).

V. An Assessment for the poor of the liberty of Southwark, (April 6, 1609).

And to these may be added a genuine document, but one that has been falsified, if not tampered with, by Mr. Collier, viz.:

VI. A Letter to Edward Alleyn from his wife, (Oct. 20, 1603).

There is no evidence that any of these documents except no. IV. (as to which there is some little doubt) was known to Malone. Mr. Collier, indeed, says,[1] that the Assessment (no. V.) was known to Malone;

[1] Letter in the Athenæum of Feb. 18, 1860.

Spurious verses on Edward Alleyn.

Sweete Nedde nowe wynne an other wager
Ffor thine olde frende and fellow stager.
Tarlton himselfe thou doest excell
And Bentley beate and conquer Knell
And nowe shall Kempe orecome aswell
The moneyes downe the place the Hope
Phillippes shall hide his head and Pope.
Ffeare not the victorie is thine
Thou still as macheles Ned shall shine.
If Rossius Richard foames and fumes
The globe shall have but emptie roomes
If thou doest act, and Willes newe playe
Shall be rehearst some other daye.
Consent then Nedde, doe us this grace
Thou cannot faile in anie case
Ffor in the triall come what maye
All sides shall brave Ned Allin saye

Ashbee & Dangerfield [illegible]

and I am also aware that Mr. Collier[2] professes to have evidence in his possession that the List of Players (no. IV.) was also known to Malone: but the former statement is a "total mistake;" and the evidence in the latter case is such as cannot be received, as I shall hereafter shew.

I believe all these documents were first made public by Mr. Collier. I will take them *seriatim*. Verses on Edward Alleyn.

I. These verses are *verbatim* as follows:—

"Sweet Nedde nowe wynne an other wager
For thine old frende and fellow stager.
Tarlton himselfe thou doest excell
And Bentley beate and conquer Knell
And nowe shall Kempe orecome aswell.
The moneyes downe the place the Hope
Phillippes shall hide his head and Pope.
Feare not the victorie is thine
Thou still as macheles Ned shall shine.
If Roscius Richard foames and fumes
The globe shall haue but emptie roomes
If thou doest act, and Willes newe playe
Shall be rehearst some other daye
Consent then Nedde, doe vs this grace
Thou cannot faile in anie case
For in the triall come what maye
All sides shall braue Ned Allin saye"

It is not difficult to perceive on what material this wretched doggerel was constructed; viz. on a letter to Edward Alleyn, signed W. P., inserted in Boswell's Malone,[3] which alludes to a wager laid by Alleyn that he would equal, in acting, his predecessors KNELL and BENTLEY. It concludes thus:—

[2] Reply, p. 53. [3] Vol. iii. p. 335.

"if you excell them, you will then be famous; if equall them, you win both the wager and credit; if short of them, we must and will saie, NED ALLEN STILL."

Mr. Collier introduces these verses to the public in his *Memoirs of Edward Alleyn.*[4] After quoting the letter of W. P., and some authentic verses on the subject of it, he tells us that

"there is another paper of a very similar kind, apparently referring to the preceding, or to some other like contest, but containing several remarkable allusions, which Malone did not notice. Perhaps it never met his eye, or perhaps he reserved it for his Life of Shakespeare, and was unwilling to forestal that production by inserting it elsewhere. It seems to be of a later date, and it mentions not only Tarlton, Knell, and Bentley, but Kempe, Phillips, and Pope, while Alleyn's rival Burbage is sneered at as "Roscius Richard," and Shakespeare introduced under the name of Will, by which we have Thomas Heywood's authority (in his "Hierarchie of the blessed Angels," 1635, p. 206) for saying he was known among his companions."

And subsequently, Mr. Collier remarks:

"We need feel little hesitation in believing that the couplet

—— "and Willes newe playe
Shall be rehearst some other daye,"

refers to Shakespeare; but it may be doubtful whether we should take the word "rehearst" in the sense of a private repetition before public performance, which then, as now, it signified, or in the more general sense of *acted*."

Mr. Hamilton[5] says that these verses are

"a forgery from beginning to end, *although executed with singular dexterity*."

It appears to me to be one of the worst executed of all the fabricated documents. A *very slight* tre-

[4] Page 13. [5] Inquiry, p. 95.

mulousness is observable throughout the document, which it was quite impossible to reproduce in the facsimile; but which at once betrays the fact that it was written slowly from an alphabet with which the writer was not too familiar: a conclusion confirmed by the peculiarity of the various letters. Mr. Collier's reply is still more curious than the charge,—which in substance he admits—alleging as a reason that

"it now seems to [him] that the reduplication of consonants and other points of orthography in it, might possibly raise suspicion."[6]

The "reduplication of consonants," which Mr. Collier now thinks such a suspicious circumstance, occurs in only *five* different words among the one hundred and thirteen of which the piece consists—viz., *Nedde* (twice), *wynne, excell, Phillippes,* and *triall:* and not one of these forms of spelling, except, perhaps, the last proper name, is extraordinary in writing of the time!

The List of Players appended to a letter from the Council to the Lord Mayor.

II. This is *verbatim* as follows:—

"Ks Comp
Burbidge
Shakspre
Fletcher
Phillips
Condle
Hemminges
Armyn
Slye

[6] Reply, p. 54.

Cowley
Hostler
Day"[7]

The existence of this list was first made public in a note to the *Memoirs of Edward Alleyn.*[8]

Mr. Collier says,

"Malone appears to have reserved another circumstance, of very considerable importance in relation to Shakespeare, for his life of the poet. To the last quoted document [*i. e.* a letter from the Council of the City of London to the Lord Mayor, dated 9 April, 1604], but in a different hand and in different ink, is appended a list of the King's players. The name of Shakespeare there occurs second; and as it could not be written at the bottom of the letter of the Council to the Lord Mayor, &c. prior to the date of that letter, it proves that up to 9th April, 1604, our great dramatist continued to be numbered among the *actors* of the company. Hitherto the last trace we have had of Shakespeare as actually on the stage, has been as one of the performers in Ben Jonson's "Sejanus," which was produced in 1603."

Mr. Hamilton writes,[9]

"Any one who will compare the character of the hand in which the "List" is written, with the letter signed H. S. in the Bridgewater library, will probably arrive at the conclusion I have done that they are by the same hand."

[7] This List is given on the sheet of facsimiles no. XVI., where it will be observed that the name of Shakspere is evidently written with an eye to that appended to the seal of the mortgage deed. There the reason for the abbreviation was the narrowness of the slip of parchment on which it was written; no such reason exists in the case of the "List."

[8] Page 68. [9] Inquiry, p. 96.

My readers may compare the facsimiles on sheets nos. XIII. and XVI., and judge for themselves of the correctness of Mr. Hamilton's opinion, in which I coincide. Among other similarities in the forms of the letters to those characterizing the H. S. letter, is the very remarkable g in "Hemminges."

Mr. Collier's replies.

Mr. Collier's first reply to this charge of spuriousness was founded on the mistake of confounding this impugned document with no. V. This error he points out in his *Reply*,[10] and takes credit for his candour and truthfulness. The fact, however, is that he had been accused of *intentionally* misstating the subject of Mr. Hamilton's charge, and had no option but to correct the mistake. Mr. Collier there says,

"The "list of players," which Mr. Hamilton charges as a modern addition to a genuine document, I saw and quoted with the other papers; and if the names were forged, I can only say that they must have been upon the instrument when it was seen by Malone before 1796, although he did not extract it, reserving it, perhaps, (as I said in my *Memoirs of Edward Alleyn*) for his *Life of Shakespeare*. My materials for those *Memoirs* were in great part collected while I was engaged on my *History of English Dramatic Poetry and the Stage;* and I can most distinctly aver that the "list of players" was then extant, and that it was seen by Mr. Amyot, who accompanied me in one of my earlier expeditions to Dulwich. I myself state (*Mem. of Alleyn*, p. 67) that the "list" itself is "in a different hand and in different ink," which I need not have mentioned if I had not wished to produce all the circumstances

[10] Page 52.

regarding it, that would enable a correct judgment to be formed of its authenticity. Moreover, to set this matter completely at rest, I have now before me Malone's copy of his *Inquiry* (8vo, 1796), as annotated by him for a second edition: it is full of scribbled scraps and notes with information, not contained in the first edition, and on the back of a letter addressed to "Mr. Malone, Queen Anne Street, East," is the very list of players in question. Therefore, whether it were or were not an addition subsequent to the date of the original document to which it is appended, it is certain that it was seen by Malone very many years before I was at Dulwich."

Rejoinder to them.

Could Mr. Collier have been so blind as not to see that, if he were the forger his opponents believe, the mere mention (without production) of this "letter addressed to Mr. Malone, Queen Anne Street, East," with the list of players on the back, would only be another circumstance of suspicion; and that the alleged memorandum, if it really existed, was as likely to be a forgery of Mr. Collier's as the "list of players" itself? Has it not a strong family likeness to "the direction of a letter to the Rev. Mr. Todd," which Mr. Collier says he found within the leaves of the volume of accounts of Household Expences at Bridgewater House, "to keep the place" where the forged document had been inserted?

If Mr. Collier be innocent of this charge of forgery, he has certainly taken the shortest and most efficacious means of fostering the suspicions which his previous conduct had aroused. It is certainly not incredible that this list on the back of the letter

Dedication of a Volume of Manuscript Poems of John Marston (in the Library at Bridgewater House) in the handwriting of the Poet.

Madam

If my slight Muse may sute yoͤ noble merrit
My hopes are crownd, & I shall cheere my spirit
But if my weake quill droopes, or seems vnfitt
Tis not yoͤ want of worth, but mine of witt.

The servant of yoͤ Honor'd
Virtues
John Marston.

III.

Forged letter addressed to Henslow, the Actor, signed John Marston.

Mr Hensloe at the rose on the Bankside

If you like my play of Columbus it is verie well & you shall giue mee noe more then twentie poundes for it but If nott lett mee haue it by this Bearer againe as I knowe the Kinges Men will freelie giue mee asmuch for it and the profitts of the third daye moreouer

Soe I rest yours
John Marston.

to Malone (if such a letter be in existence) may be in Malone's handwriting. But, who will believe *that*, who already believes that the "list" at Dulwich was written by Mr. Collier? Let Mr. Collier deposit this letter with Sir F. Madden or Sir Francis Palgrave for public inspection if he really wish to rebut the present charge. But it is note-worthy that Mr. Collier never takes that mode of clearing himself which a man of sense, strong in the consciousness of innocence, would naturally take.[11] If he possess the means of rebutting this odious charge, it is surely little short of insanity to withhold it.

III. This is *verbatim* as follows:—

The Letter addressed to Henslow, signed "John Marston."

"Mr Hensloe at the rose on the Bankside

If you like my play of Columbus it is verie . well & you

shall giue mee noe more than twentie poundes for it but If nott

lett mee haue it ^by this Bearer^ againe as I knowe the kinges Men will freelie

giue mee asmuch for it and the profitts of the third daye

moreover

Soe I rest yours

John Marston"

This was also made public by Mr. Collier in his *Memoirs of Edward Alleyn*, where he says,[12]

---

[11] Similarly, in the case of that abominable imposition, the *Seven Lectures*, attributed by Mr. Collier to Coleridge, Mr. Collier withholds the production of any of the short-hand notes which he professes to have, and which is the only conceivable evidence of the genuineness of the lectures.

[12] Page 154, note.

"it refers to a play by Marston on the subject of Columbus, of which we hear on no other authority. It is one of the scraps of correspondence between Henslowe and the poets in his employ, existing at Dulwich College, of the major part of which Malone has given copies, but omitting the subsequent, which is certainly one of the most interesting in the whole collection."

Mr. Hamilton pronounces this letter a forgery. This it unquestionably is. The signature, which he considers like Marston's, is to my sight very different. The reader may here judge for himself by comparing the facsimiles on sheet no. XV.

In this case there is one circumstance in which the manuscript resembles the notes in the Bridgewater and Perkins Folios. Mr. Hamilton tells us,[13]

"I soon noticed the existence of numerous modern pencil-marks underlying the ink, and on looking closely into the document, detected that *the whole of the letter had been first traced out in pencil after the same fashion as the pencilling in the annotated folio of Shakspere's Plays*, 1632;"

That this is the case my readers may judge for themselves, by inspecting the adjoining facsimile of the letter. Mr. Collier prudently passes over this case of proven fraud without a single remark.

The Complaint of certain inhabitants of the liberty of Southwark.

IV. This consists of a single slip of paper, containing a list of certain alleged inhabitants of the liberty of Southwark, in the year 1596. Whether this manuscript was published by Mr. Collier before his edition of Shakspere, 1858, was issued, I do not know; at any rate I have not been able to find earlier mention of it in any work of Mr. Collier's.

[13] Inquiry, p. 94.

II

…f Players appended to a letter
…the Council of the City of London,
to the Lord Mayor.

…e Pope
…urbadge
…hakspe…
…elder
…hillips
…ondle
…emminges
…rowne
…lye
…owley
…ostler
…ane

IV.

Complaint of Certain Inhabitants of the Liberty of Southwark.

Inhabitantes of Sowthwarke as have complaned
this Jully 1596
Mr Markes
Mr Tuggell
Mr Langorth
Wilsone the pyper
Mr Barett
Mr Shatspere
Phillipes
Tomson
Moseles Godfrey the baude
Nagoe
Fillpott and no more and soe well ended

Ashbee & Dangerfield, Facsim.
[illegible]

Whether Malone referred to it in his *Inquiry* is a matter of grave doubt. Mr. Collier introduces it to his readers in the following words:—"

"But Malone tells us—"From a paper now before me, "which formerly belonged to Edward Alleyn, the player, our "poet appears to have lived in Southwark, near the Bear-"Garden, in 1596."* He gives us no farther insight into the contents of the paper; but he probably referred to a small slip, borrowed with other relics of a like kind, from Dulwich College, many of which were not returned after his death. Among those returned seems to have been the paper in question, which is valuable only because it proves distinctly, that our great dramatist was an inhabitant of Southwark very soon after the Globe was in operation, although it by no means establishes that he had not been resident there long before. We subjoin it exactly as it stands in the original: the hand writing is ignorant, the spelling peculiar, and it was evidently merely a hasty and imperfect memorandum.

"Inhabitantes of Southerk as haue complaned this of Jully 1596

Mr Markis
Mr Tuppin
Mr langorth
Wilsone the pyper
Mr Barett
Mr Shakspor
Phellipes
Tomson
Mother Golden the baude
Nagges
Fillpott and no more and soe well ended"

" Life of William Shakespeare, 1858, chapter x. p. 126.

* Inquiry into the authenticity of certain miscellaneous papers and legal documents, 1796, p. 215.

This is the whole of the fragment, for such it appears to be, and without farther explanation, which we have not been able to find in any other document, in the depository where the above is preserved or elsewhere, it is impossible to understand more, than that Shakespeare and other inhabitants of Southwark had made some complaint in July 1596, which we may guess, was hostile to the wishes of the writer, who congratulated himself that the matter was so well at an end."

With Mr. Halliwell[15] I am strongly disposed to think that Mr. Collier is mistaken in supposing that Malone's reference was to this paper; for Malone evidently meant to say that he had a paper before him containing a reference to the Bear-Garden at Southwark, which is not mentioned in the "Complaint" of "Mr. Shaksper" and "Mother Golden the baude"!

Be that as it may, this document was last spring examined by Mr. Hamilton, Professor Brewer, and Mr. T. Duffus Hardy, who all pronounced it an abominable forgery.

V. This is *verbatim* as follows:—

Assessment for the poor of the Liberty of Southwark.

"A brief noat taken out of the poores booke contayning the names of all thenhabitantes of this liberty wch are rated and assessed to a weekely paim¹ towardes the reliefe of the poore. As it standes nowe encreased, this 6th day of aprill 1609. Deliuered vp to Phillip Henslowe Esquior churchwarden, by Francis Carter one of the late ouerseers of the same Libertie"

(Then follow the names of fifty-seven persons, with the amounts set opposite their names in which they are rated; and among them we find these three),—

[15] Life of Shakespeare, p. 163, note.

V.

Assessment of Inhabitants of the Liberty of Southwark.

A brief noat taken out of the poores booke contayning the names of all thenhabitantes of this libertie which are rated and assessed to a weekely paiment towardes the releife of the poore As it standes nowe encreased, this 6th day of aprill 1609. Deliuered vp to Phillip Henslowe Esquior churchwarden, by ffrancis Carter one of the late overseers of the same Libertie

	d.
Phillip Henslowe esquior assessed at weekely	vj
Ed Alleyn assessed at weekely	vj
The Ladie Burkley	iiij
Mr Cole	iiij
Mr Lee	iiij
Mrs Cannon	iij
Mrs White	iij
Mr Langworthe	iij
Mr Benfield	iij
Mr Cowden	iij
Mr Shawnyge	iij
Mrs Sparrowhawke	ij
Mr Mason	ij
Mr Walford	ij
Mr Badger	ij
Mr Hughes	ij
Mr Dawson	ij
Mr Hovell	ij
Mr Griffin	ij
Mr Toppin	ij
Mr Cenis	ij
Mr Lymon	ij
Mr Leonard	ij
Mr Simpson	ij
Mr Maynard	ij
Mr Burkett	ij
ffrancis Carter	ij
Mr Storke for halfe the parke	ij
hughe Robinson for halfe the parke	ij
Mr Carre	ij
Gilbert Catherens	ij

	d
Mr Shakespeare	vj
Mr Ed Collins	vj
John Burritt	vj
Roger Jones	~~x~~ iij ob
Mychaell Elsmore	~~x~~ iij ob
Mr Towne	ij ob
Mr Tubie	j ob
Mr Mansfield	j ob
John Dodson	j ob
Richard Smith	j ob
Richard Hunt	j ob
Simon Bird	j ob
Peter Nasam	j ob
Jeames Kiddon	j ob
Tho Stokes	j ob
John ~~[illegible]~~ Sarge	j ob
Phillip Philpott	j ob
Willm Stephens	j ob
Mr Godfrey Richards for the long slip of ground	j ob
Mr Coggen weekely	j ~~ob~~
Ferdynando Moses	j ~~ob~~
Edw Novell	j ~~ob~~
John Baron	j ~~ob~~
Mrs Dawson	j
Rafe Trott	j
John Judkin	j

	d
"Phillip Henslowe esquior assessed at weekly	vj
Ed Alleyn assessed at weekly	vj
* * * * *	*
Mr Shakespeare	vj "[16]

This document was first published by Mr. Collier in his *Memoirs of Edward Alleyn*, 1841,"[17] (p. 91), and has been received as genuine up to the spring of this year, when Mr. Hamilton, Professor Brewer, and Mr. T. Duffus Hardy examined it, and unhesitatingly pronounced it a modern forgery. It is certainly a very clumsy business. The writing is an extremely bad imitation of a 17th century hand; and it is on a piece of paper which had once served for the flyleaf of a book, as is evidenced by one of the edges being red. It will be remembered that similarly the gilt edge of the Daborne Warrant is one of the circumstances which concur with the suspicion of forgery which the writing excites.

The genuineness of no. V. of the Dulwich Manuscripts, as far as I am aware, was not publicly impugned till the publication of Mr. Staunton's excellent *Life of Shakspere*.[18] It is an unquestionable forgery. I have given a facsimile of it on sheet no. XVII. Mr. Collier, erroneously conceiving that Mr. Hamilton had impugned its genuineness, writes—[19]

"Mr. Hamilton also falls foul of other biographical materials which I met with, and which unquestionably exist in the same charitable Institution [*i. e.* Dulwich College]. One of them is a Player's Challenge,"[20] collated by Mr. Halliwell, and printed

[16] See Mr. Ashbee's facsimile for the rest. [17] Page 17.
[18] Page 31. [19] Athenæum, Feb. 18, 1860.
[20] He means the Verses on Edward Alleyn.

by him in 1848, as a genuine relic, of the same kind as several others that have come down to our time. Another is a sort of assessment to the poor of Southwark, dated 8th of April, 1609, in which Shakespeare appears as a contributor; and surely it is enough for me to say of this document, that it was seen by Malone when I was only seven years old, as he has himself recorded in his 'Enquiry,' 8vo. 1796, p. 215."

This statement I believe to have produced a considerable impression on the public mind, as nobody supposed that Mr. Collier would assert the thing that was not, where detection was so easy. But the fact is that the Assessment for the Poor of Southwark was not (as I have said) called in question by Mr. Hamilton in his *Inquiry;* but he might safely have done so, for it is a very modern fabrication, nor does Malone's *Inquiry*, either at p. 215, or at any other page of that interesting work, contain any allusion whatever to such a document!

In his *Reply*[u] Mr. Collier quotes from p. 215 of Malone's *Inquiry* the following passage:—

"We see hence that Shakspeare had no motive to reside in the Blackfriars before this period [March 1604-5]. The truth, indeed, I believe is that he never resided in the Blackfriars at all. From a paper *now before me, which formerly belonged to Edward Alleyn, the player, our poet appears to have lived in Southwark, near the Bear-Garden, in* 1596. Another curious document *in my possession*, which will be produced in the History of his Life, affords the strongest presumptive evidence *that he continued to reside in Southwark to the year* 1608."

Now what has this extract to do with the Assessment in question, which is dated April 8th, 1609? Even according to the obsolete ecclesiastical reckon-

[u] Page 46.

Extract from a letter to Edward Alleyn, from his Wife, being the last eight lines on the first page.

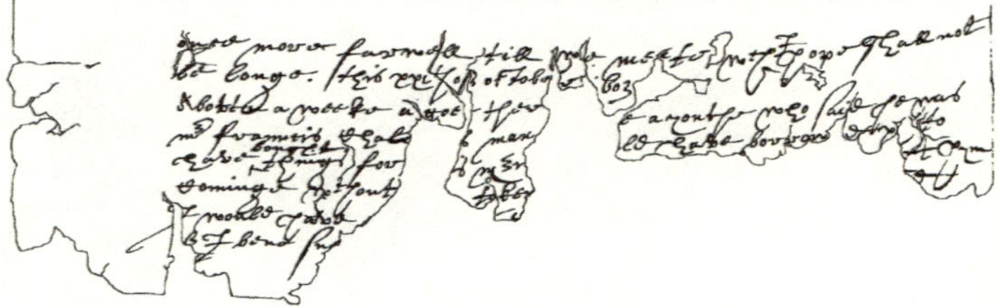

To face p. 278

ing, the year 1608 ended on March 24th of that year, so it is plain that Malone referred to some other document.[22]

The Letter to Edward Alleyn from his wife.

VI. The following is a *verbatim* copy of all that remains of the postscript to a long and interesting letter addressed to Edward Alleyn by his most excellent wife—one of those that Solomon failed to find among ten thousand, and in Shakspere's day were held to "mend the lottery well" an there were "one born but for every blazing star, or at an earthquake."[23]

> once more farwell till we meete wth I hope shall not be longe. this xxith of october [1]603.
>
> Aboute a weeke agoe ther[e] [cam]e a youthe who said he was
> Mr Frauncis Chalo[ner]s man [& wou]ld have borrow[e]d xl[s] to
> have ^bought things for [hi]s Mr[is] . . . . [trus]t hym
> Cominge wthout . . token. . . . . d
> I would have . . . .
> [i]f I bene sue[r][24] . . . .
>
> ---
>
> and inquire after the fellow and said he had lent hym a horse. I feare me he gulled hym thoughe he gulled not ^us

The line which divides the postscript marks the

---

[22] Mr. Hamilton appears to regard it as a suspicious circumstance that Mr. Collier attributes the absence of certain documents from Malone's *Inquiry* to the circumstance that he had reserved them for his Life of Shakspere, (see Hamilton's *Inquiry*, p. 95). But it is beyond question that Malone did reserve several documents for his Life of Shakspere, which he might have appropriately introduced in support of the statements in his *Inquiry*. For two examples, see Malone's *Inquiry*, 1796, p. 215.

[23] All's well that ends well, act i. sc. 3.

[24] Mr. Halliwell reads these four words ". . I bene sur"; Mr. Hamilton reads them, "& I bene su". With all the

bottom of the first page of the letter; the words "and inquire," are at the top of the second page.

Mr. Collier's falsified version of it.

Now in Mr. Collier's *Memoirs of Edward Alleyn*,[25] where this letter was first published, the postscript is given *verbatim* as follows, but not broken into lines to correspond with the original.

> . . noe more. Farwell till we meete, which I hope shall not
> be longe. This xxth of October 1603.
> "Aboute a weeke a goe there came a youthe who said he was
> Mr. Frauncis Chaloner who would have borrowed xli to
> have bought things for . . . and said he was known
> unto you, and Mr. Shakespeare of the globe, who came
> . . . said he knewe hym not, onely he herde of hym that he was
> a roge . . . so he was glade we did not lend him
> the monney . . . Richard Johnes [went] to seeke
>
> ---
>
> and inquire after the fellow, and said he had lent hym a horse. I
> feare me he gulled him, thoughe he gulled not us."

This alleged transcript was introduced by the following remarks:—

"Of this date [20th October, 1603] we have a very interesting letter from Mrs. Alleyn to her husband, written and subscribed by the person ordinarily employed; it is remarkable, because it contains a mention of Shakespeare, who is spoken of as "of the Globe;" and though it throws no new light upon our great dramatist's character, excepting as it shews that he was on good terms with Alleyn's family, any document containing merely his name must be considered valuable. The paper on which the letter was written is in a most decayed state, especially at

---

respect due from me to such authorities, I must say that I am quite certain the true lection is what I have given. The s in x[s] and that in [trus]t I have had printed in italic type to indicate that only portions of those letters are left. Mr. Collier and Mr. Hamilton agree in giving a wrong date to this letter.

[25] Page 63.

the bottom, where it breaks and drops away in dust and fragments at the slightest touch.[26] The notice of Shakespeare is near the commencement of a postscript on the lower part of the page, where the paper is most rotten, and several deficiencies occur, which it is impossible to supply: all that remains is extremely difficult to be deciphered."

That is a matter of experience. I am probably far less practised in record-reading than Mr. Collier, yet I find no difficulty at all in reading "all that remains" of this most interesting letter. My readers, however, may judge for themselves from the accompanying facsimile; in verification of which they may consult the original at Dulwich College, or Mr. Fairholt's facsimile in Mr. Halliwell's *Curiosities of Modern Shakesperian Criticism*,[27] or Mr. Frederick G. Netherclift's facsimile in Mr. Hamilton's *Inquiry*.[28] To Mr. Halliwell belongs the credit of exposing Mr. Collier's falsification of this letter: yet he did so in such very gentle terms that a careless reader, who did not examine the facsimile, would infer that Mr. Collier had done nothing worse than (to use Mr. Collier's own words) "misreading some utterly unimportant words." Mr. Hamilton is bolder, and plainly charges Mr. Collier with falsification. Mr.

---

[26] It is impossible that this could have been the case; the paper even now shews no symptoms of crumbling into dust. It is torn, indeed, and portions are wanting, where the paper has all the appearance of having been eaten away by an acid; but it is far from being rotten.

[27] Page 29. [28] Page 86.

Mr. Collier's replies concerning the letter from Mrs. Alleyn.

Collier's replies are very curious. In "The Athenæum,"[29] he writes :—

[α] "A much-decayed letter has been preserved in the Library [at Dulwich College] from Mrs. Alleyn to her husband, dated Oct. 3, [*sic*] 1603, and in one part of it, according to my reading, she mentions having seen "Mr. Shakespeare of the globe."[β] It is admitted on all hands, that the letter is very rotten, and that portions of it are deficient in this place; but the gist of the imputation is, that Shakespeare was never spoken of in it, but that I, taking advantage of the defects in the old paper, purposely misrepresented the matter. It is added[30] that for the accomplishment of this fraud, I misread and misrepresented the contents of the letter. Now inasmuch as the old decayed paper is here indisputably defective, Mr. Hamilton could not possibly know whether Shakespeare's name had or had not been visible when I saw the letter thirty years ago.[γ] I may or may not have mis-read some utterly unimportant words,[δ] nor does it signify at all, as regards his biography, whether Shakespeare was or was not in Southwark on the 3rd of October, 1603; but I assert most distinctly, that the name was contained in this part of Mrs. Alleyn's letter, and a dear and dead friend of mine could bear witness to the fact were he fortunately now alive."

In his *Reply*,[31] Mr. Collier writes:—

"One of the first documents I looked at was, I think, a letter from Mrs. Alleyn to her husband, dated 3rd [*sic*] Oct., 1603, upon which has now been founded the charge that I interpolated a passage not met with in the original. It was in one place in so decayed and crumbling a condition from the effects of damp and time, that I was obliged to handle it with the utmost cau-

[29] Feb. 18, 1860.

[30] I apprehend this *addition* is a clerical error. The addition is a mere repetition of the last clause.

[31] Page 47-50.

tion. I did not read it nor examine it closely until afterwards, how long I do not pretend to say, but a friend, now unfortunately dead, was with me, and we then read as follows, in the latter part of the letter."

[Here follows Mr. Collier's version of the postscript as in *Memoirs of Edward Alleyn*, 8vo. 1841, p. 63.]

[β] "Now the question is, and the only question of the slightest importance (though that is in truth of little moment) whether the name of "Mr. Shakespeare of the globe" occurred in the most rotten and fragmentary part of the letter at the time when I copied it. Whether it did or did not is not of the smallest interest, as regards the biography of our poet, especially as there were two, if not three, other Shakespeares "of the Globe" Theatre, then resident in Southwark. However, the charge is that from the mere love of deception (for I could have no other motive) I imagined the part of the letter in which the name of Shakespeare occurs, and corrupted the immediately adjoining portions for the purpose of giving my invention support.

It is indisputable that since I first saw and copied the letter at Dulwich, portions of it have crumbled away and entirely disappeared; so that Mr. Hamilton's account of the contents differs from mine; he accuses me not only of inaccuracy, but of fraud and wilful misrepresentation.[γ] I do not deny that it is possible I misread some utterly unimportant letters or words: the paper was in such a state of demolition that it was extremely difficult to make any sense out of the latter part of it; but I did my best to give a faithful transcript, and I am absolutely certain that "Mr. Shakespeare of the globe" was spoken of in it, and in the way I stated [ε] * * * Mr. Hamilton insists that the name of Shakespeare never was to be seen on any part of the paper which is now rotted away; but how can he tell whether it did or did not exist there, when he cannot deny that much of what was originally written on that part of the paper has been utterly annihilated ?"

To the allegations which I have distinguished by Greek letters, I will reply *seriatim*.

Rejoinder to them.

The statement marked (α) is not accurate. In the letter referred to, Mrs. Alleyn does not, according to Mr. Collier's reading, or any one else's reading, mention "having seen 'Mr. Shakespeare of the globe';" but simply that Mr. Shakespeare of the globe "came .... said he knew him not," &c. It is strange that Mr. Collier even garbles his own falsified version of this letter.

(β) Admitting the defective and decayed state of the bottom of the first page of this letter, it is certainly NOT the gist of the imputation that Shakspere was never spoken of in it. Mr. Hamilton never made any such a statement. His statement[23] is that

"portions of the three damaged lines are still legible, which are incompatible with the *Shakspere paragraph*,"

That is the gist of the imputation. Neither Mr. Hamilton nor any one else who does not remember the letter in a more perfect condition than that in which it is at present can say whether or not Shakspere's name was originally in the letter. For all we know to the contrary Ben Jonson's name may have occupied one of the missing portions. But, be this as it may, *the only portion which is defective*

[23] Inquiry, p. 88.

contains enough that is perfectly legible to render it certain that Mr. Collier's paragraph about "Mr. Shakspeare of the globe," never was there. Fortunately NO ENTIRE LINE IS WANTING. Counting from and after the words "things for," the last four lines on the page contain *nine entire* words which are still perfectly legible. None of these words are in Mr. Collier's version of those last four lines. Mr. Collier's version of those portions contains *forty-five* words, (besides one in crotchets) not one of which is found among the *nine* yet remaining. But more than this. In the identical place where Mr. Collier tells us that he and his friend read "unto you and M^r^ S*hakes*peare" (which is half a line) "cominge w^th^out . *token* . . ." yet remains unimpaired, and perfectly legible.

(γ) This extraordinary falsification is to Mr. Collier nothing more than misreading some utterly unimportant words!

(δ) What Mr. Collier's object may have been in perpetrating this falsification, it is quite impossible for any one but himself to say: but admitting what he contends for, that it does not signify at all, as regards Shakspere's biography, whether Shakspere was or was not in Southwark on the 21st of October, 1603, it still would be doubtless an interesting fact, (if it were a fact at all), as Mr. Collier points out,[33] that Shakspere "was on good terms with Alleyn's family"; but the anecdote has nevertheless a significant bearing, as we shall shortly see.

[33] Memoirs of Alleyn, p. 62.

(ε) This statement is incorrect, as Mr. Collier, with Mr. Hamilton's *Inquiry* before him, had the means of knowing.

Mr. Collier's replies continued.

But Mr. Collier further says,[34]

[ζ] "Let it not be forgotten that if my object had been to commit the imputed fraud, nothing could have been more easy than for me to have rubbed away a little more of the crumbling paper, and who then could have detected the trick?"

And again:—[35]

[η] "Here allow me to ask this question: If I had purposely misstated the import and contents of the letter, adding that it was in a state of ruinous decay, what would have been the natural course for me to have pursued? Would it not have been to have left the letter as it was, in the hope that when it was next seen and consulted, as much of it might have disappeared as possible? Instead of doing so—instead of leaving it still to be exposed to the action of air and accident, I carefully enclosed it in paper, and either I or my friend wrote on the outside, that within was a document of value which should not be roughly handled, * * as if to make sure that the next person who opened the paper should see that I had been guilty of fraud.[ζ] If, indeed, I had so misrepresented the contents of the crumbling relic, what was to prevent my rubbing away a little more of the old paper, and who then would have been able to detect the trick I had played?"

Further rejoinder.

As to the paragraphs marked (ζ) and (η) taken together, I have simply to call the reader's attention to the fact that they are inconsistent. If, as in (η), the "natural course" for Mr. Collier to have taken for avoiding detection was "to have left the letter as it was," he certainly would not have yielded

[34] The Athenæum, Feb. 18, 1860. [35] Reply, p. 50.

to the temptation described in (ζ), viz. "to have rubbed away a little more of the crumbling paper."

To the single paragraph marked (ζ), I remark further, that the paper not being in a crumbling state, Mr. Collier must have done something more than "rubbed" at it; he must have torn out the tell-tale portions, and that would have been as easily detected as performed. In the second place, I will quote the reply of a writer in "The Critic."[86]

"What have we to do with motives when we have facts which are not to be controverted? Mr. Collier very aptly and clearly sees how he might have removed the proofs; but he does not deny that he is the author of the spurious version, and in that and in the original the proofs still exist. If we are to say that it is impossible that an educated man can be guilty because he has not destroyed the traces of his guilt, then can no educated man be convicted of anything whatever—then have Dr. Dodd, Mr. Fauntleroy, and Sir John Dean Paul been wrongfully condemned."

In reply to the single paragraph marked (η), I must inform the reader that the envelope is still in existence; but that the superscription, so far from being, as Mr. Collier says, in his own writing, or even in that of Mr. Amyot,[87] the "dear and dead friend" referred to, seems to be in that of Mr. Halliwell, who,

---

[86] March 3, 1860.

[87] The editor of "Notes and Queries" says, without qualification, that the superscription is in Mr. Amyot's writing. No one who has ever seen Mr. Amyot's writing could, I am positive, trace the slightest resemblance between it and that in which the superscription is written.

I believe, enclosed the letter in it since the publication of Mr. Collier's *Memoirs of Edward Alleyn.*

The anecdote not original.

The only question remaining to be considered in relation to this letter, is, Whence did Mr. Collier obtain the anecdote about Shakspere's purse-proud sneer at the poor hack who "would have borrowed x^{s}" of Mrs. Alleyn? Did Mr. Collier invent it? Not a bit of it. I do not believe the story to date from recent times. At present I have not been successful in tracing it to head-quarters; but it was characteristically (possibly in a genuine form) cited by a writer in the "Prospective Review,"* who, so far from thinking, as Mr. Collier does, that "it is not of the smallest interest as regards the biography of our poet," pronounced it "the only antiquarian thing which can be fairly called an anecdote of Shakespeare"! The "Prospective Review" gives the anecdote in these words:

> "Mrs. Alleyne, a shrewd woman in those times, and married to Mr. Alleyne, the founder of Dulwich Hospital, was one day, in the absence of her husband applied to on some matter by *a player* who gave a reference to *Mr. Hemmings*, (the "notorious" Mr. Hemmings the Commentators say), and to Mr. Shakespeare of the Globe, and that the latter, when referred to, said, "*Yes, certainly, he knew him, and he was a rascal, and good-for-nothing.*"

The Review calls this reply "the proper speech of a substantial man."

* Vol. ix. p. 446.

CHAPTER XII.

The Forged State Paper.

Besides the libraries of Devonshire House, Bridgewater House and Dulwich College, one of the branch repositories of Her Majesty's Public Records, viz. the State Paper Office in Duke Street, Westminster, is a *locus in quo* the forger's handiwork is visible. In fact, there is one document contained in a parcel marked 'Bundle, No. 222, Elizabeth, 1596,' which is a forgery.

The Petition of the owners and players of the Black-friars Theatre to the Privy Council.

This forged State Paper purports to be a petition from the owners and players of the Blackfriars Theatre to the Privy Council, (n. d.) and from Mr. Collier's account a reader might infer that it had been discovered by himself. He gives the following account of it in his *History of English Dramatic Poetry and Annals of the Stage.*[1]

"The Blackfriars Theatre, built in 1576, seems, after the lapse of twenty years, to have required extensive repairs, if indeed, it were not, at the end of that period, entirely rebuilt. This undertaking, in 1596, seems to have alarmed some of the inhabitants of the Liberty; and not a few of them, 'some of honour,' petitioned the Privy Council, in order that the players might not be allowed to complete it, and that their farther performances in that precinct might be prevented. A copy of the

[1] Vol. i. page 297.

document, containing this request, is preserved in the State Paper Office, and to it is appended a much more curious paper—a counter petition by the Lord Chamberlain's players, entreating that they might be permitted to continue their work upon the theatre, in order to render it more commodious, and that their performances there might not be interrupted. It does not appear to be the original, but a copy, without the signatures, and it contains, at the commencement, an enumeration of the principal actors who were parties to it. They occur in the following order, and it will be instantly remarked, not only that the name of Shakespeare is found among them, but that he comes fifth in the enumeration:—

'Thomas Pope,
'Richard Burbage,
'John Hemings,
'Augustine Phillips,
'William Shakespeare,
'William Kempe,
'William Slye,
'Nicholas Tooley.

This remarkable paper has, perhaps, never seen the light from the moment it was presented, until it was very recently discovered. It is seven years anterior to the date of any other authentic record, which contains the name of our great dramatist, and it may warrant various conjectures as to the rank he held in the company in 1596, as a poet and as a player.*

* Malone had nothing upon which to found himself, but the list of actors in some of Ben Jonson's plays, and the eumeration in the licence of 1603. The name of Shakespeare is, in the latter, preceded only by that of a person (Lawrence Fletcher) not mentioned in 1596, as having anything to do with the company: Burbage, Phillips, and Hemings, who stand before him in 1596, were postponed to him in 1603, to such importance does he seem to have risen in the interval. It is not necessary to point out other differences.

It is in these terms :—[a]

'To the right honorable the Ll of her Maties most honorable priuie Counsell

'The humble petition of Thomas Pope Richard Burbadge
'John Hemings Augustine Phillips Willm̄ Shakespeare Willm
'Kempe Willm Slye Nicholas Tooley and others seruaunts
'to the right honorable the L. Chamberlaine to her Matie—
'Sheweth most humbly that yor petitioners are owners and
'players of the priuate house or theater in the precinct and
'libertie of the Blackfriers wch hath beene for manie yeares
'vsed and occupied for the playing of tragedies commedies his-
'tories enterludes and playes That the same by reason of
'hauing beene soe long built hath falne into great decaye and that
'besides the reparation thereof it hath beene found necessarie to
'make the same more conuenient for the entertainement of audi-
'tories comming thereto That to this end yor petitioners haue
'all and eche of them putt downe sommes of money according to
'their shares in the saide theater and wch they haue iustly and
'honestlie gained by the exercise of their qualitie of Stage
'players but that certaine persons (some of them of honour)
'inhabitants of the precinct and libertie of the Blackfriers
'haue as yor petitioners are enfourmed besought yor honorable
'Lps not to permitt the saide priuate house anie longer to re-
'maine open but hereafter to be shut vpp and closed to the
'manifest and great iniurie of yor petitioners who haue no other
'meanes whereby to maintaine their wiues and families but by
'the exercise of their qualitie as they haue heretofore done.
'Furthermore t[h]at in the summer season yor petitioners are
'able to playe at their newe built house on the Bankside callde
'the Globe but that in the winter they are compelled to come to
'the Blackfriers and if yor honorable Lps giue consent vnto that
'wch is prayde against yor petitioners they will not onely while

[a] I have corrected Mr. Collier's version of this State Paper, as I did that of the Complaint of certain inhabitants of Southwark, at p. 275 of this work.

'the winter endureth loose the meanes whereby they nowe sup-'port them selues and their families but be vnable to practise 'them selues in anie playes or enterluds, when calde vpon to 'performe for the recreation and solace of her Matie and her 'honorable Court as they haue beene hertofore accustomed. The 'humble prayer of yor petitioners therefore is that yor honble 'Lps will graunt permission to finishe the reparations and altera-'tions they haue begunne and as yor petitioners haue hitherto 'beene well ordred in their behauiour and iust in their deal-'inges that yor honorable Lps will not inhibit them from acting 'at their aboue named priuate house in the precinct and libertie 'of the Blackfriers and yor petitioners as in dutie most bounden 'will ever praye for the encreasing honour and happinnesse of yor 'honorable Lps."

This document was also published by Mr. Halliwell in his Folio Edition of Shakspeare,[3] as a genuine document, and he there gives a facsimile of it executed by Mr. Ashbee. The fact is that its spuriousness was not suspected till the winter of 1858-59 when it excited the suspicions of Mr. Staunton. These suspicions were at once communicated to Sir F. Madden, who did not seem to attach much weight to them. Ultimately Mr. Staunton induced Mr. Hamilton and Mr. Hardy to accompany him to the State Paper Office, when both those gentlemen unhesitatingly pronounced the document a forgery executed by the same hand as appears in such "wanton heed" and elaborate stupidity on the margins of the Perkins Folio.

Mr. Hamilton[4] says of this pseudo-State Paper,

"Its execution is very neat, and with any one not acquainted

---

[3] Vol. i. p. 137. [4] Inquiry, p. 96.

with the fictitious hand of these Shakspere forgeries it might readily pass as genuine. But an examination of the handwriting generally, the forms of some of the letters in particular, and the spurious appearance of the ink, led me to the belief not only that the paper [i. e. document] was not authentic, but that it had been executed *by the same hand* as the fictitious documents already discussed."

This conclusion is point blank denied by Mr. H. Merivale,[5] who recklessly asserts that,

"The handwriting is not only not the handwriting of the Corrector, but it is of an essentially different character and period."

Palæographic examinations of it.

As this assertion can be very easily disproved, I have furnished the reader with the evidence on which the judgment of the palæographists rests, in the shape of three facsimiles, viz. of the State Paper in question, of two of the longer pieces of manuscript in the Perkins Folio, and of the Certificate of Players at Bridgewater House. These three facsimiles are on sheet no. X. The reader is thus enabled by inspecting one sheet to form an opinion for himself on the identity of the handwritings; on this point there can be, I apprehend, but one intelligent opinion. But independently of any such inference, the document in question is a condemned forgery. On the 30th of January last, in obedience to the instructions of the Master of the Rolls, five palæographists, viz. Sir Francis Palgrave, Sir Frederic Madden, Professor Brewer, Mr. T. Duffus Hardy, and Mr. N. E. S. A. Hamilton met at the State Paper Office, and having

[5] The Edinburgh Review, Ap. 1860, vol. cxi. p. 484.

subjected the document to a palæographic examination arrived at the following unanimous decision on its character, which is appended to the document.

The opinion of five leading palæographists upon the question of its genuineness.

"We, the undersigned, at the desire of the Master of the Rolls, have carefully examined the document hereunto annexed, purporting to be a petition to the Lords of Her Majesty's Privy Council, from Thomas Pope, Richard Burbadge, John Hemings, Augustine Phillips, William Shakespeare, William Kempe, William Slye, Nicholas Tooley, and others, in answer to a petition from the Inhabitants of the Liberty of the Blackfriars; and we are of opinion, that the document in question is spurious.

30th January, 1860.

(Signed.) FRA. PALGRAVE, K.H., Deputy-Keeper of H.M. Public Records.
FREDERIC MADDEN, K.H., Keeper of the MSS., British Museum.
J. S. BREWER, M.A., Reader at the Rolls.
T. DUFFUS HARDY, Assistant Keeper of Records.
N. E. S. A. HAMILTON, Assistant, Dep. of MSS., British Museum.

"I direct this paper to be appended to the undated document now last in the Bundle, marked 222, Eliz. 1596.

2nd February, 1860.

(Signed.) JOHN ROMILLY, Master of the Rolls."

It is a remarkable instance of the fact that the same evidence affects different kinds of mind differently, that with full knowledge of the foregoing opinion arrived at by five eminently qualified palæographists taken from several departments of the state, the editor of "Notes and Queries" arrives at this conclusion, respecting the document in question, "in all probability it is genuine;"[6] and that simply because Mr. Lemon, one of the juniors of the Record Office, at the request of the editor of "The Athenæum," contributed to the columns of that periodical[7] the following effusion, which Mr. Collier dignifies with the name of an "important and indisputable piece of evidence."[8]

"State Paper Office, Feb. 14, 1860.

Mr. Lemon's letter to the Editor of the Athenæum.

Dear Sir,—In reply to your question, I beg to state that the Petition of the Players of the Blackfriars Theatre, alluded to in your note, was well known to my father and myself, before Mr. Payne Collier began his researches in this Office. I am pretty confident that my father himself brought it under the notice of Mr. Collier, in whose researches he took great interest.

I am very faithfully yours,

R. Lemon.

"The Editor of the Athenæum."

It must at first strike every one as extraordinary that the editor of "The Athenæum," while he was examining Mr. Lemon, should have omitted to ask that palæographist whether he believed the 'Players' Petition'[9] to be a genuine document. But on second thoughts that omission will cease to surprise any one: for it is now beyond a doubt that even if Mr. Lemon had refrained from denouncing the document as spurious, he had too much honesty and knowledge combined to allow him to speak of it otherwise than

[6] Notes and Queries, March 24, 1860.
[7] Feb. 18, 1860. [8] Reply, p. 59.
[9] *quasi* 1596.

as a very suspicious affair. Much as both Mr. Lechmere and Mr. Lemon have been "badgered" to pronounce an opinion counter to the sentence of Sir F. Palgrave, Sir F. Madden, and Messrs. Hardy, Brewer and Hamilton, they have found it expedient to preserve an unbroken silence; well knowing that they could not conscientiously dissent from the verdict of forgery, however much they might be disposed to acquit Mr. Collier of all participation in it.

But Mr. Lemon, in his anxiety to exonerate his father's friend from that serious charge, if he proves anything, proves too much. He says,

"I am pretty confident that my father himself brought it under the notice of Mr. Collier, in whose researches he took great interest."

Mr. Collier's reply.

Mr. Collier hunts the game thus started by Mr. Lemon: he says,[10]

"Mr. Lemon, senior, undoubtedly did bring the Players' Petition under my notice, and very much obliged to him I was, that he took so much trouble to assist me in my literary investigations."

If this be true, it indeed vindicates Mr. Collier's character from the charge of having forged this State Paper; but it does so by utterly destroying his credit for accuracy. It seems that Mr. Collier, as we have seen, was the first person to publish this forged document.

He writes:—

---

[10] Reply, p. 59.

"This remarkable paper has, perhaps, never seen the light from the moment it was presented, until it was very recently discovered."

"Very recently discovered"—*i.e.* recently in 1831, can hardly be understood to mean that the document had been discovered three—much less, sixteen—years before that date. Now, the period when Mr. Collier "began his researches," at the State Paper Office, was in the year 1827 or 1828, according to his account.[11] Therefore, according to Mr. Lemon, the document in question was well known to himself and his father before 1828 at latest. Nay, further; since Mr. Lemon was not in the State Paper Office from 1825 to 1835, the document in question must have been known to him (if at all) before 1825. Consequently, not only had it "seen the light," but was "well known" sixteen years before the period when, according to Mr. Collier, it was first discovered.

Certainly it may be said that Mr. Collier had made a mistake in supposing that it was recently discovered when he began his researches at the State Paper Office; but to my mind it is much more likely that Mr. Lemon, who was not in the State Paper Office at that time, has committed an oversight in speaking positively to a circumstance of which he could not have had any personal knowledge: and that such is the case will be apparent from the following considerations:—(I quote from Mr. Hardy's tract)—[12]

---

[11] Reply, p. 56. [12] Review, &c. p. 49.

Mr. Hardy's remarks.

"He is only "pretty confident," he says, that his father first brought this document under the notice of Mr. Collier; but he speaks positively, or at all events seems to do so, as to the fact that this document "was well known to his father and himself *before* Mr. Collier began his researches in the office." Now it seems no more than reasonable to suppose that if he is only "pretty confident" in the one case, he can hardly be *more* than "pretty confident" in the other, which is more distant in point of time, and dating [*sic*] from a period prior to the alleged commencement of Mr. Collier's researches at the State Paper Office in 1829; a period at which, if we are not much mistaken, Mr. Lemon had nothing whatever to do with the State Paper Office in an official capacity, he having resigned his situation there in 1825, at the direction of the Under Secretary of State, "in order that he might devote his time exclusively to the Commission for printing and publishing State Papers," to which he had been appointed Assistant Secretary. This office he held until 1835, in which year he was appointed Second Clerk in the State Paper Office.

"Under these circumstances, without meaning the slightest offence to Mr. Lemon, we cannot but be of opinion that he has spoken somewhat too hastily upon subjects *which could hardly have come within his knowledge;* viz., the existence of one document in particular, out of very many thousands, at a certain period of time, upwards of thirty years ago, the period of Mr. Collier's first admission into the State Paper Office; if indeed his letter can be construed to speak positively as to the latter point, which, after all, seems somewhat uncertain. Mr. Lemon, doubtless, is speaking the truth to the best of his belief; but not one iota beyond this can we admit.

* * * * * * * *

"But supposing for a moment that the "Players' Petition" was a genuine document, and that the fact of its existence had been discovered by Mr. Lemon [senior], his first duty, on such discovery, would be [*sic*] to communicate the fact to Mr. Hobhouse, the head of his office, and to make an entry of the purport of the document in the official Repertory. There is no evidence that he did either; on the contrary, the Petition was never heard of by the public until Mr. Collier printed it in 1831. Viewing the matter, too, as one of feeling, and laying aside all considerations of duty, if Mr. Lemon, Senior, had indeed discovered this precious document, and been convinced of its genuineness, no reasonable doubt can be entertained that he would have been too eager to announce the fact to the public, and that the whole of literary England would have rung with the intelligence of his good fortune. He, of all men, was not the person to conceal it from the chief of his office, from his colleagues, from his personal friends, and from the whole body of Shakespearian scholars. He was much too alive to the pleasure of congratulation to have kept such a discovery a secret for a period of four years (1825 to 1829), and then to have communicated it to Mr. Collier, at that time an unknown individual, and recently introduced to him by a mere acquaintance. Such, however, is Mr. Collier's statement. But how comes it that he never thought of this before? One would certainly suppose that Mr. Collier would have made some mention (as he has done in instances where Mr. Lemon* had introduced a document to his notice) of Mr. Lemon's kindness in placing a document of such surpassing interest as this before him; but, on the contrary, not the slightest allusion is there made to him in connexion with the "Players' Petition," although Mr. Collier states that it had been very recently discovered in the State Paper Office. Why should he *then* have concealed the fact that he *now* vouchsafes to tell us?"

Yet one literary man, professing some knowledge of palæography, (though his profession is singularly

* "The Minute in the Registers of the Privy Council (pointed out to us by Mr. Lemon) is this," &c. Again, "This new and valuable piece of information was pointed out to us by Mr. Lemon."

belied by his obvious ignorance and incompetence) has been found to defend the genuineness of this pseudo-State Paper. Mr. H. Merivale writes:—[13]

Mr. Merivale's opinion.

"Sir Frederic Madden and Mr. Hamilton have actually certified that a document, in the State Paper Office is a spurious document; although its authenticity has since been confirmed by evidence which appears irresistible." "In spite of this verdict, to which Sir F. Madden and Mr. Hamilton have pledged whatever reputation they enjoy as palæographers, the authenticity of the paper is still maintained by the best authorities in the State Paper Office to be equal to that of any other document in the collection; and this opinion is curiously confirmed by the fact, that there are spots of corrosion by rust on the paper, which have eaten away not only the paper *but the ink*, showing that the *writing* as well as the paper *is old*."

Mr. Hardy's reply to Mr. Merivale.

To these allegations Mr. Hardy gives the following sufficient reply:—

"In the first place, there is abundant reason for denying that "the authenticity of the paper is still maintained by the best authorities in the State Paper Office." Of the three Assistant Keepers of Public Records at the State Paper Branch Office, Mr. Lechmere, the chief, has hitherto declined to offer any opinion at all upon the subject; Mr. Lemon himself can at most be said to have expressed only by *implication* his belief in its genuineness; while the remaining Assistant Keeper, Mr. Hans Claude Hamilton, has stated his conviction that the so-called "Players' Petition" is an indubitable forgery.

"Again, it is not the fact that "there are spots of corrosion by rust in the paper, which have eaten away not only the paper but the ink;" though, if there were such, it would point to an exactly opposite conclusion, as we could convince the Reviewer in two minutes, by affording him ocular demonstration. Fur-

[13] The Edinburgh Review, April 1860, vol. CXI. pp. 455 and 484.

ther than this, our belief is, that the liquid with which the document was written was not what is commonly called 'ink,' or, at all events, the ink in use at that period.

* * * * * * * *

"As Mr. Collier and his supporters, however (notwithstanding the contradiction previously noticed), seem to hesitate at maintaining that the Players' Petition is genuine, it would be little better than a work of supererogation to prove that it is spurious. We therefore content ourselves with asserting that, be it original or copy, it was not written in the reign of Elizabeth or of James the First,—reigns which, of course, we particularly mention, because the handwriting is ostensibly an imitation of the handwriting of that period, and the context is intended to bear reference to the first of them. The orthography of the petition, the ink or pigment in which it is written, are not of those reigns, and the writing itself is tainted with clerical anachronisms; while the paper is, to all appearance, *the fly-leaf cut out of a book*, and certainly would never have been used either for an original Petition to the Council, or for an official copy of one. These assertions the officers of the State Paper Office, it is believed, will not be disposed to contradict. As yet they have shown no inclination to do so—(for even supposing Mr. Lemon's memory to be accurate in every respect, his evidence goes no way whatever towards establishing the genuineness of the document),—though, on the other hand, the reserve shown by them on this point (with the exception of Mr. H. C. Hamilton), is not unlikely to be misconstrued as seeming to give countenance to the statements circulated in reference to the great literary value of this spurious production. That they entertain such an opinion in reference to it, it would really be an ill compliment to suppose; but if so [*i.e.* if they do], why did they not, immediately upon reading the certificate impugning the genuineness of the document, send to the Master of the Rolls a counter-certificate, declaring their own belief in its genuineness, and protesting against such a certificate being appended until further consideration had been given to the subject? Why, in such case, have they allowed Mr. Collier's assertions to be called in question, and himself defrauded of that testimony, whatever its value, to which he has a right at their hands, if they believe in its genuineness? This, if ever there was one, is a matter in which the semblance even of a mistake should not be allowed to exist."

It is worth noticing that in Mr. Merivale's rejoinder to Mr. Hardy's *Review*, in "The Athenæum,"[14] he carefully eschews all reference to the remarks of Mr. Hardy which I have quoted; from which it may be reasonably inferred that they are unanswerable. Mr. Merivale does indeed mention the Players' Petition, but for no other purpose than to reply to an allegation of Mr. Hardy's respecting the constitution of the Record Office; which, indeed, has a bearing, though a very subordinate one, on the question at issue: but on the question of the authenticity or genuineness of that State Paper, or on the collateral question of the judgment thereupon of the officials of the State Paper Office, which in "The Edinburgh Review" he had grossly misrepresented, Mr. Merivale has not a word to say, but prudently, perhaps, backs out of a discussion which has not hitherto brought him any κῦδος, and the further entertainment of which could not possibly bring him any credit, unless he were candidly to confess that he had rashly stated what he had no means of knowing to be true. Such candour is not to be looked for till time has made an oblivion of those private interests which are opposed to the truth.

[14] August 25, 1860.

CHAPTER XIII.

SUPPOSITITIOUS AND SUSPECTED DOCUMENTS.

BESIDES the documents which have been already considered, there are at least seven cases in which documents, cited or quoted by Mr. Collier, have been searched for in the depositories indicated by him, and cannot be found. These alleged documents are,

1. A Certificate of the Justices of the Peace of the County of Middlesex about the Blackfriars, (assigned date Nov. 20, 1633).

2. A letter from Samuel Daniel, the poet.

3. A letter signed "W. Ralegh."

4. A manuscript description of an impersonation in a masque.

5. A Petition from the Inhabitants of the Liberty of the Blackfriars to the Privy Council, (assigned date 1576).

6. A Petition from the Inhabitants of the Liberty of the Blackfriars to the Privy Council, (assigned date 1596).

7. A letter from Lord Pembroke, (assigned date August 27th, 1624).

The first three of these documents ought to be at Bridgewater House, if they be not purely mythical: No. 4, if it ever existed, ought to be at Devonshire House: and the last three, unless they are myths, ought to be in the State Paper Office. But none of these can be found in the localities specified. Let us consider them *seriatim*.

The Certificate from the Justices of the Peace for the County of Middlesex about the Blackfriars.

1. This document was published by Mr. Collier in his *New Facts*, p. 27, where it is given *verbatim* as follows:—

Certificate from the Justices of the Peace of the County of Middlesex about the Blackfryers.

May it please your Lordshipps. According to the order of this honorable Board of the 9th of October last wee haue had diuers meeteings at the Blacke-Fryers, and haueing first viewed the Playhouse there, we haue called vnto us the chiefe of the Players, and such as haue interest in the said Playhouse and the buildings thereunto belonging (which wee alsoe viewed) who pretendinge an exceeding greate losse, and allmost vndoing to many of them, and especially to diuers widowes and orphanes hauing interest therein, if they should be remoued from playing there, we required them to make a reasonable demaund of recompense for such interest as they or any of them had therein: Whereupon their first demaund being in a grosse sume of 16000li wee required them to sett downe particularly in writing how, and from whense such a demaund could arise, and gave them time for it. At our next meeteing they accordingly presented vnto us a particular note thereof which amounted to 21,990li But wee descending to an examination of their interest in their houses and buildings they there possess, and the indifferent valuation thereof, haue with their owne consent valued the same as followeth.

First for the Playhouse itselfe, whereof the Company hath taken a Lease for diuers yeares yet to come of Cuthbert Burbidge and William Burbidge (who haue the inheritance thereof) at the rent of 50li per Ann, wee value the same after the same rate at 14 yeares purchase, as an indifferent recompence to the Burbidges, which cometh to 700li.

For 4 Tenements neare adioyning to the Playhouse, for the which they receive 75li per Ann rent, and for a voide piece of ground there to turne coaches in, which they value at 6li per Ann, makeing together 81li per Ann, the purchase thereof, at 14 yeares likewise, cometh to 1134li.

They demaund further in respect of the interest that some of them haue by lease in the said Playhouse, and in respect of the shares which others haue in the benefit thereof, and for the damage they all pretend they shall sustaine by their remoue, not knowing where to settle themselves againe (they being 16 in number) the sume of 2400li viz to each of them 150li But wee conceive they may be brought to accept of the sume of 1066li 13s. 4d. which is to each of them 100 markes.

All which we humbly leave to your Lordshipps graue consideration, Your Lordshipps most humbly to be commanded.

He: Spiller.

Will. Baker,
Humphrey Smith,
Lawr. Whitaker,
Willm. Childe.

20 Nov. 1633.[1]

---

[1] Ten years before, according to one of the Bridgewater Manuscripts (see page 246 of this work) the value of this property was

	£	s.	d.
For 20 shares	4666	13	4
„ the Fee	1000	0	0
„ wardrobe and properties .	500	0	0
	£6166	13	4

[But in

Mr. Collier[1] makes special mention of the discovery of this document, apart from his general remarks on the Bridgewater manuscripts: he says,

"Besides the manuscripts found at Bridgewater House, which formed the main substance of my *New Facts*, another document (at what date I am uncertain) subsequently turned up in the same collection, which rendered it most probable that the account of the claims of the Players and Proprietors of the Blackfriars Theatre, on their proposed removal from that precinct was authentic: Lord Ellesmere insisted that I should keep it, as it was no necessary part of the other documents.[2] It was a sort of summary of the account of the claims, in an Italian hand of the period, and underneath, in the hand-writing of Sir George Buck, the Master of the Revels to James I. was his memorandum that the Players and Proprietors demanded more than their interest was worth by £1500: he first wrote £2000, but subsequently altered the sum to £1500."

With the knowledge already acquired of the spuriousness of the valuation of the shares of the Black-

---

But in the Document of 1633, where the valuation of wardrobe and properties does not appear, we have,

For 16 shares	£2400
„ the Fee	£1834
	£4234

Yet these proprietors first demand £16,000, and afterwards, £21,990! Or, according to Mr. Collier's account of Sir George Buck's Memorandum, £6234 and £5734!!

[1] Reply, p. 39.

[2] From this it might be inferred that Mr. Collier *accepted* this document, and has it at present in his possession. If so, and if it be not one of the Perkins series, it would be best for all parties that he should send it to the Record Office or the British Museum for examination.

friars proprietors at Bridgewater House, we might be led to suspect the spuriousness of this document also (if any such exist) on internal evidence. Nevertheless this may be an unjust suspicion, and the document on production may turn out to be genuine: and if so, it is conceivable that it may have furnished the hint for the fabrication of the one at Bridgewater House.

2. A second letter from Samuel Daniel, the poet, is introduced to our notice by Mr. Collier in his *New Facts*[4] in the following words:— The suppositítious letter signed "Samuel Danyel."

"At Bridgewater House are preserved two original letters from Samuel Daniel to Lord Ellesmere, both of them very interesting, but one of them especially so, inasmuch as one paragraph in it refers expressly to Shakespeare, though not by name. They are both without dates, but circumstances enable us, I think, to fix them pretty exactly.

* * * * * *

"You will observe that Daniel [in the first letter[5]] adverts to his "brother's advancement" by the instrumentality of Lord Ellesmere; and the principal object of the second letter of the same poet, preserved at Bridgewater House, is to thank the Lord Keeper for "this preferment." What was the nature of it we are not informed, but it was probably procuring for him a Patent for a company of theatrical children: there is no doubt that this letter was shortly anterior in point of date to that above quoted. Daniel also mentions his incomplete poem, "The Civil Wars between the Houses of York and Lancaster," which he intended to bring down to the reign of Henry VII., but never carried further than the marriage of Edward IV. The letter contains nothing regarding Shakespeare, but

[4] Page 47—53.

[5] This is given at length at p. 247 of this work.

at the same time, it is so interesting, on account of the distinguished writer, the subject, and the person to whom it was addressed, that I shall not hesitate to insert a copy of it. Communications of the kind, by poets of eminence of that day, are the rarest, and to me the most precious, relics.

"'Right honorable. Amongst all the great workes of your worthynes it will not be the least that you have donne for me in the preferment of my brother, with whome yet now sometimes I may eat whilst I write, and so go on with the worke I have in hand, which God knowes had long since bene ended, and your Honor had had that which in my harte I have prepared for you, could I have but sustayned my self and made truce within, and peace with the world. But such hath bene my misery, that whilst I should have written the actions of men, I have been constrayned to live with children; and contrary to myne owne spirit put out of that scene which nature had made my parte. For could I but live to bring this labor of mine to the Union of Henry VII., I should have the end of all my ambition in this life, and the utmost of my desyres: for therein, if wordes can worke any thing vppon the affections of men, I will labor to give the best hand I can to the perpetuall closing up of those woundes, and the ever keeping them so, that our land may lothe to looke over those blessed boundes (which the providence of God hath set vs) vnto the horror and confusion of farther and former claymes. And though I know the greatnes of the worke requires a greater spirit then myne, yet we see that in theas frames of motions, little wheeles move the greater, and so by degrees turne about the whole, and God knowes what so pore a Muse as myne may worke vppon the affections of men. But howsoever I shall herein show my zeale to my country and to do that which my soule tells me is fit. And to this end do I now purpose to retyre me to my pore home, and not againe to see you till I have payd your Honor my vowes; and will onely pray that England which so much needes you may long injoy the treasure of your councell, and that it be not driven to complayne with that good Roman *videmus quibus extinctis jurisperitis, quam in paucis nunc spes, quam in paucioribus facultas, quam in multis audacia.* And for this comfort I have received from your goodnes I must and ever will remayne your Honors in all I ame,

SAMUEL DANYEL.""

I see nothing in the contents of this letter to throw any doubt on its genuineness. But, be that as it may, the letter cannot be found at Bridgewater House.

The letter signed "W. Ralegh."

8. Of the letter signed "W. Ralegh," we know no more than Mr. Collier tells us in his *Catalogue of Early English Literature forming a portion of the Library at Bridgewater House*, 1837; where this letter is given *in extenso*, and subjoined to it is a facsimile of the signature. From its entry here it is evident that the letter, if it were not a myth, was in Lord Ellesmere's library in 1837; and it ought to be there now: but it cannot be found. If found, it would probably turn out to be spurious; for the signature has no resemblance in the world to that of Sir Walter Ralegh. I have given a copy of Mr. Collier's facsimile in sheet no. II., and alongside of that I have placed the impossible E in the Ralegh signature, and the almost exactly similar E which occurs in the emendation *End, vice* "And", in the Bridgewater Folio. By means of this monstrous letter we are enabled to trace the chain of forgery from the Perkins Folio through the Bridgewater Folio, to the perpetration of the abomination at the foot of the Ralegh letter.

The MS. description of an impersonation in a masque.

4. Mr. Hamilton[6] calls attention to the suspicious character of the language of a description which Mr. Collier states that he discovered at Devonshire House annexed to a collection of designs for masques, by Inigo Jones. The following is Mr. Collier's account of the discovery:—

"When first I obtained permission to look through the Bridgewater MSS. in detail, I conjectured that it would be nearly impossible to turn over so many state-papers, and such a bulk of correspondence, private and official, without meeting with something illustrative of the subject to which I have devoted so many years; but I certainly never anticipated being so fortunate as to obtain particulars so new, curious, and important, regarding a Poet who, above all others, ancient or modern, native or foreign, has been the object of admiration. When I took up the copy of Lord Southampton's letter and glanced over it hastily, I could scarcely believe my eyes to see such names as Shakespeare and Burbage in connection in a manuscript of the time. There was a remarkable coincidence also in the discovery, for it happened on the anniversary of Shakespeare's birth and death. I will not attempt to describe my joy and surprise, and I can only liken it to the unexpected gratification I experienced two or three years ago, when I turned out, from some ancient depositories of the Duke of Devonshire, the original designs of Inigo Jones, not only for the scenery, but for the dresses and characters of the different

[6] Inquiry, p. 84, note. Also at p. 104, Mr. Hamilton calls upon Mr. Collier to produce a document (containing the play of Richard II., and the Rebellion of the Earl of Essex) the discovery of which the latter had communicated to "The Athenæum," of Dec. 6th, 1856, leaving his readers to suppose that it was in his own possession. The fact is that the document in question is in the State Paper Office, and is genuine.

masques by Ben Jonson, Campion, Townsend, &c. presented at Court in the reigns of our First James and Charles. The sketches were sometimes accompanied by explanations in the handwriting of the great artist, a few of which incidentally illustrate Shakespeare, who however was never employed for any of these royal entertainments: annexed to one of the drawings was the following written description, from whence we learn how the actor of the part of Falstaff was usually habited in the time of Shakespeare.

'Like a Sir Jon Falsstaff: in a roabe of russet, quite low, with a great belley, like a swolen man, long moustacheos, the sheows [shoes] shorte, and out of them great toes like naked feete: buskins to sheaw a great swolen leg. A cupp coming fourth like a beake—a great head and balde, and a little cap *alla Venetiane*, greay—a rodd and a scroule of parchment.'"[7]

Neither these designs—nor any one of them—nor the "annexed" description can be found at Devonshire House.

5. All we know about this memorial is from a remark of Mr. Collier's in his *History of English Dramatic Poetry*,[8] from which we learn (if we can be said to *learn* anything at all) that this memorial was in the State Paper Office in 1831, and that to it was annexed the spurious petition of the Blackfriars Theatre, of which I have given an account in the last chapter. No such memorial, however, is in the State Paper Office now; nor, as far as can be ascertained, was any such a document ever there.

The supposititious Blackfriars Petition of 1576.

6. For an acquaintance with this petition, we

The supposititious Black-

[7] New Facts, p. 38—9. [8] Vol. i. p. 297.

friars Petition of 1596.

are indebted to Mr. Collier, who gives us the following account of it:—[9]

"The orders of the Common Council of 1575 drove the players, at least for a time, from places within the jurisdiction of the city authorities, and without delay they sought a situation beyond that jurisdiction, but at the same time as near as possible to its boundaries. For this purpose they fixed upon the Precinct of the dissolved Monastery of the Blackfriars, and here James Burbage (who, with others, obtained the licence of 1574, already inserted) bought certain rooms near the houses, at that time, occupied by the Earl of Sussex, Lord Chamberlain, and Lord Hunsdon, who succeeded him in that office: these rooms he converted into a play-house; and while he was in the act of making the alterations, a petition to the Privy Council was prepared by certain of the inhabitants, praying that Burbage might not be allowed to proceed in his enterprise. It was signed by the Dowager Lady Elizabeth Russel, by Lord Hunsdon, and by twenty-eight other inhabitants of the Liberty of Blackfriars, and it set out the particulars above given in the following form.

'To the right Honble the Lords and others of her Maties 'most honble privy Councell.

'Humbly shewing and beseeching your Honours: the Inha'bitants of the Precinct of the Blackfryers London. That 'whereas one Burbage hath lately bought certaine Roomes in 'the same Precinct, neere adjoining unto the dwelling houses 'of the right honble the Lord Chamberlaine, and the Lord of 'Hunsdon; which Romes the said Burbage is now altering, 'and meaneth very shortly to convert, and turn the same into 'a common Playhouse; which will grow to the very great 'annoyance and trouble, not onely to all the Noblemen and 'Gentlemen there about inhabiting, but also a general incon'venience to all the inhabitants of the same Precinct, both

---

[9] History of English Dramatic Poetry, vol. i. p. 226.

'by reason of the great resort, and gathering together of all 'manner of vagrant and lewde persons, that under cullor of 'resorting to the Playes, will come thither and work all man- 'ner of mischiefe, and also to the great pestring and filling up 'of the same Precinct, if it should please God to send any visi- 'tation of sicknesse, as heretofore hath beene; for that the 'same Precinct is already grown very populous. And besides 'that the same Playhouse is so neere the Church, that the 'noyse of the drummes & trumpetts will greatly disturbe and 'hinder both the Minister, and the Parishioners in tyme of 'divine service & sermons. In tender consideration whereof, 'as also for there hath not at any tyme heretofore been used 'any Common Playhouse within the same Precinct; but that 'now all Players being banished by the Lord Maior from play- 'ing within the Cittie, by reason of the great inconvenience 'and ill rule that followeth them, they now thinke to plant 'themselves in the Liberties. That therefore it would please 'your Honours to take order, that the same roomes may be 'converted to some other use, and that no Playhouse may be 'used or kept there. And your suppliants, as most bounden, 'shall & will dayly pray for your Lordships in all honor and 'happiness long to live.' "

This document is *not* in the State Paper Office, and is not known to have ever been there. The authorities there are understood to repudiate it altogether. If it ever had an existence, which is, to say the least, very doubtful, it must have been spurious. No petitions to the Privy Council of that period were signed by such an overwhelming array of names, as would seem to have been appended to the one in question,—viz., those of thirty persons, two being "of rank." But further than this: it was the custom of that period to present petitions unsigned: of which a great many may be seen in the Record Office.

The supposititious letter from Lord Pembroke.

7. This letter is cited by Mr. Collier in his *New Particulars*,[10] in the following words:—

"It appears by an original letter from Lord Pembroke, then Lord Chamberlain, dated the 27th of August, 1624, preserved in the State Paper Office, and which was discovered there only recently, that the King's Players at the Globe were silenced for about a week, and that they were not allowed to play again until they had given bond in £300 not to repeat the performance of the *Game at Chess*."[11]

This letter, like the two petitions, last-mentioned, is not to be found in the State Paper Office. From its contents, it would appear to be a fabrication, unless indeed it be altogether mythical, and never had any pen and ink existence.[12]

---

[10] Page 49 note.

[11] Middleton's *Game at Chess* gave offence to the Spanish Ambassador. The Globe Players produced it in August, 1624.

[12] It must be further mentioned that at page 190 of Mr. Collier's *Catalogue of Early English Literature*, &c. (referred to at page 309 of this work) that gentleman calls attention to a unique copy of Marlow's *Hero and Leander*, Edition 1629, "containing some peculiarities of Marlow in the hand-writing of Gabriel Harvey." Where is this copy? Does it really exist? If so, whoever has it now should at once submit the writing to a palæographic scrutiny. I have no doubt that a great number of these fabrications yet remain unsuspected.

CHAPTER XIV.

THE VINTAGE.

Recapitulation.

Let us now look back on the ground we have traversed. We have passed in review the arguments adduced against the genuineness and authenticity of the manuscript corrections in a copy of the folio edition of Shakspere, 1623, and in one of the folio edition of 1632:[1] and we have seen on what grounds it has been affirmed that these two sets of corrections are by one hand, viz. (α) the similarity of the ink-writing in the one to that in the other; (β) the fact of nearly half the corrections in the former being in the latter also; (γ) the concurrence of two sets of corrections being both written upon pencil instructions; and (δ) both sets of corrections being discovered and turned into "hard cash" by one man. We have also examined the claims to genuineness and anti-

[1] Mr. H. Merivale, in the Edinburgh Review (April 1856, vol. CIII. p. 360), thus gracefully and fairly describes Mr. Collier's discovery of this folio:—"If we were told by some scholiast of ancient days, that Aristarchus the critic, while wandering in the market-place of Alexandria with his head full of Homer, had purchased a bargain of figs, and, on returning home, found them wrapt up in a papyrus containing the genuine text of the poet, we should smile at the simplicity of the myth; and yet the romance of Mr. Collier's discovery is almost as marvellous."—For once I cordially agree with Mr. Merivale: except that for "almost as marvellous," I propose to read *quite as incredible*.

quity of seven documents, deposited in the Library at Bridgewater House, of six documents preserved —or rather left to the ravages of dirt and mischance —in the archives of Dulwich College, and of one document in the State Paper Office. We have seen that as to six of the former seven, and five of the other six, and the State Paper in question, the palæographists of all our public depositories are unanimous in the imputation of spuriousness.

We have further seen how all these cases are connected, more or less, inevitably together. The questions now to be considered are these:—Did one man fabricate all these classes of manuscript matter? Who is specially pointed at as the fabricator? The hinge on which the answer to these questions turns is the Perkins Folio. For this reason, among others already mentioned, I have devoted the greater part of the foregoing pages to the discussion of that one case: and for that reason I must now again call attention to the external evidences of forgery in that case. All that the internal evidences can do—*and this they do most unequivocally*—is to demonstrate that some of the manuscript corrections are not so old as, from the character of the hand in which they are written in ink, one would be led to infer—indeed, that they are very modern;—and that some of them, in connection with the conduct of him who first discovered them and made them public, betray the source from which, as well as the person by whom, they had been surreptitiously obtained. But the extrinsic evidence goes much farther than this, and is more direct than the internal evidence can be. In what does it consist? As I have said,[2] the primal evidence of forgery here lies in the ink-writing: our proverb says, "When doctors differ who shall decide?" But here we have a case in which, fortunately for the speedy settlement of the question, the "doctors" are unanimous. All the palæographists of the Department of Manuscripts of the British Museum, of the Rolls, the Public Record Office, and the State Paper Office, who have spoken at all, have denounced the genuineness of the ink-writing. No wonder Mr. H. Merivale, who is so bent upon conserving his own opinion of 1856, if not of saving his friend Mr. Collier, would fain discredit palæography altogether;[3] but he might as well attempt to discredit astronomy, and insist on the orbitual motion of the sun.

The compound inference.

We have then the established fact of the spuriousness of the ink-notes. Then the pencil-marks and words are indeed significant. *Independently of the evidence of the ink-notes written beside or over those pencillings, our senses and common sense concur in the decision that the latter are written in a very modern cursive,* which, I may add, in my opinion indistinguishably resembles Mr. Collier's ordinary handwriting. We may now reverse the process of reasoning, as Mr. Hamilton did,[4] and say that

[2] Page 114 of this work. [3] The Athenæum, August 25, 1860.
[4] See the note at p. 109 of this work.

because in particular cases the ink-writing is *over*, (*i.e.* on the top of) the pencil-writing, the pencil-writing, though a modern cursive, must have been written before the ink-notes. This argument of precedence of the pencil-writing over the ink-writing, is well illustrated by a case cited in "The Critic,"[1] where it is given in the following words:—

The case of the Will of Panton.

"A curious case in illustration of this occurred twenty-two years ago, when Mr. THOMAS WILLIAMS and his two servants were tried for forging the will of Mr. JONES PANTON. In the course of the trial it was proved that the will was written upon the paper which had once contained some plans of property drawn in pencil, and the charge on behalf of the prosecution was, that the deceased had signed these plans in ink, and that the prisoners, having rubbed out the pencilled outlines, had written the will upon the sheets of paper above the signature. At the trial, Mr. NETHERCLIFT, senior, was himself a very important witness, and his testimony which was of considerable length, occupying nearly thirty pages of the printed report of the case, went entirely to prove and that upon oath that, although the pencil marks had been rubbed out, they were still there, and he could make them out distinctly *under the ink writing of the will*. In the course of his summing up, Mr. Baron PARKE very pertinently told the jury that "if the pencil writing is under the ink, as it seems to be, it is impossible it could have been written after."

The argument from the modern-looking pencil marks and words to the apparently older, but really more recent ink-writing, is the popular mode of verifying the palæographic conclusion that the ink-writing is in a simulated hand. The primal argu-

---

[1] March 3, 1860.

ment from the ink-writing (which is the one mainly relied on by the palæographists), proves that the ink-writing is, in a double sense, an imposition. The popular argument from the pencil-writing proves that the ink-writing (old as it looks to inexperienced eyes) was written after it. These conclusions taken together, prove that the pencil-marks and words were instructions for a fabrication of which the ink-words are the elements.

The Editor of the Athenæum draws on his invention.

This result is naturally one that Mr. Collier's partisans have desperately striven to evade. Every scheme that ingenious and disingenuous men could conceive, they have essayed, to obviate, if it were possible, the seemingly inevitable conclusion, that Mr. Collier, who, it would appear, wrote the pencil instructions, must have concocted, if not executed, the whole imposture. The editor of "The Athenæum" first tried to set up a counter authority. He had no fear of his men. The Fellows of the Society of Antiquaries would vouch for anything if necessary. But he reckoned without his host. In "The Athenæum" of Sept. 16, 1859, the editor announced that the Duke of Devonshire had "permitted four eminent Fellows of the Society of Antiquaries to make a careful investigation" of the Perkins Folio; that the folio was then in the hands of the Duke's solicitor; that the four gentlemen in question would make known the result of their investigation in their own way; but that the facts they had elicited tended to prove how hasty and superficial had been the inquiry which had resulted in the impeachment of the genuineness of the notes. This statement, which, as far as concerned the Duke's permission, was *a pure fabrication*, was immediately contradicted, on authority, in "The Literary Gazette," and "The Critic," and also in at least two provincial newspapers. The authoritative contradiction in one of the latter having been communicated to the editor of "The Athenæum," he, in the week following, most positively reiterated his previous statement. The Duke of Devonshire, as I have said, never granted "permission to four eminent Fellows of the Society of Antiquaries to make a careful investigation" of the folio; but without waiting for any such permission, I believe some of the Fellows did examine the folio, and the result was such that they did not deem it prudent to take the field against the palæographists of the British Museum, the Rolls, the Public Record Office, and the State Paper Office.

General conclusions on the Controversy.

Here then we have a case in which 30,000 manuscript notes, written on the vacant spaces of a copy of the second folio of Shakspere, are simulations of handwritings of the seventeenth century, and written sometimes on the top, sometimes by the side of half obliterated pencil marks and words—such pencillings being in almost every case instructions for the superposed, or at least after-written, ink corrections. Here then—in the correspondence of the pencil and ink—we have the key-stone of the arch. To the pencillings is attached Mr. Collier's "plain round

English hand," in which, indeed, those pencillings appear to be invariably written, and to the various forms of the ink-writing are attached (in order of cogency),

1st. The two documents facsimiled on sheet no. X. and that on sheet no. XVII.
2nd. „ document on sheet no. XII.
3rd. „ „ „ „ „ IX.
4th. „ „ „ „ „ XIV.
5th. „ documents on sheets nos. VIII. and XIII., and the 1st on sheet no. XVI.
6th. „ document on sheet no. VII., and the 2nd on sheet no. XV.
7th. The ink corrections of the Bridgewater Folio, for which see sheets of facsimiles nos. I. and II.

On this 7th class hangs the Ralegh letter, of the signature to which a facsimile is given on sheet no. II.[6]

Now in this chain the following links are perfectly indisputable:—

Mr. Collier's handwriting=the pencil-writing of the Perkins Folio=the ink-writing of the Perkins Folio=the Certificate of the Blackfriars Players=the Petition of the Blackfriars Players=the Assessment for the Southwark poor. This portion of the

[6] The second document on sheet no. XVI. I will not undertake to class. It is the only manuscript in the series as to which it is possible to doubt the connection with the other forgeries; yet it is the worst executed, and most easily detected of all.

chain *alone* connects Mr. Collier, on very strong probable evidence, with the fabrication of the manuscript corrections of the Perkins Folio, with the fabrication of one of the Bridgewater House documents, and with that of one of the Dulwich College documents, as well as of a State Paper. So far I cannot say that I entertain so much doubt as to justify even the verdict of *not-proven*. Imagine a stranger to this unhappy controversy approaching it on this side:—

1. One man discovered two folios corrected in manuscript, and (to put the case mildly, say) *three* documents bearing on the life of Shakspere.

2. All the annotations and documents so discovered are forgeries.

3. All the annotations of both folios, and all the documents, appear to be in one handwriting, (or in other words one man forged them all).

4. Lying underneath or alongside the ink-corrections of one of the folios, are found pencil instructions for those corrections in one man's handwriting.

Now in the first and fourth sections, two men are spoken of. Add to those,

5. The two men spoken of are *one* man.

6. The man in question occupied the foremost place as editor of Shakspere, and commentator on Shaksperian literature.

At this point the stranger I have supposed could have but one point to urge why that editor should not be credited with the whole fabrication; it is this: Can it be believed that a man of Mr. Collier's moral character could have done this? Is not character to be allowed its weight against the accumulated circumstantial evidence? It remains then but to add,

7. The editor in question has been already convicted of falsifying a document (viz., the letter, the essential part of which is given in facsimile on sheet no. XVIII.), which so falsified was made to have a curious and interesting bearing on the life and character of Shakspere; but in its pristine integrity had no *such* bearing on Shakspere.

The Editor of the Athenæum again resorts to misrepresentation.

Now this is the case against Mr. Collier. It is on this evidence that he stands charged with being himself the *παραδιόρθωτης* (as De Quincey would have called him) of the Perkins Folio, and the concoctor and prime instigator, if not the fabricator, of various documents, all bearing on the life of Shakspere. Mr. Collier's partisans have also laboured to deliver him from the 7th position: but, as might be expected, with no success. The editor of "The Athenæum," finding the case hopeless, resorted here, as in the case of the Perkins Folio, to the grossest misrepresentation. Like a prudent man, he relied on no facsimiles, but went off to Dulwich College, where the Master shewed him the famous letter of Mrs. Alleyn, in which Mr. Collier had contrived to

"find void places in the paper
To steal in something to entrap her"—

or rather to entrap a confiding public in general, and

the Shakespeare Society in particular. Well, what did the editor of "The Athenæum" take by his motion? Why, he verified Mr. F. G. Netherclift's facsimile of the postscript. Mr. H. Merivale, *without taking that trouble*, had, shortly before,[7] insinuated doubts of the fidelity of the facsimile. The editor of "The Athenæum" satisfied himself, by inspection, that the original contained the same damnatory evidence as the facsimile. Having arrived at this painful conclusion, he again attempted to defend Mr. Collier from the imputation of having falsified the letter, and, to do this, he resorted to the grossest misrepresentation. In the very next number of "The Athenæum,"[8] he wrote:—

"Since our article of last week on the Collier controversy, we have been to Dulwich, and by the courtesy of the Rev. Alfred Carver, have seen Mrs. Alleyne's letter. The paper is worn and rotten; at the lower end, where the words "Mr. Shakespeare of the Globe" were found by Mr. Collier, most of all. Nearly the whole of three lines has dropt away, *so that the fragments which remain are incapable of yielding any decisive proof either way.*"

When the editor of a periodical of such a position as that of "The Athenæum" has recourse to misrepresentation to support a falling cause, it may well be inferred that the cause is *in extremis!*

Mr. Collier's present position.

Of all the offences with which Mr. Collier stands charged, the fabrication of the Perkins notes is the worst. Shame to the perpetrator of that foul libel on the pure genius of Shakspere! The texts of

[7] The Edinburgh Review, April, 1860. [8] February 25th, 1860.

Shakspere and of the English Bible have been justly regarded as the two river-heads of our vernacular English. Gallicisms are constantly percolating into it, as our *social* changes demand the admixture (for no other changes can render the use of French words necessary, much less expedient), and its purity is being constantly violated by the importation of native and (still worse) American slang, and the cant and shibboleth of professions and sects. To the texts of Shakspere and of our Bible we must cleave, if we would save our language from deterioration. Yet it is one of these texts that a tasteless and incompetent peddler has attempted to corrupt throughout its wide and fertile extent. What is the result?

> "The fly-blown text conceives an alien brood,
> And turns to maggots what was meant for food."[9]

The other fabrications merely vitiate our Elizabethan history. That is a grave offence, but less grave than the other. THE MAN WHO LIES UNDER THESE APPALLING SUSPICIONS IS THE RECIPIENT OF A GOVERNMENT PENSION. Is this scandal to continue? Is no tribunal to be constituted by the Government for the investigation of the charges preferred against Mr. Collier? His friends as well as his opponents have urged him to refer his case to arbitration:

> ὡς δὲ πέτρος ἢ θαλάσσιος
> κλύδων ἀκούει νουθετούμενος φίλων.

---

[9] Dryden's Religio Laici.

For reasons best known to himself he evades inquiry.[10] If the case is not to be referred to a literary tribunal, it may now be considered as practically settled.

The *complete view* comprized in the foregoing pages will hand down to posterity the real merits of this case. On these merits it will sooner or later receive the adjudication of the public. They are not likely to be far from doing justice in the long run. To them I gladly commit the task of returning a verdict according to the evidence adduced.

One word more I will offer in anticipation of a possible charge against me—viz., that of striking a man who is down. Mr. Collier is not down. He is not, indeed, upon his legs: but he is bolstered up by the officious aid of his numerous partisans and friends. When they "let him slip down"[11] we will not strike another blow. "Non nostrum est *κείμενοις ἐπεμβαίνειν.*"

---

[10] It would have been better for him to have sooner taken the advice of his own heraldic motto—"Ben tacer parlar bene." It is *now* too late.

[11] See page 126 of this work.

APPENDIX.

I COULD not, without "travelling out of the record," have introduced into the body of this work the substance of the two charges which Mr. Collier has, by way of retaliation for a supposititious injury, brought against Sir Frederic Madden, forasmuch as those charges relate to matters in no way connected with the alleged Shakspere Forgeries. Sir F. Madden's reply was published in "The Critic," and has certainly not been circulated as extensively as Mr. Collier's attack. Accordingly I reprint Mr. Collier's charges, and Sir F. Madden's letter, by way of Appendix. The latter, indeed, contains a narrative of facts which I have already given in chapters III. and V.; but I do not see that anything is to be gained by omitting any part of that letter, so it is here reprinted *in extenso*.

MR. COLLIER'S CHARGES AGAINST SIR F. MADDEN.

How and why the Manuscript authorities of the British Museum have been heated into such animosity towards me I cannot pretend to explain. I was always upon good terms with Sir F. Madden, whom I have known for more than a quarter of a century, and upon two occasions I was of some service to him. Of one of them I can say no more; but of the other I may remark that it occurred within the last two or three years, and it was when he had involved himself in an awkward scrape by purchasing manuscripts, which he ought to have known had been dishonestly come by. They had in some way escaped from Lord Ellesmere's Collection, and the most obvious and important of them had actually been printed in a volume, with which Sir F. Madden ought to have been well acquainted. The late Earl Ellesmere heard of the strange circumstance, put the matter into the hands of his solicitor, and asked me to inquire of Sir F. Madden as to the facts. I did so; and finding, as I of course expected, that Sir F. Madden had innocently, though (*sic*) ignorantly and most incautiously, become possessed of the documents, they were restored to the noble owner, and the matter was dropped. Sir F. Madden showed me some of the manuscripts he had thus purchased, possibly all. One of them was an entire volume relating to the Mint in the reign of Elizabeth, with the handwriting of Sir Thomas Egerton (afterwards Lord Chancellor and Baron Ellesmere) on nearly every page, which Sir F. Madden, with his great skill and experience in palæography, might have recognized; and the other was a very remarkable document on parchment—so remarkable, that it is astonishing how Sir F. Madden could have become possessed of it without suspicion. It was an Address from all the Members of Lincoln's Inn to the Queen in 1584, declaring that they would defend her to the last against Spain, and against all her open or concealed enemies; and the very first name at the bottom of the instrument (and it contained very many) was that of Sir Thomas Egerton, then Solicitor-General. This document was printed at full length in the *Egerton Papers* by the Camden Society in 1840, and when it was printed it attracted much attention. Nevertheless, Sir F. Madden had bought the original; and the late Earl of Ellesmere wished the matter to be investigated, though, as far as I am aware, it was never his design to prosecute. Really and truly, if Sir F. Madden had then been indicted for receiving stolen goods, knowing them to have been stolen, it might have gone hard with him. I should willingly have been one of his witnesses to character.

Some men can forget an injury who never can forgive an obligation; but I assure Sir F. Madden that he was not in the slightest degree indebted to me on the occasion: ["upon two occasions I was of some service to him. Of one of them I can say no more; but of the other" &c. *See p.* 328!] all along the Earl of Ellesmere was convinced that the Keeper of the Manuscripts had only acted carelessly, not criminally. The crime indeed lay elsewhere. Therefore I cannot for a moment suppose," &c., *more suo.*—*Reply*, pp. 28—30.

"and if the Trustees of the British Museum would give me leave, I could promise, with no other means, to expunge every vestige of the famous signature, "Willm Shakspere," in the Montaigne's *Essays* by Florio, 1603, for which alone Sir F. Madden paid out of the public purse no less a sum than £130."—*Reply*, p. 55.

SIR F. MADDEN'S REPLY,

FROM "THE CRITIC" FOR MARCH 24, 1860.

THE SHAKSPERE DOCUMENTS.

To the Editor of the Critic.

SIR,—I have been very unwilling to enter into the arena on which the question respecting the SHAKSPERE forgeries has been so warmly debated; but the language used by Mr. COLLIER in his recently-published "Reply" to Mr. HAMILTON'S "Inquiry" leaves me no longer any choice. Silence would now only be weakness, and a sense of duty compels me to notice what a sense of injury might probably have induced me to pass over in silence. The audacity of the statement made by Mr. COLLIER, if not contradicted, might well pass current with the multitude as the proof of his confidence in a good cause—

Nam, cum magna malæ superest *audacia* causæ,
Creditur a multis *fiducia*.

Mr. Collier is not content with using the legitimate weapons of defence, but has not hesitated to ascribe to myself and others the most unworthy motives for the opinions we have given. He has gone even further; he has, in no obscure terms, insinuated (although, in his usual style of writing, pretending to disbelieve the insinuation) that the pencillings on the margins of the Collier Folio "originated" at the British Museum, and did not exist in the volume before it was entrusted to my care; and if "a fancy" should cross the mind of any one that those pencillings resemble his own handwriting, the likeness, Mr. Collier says, can only be explained by the circumstance that his hand was familiar to many at the Museum! In answering this accusation, I beg to give a narrative of the circumstances which led to the Collier Folio having been placed in my hands by his Grace the Duke of Devonshire.

During the summer and autumn of 1858 Dr. Mansfield Ingleby and Mr. Staunton had called more than once on me, to ask my opinion of the genuineness of the notes of the "Old Corrector," as printed by Mr. Collier, and also at the same time to express their opinion, from internal evidence, that the notes were of recent origin. So far from my having at that time "aided the case" against Mr. Collier, as falsely asserted by him (p. 70 of his Reply), I call upon the two gentlemen above named to bear witness whether I did not express my great surprise at their statement, and manifest the utmost unwillingness to believe that so large a body of notes could have been fabricated, or, if fabricated, could escape detection. These interviews, however, led me to address a request to Mr. Collier, on Sept. 6, 1858, that he would procure me a sight of the Folio, which of itself ought to prove that I could at that time have entertained no doubt of his integrity in the matter. To this request I never received any answer, nor indeed, to the best of my belief, did Mr. Collier write to me at all subsequently; and, although I thought it strange, yet I certainly never took offence at it. I resolved, however, in my own mind, to prefer my request to the DUKE of DEVONSHIRE himself; but official and other business constantly interfered to prevent my carrying out my intention until May, 1859, when Professor BODENSTEDT was introduced to me by Mr. WATTS of the Museum, and having expressed his great desire to see the Collier Folio, I promised them to gratify, if possible, their and my own wishes on the subject, as well as to give several of my Shaksperian friends an opportunity of examining the volume. Accordingly, on the 13th of May, I wrote to the DUKE, requesting the loan of the volume for a short time, and by his Grace's liberality it was sent to me on the 26th of the same month, late in the day. In the evening of the same day I wrote letters to Professor BODENSTEDT, the Rev. A. DYCE, Mr. W. J. THOMS (a friend of Mr. COLLIER), and I believe Mr. STAUNTON, inviting them to see the volume.

Having thus succeeded in obtaining the volume, my next step was to examine it critically on palæographic grounds, and this I did on the following morning very carefully, together with Mr. BOND, the Assistant-Keeper of my Department, and we were both struck with the very suspicious character of the writing—certainly the work of one hand, but presenting varieties of forms assignable to different periods—the evident *painting* over of many of the letters, and the artificial look of the ink. The day had not passed before I had quite made up my mind that the "Old Corrector" never lived in the seventeenth century, but that the notes were fabricated at a recent period. On the 28th Mr. DYCE came to see the volume in my study; on the 30th, Mr. FORSTER; on the 31st Professor BODENSTEDT; and on the 1st and 2nd of June, Mr. BRUCE (another friend of Mr. COLLIER). On the latter day, also, Mr. HAMILTON called my attention to the numerous words deleted in the margin, either with an acid or rubbed out, apparently with the finger, and many more half effaced. The motives of the "Old Corrector" in this proceeding began to appear most enigmatical. One instance I recall to mind (not noticed by Mr.

COLLIER, but certainly important to form an opinion of the "authority" of the Corrector) was in "As You Like it" (act iii. sc. 4), where Rosalind says, "His kissing is as full of sanctity as the touch of holy *bread*." The "Old Corrector" had written "*beard*" in the margin as the emendation, and then partially rubbed it out. This weak and unnecessary correction was, in fact, suggested by Warburton, from whom, in my humble opinion, it was borrowed. From the commencement of June not a day passed without the volume having been inspected constantly in my study by literary and other persons, and almost always in my presence. There was no preference given, nor am I aware that any special "invitations," besides those already mentioned, were sent out (as Mr. COLLIER says) to any one to come and examine the book.

It was on the 6th of June, when Dr. MANSFIELD INGLEBY was examining certain passages of the volume very closely, that he first directed my attention to a pencil mark which appeared to him to be under the ink; but I did not then pursue the inquiry. Within a week, however, afterwards, Mr. HAMILTON again spoke to me on the subject of the pencillings he had discovered on the margins, some of which seemed to be underneath the writing. On this being pointed out to me, I again looked through the volume page by page, and was inexpressibly astonished to discover hundreds of marks of punctuation and corrigenda in pencil, more or less distinct, in an apparently modern hand, which were evidently intended as a guide to the "Old Corrector," and in all cases followed by a corresponding alteration of the text in ink. Entire words were also found written in pencil by the same hand, followed by a similar correction in ink; and to my eyes, as well as to those of Mr. BOND and Mr. HAMILTON, it seemed undeniable that several of these pencillings *did underlie the ink*. The scientific assistance of Professor MASKELYNE (who now saw the book for the first time) was then suggested, and the result of his examination by the microscope was to prove the fact, which to a practised eye had previously appeared all but certain. Now then I would ask, by whom and at what time could these recent pencillings have been made? Certainly not at the Museum. It is a simple impossibility; but if any further denial is required, I declare positively that the whole of these pencillings, together with the ink notes, must have been in the volume when it was first sent to me, and that during the time it was in my care it was kept in the strictest custody. The charge so boldly advanced by Mr. COLLIER, that "thousands of specks and atoms" might have been made in the volume in the Department of Manuscripts, and then construed into letters, as well as his insinuation that the fac-simile, so faithfully executed by the lithographer, Mr. F. NETHERCLIFT, jun., and published by Mr. HAMILTON, is unfair or imaginary, are absolutely and wholly void of foundation. But, writes Mr. COLLIER, he expected different treatment from Sir F. MADDEN. And wherefore? It is true that for nearly thirty years I had been on terms of literary friendship with Mr. COLLIER; but is it on that account I am not to be allowed to give an opinion on a forged document, if he happens to have printed it? Other editors and lovers of SHAKSPERE have been and are still my friends, besides Mr. COLLIER, and why I should disregard their wishes, for the sake alone of Mr. COLLIER and his "Old Corrector," I am at a loss to conceive. From my official position, I felt bound to examine the volume and give a conscientious opinion of it, and to that opinion I adhere. The most absurd reasons have been assigned by Mr. COLLIER and his party for my conduct—in one place, that I was hostile to him, because he had been proposed to be the Head of the Museum; and in another, because he had given his folio Shakspere to the DUKE of DEVONSHIRE, instead of depositing it in the Museum! As to the former, I can only say, I never heard of such an intention until I read it in the *Athenæum* of the 18th of last February; and as to the latter, I assert that I knew not that the folio had been given to the DUKE, until so informed by Dr. INGLEBY, in 1858.

I now proceed to notice some other portions of Mr. COL-

LIER's "Reply," which are equally at variance with the facts. At p. 18 (and previously in the *Athenæum*) he speaks of Mr. PARRY's visit to me on the 13th (not 14th) of July, and, in regard to that gentleman's opinion respecting his own folio, makes the following extraordinary misrepresentation: "When he went there (to the Museum) on the 14th July last, for the purpose of inspecting the PERKINS Folio, *in the presence of* Sir F. MADDEN, Mr. HAMILTON, Mr. MASKELYNE, *and others, he may easily have been confused by the rapid passing and repassing of the folios of* 1623 *and* 1632 *before his eyes; and at last he may not have been able to remember which edition had really been his own book.* He spoke to the best of his memory, but his memory was bad; and he may have been, as it were, *cajoled out of his own conviction.*" This is really too bad; but I will not condescend to retaliate, otherwise than by a plain statement of facts. Mr. PARRY came of his own accord to see me, and I received him in my study. On his entry, there was no one else present, and I placed the COLLIER Folio on the table before him, and requested him to examine it and tell me if it was the copy formerly in his possession. Mr. PARRY looked at it externally and internally, and then, without the slightest hesitation, declared that *it was not his book*, and that he had never been shown this folio by Mr. COLLIER. His only doubt seemed to be whether this was really the copy that had been represented as once belonging to himself. I was astonished at this declaration, and sent for Mr. HAMILTON, who having been introduced to Mr. PARRY, the latter repeated his statement, and, at my request, wrote down as follows:

British Museum, July 13, 1859.

On being shown an old edition of Shakespeare's plays, I think I can positively say that it is not the book which Mr. Gray gave me in or about 1806. Sir Frederick Madden stated to me that this copy of Shakespeare, which he now produces to me, was once in Mr. Collier's possession.

(Signed) FRA. CHAS. PARRY.

I may add that Mr. PARRY declared, in the hearing of Mr. HAMILTON and myself (as he subsequently did to others), that this volume was of the edition 1623; that it was in smooth dark binding, with a new back lettered with the date; that it had no writing on the upper cover, was not so thick, and had a broader margin. Will this satisfy Mr. COLLIER? If not, and as a complete refutation of the juggling trick, of which Mr. COLLIER has ventured to accuse me and my colleagues, I have since received the following letter from Mr. PARRY:

March 12, 1860.

I have this instant received your note requesting me to say whether the statement made by Mr. Collier in the *Athenæum* of Feb. 18 last, namely, that you had confused me by passing and repassing several folio Shakespeares before me, was true. I have no hesitation whatever in flatly contradicting that assertion. While I was conversing with you on the subject, you brought a large old book and placed it on the table. I looked at it several times whilst we were speaking together, and was greatly surprised when at length you took it up and said that was the book in question. I felt perfectly assured that I had never seen that book before. I also now must add that you did not show me any other book whatever, or speak of any other book on that occasion.

I am, &c.
(Signed) F. C. PARRY.

In another part of the "Reply" Mr. COLLIER speaks of what he terms "a mighty fuss" made by Mr. HAMILTON in his first letter "regarding the water-mark on the fly-leaf;" and then proceeds distinctly to charge Mr. HAMILTON, "or somebody else," with the crime (for crime it would be) of having abstracted this fly-leaf from the volume. I deny the charge. It is a pure invention. No fly-leaf was in the book when I received it, nor does Mr. HAMILTON speak of any fly-leaf, but only of the "water-mark of the leaves pasted inside the covers." Mr. COLLIER is pleased to convert these leaves into a "fly-leaf," and then to accuse some person in my Department of abstracting a leaf that had no existence!

As to the personalities indulged in by Mr. COLLIER towards myself, my answer shall be as brief as is consistent with a due explanation of the facts. For the sake, apparently, of diverting the attention of the public from the real points at issue, he has not scrupled to bring a charge against me which he must have known to be false. He commences by asserting that on two occasions he was "of some service to me," but of one of these he "can say no more." Why not? I call upon Mr. COLLIER to speak out. Surely there is no service really rendered to me by Mr. COLLIER that he need be reluctant to mention, or I myself, if true, to acknowledge. But with regard to the other service, he refers to the purchase by me of certain documents which "had escaped from Lord ELLESMERE's collection," and his charge is, that I bought manuscripts which "I ought to have known had been dishonestly come by." He then proceeds thus: "The late Earl ELLESMERE heard of the strange circumstance, put the matter into the hands of his solicitor, and asked me to inquire of Sir F. MADDEN as to the facts. I did so, and finding, as I of course expected, that Sir F. MADDEN had innocently, though ignorantly and most incautiously, become possessed of the documents, they were restored to the noble owner, and the matter was dropped." Mr. COLLIER then concludes that, "if Sir F. MADDEN had been indicted for receiving stolen goods, knowing them to have been stolen, it might have gone hard with him." Never was any transaction so wilfully misrepresented! The facts are these: In October, 1854 (not two or three years ago, as Mr. COLLIER states) some circumstances occurred which induced me to doubt whether a number of loose papers and an original document on parchment in a very damaged state, which had been purchased some time previously from a person of great apparent respectability (and who stated he had bought them at Shrewsbury), were fairly come by, and whether the parchment document might not have "escaped" from Lord ELLESMERE's library. As soon as this doubt arose I wrote to Mr. COLLIER, and requested him to come as soon as possible to examine these manuscripts, as I wished to communicate the result to Lord ELLESMERE before I brought it to the notice of the Trustees. Mr. COLLIER came a day or two afterwards, and was shown the whole of the documents purchased. Mr. COLLIER then wrote to Lord ELLESMERE, who knew nothing of the matter, but expressed his obligation to myself; and it was only by means of a letter from the individual of whom I had bought the papers (communicated to me by Mr. COLLIER) that it was ascertained how they had been lost. It was at my suggestion that Lord ELLESMERE applied to the Trustees for the restoration of the manuscripts; and it was not till after the meeting of the committee, on the 11th November, that Lord ELLESMERE thought of referring the matter to his solicitor, and, after some legal discussion, the whole of the manuscripts were finally restored to Bridgewater House. What the "service" was, rendered to me by Mr. COLLIER in this affair, I am at a loss to understand. On the contrary, I have good reason to believe that Mr. COLLIER prejudiced Lord ELLESMERE's mind against me. I had acted throughout openly and without reserve. I had bought the manuscripts of a respectable individual; I was quite unconscious of the real ownership; I was the first subsequently to suspect it; and then took all the steps in my power to assist in the restoration of the manuscripts to the owner. But Mr. COLLIER says, that, though "innocently," I obtained the documents "ignorantly;" and that I "ought to have been well acquainted" with a volume of "Egerton Papers," published by the Camden Society in 1840. Now, I have to observe that this volume was printed *thirteen* years previous to the purchase of the papers, that it is a quarto of 485 pages, and that it contains no less than 219 miscellaneous articles on all sorts of subjects. In this volume were printed two (and two only) of the whole collection of manuscripts purchased. Is it not requiring rather too much, even of the most accurate memory, to recall to mind two papers in the middle of a thick quarto volume, after such a lapse of time? Could Mr. COLLIER himself do it? But the real fact remains to be told. In the year of the publication of the Camden volume, I was too much occupied by literary labours to be able to devote much attention to works not connected with them, and when I received Mr. COLLIER's volume from the Camden Society, I did what I doubt not some other members might have done, that is to say, place it on a shelf of my library unopened. In confirmation of what I have above written, I can produce letters and reports still in my hands; and Sir Henry Ellis and Mr. Hawkins (both of whom were consulted throughout) would, I am confident, confirm my statement. And so much for the "obligation" which Mr. Collier says some men (meaning myself) can never forgive!

There is one more point I must mention before I conclude, although a very slight matter. At p. 53 of his "Reply," Mr. Collier alludes to the autograph signature of Shakspere in Florio's Montaigne, which he declares he could easily "expunge," if permitted, and for which, he says, "Sir F. Madden paid out of the public purse no less than 130*l*." I certainly wrote an article in 1837, to endeavour to prove this signature to be genuine, and Mr. Collier himself ("Life of Shakespeare," p. ccxxxvi. edit. 1844) fully admits it to be so; but as to the purchase for the Museum, I had nothing to do with it. It was bought by the Head of the Department of Printed Books, and has belonged ever since to that Department.

The literary public, I am sure, will not take much interest in personal disputes of this kind; and I think it would have been a far preferable course if Mr. Collier and his friends had proposed the nomination of a tribunal of competent persons, who should hear and examine the evidence connected with the whole of the Shakspere forgeries, and pronounce definitely on them.

I am, Sir, your obedient servant,

F. Madden.

British Museum, 20th March, 1860.

THE BIBLIOGRAPHY

OF THE

SHAKSPERE CONTROVERSY.

N.B. An asterisk (*) prefixed to the designation of a book or an article indicates that it is against the genuineness of the manuscript notes in the Perkins Folio; or of any of the documents in question. On the contrary a dagger (†) indicates it is in favour of their genuineness. The absence of both signs is an indication of neutrality.

I.—BOOKS AND PAMPHLETS.

* The History of English Dramatic Poetry to the time of Shakespeare: and Annals of the Stage to the Restoration, by J. Payne Collier, Esq., F.S.A. 3 vols. . . 1831

* New Facts regarding the Life of Shakespeare, in a letter to Thomas Amyot, Esq., F.R.S. Treasurer of the Society of Antiquaries, from J. Payne Collier, F.S.A. . . 1835

(25 copies also were printed on large paper.)

* New Particulars regarding the Works of Shakespeare, in a letter to the Rev. A. Dyce, B.A., Editor of the Works of Peele, Greene, Webster, &c. from J. Payne Collier, F.S.A. 1836

(25 copies also were printed on large paper.)

* A Catalogue, Biographical and Critical, of early English Literature; forming a portion of the Library at Bridgewater House, &c. Edited by J. Payne Collier, Esq., F.S.A. 1837

* Further particulars regarding Shakespeare and his Works, in a letter to the Rev. Joseph Hunter, F.S.A., from J. Payne Collier, F.S.A. 1839

(25 copies also were printed on large paper.)

* Memoirs of Edward Alleyn, Founder of Dulwich College: including some new particulars respecting Shakespeare, Ben

Jonson, Massinger, Marston, Dekker, &c., by J. Payne Collier, Esq., F.S.A. 1841

Printed for the Shakespeare Society.

* Reasons for a New Edition of Shakespeare's Works, containing notices of the defects of former impressions, and pointing out the lately acquired means of illustrating the Plays, Poems, and Biography of the Poet, by J. Payne Collier, Esq., F.S.A. 1841

2nd Edition, 1842.

* The Works of Shakespeare. Edited by J. Payne Collier, Esq., F.S.A., 8 vols. . . . . . 1841—1844

The Alleyn Papers. A Collection of Original Documents, illustrative of the Life and Times of Edward Alleyn, and of the early English Stage and Drama. With an introduction by J. Payne Collier, Esq., F.S.A. 1843

Printed for the Shakespeare Society.

* Notes and Emendations to the text of Shakespeare's Plays, from early manuscript corrections in a copy of the folio, 1632, in the possession of J. Payne Collier, Esq., F.S.A. . 1852

Printed for the Shakspere Society, pp. 512.
Published January, 1853.
2nd Edition, pp. 528, 1853.

Translated into German, by Dr. Leo (1853), and forming the substance of Dr. Julius Frese's supplementary volume of Shakespeare's Dramatic Works (1853), and of Dr. Delius' "English Theatre in Shakspeare's Time."

A Few Remarks on the Emendation, "Who smothers her with painting," in the Play of *Cymbeline*. Discovered by *Mr. Collier*, in a Corrected Copy of the Second Edition of *Shakespeare*. By J. O. Halliwell, Esq., F.R.S., &c. . 1852

Petulantly replied to by Mr. Collier in the *addenda* to his Notes and Emendations, 1st Edition.

† Curiosities of Modern Shaksperian Criticism. By J. O. Halliwell, Esq., F.R.S., &c. . . . 1853

This is an able exposure of the misrepresentations of a review of Vol. I., of Mr. Halliwell's Folio Shakespeare, in "The Athenæum." This rejoinder was noticed in that periodical for August 13, 1853, where the writer refuses "to retract or to alter" any of his statements. These articles form a most instructive example of the excess to which the partisanship of reviewers can run.

† The Text of Shakespeare Vindicated from the interpolations and corruptions advocated by John Payne Collier, Esq., in his Notes and Emendations. By Samuel Weller Singer. 1853

This was the first publication that took the field against the genuineness of the Perkins manuscript notes, on internal evidence. It has the virtue of earnestness, and the vice of intemperance. In a critical point of view it is nearly valueless. It was severely reviewed in "The Athenæum," May 28 and June 4th, 1853.

Observations on some of the Manuscript Emendations of the text of Shakespeare, *and are they copyright?* By J. O. Halliwell, Esq., F.R.S., &c. 1853

† Observations on the Shaksperian Forgeries at Bridgewater House; illustrative of a facsimile of the spurious Letter of H. S. By James O. Halliwell, Esq. pp. 8. . 1853

Printed "for private circulation only."

A Few Notes on Shakespeare; with occasional remarks on the emendations of the manuscript corrector in Mr. Collier's copy of the folio, 1632. By the Rev. Alexander Dyce 1853

A few Words in reply to the Animadversions of the Rev. Mr. Dyce on Mr. Hunter's "Disquisition on the Tempest" (1839); and his "New Illustrations of the Life, Studies and Writings of Shakespeare" (1845); contained in his work entitled "A Few Notes, &c. &c." By the author of the Disquisition and the Illustrations 1853

* Old Lamps, or New? A plea for the original Editions of the Text of Shakspere: forming an introductory notice to the Stratford Shakspere. Edited by Charles Knight . 1853

* The Plays of Shakespeare. The text regulated by the old copies, and by the recently discovered folio of 1632. By J. Payne Collier, Esq., F.S.A., 1 vol. . . . 1853

"It would almost seem that the one volume had been printed from some modern copy, (certainly it is not from Mr. Collier's own edition in eight volumes) with the insertion of all the alterations that had been published in *Notes and Emendations*; that afterwards the volume had been collated with the folio of 1632, and where any further deviations from that text had been discovered in the one-volume edition, they had been inserted, first in the margin of the folio (!), and then in the "List" of all the MS. Emendations." Mr. T. J. Arnold.—*Fraser's Magazine*, Feb. 1860.

† Shakespeare's Scholar, being Historical and Critical Studies of his Text, Characters and Commentators, with an Examination of Mr. Collier's Folio of 1632, by Richard Grant White, A.M. 1854

Reviewed in "The Athenæum" for September 9th, 1854.

† Literary Cookery, with reference to matter attributed to Coleridge and Shakespeare. A letter addressed to "The Athenæum." With a postscript containing some remarks upon the refusal of that journal to print it. . . 1855

For this publication Mr. Collier prosecuted the publisher, and failed.

* Seven Lectures on Shakespeare and Milton. By the late S. T. Coleridge. A List of all the MS. Emendations in Mr. Collier's Folio, 1632, and an Introductory Preface. By J. Payne Collier, Esq. 1856

It was against forestalled extracts from these seven lectures as published by Mr. Collier, in "Notes and Queries," that the pamphlet called *Literary Cookery* was directed. The "List" was added, I suppose, to make a small book saleable at a large price.

* The Works of Shakespeare. Edited by J. Payne Collier, Esq., F.S.A., 6 vols. 1858

This Edition was a signal disgrace to the Republic of Letters. It is in no sense an Edition of Shakspere.

† Strictures on Mr. Collier's New Edition of Shakespeare, 1858. By the Rev. Alexander Dyce . . . 1859

A severe but just exposure of Mr. Collier's misrepresentations of Mr. Dyce's Works. Mr. Collier feigns not to reciprocate the malice of his *quondam* friend, and says "I still say of him as the great Saint said of the greater Sectary, 'I loved thee once; I almost love thee still.'" (*Reply*, p. 67.) Would not Edgar's phrase be more in point, "Wine* I loved deeply; *Dyce* dearly."? (*Lear*, iii. 2.)

† The Shakspeare Fabrications, or the MS. Notes of the Perkins Folio shewn to be of recent origin, with an Appendix on the authorship of the Ireland Forgeries. By C. Mansfield Ingleby, Esq., LL.D. . . . 1859

---

* I mean of course the metaphorical wine of Shakspere's genius, commonly called "the flow of soul."

† An Inquiry into the Genuineness of the Manuscript Correction in Mr. J. Payne Collier's annotated Shakspere, Folio, 1632; and of certain Shaksperian Documents likewise published by Mr. Collier. By N. E. S. A. Hamilton . 1860

* Mr. J. Payne Collier's Reply to Mr. N. E. S. A. Hamilton's "Inquiry" into the imputed Shakespeare Forgeries . 1860

† The Preface to Mr. Staunton's Edition of Shakespeare's Works, (1857-1860.) . . May, 1860

† The Life of Shakspeare, by H. Staunton May, 1860

* Strictures on Mr. N. E. S. A. Hamilton's Inquiry into the genuineness of the MS. corrections in Mr. J. Payne Collier's annotated Shakespeare, Folio, 1632. By Scrutator . 1860

A very remarkable pamphlet! It is thickly studded with Latin phrases. Of these one only extends to three words, and one only to four words; the former containing two bad blunders, and the latter one. So much for Scrutator's scholarship. As for his honesty, see p. 25, where he tells us that "the tail" of the Alleyn Letter "is gone;" though he knew from the facsimile that it was not; and defends the genuineness of the letter, well knowing that nobody had ever questioned it. The whole pamphlet is a proof *ad nauseam* of the writer's incapacity and inexperience.

† A Review of the present state of the Shakespearian Controversy. By Thomas Duffus Hardy, Assistant Keeper of the Public Records 1860

† Collier, Coleridge, and Shakespeare. A Review. By the author of "Literary Cookery" . . . 1860

This may be regarded as the finishing stroke in the demolition of the genuineness of the "Seven Lectures," which Mr. Collier in 1856 published as Coleridge's.

In 1854, "The Athenæum" (October 6th) called "Literary Cookery," "a mere waste of words." In 1860 (August 11th), the same journal calls "Collier, Coleridge, and Shakespeare," a "mere waste of passionate words." It would be difficult to find a publication which is more thoroughly characterized by calmness and deliberation.

II.—ARTICLES IN PERIODICALS.

† The Neology of Shakspeare. A Lecture delivered by Dr. Ingleby, at the Theatre of the Birmingham and Midland Institute, November 24th, 1856, reported in "The Birmingham Journal" for November 29th, 1856. The manuscript notes of the Perkins Folio are here pronounced to be fabrications.

* Article in "The Athenæum," July 9th, 1859.

† Article in "The Bulletin," June 11th, 1859.

† A new affaire du Collier. "The Saturday Review," July 23rd, 1859. This is an exceedingly smart and witty article ironically vindicating Mr. Collier's integrity. It speaks of the Perkins Folio as "a volume which, under the name of the Collier folio Shakspeare, will probably have a chapter in history to itself next in place to that of a certain diamond necklace —— the main difference, perhaps, being in the uncertainty as to who plays the part of Cagliostro in the events which that chapter will record." Hence the very curious heading.

† Mr. Collier's Shakspeare (signed, Eton, W. W. T.), "The Bulletin," July 23, 1859.

† Literary Forgery. "The New York Daily Tribune," Aug. 6th, 1859. The writer thus sums up his case:—"Thus falls to the ground a literary imposture which, from the fame of the author to whose works it related, and the distinguished position of its first and most eminent dupe and innocent apostle, Mr. Collier, has excited a more general interest in the reading world than any other upon record. Its author, who must be a very clever and dextrous fellow, may be yet alive, and chuckling, like his prototype Ireland, over the credulity of his victims. But how characteristic it is of dear old England that he should have been obliged to wait so long to be found out! Who believes that, had that old folio been brought for-

ward in New-York instead of London, five long years would have elapsed before the array of internal evidence against the authority and the antiquity of its corrections produced by the American critic [Mr. R. Grant White], would have been sustained by the tests of the microscope and the laboratory."

This is by far the richest joke that has ever been perpetrated in connection with this controversy. In 1854, Mr. R. Grant White, it seems, demolished—in pure Yankee, "catawampously chawed up"—the "old corrector," on internal evidence only; and in 1860, that same critic maintains in "The Athenæum" the genuineness of the manuscript notes! In 1859, Messrs. Hamilton and Maskelyne are hailed as the demolishers of the "old corrector," on external evidence; and in 1860, these very gentlemen who sneer at "dear old England," for having allowed five years to elapse before they subjected the volume to a palæographic or scientific examination, re-publish, in the form of a pamphlet, Mr. Collier's two replies, and send over to England a cart load of the reprint for gratuitous circulation among the dupes of Messrs. Hamilton and Maskelyne! Verily these Americans are comical fellows.

† THE SHAKESPEARE CONTROVERSY. "The Universal Review," Saturday, September, 1859.

† Two short articles in "The Literary Gazette," Sept. 24th, and October 1st, 1859.

* THE COLLIER-FOLIO SHAKESPEARE. IS IT AN IMPOSTURE?—A clever defence of the genuineness of the manuscript notes of the Perkins Folio by Mr. R. Grant White, in "The Atlantic Monthly Advertiser," October, 1859. It is to be hoped that Mr. White's "Prolegomena," will contain something more satisfactory on this subject than the article in question. But I am sure that whatever he writes will be conscientious, genial and gentlemanly.

† THE SHAKESPEARIAN DISCOVERY, by T. J. Arnold, Esq., Police Magistrate. "Fraser's Magazine," January, 1860.

† THE 'OLD CORRECTOR,' by T. J. Arnold, Esq., "Fraser's Magazine," February, 1860.

* THE IMPUTED SHAKSPEARE FORGERIES. Mr. J. PAYNE COLLIER'S REPLY. "The Athenæum," Feb. 18, 1860.

† Article in "The Press," Feb. 25, 1860.

* THE SHAKSPEARE CONTROVERSY. "Notes and Queries," March 24, 1860. (2nd Series, vol. ix. p. 210.)

† THE SHAKSPERE DOCUMENTS. A long and important letter from Sir F. Madden, K.H., Keeper of the Manuscripts of the British Museum. "The Critic," March 24, 1860.

The letter is reprinted in the Appendix to this book.

† A FEW POINTS CONNECTED WITH THE SHAKESPEARE DOCUMENTS. "The Critic," March 31, 1860.

* Mr. COLLIER AND HIS SHAKSPERE. "The Saturday Review," April 21, 1860.

† THE ALLEGED SHAKSPEARE FORGERIES. "The Literary Gazette," April 28, 1860.

† Mr. COLLIER'S REPLY, by T. J. Arnold, Esq. "Fraser's Magazine," May, 1860.

† THE SHAKSPEARE CONTROVERSY. "The Literary Gazette," May 12, 1860.

† THE SHAKESPEARE DOCUMENTS. A letter from T. J. Arnold, Esq. "The Critic," May 26, 1860.

* A Letter in "The Athenæum," August 25, 1860, from Herman Merivale, Esq. (signed "An Edinburgh Reviewer") in reply to Mr. T. Duffus Hardy's "Review of the present state of the Shakespearian Controversy."

III.—REVIEWS IN PERIODICALS.

Among the numerous notices of Mr. Collier's *Notes and Emendations*, the following seem most note-worthy.

* The Athenæum, January 8th, 1853.

† Blackwood's Edinburgh Magazine, August, September, October, 1853.

Three slashing articles manifesting intelligence and good sense. But the writer did not give himself time to arrive at a sound judgment, and if had not "more zeal than knowledge," he, at least, allowed his zeal to overrun his discretion.

The North British Review, February, 1854.

This review does not exhibit much critical sagacity.

* The North American Review, April, 1854.

This article is highly praised in the following paper in "The Edinburgh Review," but "for which of his vices," it would be difficult to say. A more wretched affair never disgraced periodical.

* The Edinburgh Review, April, 1856.

Besides these reviews, I may notice two articles in the Literary Gazette, for January 8th, and June 11th, 1853. The first is a review of *Notes and Emendations*, and the second of that and Mr. Hunter's *Few Words* (or *Many Words*, as it should be called from its title-page). The first article favours Mr. Collier's book—the second is dead against it.

The Athenæum has two reviews of Singer's *Text of Shakspere Vindicated*, May 28th, and June 4th, 1853; both pro-Collierite, of course; and the Literary Gazette has a *neutral* review of that work (and Mr. Dyce's *Few Notes*), June 4th, 1853.

Besides these reviews, which relate directly to Mr. Collier's *Notes and Emendations*, I will simply mention two that have an indirect bearing on the subject, and are worth perusal, viz. An article on Mr. Dyce's Shakspere in the Quarterly Review, January, 1859, and an article on Mr. R. G. White's Shakspere, in the North American Review, January, 1859.

These articles have, of course, no reference to the controversy which arose out of the publication of Mr. Hamilton's *Inquiry*, and my *Shakspeare Fabrications*.

The following is a tolerably complete list of Reviews of those works:—

Reviews of Dr. Ingleby's *Shakspeare Fabrications*.

* *The Athenæum*, Aug. 20, 1859.
* *The Critic*, Aug. 27, 1859.
* *The Atlas*, Sept. 10, 1859.

† *The Literary Gazette*, Sept. 17, 1859.

The Hamilton Correspondence in *The Times*.

† From Mr. Hamilton, July 2, 1859.
† „ Looker-on „ 5, „
* „ Mr. Collier „ 7, „
† „ Prof. Maskelyne „ 16, „
† „ Mr. Hamilton „ 16, „
* „ Mr. Collier „ 20, „
† „ Mr. Parry August 1, „
† „ Sir F. Madden March 22, 1860.

Reviews of Mr. Hamilton's *Inquiry*.

† *The Critic* . . . Feb. 11, 1860.
* *The Athenæum* . . Feb. 18, 1860.
† *The Critic* . . Feb. 25, 1860.
† *The Critic* . . . March 3, 1860.
† *The Literary Gazette* . March 17, 1860.
† *The Spectator* . . Feb. 25, 1860.
† *The Spectator* . . March 3, 1860.
† *Colburn's New Monthly Magazine* April, 1860.
† *The New Quarterly Review* April, 1860.

Reviews of Mr. Collier's *Reply*.

† *The Critic* March 17, 1860.
* *The Literary Gazette* March 24, 1860.

Review of Mr. Hamilton's *Inquiry*, Dr. Ingleby's *Shakspeare Fabrications*, and Mr. Collier's *Reply*, *collectively*.

* *The Edinburgh Review*, April, 1860.

This review is from the pen of Mr. Herman Merivale. It professes to be a continuation of an article in "The Edinburgh Review" for April, 1856.

SUPPLEMENTAL NOTES.

p. 16, l. 7.—As to Shakspere's authorship of parts of *The Two Noble Kinsmen*, see "The Quarterly Review," vol. 83, p. 403 (1848).

p. 104, l. 4.—The account given in "The Gentleman's Magazine" for March, 1856 (vol. 45, New Series, p. 269), might have authorized me in carrying the parallel still further. We there read, "Another statement says that the pencil marks on which the Uncials were traced came out plainly by these tests."

p. 144, *note* [8].—Though the first edition of Hudibras bears the date 1663, it must have been published in the previous year; for we learn from Pepys' Diary, under Dec. 26, 1662, that he fell into discourse with a Mr. Battersby "of a new book of drollery in use, called *Hudibras*." He bought a copy the same day for 2*s* 6*d*, but growing "ashamed of it" he sold it shortly after for 1*s* 6*d*. On Feb. 6, 1662-3, however, he bought another copy.

p. 181, l. 2.—Mr. Halliwell unaccountably says of the monstrous compound *busy-less*, "it is so *naturally* (though perhaps not quite grammatically) formed, its *rare occurrence* is not, in itself, a sufficient reason for its rejection." (Fo. Shakespeare, Vol. I.) Probably not: but it will be time enough to discuss that point when Mr. Halliwell has made good his allegation of the "rare occurrence" of the word in question by producing a *single instance* of its use in any author of the period. In the meantime I must be allowed to say that *busy-less*, so far from being "naturally formed," is a compound (manufactured by Theobald—

probably when he was half-drunk—) which violates at once the rules of English grammar and the genius of the English language. *Busy-less* could not have meant *unemployed*, unless *busy* were either a noun substantive meaning *employment*, or an intransitive verb meaning *to labour*.

p. 198, l. 4.—In fact soon afterwards a similar stage-direction is inserted in ink, "Long and selfe struggling." See Perkins Folio, p. 57, col. 2. See also the facsimile of the shorthand, on sheet no. IV.

p. 239.—Mr. Dyce's adoption of *bisson multitude*.

Mr. Dyce persists in the ordinary punctuation. Had he consulted either the original text of Plutarch, or even North's translation of it, he would have been saved from this wretched blunder. It is wonderful that Dr. Farmer should have missed the point; for he would have been only too glad to have included this case in his list of blunders into which the poor simpleton Shakspere had been betrayed through the ambiguity of some of North's expressions. Shakspere simply *could not* have written the ignorant perversion of the sense and meaning of the text in Plutarch —even according to North—which Mr. Dyce's punctuation would impute to him.

THE END.

G. NORMAN, PRINTER, MAIDEN LANE, COVENT GARDEN.

ADDITIONAL CORRECTIONS.

Page xiii, line 6 from bottom, *for* * *read* †
„ 21, line 9, *for* worse *read* worst
„ 35, line 29, *for* inconsistent *read* consistent
„ 102, line 7 from bottom, *for* excellent *read* exquisite
„ 107, line 6 of *note*, *add* See facsimile on sheet no. II.
„ 179, line 14, *after* approval *read* in his Introduction
„ 184, line 14, *for* we *read* one
„ 237, line 17, *for* disturbed *read* distorted
„ 239, line 1, *for* antecedents *read* antecedent
„ 247, line 2, *for* £5000 and £6000 *read* £3000 and £4000
„ 297, lines 6 and 17, *for* sixteen *read* six
„ 346, *at the end of* "Articles in Periodicals" *add*

† The Shakspeare Controversy. A letter in "The Athenæum," September 1st, 1860, from T. Duffus Hardy, Esq. in reply to Mr. Merivale's letter in that periodical.

„ 347, line 5, *after* if *read* he

The facsimile intended to face the title has been unavoidably withdrawn.

CORRECTIONS.

Before perusing this work the reader is requested to make the following corrections :—

p. 16, l. 18.—*After* copies *insert* having the title
p. 27, l. 8.—*Before* Shakspere *insert* the plays of
p. 54, *last line of note* [4].—*For* the *read* some
p. 97, l. 8.—*Before* rather *read* which he preferred to do
p. 123, *note* [4]—*Transfer the* ["] *from the second* to *to the first* to
p. 126, l. 1 *of extract.*—*For* Fortunes *read* Fortune,
p. 135, l. 4 *from bottom.*—*For* special *read* specious.
p. 150, l. 2 *from bottom.*—*Before* immediately *read* he
p. 151, l. 15.—*For* " three " cheers *read* " three cheers "
p. 152.—*After the first example in class* 2, *add* Sylvester's *Dubartas*, 5th day, 1st week, p. 105, ed. 1618
p. 201, l. 10.—*For* on *read* no
p. 215.—*Erase the last example in Class III. and in the next line for* nine *read* ten
p. 217, l. 9.—*After* manuscript *read* copies
p. 232, l. 10 *from bottom.*—*For* moral *read* real
p. 244, l. 9.—*For* have *read* has

VII. The Perkins Folio:—Philological Tests. VIII. The Perkins Folio: —Mr. Collier's Dealings with the Emendations. IX. The Perkins Folio: —Value of the Emendations: Mr. Collier's claim of Originality for the "Old Corrector." X. The Bridgewater Manuscripts. XI. The Dulwich Manuscripts. XII. The Forged State Paper. XIII. Supposititious and Suspected Documents. XIV. The Vintage. Appendix, containing Mr. Collier's Charges against Sir F. Madden, and his Reply; Bibliography of the Shakspere Controversy. Supplemental Notes.

Bunyan's Pilgrim's Progress, with Memoir of the Author by Dr. Geo. Cheever, Bogue's beautiful illustrated edition, elegantly printed ou toned paper in 8vo. and profusely illustrated, with portrait and upwards of 300 beautiful woodcuts by Dalziel from designs by William Harvey, *cloth gilt, gilt edges,* (pub. at 12*s* 6*d*) 9*s* *Bogue,* 1857

—— *calf, antique style, red edges,* 13*s*

—— *morocco extra, gilt edges,* 14*s* 6*d*

—— *morocco, antique style, gilt edges,* 15*s* 6*d*

Early English Prose Romances, with Bibliographical and Historical Introductions, edited by W. J. Thoms, F.S.A.; second edition, revised, elegantly printed in 3 vols. crown 8vo. *half bound morocco, uncut, in the Roxburghe style,* £1. 7*s*; *or tree-marbled calf extra, gilt edges,* £1. 18*s* 1858

—— 3 vols. 8vo. LARGE PAPER, *of which only 50 copies are printed, half bound morocco, uncut,* £2. 5*s*; *or tree-marbled calf extra, gilt edges, by Riviere,* £3. 1858

CONTENTS: Lyfe of Robert the Deuyll; from an edition by Wynkyn de Worde—Thomas of Reading, or the six Worthie Yeomen of the West, by T. Deloney, 1632—Famous Historie of Fryer Bacon (1630)—Historie of Frier Rush, 1620—Lyfe of Virgilius; from an unique copy printed at Antwerp by Johnn Doesborcke—Noble Birth and Gallant Atchievements of Robin Hood, in Twelve several Stories, 1678—History of George a Green, Pindar of Wakefield, 1706—History of Tom a Lincolne, the Red Rose Knight, 1635—History of Helyas, Knight of the Swaune; from an unique copy printed by Copland—The Damnable Life and Deserved Death of Dr. Faustus, 1592—Second Report of Dr. Faustus, containing his Appearances and the Deeds of Wagner, 1594.

"We notice with much satisfaction this reprint of the popular literature of our ancestors. It is not the mere antiquary who is gratified by being able to procure those romances which were once the mental recreation of society, and unquestionably form part of our national literature, but the general reader, who is possessed of the least curiosity, will gladly become acquainted with what may be termed the 'WAVERLEY NOVELS' of their day."—RETROSPECTIVE REVIEW. *Notice of the First Edition.*

Dr. Syntax's Three Tours, in Search of the Picturesque, in Search of Consolation, and in Search of a Wife, [in Hudibrastic Verse], by Wm. Combe, illustrated with eighty-one humourous COLOURED engravings by Rowlandson, 3 vols. royal 8vo. *cloth gilt,* (pub. at £3. 3*s*) £1. 11*s* 6*d*

Brougham's (Lord) Lives of Men of Letters and Science who flourished in the Time of George III. with 8 fine portraits, 8vo. *cloth,* (pub. at £1. 1*s*) 5*s*

CONTENTS: Voltaire, Rousseau, Hume, Robertson, Joseph Black, Jos. Watt, Dr. Priestley, Sir Humphry Davy, Simson.

Blake's Illustrated Edition of Blair's Grave.

The Grave, a Poem, illustrated with Twelve Plates from Designs by Wm. Blake, and a fine Portrait of Blake engraved by Schiavonetti, 4to. *cloth lettered,* £1. 1*s*

—— 4to. *half bound morocco extra, uncut, top edges gilt,* £1. 6*s*

—— royal 4to. large paper, *with proof impressions of the plates, cloth lettered,* £2. 2*s*

Britton's Cathedral Antiquities of England.

Each Cathedral is sold separately, in cloth.

	Plates.	Reduced. £.	*s.*	*d.*	Pub. at £.	*s.*	*d.*		Plates.	Reduced. £.	*s.*	*d.*	Pub. at £.	*s.*	*d.*
Norwich .	26	0	15	0	2	10	0	Exeter . .	22	0	15	0	2	10	0
Winchester .	30	0	16	0	3	3	0	Peterborough	16	0	12	0	1	18	0
Lichfield .	16	0	12	0	1	18	0	Bristol . .	12	0	9	0	1	4	0
Oxford . .	11	0	9	0	1	4	0	Hereford .	16	0	12	0	1	18	0
Canterbury .	26	0	16	0	3	3	0	Worcester .	16	0	12	0	1	18	0
Wells . . .	24	0	15	0	2	10	0								

On Large Paper only the following can be had:—

	Reduced to £.	*s.*	*d.*	Pub. at £.	*s.*	*d.*		Reduced to £.	*s.*	*d.*	Pub. at £.	*s.*	*d.*
Oxford . . .	0	16	0	3	3	0	Canterbury . .	1	8	6	5	5	0
Salisbury . .	1	8	0	5	5	0	Worcester . .	1	5	0	3	3	0
Winchester .	1	8	0	5	5	0	Oxford, folio .	1	1	0	5	0	0

Britton's Picturesque Antiquities of the

English Cities, consisting of a Series of Engravings of Ancient Buildings, Street Architecture, Bars, Castles, &c. with Historical and Descriptive Accounts of the Subjects, and of the Characteristics of each City; with 60 plates by J. Le Keux, from Drawings by W. H. Bartlett, and 24 woodcuts, 4to. *cloth gilt, gilt edges,* £1. 1*s*

Burke's (Rt. Hon. Edmund) Correspon-

dence, from 1774 to his decease in 1797, edited by Earl Fitzwilliam and Sir R. Bourke, fine portrait, 4 vols. 8vo. *cloth,* (pub. at £2. 8*s*) 12*s* 1844

This valuable and interesting work contains numerous Historical and Biographical Notes, and Original Letters from the leading Statesmen of the period, and forms an *Autobiography* of this celebrated Statesman and Writer. It is also necessary to complete the edition of Burke's Works in 16 vols. 8vo. which does not contain the Correspondence.

Coney's (J.) Beauties of Continental Archi-

tecture, in a series of Views of Ancient Cathedrals and Public Buildings in France, the Netherlands and Germany, 28 plates and 56 vignettes, imp. 4to. *half bound morocco extra, gilt edges,* (pub. at £4. 4*s*) £1. 16*s*

Cotman's Architectural Antiquities of Nor-

mandy, with Descriptions by Dawson Turner. One Hundred Plates, 2 vols. in 1, folio, *half bound morocco extra, uncut, top edges gilt,* (pub. at £12. 12*s*) £4. 4*s*

—— 2 vols. imp. folio, Proofs on India Paper, *cloth,* (pub. at £21.) £7. 7*s*

***Clutton's (Henry) Illustrations of Mediæval** Architecture in France*, from the Accession of Charles VI. to the Demise of Louis XII.; with Historical and Professional Remarks, 16 beautiful lithographic engravings, executed in coloured tints, and 28 woodcuts, folio, *half bound morocco, uncut*, (pub. at £3. 3*s*) £1. 11*s* 6*d* 1853

It is more particularly the object of the present work to draw the attention of English Architects and Antiquarians to a phase of Mediæval Art wholly distinct from anything to be found in this country, and to point out from the published examples, certain principles in its construction and details, which may, perhaps, be advantageously adopted in modern practice. At the same time historical notices have been introduced, together with much antiquarian information, illustrative of the Domestic Life of the 15th Century, derived from a careful comparison of the works of the Chroniclers, with the remains of the edifices of that period.

***Cooper's Groups of Cattle, drawn from** Nature*, 26 large and beautiful lithographic engravings, royal folio, *half bound morocco, uncut*, (pub. at £4. 4*s*) £2. 16*s*

***Cuitt's (Geo.) Wanderings and Pencillings** amongst Ruins of the Olden Time, in England and Wales.* A Series of Seventy-three Etchings (*in the style of Piranesi*), with descriptive letterpress, Archæological, Legendary, and Architectural, Seventy-three plates, folio, *half bound morocco extra, gilt edges*, £3. 13*s* 6*d*

"These Plates are etched with great freedom, and will remind the spectator of them, or reader of the book, of the Etchings of Rome (*by Piranesi*), to which they come nearer than any modern work of British Art of a similar class. Etching represents rugged grandeur, decay, dilapidation, and ruin admirably well, and has been happily chosen by the artist to depict what he had seen. The letterpress is well written, and the work is an addition to the Fine Arts, and the knowledge of the antiquary."—TIMES.

Flaxman's Compositions from Dante. One Hundred and Eleven Plates in Outline, oblong 4to. *half bound morocco*, (pub. at £4. 4*s*) £2. 2*s*

"The designs of Mr. Flaxman are the noblest productions of art, and frequently display a sublime simplicity which is worthy of his great original. Indeed, he who is so able to transfer such creations from one fine art to another, seems of a mind little inferior to his who could first conceive them. To borrow the words of an excellent Italian sculptor—"Mr. Flaxman has translated Dante best, for he has translated it into the universal language of Nature."

***Flaxman's Anatomical Studies, of the Bones** and Muscles*, for the use of Artists, Portrait and 21 Plates by Landseer, folio, *cloth*, £1. 1*s*

***Fielding's (T. H.) Art of Engraving, with** the Modes of Operation*, viz.: Etching, Line Engraving, Chalk and Stipple, Soft Ground Etching, Aquatint, Mezzotint, Lithography, Wood Engraving, Medallic Engraving, Electrography, Photography, with 10 Plates of the different Styles, and 8 Woodcuts, royal 8vo. *cloth gilt*, (pub. at £1. 16*s*) 9*s*

Grant's (Mrs., of Laggan) Letters from the Mountains; being the Correspondence with her Friends between the years 1778 and 1803, Sixth Edition, 2 vols. post 8vo. *cloth*, (pub. at £1. 1*s*) 10*s* 6*d*

Grant. Memoir and Correspondence of Mrs. Grant, of Laggan, Second Edition, portrait, 3 vols. post 8vo. *cloth*, (pub. at £1. 11*s* 6*d*) 12*s*

Grey's (Earl) Colonial Policy of Lord John Russell's Administration, second edition, with additions, 2 vols. 8vo. *cloth*, (pub. at £1. 8*s*) 9*s*

"A handbook of modern colonial policy, which no person desirous of understanding the present state and future prospects of our Colonies can omit to read."—EDINBURGH REVIEW.

Hall's (Mrs. S. C.) Sketches of Irish Character; fifth edition, with a New Introduction, elegantly printed in crown 8vo. and beautifully illustrated with five plates by Maclise, and fifty-six woodcuts, *handsomely bound in cloth gilt*, 8*s*—or, *cloth gilt, gilt edges, for presents*, 9*s*

"Mrs. Hall has already shewn her fitness for the task, by an intimate acquaintance with that class of Irish life which affords the animated portion of her descriptions. She paints the peasantry and working classes of the country with fidelity, and her pen is wonderfully assisted by the productions of the pencil which she has called to her aid. The woodcuts are clever, and well selected for the purpose of exhibiting the more common forms which present themselves in Irish scenery and Irish life. Industry is manifest in the collection of picturesque facts and characteristic anecdotes, and good-will in the elaboration."—ATHENÆUM.

Keppel's (Capt. the Hon. Henry) Account of the Expedition to Borneo of H.M.S. Dido, for the Suppression of Piracy: with Extracts from the Journal of James Brooke, Esq., of Sarawak; third edition, with an additional Chapter, by W. K. Kelly, 6 maps and 11 plates, 2 vols. 8vo. *cloth*, (pub. at £1. 12*s*) 10*s* 6*d*

Lawrence's (Sir Thomas) Works. Engravings from the choicest Works of Sir Thomas Lawrence, P.R.A. a Series of Fifty Plates, engraved in Mezzotints, in the First Style of the Art, by S. Cousins, Ward, Giller, Coombes, Humphreys, &c. with Biographical and Critical Notices to each Plate, folio, PROOFS, *half bound morocco extra, gilt edges*, (pub. at £18. 18*s*) £5. 15*s* 6*d*

Lepsius' (Dr. R.) Discoveries in Egypt, Ethiopia, and the Peninsula of Sinai, in 1842-45, edited with Notes by Kenneth Mackenzie; second edition, with additions, map and 2 plates, 8vo. *cloth* (pub. at 12*s*) 5*s*

Letters of William III. and Louis XIV. and of their Ministers; illustrative of the Domestic and Foreign Politics of England from the Peace of Ryswick to the Accession of Philip V. of Spain (1697 to 1700), edited by P. Grimblot, 2 vols. 8vo. *cloth* (pub. at £1. 10*s*) 7*s* 6*d*

Library (The) of Entertaining Knowledge.

*** The following works can still be had, price 2s 3d per volume, bound in cloth.

The Menageries, Vols. 1 and 2, Monkeys.
Architecture of Birds
Habits of Birds
Faculties of Birds
Insect Miscellanies
Vegetable Substances, 3 vols.
Paris and its Historical Scenes, 2 vols.
Criminal Trials, 2 vols.
Historical Parallels, 2 vols.
Pompeii, 2 vols.
Egyptian Antiquities, 2 vols.
Elgin Marbles, 2 vols.
Townley Marbles, 2 vols.
The New Zealanders
The Hindoos, 2 vols.
The Chinese: a Description of the Empire of China, by Sir J. F. Davis, F.R.S., 2 vols.

Liverseege's (H.) Works, 37 beautiful engravings in Mezzotinto, by S. and H. Cousins, Bromley, Ward, Giller and others, folio, *half bound morocco extra, gilt edges*, (pub. at £6. 6s) £2. 12s 6d

Miles's Epitome, Historical and Statistical, descriptive of the Royal Naval Service of England, with 8 coloured Views of Shipping, &c. by W. Knell, and 14 coloured Illustrations of Flags, Pendants, and Ensigns, royal 8vo. *cloth gilt*, (pub. at 18s) 10s 6d

Moses's Select Greek and Roman Antiquities, from Vases, 37 plates, 4to. *cloth*, (pub. at £1. 1s) 10s 6d

National Gallery of Pictures, published by the Associated Artists: a Series of Twenty-nine splendid Plates, beautifully engraved in the Line Manner, by Finden, Burnett, Doo, Golding, Goodall, Humphries, Le Keux, Pye, Miller, Robinson, Watt and Greatbach, with Descriptions to each Plate in English and French, imperial folio, *hf. bd. morocco extra, gilt edges*, (pub. at £16. 16s) £4. 14s 6d

——— The same, a cheaper edition, 29 plates, folio, *hf. bd. morocco extra, gilt edges*, £2. 5s

This edition, being about one half the size of its precursor, is admirably adapted to adorn the drawing room table.

Neale's (J. P.) Mansions of England, or Picturesque Delineations of the Seats of Noblemen and Gentlemen; nearly 400 Views with Descriptions, 2 vols. 4to. *hf. bd. morocco extra, uncut, top edges gilt*, £2. 8s

Prout's Sketches at Home and Abroad, being Examples of the Interiors and Exteriors of Gothic Buildings. With Hints on the acquirements of Freedom of Execution, and Breadth of Effect in Landscape Painting; to which are added Simple Instructions on the proper use and application of Colour. Forty-eight Plates on India Paper, impl. 4to. *hf. bd. morocco extra, gilt edges*, (pub. at £4. 14s 6d) £2.

*** Mr. Prout's Hints on Light and Shadow; with his Sketches, or Hints on Breadth of Effect and the Use of Colour, and the admirable works of Mr. Pyne on Groups and Figures, form A COMPLETE CYCLOPÆDIA OF DRAWING.

Prout's (Samuel) Hints on Light and Shadow, Composition, &c., as applicable to Landscape Painting, illustrated by Examples, twenty-two plates, imp. 4to. *cloth gilt*, (pub. at £2. 2s) £1. 1s

Pyne's (W. H.) Microcosm; Picturesque Groups for the Embellishment of Landscape, in a Series of One Thousand Subjects, viz. Rural and Domestic Scenery, Shipping, Crafts, Sports, &c. 120 plates in aquatints, with descriptions, 2 vols. in 1, royal 4to. *half bound morocco, uncut*, (pub. at £6. 6s) £1. 11s 6d

Pyne's Etchings of Rustic Figures in imitation of Chalk, 36 plates, 4to. *cloth*, (pub. at £1. 16s) 9s

Pugin (A.) and Le Keux's Architectural Antiquities of Normandy, with Descriptions by John Britton, Eighty Plates by Le Keux, 4to. *hf. bd. morocco, uncut, top edges gilt*, (pub. at £6. 6s) £2. 12s 6d

Pugin and Mackenzie's Specimens of Gothic Architecture, selected from Ancient Buildings at Oxford, Sixty-one Plates, 4to. *cloth*, (pub. at £2. 2s) £1. 1s

Pugin's Specimens of Gothic Architecture, selected from Ancient Edifices in England, consisting of Plans, Sections, and Parts at large; calculated to exemplify the various Styles, and the Practical Construction of this admired Class of Architecture, with Historical and Descriptive Accounts by E. J. Willson, 114 plates, 2 vols. 4to. *half bound morocco, uncut, top edges gilt*, (pub. at £6. 6s) £3. 13s 6d

—— Another copy, 2 vols. impl. 4to. LARGE PAPER, *cloth*, (pub. at £9. 9s) £6. 6s

This work is adapted to furnish practical and useful information to the Architect, Builder, Cabinet Maker, &c. as well as to the critical Antiquary and Connoisseur.

Pugin's (A. W.) Details of Ancient Timber Houses of the 15th and 16th Centuries, selected from those existing at Caen, Beauvais, Abbeville, Strasbourg, &c. 22 plates, 4to. *cloth*, (pub. at £1. 1s) 12s

Pugin's Gothic Furniture of the 15th century, 25 plates, 4to. *cloth*, (pub. £1. 1s) 12s

Pugin's Designs for Iron and Brass Work, in the Style of the 15th and 16th Centuries, 27 plates, 4to. *cloth*, (pub. at £1. 1s) 12s

Pugin's Designs for Gold and Silver Ornaments, in the Style of the 15th and 16th Centuries, 27 plates of Cups, Chargers, Flagons, Tankards, Candlesticks, Sconces, Chalices, Crosses, Reliquaries, Candelabra, Monstrances, Feretra, &c. 4to. *cloth*, (pub. at £1. 1s) 12s

*** The above four works of Mr. A. W. Pugin may also be had, in one volume, half bound morocco extra, gilt edges, price £2. 12s 6d.

Reynard the Fox, after the German Version of Goethe, with a Bibliographical and Historical Introduction, by T. J. Arnold, Esq. 8vo. beautifully printed by Whittingham, with title-page and 12 plates, engraved on steel, after the clever and characteristic designs of J. Wolf, *half bound morocco, Roxburghe style, uncut*, 10*s* 6*d*

—— the same, with the plates on India paper (of which only 50 copies were printed), *half bd. morocco, uncut*, 15*s*

Reynard the Fox, after the German Version of Goethe, translated into English Verse by T. J. Arnold, Esq. with 70 beautiful woodcut illustrations after the celebrated designs of Wilhelm von Kaulbach, and 13 additional steel engravings from the clever and spirited designs of J. Wolf inserted, royal 8vo. beautifully printed by Clay on toned paper, *half bound morocco, uncut, top edge gilt*, 18*s*

Reynolds' (Sir Joshua) Discourses on Painting, with Notes by J. Burnet; with 12 fine engravings executed in bistre and aquatint, roy. 4to. LARGE PAPER, with proof impressions of the plates on India paper, *half bound morocco, uncut*, (pub. at £4. 4*s*) £1. 5*s*

One of the most important works on art ever published.

Thugs, or Secret Murderers of India. Illustrations of the History and Practices of the Thugs; and Notices of the Proceedings of the Government of India for the suppression of the crime of Thuggee, 8vo. *cloth*, (pub. at 15*s*) 5*s* 6*d*

Turner's Southern Coast of England. An Antiquarian and Picturesque Tour by Land and Sea, round the Southern Coast of England, illustrated with Eighty-four Plates by J. M. W. Turner, William Collins, P. Dewint, S. Owen, W. Westall, Prout, and others, engraved by George Cooke, W. B. Cooke, W. Finden, and other eminent Engravers, 4to. *half bound morocco extra, gilt edges*, £2. 12*s* 6*d*—*or half bound morocco, uncut*, £2. 10*s* 1849

Walter's (Rev. Henry) History of England, from the earliest Period to the passing of the Reform Bill in 1832, in which it is intended to consider Men and Events on Christian Principles, 7 vols. 12mo. *cloth*, (pub. at £2. 12*s*) 18*s*—*or hf. bd. calf gilt*, £1. 6*s*

—— 7 vols. royal 12mo. LARGE PAPER, *cloth*, (pub. at £3. 3*s*) £1. 1*s*—*or half bound, calf extra, marb. edges*, £1. 11*s* 6*d*

An excellent History of England, and particularly adapted to be put into the hands of the youth of both sexes.

Westwood's (J. O.) Cabinet of Oriental Entomology; being a Selection of the Rarer and more Beautiful Species of Insects, Natives of India and the adjacent Islands, the greater portion of which are now, for the first time, described and figured, 42 beautifully coloured plates, 4to. *cloth gilt*, (pub. at £2. 12*s* 6*d*) £1. 16*s*

www.ingramcontent.com/pod-product-compliance
Lightning Source LLC
Chambersburg PA
CBHW030825110726
47900CB00006B/1756
* 9 7 8 3 7 4 1 1 8 6 4 7 9 *